A Universe Upon Us
Marc B. DeGeorge

MuseMarc Studio, LLC.

Acknowledgments

A story may be written by one person, but it takes many to turn it into a novel. To that end, I'd like to thank the following for their contribution to turning my typing into reality.

First, my dedicated and awesome reading group, Ben Pick, Tracey Canole, E. Marie Robertson, Michelle Darnell, Joe Creech, Kelly Fisher and J. Logan Rice. Thank you for your critical commentary, positive support, and friendship.

My amazing editors, Joanne Machin and Ariel Anderson. Your skills have kept me from making one too many plot holes. Thank you.

Also to my wife and family, for your support and love.

Contents

TREASON

They stole my life from me. They ripped me from stasis and put a gun in my hand. I was far from alone. Every child now breathing the raw, dry air of the *Stratford* suffered my fate. We fight each other, because they forced us to. The adults did. And for that, I hate each and every last one of them.

There's the enemy, and there's us, but really, we are all the same—a terrified people, trapped on this runaway colony ship, five hundred-light-years from Earth. Maybe. No one knows for sure where or when we are on our thousand-year journey. Our fighting made the systems of the *Stratford* go from bad to worse, making it impossible to fix everything. We have become captives of this galactic coffin, victims of our own making.

And all anyone is trying to do is survive.

I had a cheery childhood once. My friends, my family, my corgi puppy. It didn't last. We wasted our planet, just like we've ravaged this ship, and there was no choice but to leave. My parents put me in a pod and told me not to worry, that I would see them soon. A thousand years in frozen hibernation would pass just like that.

But now, I will never speak with them again.

"Ceri." Efa motions for me to break left and keep down. She goes opposite, heading toward a pile of trash to use as cover.

I nod to my squad mate and choose a path through the rubble, squirming between a pair of collapsed ventilators and up into the duct. We're the point team for this clash, sent to prod the area for the Fahrasi raiding party our scouts warned us about. Our enemy is trying something new today, and we are ready to stop them—if we can.

They couldn't have picked a better place for it, really. Like the other levels, we've either powered the overhead lighting off or destroyed it for strategic reasons. Unlike other levels, we've turned this one into a wasteland of scrap, but we call them tactical positions. All of it is practical for making war.

"At point in ten seconds, Captain," I say through my comm and throw a glance toward Efa. She clicks her comm once to confirm the same, then slips into the darkness.

"What about the rest of your squad?" Captain Daga's sharp tone breaks through the comm static as if he was standing in front of me. I cringe as if he was.

"All ready."

"Good. Now stay alert and don't screw this up. They'll be coming any moment."

I grit my teeth and climb into my ambush point. Captain Daga doesn't need to threaten me like that before a battle. I know what I'm doing. That's why he made me the squad's field leader.

Footsteps approach, fast but light. This Fahrasi has experience, but I've got the height advantage. I'll jump down and ambush them. A hard slice across the face and they'll reconsider attacking my faction again.

"One coming," I say and tense. The moment they clear the heat exchanger, I'll be on them.

"Ceri, I've got eyes on your target," Efa says. *"Hold your position."*

"Why?"

"Just trust me."

"Negative, Ceri," Captain Daga says. *"Do not hold. Go the moment you see them."*

"Ceri..." Efa pleads, but I cannot disobey an order from the captain. Whatever she's concerned about will come clear soon enough.

There. A Fahrasi about my age, skinny and tall. Shaggy black hair and lanky legs. He steps with caution, his head darting from side to side. This boy may expect to slip through our defenses, but he isn't expecting me.

With a quick inhale, I fly from the duct, the blade of my knife leading the way. A sharp bang follows. *Hyuk.* My boot hit the duct. The Fahrasi startles and looks up. Can't do anything about it now.

He blocks my blade as I dive into him, buy my inertia knocks him back. We crash into the alley between the exchangers. The Fahrasi kicks out, aiming for my gut. He misses. I slice my blade across his path and scramble away.

"Ceri, I'm coming!" Efa calls.

"No! Stay in position, you stupid brat! There could be more!" the captain roars.

This boy is more agile than I estimated. He rolls forward, grabbing a metal bar as he moves. I aim my pistol at him—too slow. He knocks it from my hand before my finger can hit the trigger. I'm forced back a second time, but he's not the fighter I am. I'll get him yet.

We stare at each other, waiting for an opening. My breaths are coming fast now. So are his. I should get this over with quick, or I'll be too exhausted to handle the next one.

He grins. I step back, my blade coming up. Bish. Did his squad flank me?

"What the hyuk is that for?" I growl. "You enjoying this or something?"

"No. You just remind me of someone. You're pretty like she is."

If he's trying to distract me, he's doing a poor job of it.

"And you're about to die." I dodge right and thrust my blade at his side. It catches him off guard. He barely gets his bar on my knife. The tip of it scratches his ribs, and he sucks a breath in through his teeth. The boy backs off, and I follow, cutting at his chest. He throws his arms up to avoid losing his guts and gets in a lucky block.

I attack again and again, but he evades. We're both getting tired. Good. This won't last long. Either he exhausts himself and retreats, or I skewer him and teach him the lesson all Fahrasi should learn: keep away or die.

Then it happens—he steps wrong and trips. I'm on him in an instant. My knife goes over my head, ready to plunge it into his chest. I swing down, but he catches it on his bar, holding it in both hands. Wrong move. I slide my blade off it and continue down. He's done.

"No!"

Efa's body slams into me before her voice reaches my brain. I fall over, crushing into the hard composite of the exchanger's chassis. Sparks cross my vision, and I'm blinded. My arms flail out, hoping to protect myself from her sudden attack. Efa keeps her arms wrapped around me as if her petite frame is going to stop me from fighting. But why?

I shove Efa aside and jump to my feet, my blade slicing the air in front of me. As soon as I finish this bish-head off, I'm going to skewer my squad mate with as many curses as I can think of.

The boy only stares, wide-eyed, and I consider caution. Another Fahrasi could come any second. I need to be on my guard.

I charge, my blade coming up. He moves then, taking a few steps back. It doesn't matter. I'll still reach him and slice his fingers off. If he doesn't want to fight, then he'll just have to take my punishment. Losing a finger or two will make him think twice about stealing our food.

"Ceri, stop!" Efa entangles my legs, and I crash, face first, into the deck.

And right in front of the Fahrasi.

My brain screams alarm. I twist and kick off the deck, putting as much distance as I can between me and my enemy. But I've lost my blade. I'm weaponless. Even with the two of us here, he's got the advantage now.

I drop into a stance, ready to battle him hand to hand. He just stands there frozen. Battle panic? No. He was ready to take me out before. Something's wrong, especially with my squad mate.

"Let him go," Efa says, breathless.

"Why the hyuk would I do that?" I challenge.

"Just trust me!"

"Why?"

The boy shifts and tenses. He was watching Efa and me spit words back and forth. Now he's ready to attack or run. I'm not sure, nor do I care, which. All this standing around is getting to me.

With a last look at Efa, the boy turns and bolts. Fine. I'll just find my weapons so I can kill my squad mate with them instead. To stop me from hurting myself is one thing. To stop me from hurting the enemy is treason. There'd better be an extraordinary reason for this, or I'm going to do damage to something, and it could be her.

"Efa, what the hell?" I say and pound my fist on the floor. "I had him! Why did you stop me?"

"Ceri." Efa backs away, her hands pressing together as in prayer. "I'm sorry. I just didn't want you to hurt him."

My forehead gets tight. Not want me to hurt him? This, from the girl who took her first life at fourteen, two years before I did.

"That won't cut it! You either tell me why now, or I'm going to drag you straight to Captain Daga and make you explain it to his face! Do you realize what he could do to you? This is hyuking treason, Efa! You want to be executed?"

Efa grimaces and ducks her head. Good. The threat of punishment had better terrify her. I don't want to see her die any more than she does, so she better give me something now, or I might just carry out her sentence right here.

"Ceri, Efa! Respond!" The captain is angry. That's normal for him, but his tone adds another level of fury that I'm reluctant to confront, especially when I don't know what's going on with my squad mate.

"Go ahead, Captain," I say, attempting to keep my tone calm so I don't provoke him.

"Give me status! Efa, are you holding position? I will skin you alive if you moved."

Efa stares at me, the whites of her eyes making a ring about her pretty brown irises. I've always envied them. I hate blue with a passion. It's the color that the Fahrasi wear on their armbands.

As I glare down at her, Efa's gaze turns pleading, and I curse under my breath. After the bish she just pulled, she wants me to cover for her, too. I have every right to report the truth. The captain is no friend of mine, but I know better than to get on his bad side, like I have many times before. I should tell him what a screw-up Efa's been.

But then, tomorrow, my squad mate of seven years would be dead.

Efa's lower lip trembles when she reads the intention behind my eyes. It shakes my resolve, and I sigh, my shoulders relaxing. I can't commit her to punishment. Not from an adult. They've already hurt us enough.

"*Well?*" the captain says.

"She's still in position, Captain. Standby," I reply, my eyes locked on Efa's.

"*Like hell I'm going to standby. What's your status, Ceri?*"

"Enemy combatant repelled. No signs of others."

"*Understood. Pull back to delta position and await further orders. I may need you two for backup. Send the rest of your squad back to base.*"

I level an expectant look at Efa, who continues to shrink from my gaze. She's always looked at me as her big sister. I don't enjoy playing that role, but I care about her, and so I've allowed myself to be a pushover when it came to her requests. Even when they put us both at risk. Like now.

She's crossed the line this time, and I will make sure she remembers that for a long time. A very long time.

I pick up my weapons and return to her, the rage in my body only slightly diminished. Efa presses her lips together, stepping back as I approach. Three steps later and her back is against the tall side of an atmospheric scrubber.

The heels of my hands slam the machine on each side of her head. Efa winces as the boom of the impact echoes throughout the level. I just gave away our position. Efa knows I'm showing her how furious I am.

"Now we're going to delta position, and when we get there, you're going to tell me just what was so important that you put me at risk, not even twice, but three hyuking times!"

"I can't, Ceri."

A tear drops from her eye, followed by another. If it's meant to get sympathy from me, it won't work. She can cry herself dry for all I care.

"I just lied to the captain to save your dimply ass. *Can't* doesn't exist in your vocabulary right now." I jab my finger in her face. "You will tell me, or I'm going to gut you and throw your body to the Fahrasi to eat."

Efa looks up at me in the murky light of the status bulbs of the exchangers, wondering if I'd really do what I just threatened to. I'm not sure myself. I've never been this mad at her.

"Okay." She sniffles. "I will. I'll tell you."

CONFESSION

WE PULL BACK AS ordered, in silence, as required, meandering through the broken piles of scrap on level eight—no one's ground. Only battles happen here. Only blood and death. There is no other reason to be here. Life is elsewhere. Our faction holds the aft and parts of the upper levels, while the Fahrasi have command and control at the fore and most of levels twenty-seven through twenty-nine, where many of their people remain in stasis. There are many more levels below, but no one has ever been there.

It's standard to retreat in quiet, but this stillness is a disquiet between us. Now that Efa has betrayed my trust, my mind has turned restless. It will affect my ability to decide things in the heat of battle, but I have already made the worst choice I could. I have broken the chain of command by lying to my captain.

Delta position is nothing more than a haphazard collection of tipped-over tables, torn screens, and broken ductwork, all piled together to create the sense of a secure place. It's not. We have taken it from the Fahrasi as many times as they have reclaimed it. It is likely the one construction, however pathetic, on this ship that has had any level of collaboration between factions.

"Delta is clear, Captain," I say through the comm. Perhaps it will stop our squad commander from badgering us. He has three squads under his command, yet he seems to pick on C Squad—ours—the most.

"Understood. Efa with you?"

"Affirmative."

"Good. Standby. I think we've pushed their challenge back for today. Just waiting on the report from the scouts."

That could mean a long wait. There is nothing to do other than eat or sleep. And I am not tired. Or hungry.

My body drops onto what was a whole container once. I motion for Efa to grab a seat, but she shakes her head and stands in front of me as a guilty child might. We are still children, after all. At least, according to the adults.

"Come on," I say. "Let's go. Spit it out."

Efa lets out a desperate sigh. "Can't you just trust me?"

"Do you really want to die that badly?"

Despite the near darkness, the anguish on her face is clear. My heart constricts, even as the rest of me still burns hot with rage. Ever since we met, we've held an unbroken trust between us and shared everything. The lump in my chest isn't just about anger. It hurts that she's keeping this from me.

Efa drops her pack to the floor and sits on it. Her body heaves as she lets out a shaky breath and stares at her fingers. If this is her gathering courage, I'll be patient. Just not for long.

After a minute, she sighs again and says, "I didn't mean it to happen, Ceri. I couldn't control my feelings."

I blink. "What? What do you mean, your feelings?"

"That boy you almost killed...his name is Merek."

Efa's tears fall again, but she holds her head up as she stares off into the distance. She's made peace with her confession. I, on the other hand, feel a storm surging up inside of me.

"How in the hyuk do you know his name?" I ask, fearing the answer. "What's so special about him?"

"We're in love."

The ship spins before my eyes as her words solidify in my mind. I shake my head with a fierce energy, stuck between yelling at her for making things up and trying to comprehend the possibility of it. Efa? In love with the enemy? It couldn't be true. She doesn't know what that kind of love is.

As I struggle to grasp her simple declaration, Efa looks at me, the desire to be understood deep within her eyes. Maybe she doesn't realize what she's saying, but she believes it. And that's worse.

"And, *dithdi*, we need your help," Efa adds. She moves off her pack and kneels before me, reaching out for my hands. Her touch breaks me from my confusion and snaps my mind back to reality. I snatch my hands away and frown at her addressing me formally as her older sister.

"Yeah, you need my help, alright—to get your brain examined. Do you even realize what you just said? How could you be in love with...with...a Fahrasi?"

"Please, Ceri." Efa presses on my knees, her eyes once again pleading with me. "You asked me to tell you. I am. Can't you see how hard this is for me?"

"I didn't ask," I grumble and look away. My fury is waning, even as I fight to keep it burning. I'm still mad that she kept this from me, but now that it's clear she's not about to switch sides or spy for the enemy, my empathy for her situation is increasing. "Fine. Tell me, then," I say.

"I know you think I'm being foolish."

"So you noticed that?"

"Come on!" Efa whines as she slaps her hands on my thighs. "I've thought about this, Ceri. A lot. I know how I feel. And I wouldn't be in love with him if I thought he was our enemy. But he's not like the others. He doesn't want to fight us. And...he loves me. He's said so."

Efa's face brightens when she talks about him. It's as if this is the first time she's realized his feelings for her are real. I still have doubt, but my thoughts are turning from killing my squad mate to protecting her. There's more danger in her fantasy than she realizes, and not all of it is physical.

"We're not stupid," Efa continues. "We know, as things are, there's no way for us to be together. But I...we want to change that."

"Change what?"

"I want you to help Merek and me find a place to hide." When she sees I don't quite understand, she adds, "*To live. Our lives.* Together. Away from all this. That's how we'll change our situation."

Her words come clear to me and my stomach tightens. She's not being foolish; she's utterly delusional. Sure, there are plenty of levels on this ship that no one's been to in hundreds of years, but there's a reason for that. No one awake needs to go there. Or would want to.

"You are out of your mind," I say. "And you want me to support such an idiotic idea?"

Efa shakes her head, denying the truth of my question. "I'm not crazy, Ceri. I just want to be with him, and I need you to help me."

"Forget it. I won't help you kill yourself. And that's what's going to happen if you try to escape."

A whimper escapes her throat. "Ceri, please! You've never been in love, so—"

"That won't help you convince me."

Efa huffs and sits back, hugging her knees to her body. She's trying to get through to me, and I'm not making it easy. Why should I? What she wants is beyond stupid. Even if this boy is some kind of pacifist, which I doubt, he can still hurt her. I don't think she gets that.

"Then how can I?" Efa pleads.

"How can you what?"

"Convince you."

"Efa, how did you spend enough time with a Fahrasi boy to fall in love with him? How'd you even meet him? And how long have you kept this from me? I've been trying not to blow up about that, you know. Why didn't you trust me with this? I've got your back, Efa. And you'd better have mine, too. So give me everything, or I'm done talking."

Efa looks down, regretful. Of her own actions? Or my response? I'm unsure. I feel bad about slamming on her so much, but if I don't, she'll step right on a bomb. And I need my squad mate—my friend—to survive. If we weren't awaiting orders, I'd march her straight back to base and lock her in the toilet until she got her sense back.

Is this what being in love is like?

"It was all an accident," Efa says. "At least at first. You remember those comms we stole from the Fahrasi so we could listen in on their operations?"

I nod. That was only a few months ago.

"Well, I was testing one out when I keyed the mic without knowing it. I must have been talking nonsense to myself for three minutes before I realized my mistake. Then I hear this voice get on and blast me for being dumb. But Merek was kind after that, and I took a liking to him. We must have talked at the end of every shift for two weeks before we agreed to meet."

Efa shies and distracts herself by playing with a strap on her pack. I lean forward, reaching to touch her hands, encouraging her to continue when she looks at me. After a moment, she does.

"It was only then that we realized we were on opposite sides." Efa chuckles. "I almost shot him before he identified himself! He didn't even have a weapon on him. I mean, who's the dumb one, right? I don't even remember what we talked about. It was just nice to be doing something besides fighting for once. After that, we met once a week. Merek even brought me little gifts."

"Like what?"

"Oh, whatever he could get his hands on, I guess. Trinkets, mostly, though there was this one time he brought me ice cream."

I lean forward. "What's ice cream?"

"Ceri, you'd love it!" Efa's face lights up, and she grabs my hands to shake them. "It's luscious and sweet and has the most amazing flavors! Nothing like I've ever tasted! I think it was called mint chocolate."

I try to imagine ice cream. It didn't exist on Earth, and nothing I've ever eaten here has given me a pleasure equivalent to what I see in Efa's animated eyes. No one has. *Enjoyment* is a word seldom used on the *Stratford*.

"Ceri, Efa. Call in."

"Go ahead, Captain," I say.

"Legs up, ladies. I'm sending the two of you back in. Scouts report more activity on level nine. Looks like they caught B Squad sleeping. You're the only two not otherwise engaged, so you're up. Get in there and clean up that mess."

"Acknowledged. We're on our way."

"Wait!" Efa jumps on me before I can move. "You haven't given me your answer! I'm not going until you do."

"Efa, stop being a fool."

"I'm not!" She reaches up and takes my face in her hands, tilting it until our eyes connect. "Look at me! I'm serious about this. You may not understand why, and sometimes I don't get it either, but I know how I feel! So please...*please*, Ceri. Tell me you'll help us be together!"

I pull her hands away from my face but hold on to them. I feel like she's about to run away from me to be with this...this Fahrasi. That she'd choose him over me makes my chest burn something fierce.

"You've got some real cheek to ask me like this, Efa," I say. "Did you ever consider that he could just be using you for intel? Every little innocent question he asks could add to a Fahrasi plan. Is that what you want?"

"No! Merek would never do that! He's not our enemy!"

"Maybe and maybe not. I believe you when you say you love him, but you aren't thinking like a soldier right now. And there's a million other reasons for me to say no. So no."

"That's not fair!"

"The adults forbid relations between soldiers on the *same side*, Efa. What do you think would happen if they caught you with the enemy? I'm not doing this and neither are you."

"No!" Efa collapses into me with a sob. "Why can't this just be simple? Why can't we just be together?"

It's not a question that needs an answer. Not from me, anyway. She will have to work this out on her own until she can accept reality. All I can do is help her through it, like a big sister might.

"Come on," I say, rubbing her back. "We've got a job to do. The captain is expecting us, and we need to stay off his bish list."

Efa remains on me for another minute, and I keep my protest to myself. I much prefer she stays close to me, so I can keep my eye on her. It comforts me, too. There's no one else I trust like Efa.

"Okay." Efa sniffles and lifts from my lap, catching my eye as she does. "I don't blame you. I know you're just trying to protect me. Thank you for that."

When she remains quiet after, I wonder but leave it at that. I have a feeling I will need to keep my eye on her.

DEATH

WE ARRIVE TO A mess. Not the typical clutter that covers most decks—this is a failure of execution. B Squad didn't position themselves well, and the enemy flanked them. Now Efa and I must take charge, or the babies of B Squad will have more to worry about than just avoiding the wrath of Captain Daga.

"That's it? Just you two?" Deryn, D Squad's pip-squeak field leader, stares at us as we march into his position. He should do a better job of keeping his surprise hidden, but he didn't hide his squad well either, so I'm not surprised at his lack of emotional control. Deryn's only fifteen. I shouldn't expect much of him in terms of maturity. Still, he's responsible for eight lives. The least he could do is keep his mouth from hanging open like that.

"You wouldn't need us if you'd deployed your team correctly," Efa says, putting her fist under his jaw and lifting until Deryn's teeth snap together. Then, to press her insult more, she pats his cheek.

"Like you've done any better!" Deryn pulls away from Efa's hand and swats at it. "If it wasn't for you letting them get past, my squad wouldn't need support!"

"What did you say?" I move forward, leveling my gaze at him.

Deryn sneers at me. "I don't repeat myself. Pay attention next time."

If there is one thing that bothers me to no end, it is someone attempting to blame me for their own mistake. I step up to Deryn, using my height advantage to stare him down. He tries not to be intimidated, but judging by his quickened respiration, I am effective in my ploy.

"If *you* were paying attention, C Squad repelled the attack on level eight. That means the Fahrasi infiltrated this level from *below*. So if you were thinking you should deploy your squad to defend against an attack from above, then you're a bigger idiot than I assumed."

Deryn's eyes widen, and he steps back. His lower lip even trembles a bit. I could have been gentler, but really he deserved worse. Deryn needs to learn group tactics, and if he can't, he shouldn't be field leader.

"Easy on him, Ceri," Efa says. "He knows what he did wrong."

"Then he had better not mess up again," I reply, giving Deryn a hard glance. He attempts to stand up to my warning, but his motions are hesitant. Reluctant even. Good. A little fear might make him remember for next time.

I've been where he is right now. All field leads have. During my first command at sixteen, I nearly made the same mistake. It was only by accident that I realized my squad was in the wrong position and rushed to reposition them. I got chewed out hard by the captain for my stupidity, then I found a hole to cry in so no one would see me. I straightened up quick after that.

"*Deryn, Deryn!*" one of his squad calls over the comm.

"What is it?"

"*Enemy sighted! Four...no...five!*"

"Hyuk!" Deryn looks at me. He wants me to go solve his problem for him. In the interest of his team, I will. We might compete, but we're all Tarakh. I don't want his squad to die any more than my own.

"Pull them back," I say. "Defensive positions! Make sure they can see each other."

"Yeah, yeah, I know! I know!"

"Then do it!"

He gets back on comm and, with a little help from Captain Daga, gets his team situated.

"*Ceri, Efa,*" the captain says. "*Get out there and push those bastards back.*"

"I'm coming with you," Deryn says.

"Then I'll take point," Efa adds. I know why. But she won't see him again. Not today. Merek, or whatever his name is, knew I had him. He'll keep away from the front for now.

We race toward the center of the level, where Deryn's positioned three of his team. If they've situated themselves well, they should be fine facing superior enemy numbers. Level nine isn't a big open space like eight is. It's a labyrinth of corridors, around which anyone could wait in ambush. That's to our advantage.

Efa darts ahead of us, keeping to cover twenty paces away, as per our training. She's a solid point person and knows this level better than I do. Efa knows most levels better than me. If she wanted it, she could be the field leader of C Squad. Sometimes I think she turned it down because she wanted me to have it. Though it isn't much of a command. Captain Daga keeps a tight leash on all of us.

"*Deryn!*" Cai, Deryn's point, shouts out. "*They're after Yale!*"

"Hold," Deryn replies. "We're almost there. And keep your voice down!"

"*All of you keep your voices down!*" Captain Daga hisses. "*Noise and light discipline!*"

I put my hand on Deryn's back and push him along as Efa speeds up. She hits the last turn and pulls out her pistol, covering me. I move forward when she signals. We'll alternate leads until we come into contact with the enemy. Then we'll close in and take them down.

"*Deryn!*" Cai's twelve-year-old voice cries. "*Yale's in trouble!*"

"Where is he?" I ask before Deryn can respond. If he shouts out of worry, he'll give us away.

"*Ceri! He's in bay twelve! I just lost visual! Please help him!*"

"I'm going," Deryn says. I grab his uniform as he tries to pass. Deryn yelps, his arms flailing about. I throw him behind me with a glare. He can get himself killed all he wants, but he's not putting Efa and me in danger. Or his team.

A pained cry shatters the quiet. Then movement. A dark shape emerges from the bay. It's a Fahrasi! With a sharp breath, I raise my pistol and fire.

My dart scrapes the wall, sparking as it does. The Fahrasi throws their hands up and sprints away. Efa fires a shot in vain. Our opponent is already gone. We'll need to remain vigilant, however. A few could still be around.

Deryn slips by me on his second try, racing toward the bay and diving in. My jaw tightens, but I stay put. I should chase him down and beat him for breaking formation. There's no need. The captain will do it twice over once he returns to base.

He might wish it was me, though. I'd be less harsh on him than any adult.

Efa takes point again, covering me as I move up and slide into the bay. She's behind me a second later. I scan the room, weapon up. It's clear. Only Deryn is there. Deryn and a body on the floor.

As I approach, he sniffles. It doesn't take much to know what happened. I can do little more than pat his shoulder as we stare down at Yale's lifeless form. There is no way to resurrect the dead.

Our everyday life is violence. Wake up, fight, sleep, fight again. I've become so numb to it I struggle to feel anything about the murder of yet another soldier, even one of Yale's age. But I can't afford to cry over every child. I'd grieve so often, I'd become useless, and if I want to survive, I need to remain valuable to the adults.

"Hyuk it all!" Deryn says in between sobs.

There are a thousand kind things I could say about Yale. None of them matter. He won't hear them. All we can do is build that wall around our hearts like we've always done and keep moving. Every child woken up to fight was dead the moment they opened their eyes.

"Deryn, take Yale and return to base with your squad," the captain says, his voice staying calm. *"I'm bringing A Squad up from seventeen. Efa and Ceri, you hold until they arrive."*

"Negative, Captain," I reply. "We're going after them."

"Since when do you give orders to me, grunt?"

Bish.

I would be smart to keep my mouth shut. Not like I have in the past. He's just waiting for an excuse to pound my head into the deck for speaking my mind.

"Stay put and wait for A Squad. Deryn, get moving," the captain adds when I stay silent.

I give Deryn's shoulder a gentle squeeze. He acknowledges my sympathy with a nod and wipes his nose with this sleeve. Then, with a breath, he scoops his fallen comrade up and heads out.

Once he's clear, I give Efa a sign to mute her comm. She raises an eyebrow but complies and gets close.

"You want to get that Fahrasi before A Squad does, don't you?" Efa whispers, her gaze pained.

"I'm glad I made it obvious."

"Aren't you in enough trouble with the captain already?"

"No more than you."

She catches my stare and wrinkles her nose. It's me she's in trouble with, really. The captain doesn't know about her indecent meetings with an enemy combatant. I will keep it that way if she follows my suggestions to get rid of him.

"Okay," Efa says, a hint of reluctance in her voice. "Then you take point."

We push forward, flowing through the corridors as fast as is safe. It's not. I can't see much past my outstretched hand. The next turn I take could put me face to face with a Fahrasi. I keep my pistol in one hand and my blade in the other, and hope that I am faster than my enemy.

A pair of voices up ahead stops me in my tracks. They're Fahrasi, for certain. Perhaps not the one I'm looking for, but it doesn't matter. Any hit is proper revenge for Yale.

I motion Efa forward, then drop to a crouch. She nods when she hears them talking. They should keep giving away their position like that. It makes them easy to target.

Efa motions toward a junction and moves off. She'll go around and hit them from the side. They might turn and fire back, or they'll run in my direction. Either way, they're done.

I search the darkness, straining my eyes to locate our opponents. I saw little of the fleeing Fahrasi who got Yale, but I remember the manner of his movement. That's more important than the details of pure sight in this dim light. If he's out there, I'll pick him out. He'll be the one cringing behind the others.

The whine of flying darts fills the air. It's Efa's gun. The Fahrasi turn and fire back, retreating towards me. I've got a clear shot, and I take it. A volley of darts bursts from my pistol. A second later, one of them cries out.

They fire back, blind to my position. I open up with another clip, covering the breadth of the corridor. They run, and I charge after, whistling to bring Efa forward.

There's a thump ahead of me—one of them's fallen. Were they hit? I aim for the sound and fire, rewarded by a sharp moan.

I chance my light, turning it on full to blind anyone dumb enough to be staring my way. The wounded Fahrasi is there, kneeling on the deck. His hands go up to block the light, one of them dripping blood. I shine my light down the hallway, but his partner is long gone.

"Mercy," he croaks. "Please! Let them take me back!"

My eyes narrow as I feel my heart harden to his plea. I'm far past forgiveness.

"Yale," I hiss, and the Fahrasi lowers his hands, confused. "Did you give Yale mercy?"

His eyes go wide as I raise my gun, my teeth clench. A second later, I pull the trigger, and the Fahrasi—a boy about my age—collapses. My light goes out once it's done, and I slide to the floor as my breath comes up short. My body turns numb as I stare into the darkness. I'm glad for my lack of vision. The absolute nothing of deep black is comforting. And right now, I need it.

I wish I hadn't seen his eyes. It's always harder that way. Not that killing is ever easy. It's just another part of the day, and perhaps that makes it worse. No one should have ending a life as part of their normal routine. Though, I wish someone would explain what is normal about any of this.

"Ceri," Efa whispers as she snatches my arm and tugs me up. I relax my muscles and let her pull me along. We still need to return to the staging area and rendezvous with A Squad to finish clearing the level of Fahrasi infiltrators.

I hope we find no one else.

APPEAL

THE CAPTAIN HAD THE wisdom to call Efa and me back to base. Maybe he heard the weariness in my voice, or maybe he had intel that said we'd done our fighting for today. I am thankful no matter the reason.

I put my hands and feet on the sides of the ladder to fourteen and let gravity take me down. It's not really gravity, but I know no other word to call it. They built the *Stratford* like a tower: command and control near the top, and the engines where the basement would be. Constant, gentle acceleration keeps our feet pressed against the deck. If we ever get this ship back on course, then one day we will decelerate, and for the short time it takes to flip the ship around, our gravity will disappear.

Today, though, it is not a problem for me to worry about.

"You should wash up first," Efa says to me when I fall into my sleep nest. "You've got blood on your face."

"And it will still be there when I wake," I reply.

Efa looks down at me, pity on her face as if I am some small, hungry child. I attempt to ignore her and reach to undo the laces on my boots. But as I stretch my arms out, she grabs them and tugs me up. I make a feeble attempt to resist and fail.

"Efa, leave me alone," I say.

"After I wash that stuff off your face. Besides, I want to talk to you."

"Aren't you exhausted of talking?"

Efa remains quiet as she drags me to the toilet facility, my hands still held captive in hers. I can barely stand and struggle not to crash into her. It's not common for her to be so adamant, so it must be important. As much as I want to simply close my eyes, I owe it to her to at least listen. I am wary of her demand, however. I don't want to talk anymore about this Merek boy, if that's what she wants. Yet I suspect that's exactly what this conversation will be about. Whatever it is, it better be quick.

Once we're inside, Efa glances down the corridor before sliding the door shut and locking it. Then she pushes me down onto the toilet and grabs a rag, soaking it under the faucet with warm water and adding the sanitizing chemical that substitutes for soap here. Its scent is barely pleasant. It's still better than smelling of sweat and death.

Efa takes my chin with one hand and presses the rag against my face as I watch my surrogate mother care for me. I have done the same for her more often than not. Our actual parents remain frozen, their lives suspended in stasis until we arrive on our new homeworld. The only adults awake are those required to keep the ship running. They've sacrificed their chance to step foot on a new planet so that others can arrive safely.

They sacrificed our chance, too, without even asking. Not that they could have. Once pulled from stasis, there's no returning. Perhaps they thought children were expendable. We don't have the knowledge or expertise to build a new world. And adults can always make more children.

"Hold still," Efa says, gripping my chin tighter. I resist, but there is little point. It's simpler just to let her finish.

"So why lock the door?" I ask.

"Why do you think?"

"No games, Efa. If you have something to tell me, then say it. Otherwise, let me sleep. You should too. There's no telling when—"

"I want you to reconsider," Efa blurts out.

I pull my chin from her grasp and let my gaze penetrate hers. She turns from me, stepping away. Now my tired brain understands what it is she wants. I have no interest in changing my mind, however. I'll let her say what she needs to, then I will collapse into my nest.

"Talk then," I say, my voice growing hard. "Tell me why you think I'm wrong."

"Why, Ceri?"

"That is what I am asking you."

"No." Efa pivots back. "I mean, why do we have to fight each other? Why are the Fahrasi our enemy? Who decided that?"

"People who are long dead. You won't be getting an answer from them. And they've told you the same things they told me when we woke from stasis."

Efa shakes her head. I expect that wasn't the answer she was hoping for. If she wants me to play along, she'll need to try harder than that. I won't make this easy. Efa needs to understand the danger her desire has put her in.

My squad mate sets her jaw and stares. She's going on the offensive. I should commend her for that, if I could find it in me to do so. But she's about to attack me, and I can't be lazy about it, or Efa's words will beat me back.

"Do you think that boy you killed today was any different from us?" Efa says, crossing her arms.

"Why bring him up?" I reply as my stomach twists. Now his face is in my head, and suddenly sleep is a scary notion.

"Just answer me."

I tilt my head to the side and let it hang there for a moment. What I should be doing is considering my reply so I can speak with honest intention. That won't happen now. That boy's terrified stare has replaced all reason and logic in my mind.

"No, he's not," is what I can muster. It's the truth. I don't hate the Fahrasi. Not really. I don't like them, either. All I know of them is that they're capable of two things: fighting and stealing.

"Exactly," Efa says. "So, isn't it possible that they have no more interest than we do in killing?"

A sigh escapes my lips. Efa is attempting to reason me into supporting her. Perhaps I need to give her a stronger response. For her sake, I will try to manage one.

"And what does that have to do with you falling for this boy?"

"His name is Merek. Please call him by his name."

"Why? Am I supposed to like him now that I know his name?"

"No. I just want you to understand he's a person."

"A person you love, is that it? So I should just give him permission to do whatever he wants to you?"

Efa's cheeks turn red as she presses her lips together and ducks her head. Now I know they've done more than talk. And it makes me like him even less than when I was about to stick him with my blade.

Still, I'm curious. Adults tell us little about courtship, and what information we know we've had to beg for. I can imagine some, but that's all that gets to happen. The punishment for anything beyond talk is a month's worth of solitary isolation and some harsh chemical injection. Efa's the first to take the risk.

"So you've kissed him," I say as a prompt for her to tell me more.

"Come on." Efa's tone begs me not to press. Now I must know.

"Have you done more than that?"

"Ceri!" Efa's jaw goes slack, and she pulls away from me as if I just suggested heresy. I still have my answer, and it fits my assumption. But kissing is bad enough. I worry about what happens when the two of them really give in to their throes of passion.

"You need to keep his lips away from yours," I warn. "It will lead to...other things."

"When did you become an expert?" Efa fires back. "You've kissed no one. Not even me."

"Why would I kiss you?" I pull back and frown.

"I just mean you shouldn't lecture me on what to do with a boy when you've never even looked at one with anything more than suspicion!"

"Keep your voice down, Efa."

"Then you keep your mouth shut!"

My mouth closes then. Not because Efa ordered it. I've pushed her too hard, and this is her reaction to my lack of tact. I'm exhausted and not thinking straight, so I've relied on what I do best. Fight. But this is a sensitive issue for her. I should be more aware of her feelings.

"Okay," I say, pressing my knees together as my hands slide over them. "I'm sorry. I will be more considerate."

"You'd better!" Efa's warning is only half-serious, and a moment later, she smiles and chuckles, unable to hold her anger against me. I join in the second I feel the tension break between us. We've argued before but could never remain angry with each other for long. I am still sore from her betrayal, but instead of finding reasons to be mad at her, I'll look for ways to settle the argument. If that means giving in to her a little, I will. But only a little.

"Efa," I say after our laughter has died off. "As much as you may want it to, or as much as I want happiness for you, you have to know, this won't end well. The one time you're careless about sneaking off to see him might be the last time. Do you understand that?"

Efa nods, her face becoming pained. She may wish for a fairy-tale ending to this, but in the back of her mind, she knows how unlikely that would be.

"Does that mean you won't help me?" she asks, her eyes finding mine. They turn misty as she waits for my reply.

"I am helping you."

"Is that what this is?"

"Come on, Efa. What do you want me to say? You and Merek should run off and be happy together? Where would you even go?"

"There are places."

"I know the places you mean. There is no life to be made there. What would you eat? What happens if you get hurt? Have you even thought about these things?"

"We've talked about them. Merek said he could take some food stores, and if I can, I'll take some medication from the base supply."

I shut my eyes and shake my head. This conversation is going nowhere. I thought that after we had our little laugh together she'd open up and see reason. That was my delusion. Love, if that is what this is, has got her stronger than I expected.

"No, Efa," I say. "If you get caught doing that, the chief will cut your hands off and throw you out an airlock."

"Ceri, Efa, respond stat!" the captain says through the comm, reminding me I've still got my earpiece in. From the frown on Efa's face, so does she.

"Go ahead, Captain," I reply.

"I need to see you two in my office now."

"We haven't even cleaned up yet," Efa says.

"You'll get your chance for downtime. This takes precedence. Come now."

Efa glares. Not at me. Just in my direction. Matters less important interrupt our conversation again. There's not a choice to be had. If we don't go, the captain will have his darlings in A Squad drag us there.

I shrug at Efa. Perhaps we've found something to agree on, though I don't know what that might be. She's got to come around and see reason at some point, but she may not. Efa is right about one thing: I know nothing about matters of the heart. My only love is for her and our squad. I have no idea how that compares to what she feels for Merek.

Merek. Wonderful. Now I am calling the Fahrasi by his name. Why Efa fell for a boy who's bish at fighting is beyond my speculation. Still, knowing his name makes him seem more human.

DECISION

THE CAPTAIN WATCHES US as we enter his office, a space that can't hold much more than three people and a desk. It is good that there is another door behind the captain's back, then. He won't have to climb over his single piece of furniture to get out.

His permanent scowl hides any hint of his current mood. I will assume since he isn't yelling at us, that he is as content as he can ever be. Yet his constant level of displeasure is not his fault. Just like us, Captain Daga was once a child whose dreams were erased by adults. That's plenty of reason for anyone to always seem like they hate the universe.

"Captain!" I say, using the tone I learned in training as I snap the heels of my boots together.

"Relax, Ceri," he says, patting the air to calm me. I don't need it. As much as I show my respect, my hands still clench whenever I face him. Efa may think I am tough, but she's never seen Captain Daga take out an entire Fahrasi squad by himself.

"Good job repelling the enemy on eight. You kept C Squad together well today. Unfortunately, Deryn still has a way to go before he's as solid as a field lead. We were lucky that A Squad could complete their mission quick enough to come up and take over."

My hands squeeze tighter. More than intimidation, the captain's love for A Squad makes me want to punch a hole in the *Stratford*'s hull and push his pet soldiers out of it. They deserve the credit for their ability, and so do we. Yet the captain has never given us more than a pat on the back. A Squad may be the best, but my team is a tight second.

"Captain," an aide says as she pops through the back door and hands him a tablet. "The report from A."

"Oh, good."

And, of course, now he will take the time to read through it while Efa and I stand here. My exhaustion already makes me unsteady on my feet. If he'd allow it, I'd drop where I am and sit.

I share a glance with Efa. She has a faraway look in her eyes, and that only adds to my tension. Of all the times to be dreaming about her enemy lover, this should not be one of them. I tap her ankle to pull her out of it, hoping Captain Daga doesn't catch my motion.

If Efa slipped about Merek, even one bit, it would draw the captain's suspicion. He'd interrogate her with every tool he's got until she gave something up, and then we'd both feel his wrath, her for her betrayal and me for allowing it to happen. He'd shut the two of us away in storage crates for months with nothing but water and cardboard to eat. I need to impose myself into Efa's situation before she gets us both punished.

"What's this?" the captain says, peering closer at the tablet. "Did you neutralize a Fahrasi?"

"Captain?" I ask, attempting to feign ignorance.

"This has to be your work, Ceri. Nobody else can hit an eye with a dart like that. Did you kill an enemy combatant?"

If Efa hadn't shuffled the moment the captain called me out, I might have been able to deny it. But he noticed, and for me to lie now would only cause me hurt. This is why I fear him learning about this Merek. Captain Daga is highly intelligent and persistent. He would stop at nothing to uproot any hint of deception among his squads. And once he did, his discipline would come swift and hard.

"I did, Captain! He was the one who got Yale," I say, trying to sound proud of my act.

"Yeah? And how did you catch him in corridor five when I told you to stay in bay twelve?"

I only press my lips together. I'm already in trouble. Trying to explain will only get me locked up. I'll just have to hope he goes easy on me because the mission was a success.

"Let me get this straight," Captain Daga says, leaning forward on his desk, "so we are clear about this. You had orders. You disobeyed them because you thought you'd play hero and avenge Yale. Is that about right?"

"Yes, sir," I answer. There are no other words that he will accept.

"And even though there were only two of you versus an entire squad, you decided it was fine to put yourselves at risk because getting back at the Fahrasi was more important than securing your position?" I drop my gaze, but the captain pounds a fist on his desk. "Look at me when I'm talking to you!"

"Sorry, Captain," I say.

His eyes dart between Efa and me as he picks up a stylus from his desk and bends it to just before its breaking point. It's good that Efa has remained quiet. Any words from her, however well intended, would snap that writing implement in two.

"This is your last warning," the captain says, pointing the now bent stylus at us. "The two of you cannot disobey me ever again. I don't care if you can take down the enemy's entire defensive line. If I give you an order, you follow it. Without question. Or I will ensure the rest of your life on this ship becomes a living hell. Got it?"

"Yes, Captain!" I reply.

"Yes, Captain!" Efa adds after he lays a narrow-eyed glance at her.

"Hit your nests, then. We're on the offensive tomorrow. Now get out of my sight!"

Without another word, Efa and I spin on our heels and move out as fast as we can without running. There is little reason to stay, as it would only irritate him more, and I have no interest in finding out what happens if we do.

There's a more pressing issue, anyway. Efa's misguided romance is more precarious than it was just ten minutes ago. Imprisonment is no longer a possibility. The captain will execute us if he finds out.

I have to bring this flirtation to an end, though I worry about Efa's response. She may do something drastic, outside of my protection, like attempt to run with Merek. The *Stratford* is large, but it is not infinite. Any determined pursuer would find them if they looked hard enough.

"Maybe he is right," Efa says once we're clear of the captain's office. "We should have held our position. Besides, you shouldn't have killed that boy like that."

Efa's comment hits me hard, like a slap across the face. I gasp and react. My hands grab her collar, and I shove her against the wall. Efa falls back, shock covering her face. Her hands fly up, and she turns her head to protect her face.

"And what about Yale?" I shout and shake her. "Didn't he deserve to live? I killed that Fahrasi because he's the enemy! I would have ended them all if I had the chance. So don't get all soft on me just because—"

Efa claps her hand over my mouth, her eyes wide. She shakes her head in a panic, and I come to my senses. A quick check of the corridor shows we're in the clear. Other than the captain and his staff, only sentries would be awake now. But if one of them were to hear...

I let her go with an apologetic shrug. That was wrong, but after everything that happened today, I've got little self control left. I need to lie down and shut my eyes, even if I get little rest from it.

As we make our way back to our sleeping space, Efa curls her arm around mine. It's her way of making peace between us, so I let her. Her nearness is comforting, too. It makes me feel like we're in this situation together, just like always.

I remember when they first woke us out of stasis. My head was a jumble of visions. The techs say the brain is still active during suspension, if only a tiny amount. But a never-ending series of dreams that constantly play through our thoughts over hundreds of years has a serious effect. The mind struggles to return to conscious thought. Efa and I helped each other through those first few days by sharing some of the dreams we had. Since then, we've been inseparable.

Now Efa's desire to be with this boy has caught the two of us in a situation where there's no easy way out. I don't want to go against my faction, and I can't betray Efa. That leaves me little choice, and like it or not, we will have to see this through, no matter the outcome.

As squad leader, Efa's survival is my responsibility. As her friend, I want her to be happy. These things are clashing hard, and there can only be one outcome. She's too caught up in her feelings for Merek to have any realistic view of the situation, so I've got to take charge and make decisions for her. Which means I need information, if I am to choose well.

And the only way to get that information, as detestable as I may find it, is to go straight to the source.

"I need to meet him," I say as I sit on my nest.

"What?" Efa freezes, her rag of a blanket halfway over her body.

Before I reply, I scan the other nests of my squad. Everyone, boys and girls alike, is fast asleep, or at least pretending to be. No way to find out without waking them, so I press my head against hers and feign cuddling up with her as we often do.

"Merek," I whisper. "I want you to set up a meeting."

Efa pulls back and stares at me with a blank expression.

"Say yes, Efa," I add.

"Yes...to what? Why do you want to meet him?"

"Because I need to know what I am dealing with."

"What does that mean? What are you dealing with?" Efa's face lights up. "You're going to help us!"

"I never said that."

"Then?"

I watch her moment of joy turn into one of apprehension and suspicion. Her eyes narrow, though, like mine, her eyelids are already hanging heavy. I take a breath to gather my thoughts once more.

"Efa, you heard the captain. We so much as turn left when he orders us right, we're going to be in a dangerous place with him. That means any slipup by you is a slipup by the two of us. I need to know what I'm dealing with so I can keep us away from his bad side."

She considers. I know it cannot be easy for her. Efa wants so much for me just to accept the two of them as connected; any other possibility is hard for her to even acknowledge.

"Okay. I get it," Efa says. "And you're right. I didn't think of it that way. I'm sorry, Ceri. Now you're wound up in this, too."

"So you'll set up a time for us to meet?" I ask.

Efa nods. "Tomorrow, after the assault."

"Good. Then don't die tomorrow, or you won't get to meet your lover."

Efa snorts and shoves me, a smile coming to her face. "Don't you die, either."

I fall back with the force of her push, grabbing my blanket and pulling up over my shoulders. Efa watches me for a moment longer, her gaze passive. Behind it, there is a torrent of emotion, but soon after, she transforms it into an upward curl of her mouth. Then, failing to sustain it, Efa lies down and covers her head with the blanket.

As exhausted as I am, I cannot help but think about what tomorrow will bring. I certainly hope I am doing the right thing. Everything ends if I am not.

MEETING

No one died during our assault. Not even the enemy. Nor did we get any supplies. I would have liked to have stolen the Fahrasi's stock of ice cream. It has been on my mind since Efa told me about it. I am surprised such a thing even exists. On the *Stratford*, it is no more difficult to make food cold than hot, yet I cannot fathom what *cream* might be. Aside from looking out for Efa, it has become my priority to sample as much of it as I can.

"How much farther?" I ask as Efa leads us through winding maintenance tunnels and complex arrangements of conduit up on level five. We are inside the triple hull of the ship, a place no one goes. Or nearly no one. That aspect of our location doesn't bother me. That we are so close to the Fahrasi's principal base does. They may not have eyes inside the hull, but they will most certainly have placed them at any entrance or exit that comes anywhere near their home.

"Almost there," Efa replies. She pauses, staring out into the dark. Then her hand comes up, halting me. My hands go to my weapons, ready to fight our way free if necessary.

When Efa turns to me and smiles, I know I won't need to draw any more blood today. Not unless this Merek tries something stupid. Then I will ensure he understands Efa is off-limits to him. Forever.

I squint and peer over Efa's shoulder. Sure enough, I recognize a lanky silhouette about twenty paces away, just behind a vertical duct that passes through the grated catwalk we're on. Merek waves to us with overenthusiastic abandon and approaches, glancing once behind him to ensure he's clear from observation. I give him credit for having the brains to at least do that.

Efa meets him halfway, and the pair throw their arms about each other. She presses into him, laying her head on his chest as he strokes her hair. I take my time getting over to them, but when they separate to look into each other's eyes and then go to connect lips, I clear my throat as a reminder to them I am here.

"Ceri!" Efa says with a squeak. She turns, moving to Merek's side so the two of them can face me. "This is Merek. Merek, meet my squad mate, Ceri."

Whether or not it is an oversight, I appreciate her not giving away the fact that I am also the squad's field leader. I prefer to remain a simple line soldier. It lessens my value to the enemy.

"You? Wow." Merek's eyes open wide before his face turns into a grin. "I thought you had me for sure."

"I definitely would have," I reply, my gaze never leaving his until he swallows and breaks our contact.

"Yeah, well, good thing Efa was there to stop you." Merek wraps his arm about her and squeezes, to which Efa beams. "Sorry about the comment."

"What comment?" Efa asks, looking between the two of us.

"I think he found me attractive," I say. It's a test for him and for Efa. I want to see if their responses tell me anything.

Merek is more skilled at deception than I would expect. Rather than flat out denying it when Efa gives him a curious glance, he just smiles and nods. His deceit is not so serious, yet my intuition makes me uneasy about his behavior. I can't yet tell why.

"Well, Efa may be the prettiest, but I bet you're the deadliest," Merek says. His smile remains, but behind his eyes is a sense of knowing about something he is unwilling to divulge.

"What makes you think that?" I ask.

"Oh, well," Merek demurs, "the way you fought me with such fierceness. I'm glad I didn't get a knife or a dart through my eye or something."

My shoulders tense. His reply is a bit too specific for my comfort. Few would know about how I took out that boy on level nine. It makes me wonder if he was there yesterday, watching us. That would mean he faked his surprise at meeting me here tonight. There is more to him than he is letting on, that is for certain. I will keep my hand by my blade, just in case.

"Hey, can we stop talking about fighting?" Efa says, breaking the tension. "That's not why we're here, right?"

I continue to watch him, even when he's returned his attention to Efa. He prefers to look at her, as he should, I suppose.

She does not give off an aggressive aura, as I likely do. We are here for different reasons: her to see the boy of her affection, me to ensure that is all he is. At least for now.

"No, it's not," Merek agrees.

An uncomfortable silence follows. Though, I should've expected it. I'm only here to listen and observe, not make small talk. That's for the two of them to do.

"Hey, do you want to see something cool?" Merek asks. "I just found it on my way here tonight."

Efa looks to me for my answer. Hers is obvious. She only wants my permission to go.

"It's clear away from any people, I promise," he adds. "Yours and mine."

I remain tense as he smiles, but if Merek was planning a trap for us, he and his faction would have sprung it the moment we became isolated in the hull wall. Now that we have familiarity with our surroundings, it would be harder for them to capture or kill us. Still, it's barely a comfort.

"Alright," I say. "You're leading the way. I'll cover our backs."

"No need for that." Merek chuckles. "We're alone."

"Would you believe me if I said that?"

My question catches him off guard, but this time, instead of hiding his surprise, he gives me a humbled grin and ducks his head.

"Yeah, fair enough," he says, then shakes his head. "But I would never put Efa in danger. You can believe me on that."

"How about me? Would you put me in danger?"

"Ceri!" Efa chides. "Give him a chance, would you?"

As I've already agreed to do so, there is little reason to change my answer. I am here for Efa. That is all. Merek won't hurt her, and even if he tries, I am close enough to skewer him through his gut with relative ease.

I motion for them to go, then do a quick check of the surroundings, in case we need to escape. The catwalk is narrow, and it would be near impossible to maneuver in a fight. That only leaves the vertical for movement if we become surrounded, but it's a far drop to the catwalk below, which is at least two levels down. It is too dark to know for sure. Up is only a little better, and that would require a good deal of climbing. I'm reluctant to use that option. Ever since our awakening, I have a tendency to get light-headed on a high climb.

Merek holds Efa's hand as he leads her around the catwalk. We're circling the hull of the ship, headed where, I don't know. I've never been on level four, much less in the hulls. We sealed all the hatches from nine to eighteen so the Fahrasi couldn't sneak up on us that way. I'm sure they would, if they could.

I must remember that Merek is one of them, though I will admit, now that I've met him in a non-violent circumstance, he seems less dangerous than I expected. There was only once that I met a Fahrasi in a peaceful situation, and that was during a prisoner swap. The boy and girl we had captured were barely teenage. They both cried when we caught them. The B Squad near-adult we got in exchange was worth way more.

"Okay, we're here," Merek says. He turns toward a hatch on the secondary hull and grabs the lever. A second later, he pulls his hand away and sucks in a breath through his teeth. The lever must be freezing. Now that we've stopped, I can feel the chill coming off the secondary hull. Past it is the main structural hull of the ship, and after that, only the absolute cold of space.

"Use your boot," Efa says, to which Merek takes a hold of the catwalk railing and lifts his leg. With a sharp thrust, he unlatches the lever, then puts the toe of his boot under and pulls toward us.

The frozen air that slips out grips my face with icy fingers, and I'm caught unprepared for the uncontrollable shiver that runs through me. I step back and turn away, careful not to inhale too deeply for fear of my lungs freezing.

Efa gasps, igniting my fear that she's swallowed the frozen air. I spin towards her but stop halfway as a bright glow blankets the area in golden illumination and stabs at my sight. My eyelids squeeze together to block the glare, yet the light still seems to pass through them. A moment later, I feel the light's warmth on me and the chill dissipates from my bones.

I've never experienced light this powerful. It's interesting in its own right, but it's also a problem. Someone could see it from all the way down at the bottom of the ship.

"Are you insane?" I hiss. "Shut that thing before someone spots us!"

"In a moment," Merek says, "once our eyes get used to it. Then you can look, but don't stare right at it. It could blind you."

"What is it?" Efa asks.

"A binary star. One smaller star orbits the other. We're transiting its system right now."

The breath leaves my body. I haven't seen a star since we left Earth, and the memory of that is so distant in my mind it is as alien as the pair of burning globes before us now. Still, to consider these as suns no human has seen before...

"How did you find this?" I ask.

"I had nothing to do while I was waiting for you, so I went exploring. I've no idea why they'd build a window into the outer hull like that. Maybe it was for ease of maintenance or something."

"It didn't occur to you that you could have been killed or captured?"

"No. Not here. No one comes here. There's nothing anyone wants." Merek shrugs. "Well, except maybe this view."

I uncover my eyes, slowly at first. The light is beautiful, though still painful to look at. Seven years of living in the dark has made our bodies adapt. Our eyes have grown more perceptive to what is in the shadows but more sensitive to light. The staggering glow we behold would overpower anyone's vision.

It's not so bad to observe when it reflects off the back wall. The rays of the two stars blend in a dance of red and blue light, combining to create a purple hue. I am captivated by how simple, yet stunning, it is.

Then the panic of reality returns.

"Okay," I say. "That's enough. Shut it."

Merek does as I demand. But when the hatch is closed, it becomes worse than dark. I'm blinded, and there's nothing

I can do about it until my eyes readjust. My stomach turns over the lack of situational awareness. We are easy targets for capture. They'd be on us before we could tell where they were coming from.

"Thank you," Efa says. The tone of her voice is sticky-sweet and breathless. I think she kisses him then. I cannot see, and lips connecting is not a sound I am familiar with. It only twists my insides even further.

"I hope you enjoyed it too, Ceri," Merek says.

"Yeah." I swallow. "Thanks...for...showing us."

It is strange that I struggle for the words. It's right of me to suspect him. He may be kind to Efa, but he is still a Fahrasi, and if I do not break the two of them apart, there will come a day where he will have to choose loyalties. Efa will be put to the same test, and I dread what the captain would command of me should Efa choose wrong.

"Come on," Merek says, putting an arm around Efa. "I'll take you two to an exit so you can get back quickly. I'm sure your squad commander will be looking for you soon."

Oh, he most certainly will be.

The three of us end up at an exit to level eight. It will be an easy climb back to our base, and it's not lost on me that Merek is putting himself at risk to get us this far. We hold most of this level and everything below it for almost twenty more. Our only chance to keep him safe would be to pretend he was a prisoner.

Efa gives me an apologetic glance, then pushes up onto her toes to kiss him once again. Her hands cup his face, and a soft moan of contentment escapes her throat. For a moment,

I forget I am being rude by watching them. And in the next, I realize I am holding my breath.

She is happy with him, of that I am certain. Happier than I have ever seen her. I suppose, for the moment, it wouldn't be a bad thing to allow her that. Efa may never find joy like that again.

The two would-be lovers take a long look at each other before separating. Merek sets his eyes on me then and approaches. I feel my body tense, unsure of his intentions.

"I'm sorry," he says, reaching out to touch my arm, perhaps to show he is honest about his feelings.

"For what?" I ask, backing away from his hand.

"Attacking you. This conflict. All of it." Merek bows his head. "I could never put my heart into the fight, and after I met Efa, I realized why. The Tarakh and the Fahrasi. We're no different. We just can't seem to agree on a way forward."

His words are pleasant and not all that original. There have been others before him who have tried to mend the wounds that separate the two factions. They did not live very long.

"Have you ever killed a Tarakh?" I ask, watching him for this response.

"I wouldn't be here now if I hadn't." Then Merek's eyes rise, pleading to me. "But you have to know how I much I regret it."

"Well, only Efa can believe you. I cannot afford to be so trusting. If we meet in battle again, Merek, know I will have no choice but to kill you. For Efa's sake, I do not wish to see you dead, but I must protect myself, and as you already know, I'm good at it."

Merek presses his lips together and nods. I am sure he wishes the situation could be different.

That is something we have in common.

DISAGREEMENT

As we cross to the ladder heading to level nine, I power on my comm, listening for any mention of Efa or me in case the captain is looking for us. There isn't, and relief comes easily. Captain Daga dismissed us from duty once it was clear our attack was a failure. He blamed it on poor intel rather than any of us. I am thankful that even he gets battle-weary sometimes and takes the simple path to the end of a mission.

"Remember," I say to Efa, "our story is that we stayed behind to scout for the Fahrasi supplies we missed, but still couldn't find anything. That way—"

"Why?" Efa grabs my shoulder, slamming me against the wall's metal plating. Sparks flash cross my eyes as the impact knocks any thought from my head. "Why did you say that to him?"

I take a moment to recover. My body is reeling from the shock and the pain. Efa is stronger than she appears, and she used it against me. I am not sure what stuns me more, her strength or her action.

"Say what?" I ask, my forehead going tight.

"Don't pretend you forgot, Ceri!" Efa seethes and slams me into the wall again. "I heard it! You told Merek that you would kill him! Why?"

I blink, staring at the fire in her eyes. I am feeling some heat of my own—no one pushes me like that. Not even Efa. And her force was intentional. My shoulder blade may be sore over the next few days, but my anger is immediate.

"You misunderstood," I say, forcing calm on myself. This is not the time or place for us to get into a fight. "I didn't say I would. I said if we meet in battle again, I'd have no choice but to."

Efa shoves me a third time, and I give her a hard glare in warning. I am only tolerant to a certain level, and she is already pressing past that line.

"Are you jealous of me? Is that it?" Efa's tone is full of acid.

"Of course not. I have no interest in Merek. Don't be stupid."

"Then why were you so mean to him?"

"When was I mean?"

"All night long! You barely thanked him for taking us up to see that amazing view!"

"But I thanked him, didn't I?"

When her hands come up to drive me against the wall again, I throw mine between her arms and pound them into her shoulders. Efa gasps but recovers quickly, her feet slipping into a fighting stance.

We've fought each other before, mostly in combat training and a few times over nonsense that only two sisters could find reason to hit each other over. The adults stopped us before it became too violent, but right now, there's none of them around. I need to act the older sibling at this moment, or things will get out of hand. Efa has not been this angry in a while. Neither have I.

"Cool down," I say, "or one of us is going to get hurt."

"I'm already hurt," Efa spits back.

"Don't exaggerate. I didn't push you hard."

"Here is where you hurt me!" Efa slaps a hand over her heart as her eyes get wet. "You know, Merek didn't want to meet you. He thought you could be a risk, but he did it anyway because I asked him to. He trusted me to bring someone who was going to understand him. But all you did was act like he was going to stab us both! And then you ended the conversation with 'don't make me kill you'? What kind of hyuk is that? Did you forget how to be a human being? He was hoping you would like him!"

"Well, I don't dislike him," I say and shrug.

"That's it?"

"What else do you want?"

"How about you tell me you're happy for me? How about saying Merek seems like he's nice? Why is it so hard for you to say that?"

"Because it would be a lie."

Efa's mouth drops open—only long enough for her to pull her fist back and swing at me. It's a lazy punch, and I've no trouble blocking it.

But I miss her knee as it comes up and gets me right in my gut. I cough and double over, the air flying from my lungs. Efa steps back, fear covering her face. It's her mistake. She never learned how to press an attack.

I feign falling over—it's easy; Efa hit me hard enough to make me sick—and step forward. I place my foot just behind her leg and spin, throwing my arms under hers, then move up and around her shoulders to clasp my hands behind her neck.

Before Efa can react, my knee goes down on the back of her leg, and I take her down backward. The two of us fall, with Efa landing in between my legs. I swing them up and lock her ankles down with my feet until she stops struggling.

We both take a few heavy breaths, letting the rage flow from us. Efa pushes against my headlock, but I'm not so willing to let her go. I don't want to get hit again. She's done enough damage to me for one night.

"Calm down and listen," I growl. "You've got no idea how messed up you are over this. You're so infatuated with this boy that you don't want to hear anything other than total support of your crazy idea. Why does it have to be you and Merek versus everyone else? All I'm trying to do is protect you, and you take his side instead. You'd be on your own if you pushed me away. I don't want that, and neither do you. And I'm still mad at you for keeping this from me. So give me a break, okay?"

Efa relaxes a little, and so do I. My hands come off her neck and slide to rest on her arms, thankful that she is at least willing to hear me out.

"Merek seems okay, honestly," I continue. "I see how much he cares for you and how happy you are together. That makes a difference to me. I would have pulled you away from him in a second if I thought he would hurt you."

"Thanks," Efa says, her voice quiet. She leans to the side and back, resting her head on my shoulder. "Sorry."

"It doesn't change that he's Fahrasi and you're Tarakh. The two of you may see past faction lines, but few others do. That puts you in real danger. The adults will see it as a Fahrasi boy taking advantage of you, and his people will see it as *you* seducing *him*. Neither is the truth, but until everyone accepts this as real, you will always be hiding your feelings for him. Is that what you want?"

"No, of course not." Efa pivots so she can look at me. The light from a status lamp on the wall highlights the wetness on her cheeks—more than I've seen in a long time. "I just want you to like him. If you could do that, it would mean everything to me, Ceri."

My breath gets shaky as a sob wells up inside my chest. I want nothing more than for her to be happy. It just may not be possible.

I brush her cheek dry with my thumb, smiling at her through worry-soaked eyes. Efa tries to smile back and fails. I shake my head at her, and she laughs. It's contagious, and after a moment of her pathetic state, I chuckle, but I have to stop when the ribs on my back ache.

"That hurt, you know," I say. "Did you really have to hit me so hard?"

"You deserved it. You were being a total bish-head," Efa replies, her face hard. Then she softens a little. "I'll steal some topical painkiller from the med office for you, okay?"

"Fine, but you're going to put it on for me."

"Fine, I will." She pats my arm and gives me a hopeful smile. "We good, then?"

"That depends."

Efa sighs as if she knew that was coming. I still have something to say, though I will try to take the edge off my words, despite the pain in my shoulder giving me reason not to. If I am too harsh, I fear she will pull away from me. Then not only will I not be able to protect her, but I will be alone. I am not sure which one scares me more.

"Tell me," Efa says.

"I won't hurt him, Efa," I reply. "That, I promise. Merek won't seek me out in a battle either, so you shouldn't have any worry about us hurting each other."

"I am not worried about *him* hurting *you* in a fight, Ceri." The grin that follows tells me why she thinks that way. So I am not the only one who recognizes his lack of battle skill.

"And I promise to be nice to him...provided he remains good to you."

"He will. Now get to the point."

I draw a slow breath as she waits for me to speak. Perhaps I am overthinking this moment. The tingle across my arms says otherwise. Still, I must say this, no matter the outcome.

"I won't stop you from seeing him, Efa, but I still think you should break it off. This will only end badly for the two of you."

Distress crosses Efa's face, and her gaze drops to the floor.

"Maybe you're right," she says, hanging her head, "but I don't think I will ever be strong enough to do that."

MISSION

"OKAY, GATHER UP," CAPTAIN Daga says, motioning to me and the other two field leaders as he strides into the armory and over to a table with a recessed screen. Deryn, Rhain—A Squad's arrogant leader—and I each take a side, while Captain Daga goes to the end to control the screen.

Rhain throws a glance at me across the table. He must have noticed my hunched-over movements and is wondering why. I won't tell him, because he'll use it against me. He won't do something as stupid as tell the captain outright. Instead, he'll leverage that threat for a favor. An extra shift, extra rations, or something like that. It doesn't matter as long as he makes me understand he will always be better than me. I wonder sometimes if he might be right.

"Where are we going today, Captain?" Rhain asks. "Up or down?"

"Down," Captain Daga replies, glancing up at him. "Way down. Level sixty-two, to be exact. Niah and her team have returned with promising evidence there could be a significant store of blankets and medicine there. Level sixty-three contains an unpopulated stasis chamber, and we believe this would be the supplies from the recovery room."

"How many stasis beds?" I ask.

"Niah estimates it at over two hundred."

I whistle out my amazement. With that many units, there could be enough blankets for the entire Tarakh faction to build themselves new nests and still have extra in case they get cold. Not to mention the medicine. We've scavenged a good assortment, but there are still things we lack, like topical painkiller. Efa couldn't find any, and I woke up this morning stiff as a composite fiber board.

"Seems simple enough," Rhain says, looking smug. If he wasn't as good as he thinks he is, I would have taken his spot a year ago.

"It won't be," the captain replies. "Niah encountered a pair of Fahrasi scouts while on patrol. They ran before she could take them out. That means we fully expect the enemy to be in the area. We're deploying all the squads for this one."

Deryn's eyes slide over to me, the edges showing a bit of white. This will be his first long-hike mission. They haven't replaced Yale yet, so he's down one squad member, too. The Captain will likely keep him in reserve.

"As I drew the short straw on this one, my squads will make the trip. D, E, and F will provide a diversion attack on the same target as yesterday. G and H are in reserve as usual. Ceri, I want your squad to take point on this one. Rhain, you will be the main counteroffensive should we need it." The captain turns to Deryn and says, "You're supporting A on this one."

"Yes, Captain." Deryn lets out a relieved sigh. "Thank you."

"That doesn't mean you get to sit around," the captain replies. "If Rhain calls for you, you go in full force. Understand?"

"Yes, Captain."

Deryn may be glad to ride behind the talents of A Squad on this mission, but my team will be out front and exposed. If there's an ambush, we'll be the ones who get hit first.

"Why us, Captain?" I ask. "We were point two days ago. Let A Squad lead the way on this one."

"We're not having a debate over who did what and when. All of you have taken point as of late. You've impressed the chief with your work, and so you get to take lead." When the captain sees my reaction, he adds, "Think of it this way. If you do well on this one, Ceri, you and your squad will be off my bish list."

This is far from the good deal he's attempting to make it sound like. I won't care about being off some list if a rusty Fahrasi blade cripples me. It will always be my preference to have the ability to walk over making Captain Daga happy. I am not even sure the man can smile.

"Alright, continuing on. There's another objective of this mission, but I will stress that this is secondary. The supplies are priority, especially the medicine. However, if you can do this, it will make your lives easier."

"We'll do it, Captain," Rhain, ever the suck-up, says. "Just name it."

"Are you familiar with the *Stratford*'s automated rail system?"

Rhain, Deryn, and I share a confused glance.

"I think the three of you are smart enough to realize the designer of this ship didn't expect us to climb ladders all the time. There are two transport systems that travel the length of the ship. One is the automated rail system, designed to move cargo around, and the other is a passenger transport system. That one is beyond repair, so we won't be touching it."

"What do you want us to do with the rail system?" Deryn asks.

"Get it to work. We know that power is active in the system, but it doesn't respond to our commands. That means it may need a security key. But if you can use it, you can send everything you get your hands on up to level fifteen with a single transport. If you can't…"

"We'll be adding our body weight in cargo to our backs," I say, envisioning the struggle to climb forty-seven levels with the Fahrasi on our heels. There's no telling how many of their squads will be down there. They might not fall for the diversion the other squads will set up.

And then my team will face an overwhelming force while we're moving at half speed. It will be a simple task for the Fahrasi to pick us off as we try to escape. In other words, this is a bish mission, and the captain must know that. He's trying to lure me into taking the risk by dangling the possibility of redemption in my face.

Deryn and Rhain realize it, too. Their squads will retreat before us, though. Last in, but first out. And that leaves my squad to cover them. Right now, I'm sure they're hoping I won't call it out, but if they think I'm going to accept this suicide operation, they're mistaken.

"Captain, A Squad is the strongest of the three of us, right?" I ask.

"Of course," he replies, raising an eyebrow. Rhain smirks and puffs out his chest. He won't be bursting with pride once he hears what I have to say.

"Then doesn't it make more sense that they take point? The faster a squad can get in and get as many supplies as possible, the more likely the mission will succeed. My team is sore from yesterday, Captain. We might not move at our best pace with such a load on our backs."

The captain's face turns stony as he realizes my intention. I did not expect him to like my suggestion right away. I only hope the logic in my suggestion is a better argument than I've been using.

"We need these supplies, Captain," I add. "I'm fine with my squad waiting for another chance to redeem ourselves for the sake of getting as much of that medication up. I think one of Deryn's squad is good at security systems. We'll cover them while she gets access to the rail system."

"What a load of bish," Rhain says. "You're the only one on your team who's sore, and I bet that's because you spent all yesterday lying on your back!"

"Yeah? And where was A Squad yesterday? In the back playing with your little toy guns, that's where. Deryn and I busted our asses looking for an imaginary store of food! You were no help at all."

The captain watches us spit words at each other, his eyes sliding back and forth between me and Rhain. He wants to see how this ends. The bastard is probably enjoying it, too.

"It's not my fault you couldn't find it," Rhain says, waving a dismissive hand. "Cut that mop off your head and you'll be able to see. What do you need hair for, anyway?"

"So I don't look like I have half an ass for a head."

Deryn throws a fist over his mouth, but it's more than obvious that he's laughing at Rhain's buzz-cut hairstyle. Rhain glares at Deryn. It's going to cost him for taking my side. I'll try to protect him from retaliation, but I can't be everywhere at once.

There's no regulation about hair, and everyone wears it as they want. I like mine long, even though it's a risk for combat. After I heard the Fahrasi strangled a boy with his ponytail, Efa and I tie ours down under caps.

"Alright, enough," the captain says, with only mild annoyance. "You three need to work together on this mission closer than you have before. That means I want none of this nonsense to go on from here on out. If I hear any of you disrespecting each other, I will feed you into the engines. Understood?"

"Yes, Captain!" the three of us shout together. Our reply isn't sincere, just well rehearsed. Captain Daga accepts it anyway. He needs to get on with the briefing, and he knows we get his message. It's far from the first time he's threatened to kill us.

"Ceri, I appreciate your logic, but I'm denying your request. You'd know why if you had kept your mouth shut and let me finish. C Squad will locate the supplies and grab what you can, then you're to get out of the way so A Squad can come in and get the bulk of the material. Deryn, your team can cover your own hacker. Once A Squad is clear, you get what's left. If you get the rail system working, send your two best up with the transport."

"Captain," I try once more.

His response is to level his narrowed gaze at me.

"The adult in the room is done talking about this, Ceri," he says in an edgy tone. "All I want from here on out is your obedience to the mission. If you can't handle that, then I'll demote you on the spot and put you under Rhain's lead. Understand?"

I bite my lower lip and duck my head, abandoning any further attempt to change his mind. He has never been one to debate anything. Especially not with the *children*. I hate when he treats us as lesser people. I likely know more about field operations than he does.

"Say it, Ceri!" the captain shouts, making me flinch. "Do you understand or not?"

"I understand, Captain."

"Good. Now go brief your squads. You're leaving in thirty minutes."

CHOICE

Level sixty-two is immaculate. From the floor to the supply cabinets and the two dozen recovery beds, there is not one speck of dust on anything. The air here smells suspended in time—clear, unmoving, with barely a hint remaining of the chemicals used to prepare this space. No human has been here to foul it up since the launch of this ship. On the other floors where we live, we are like vermin; bits and scraps of material, once part of something tangible, cover every flat surface.

I am amazed at how any of this has avoided scavenging or deterioration for so long. Each rack and crate of liquids, tablets, hypodermics is organized in perfect stacks and rows. The piles of prized blankets and pillows are so arranged that they could have come from the factory that way.

Either faction would kill to get their hands on these supplies—I know the Fahrasi will. We must be ready to do the same, without hesitation. My weapons are already out.

"Stick close," I whisper to Efa. We crouch down and move forward toward our prize. My squad of ten spreads out, moving up behind us in relative silence, while A Squad hangs back by the ladder and waits for us to spring whatever trap our enemy may have for us.

If I had a god or goddess to pray to, I might do so now. Others worship our ancestors, but my only faith is in the soldiers who surround me. Should something happen, they'd be the only ones to save my life, as I am the only one to save theirs.

I signal to the team to my right, motioning for them to move up and claim the blankets. They respond with a nod and slide forward, their eyes focused on the luxurious fabrics just ahead of them. I cannot allow myself to be so enthralled, even when I am hopeful we might escape unharmed.

But it is not to be.

The piercing whine of darts fills the air. One of the forward pair twists and drops. The other is faster and takes cover, as do we. In seconds, my gun is firing its first volley. Efa's a second later.

A collective howl comes from all directions. The pounding of boots follows. There must be hundreds. I get a chill across my back, and I snap into action.

"Pull back! Pull back!" I shout. Another of my squad gets hit, her body convulsing before she collapses in a heap. I grab Efa by the back of her shirt and drag her along as she takes aim at any hint of movement.

"*Ceri, status!*" the captain calls.

"Not now!" I reply, taking out a too-aggressive Fahrasi with a shot to his chest.

"*Dammit! Rhain, what do you see?*"

"We're about to get overrun!" Rhain responds. *"A Squad, up to sixty-one. Deryn, get your squad out of there!"*

"We're going!" Deryn responds.

"Not yet! Rhain, cover C Squad!" the captain says.

"But we're about to—" Rhain protests.

"Do it!"

"Ah, hyuk!" Rhain shouts. There's a pause. Then, *"A Squad, turn those tables over and line up!"*

The captain's order is a welcome relief. The Fahasi are close to surrounding us, even as my squad retreats at all possible speed. I'm already down two people, and we've taken out five of the enemy already, but we're still up against scores of them.

The air fills with darts that whiz over our heads. Several Fahrasi drop, but they keep coming. I've never seen so many attacking at once.

"Go, I'll cover you," I yell at Efa. She hesitates, then chases after the rest of the squad. I can only be glad of her trust in me for a second. In the next, I turn back to the fight.

Through the fray, I notice a face and curse. Merek. I had hoped he wouldn't be here. At least Efa is not here to see him.

But he's out in the open with his squad. If he doesn't get to cover, he's going to—

Bish!

Merek's body jerks and falls, his face contorting in agony as he grabs his leg. His squad flies by him as they press their attack on A Squad. They'll bring the Fahrasi advance to a halt, but only long enough for Deryn and my people to get up the ladder. Then they'll pull back the second there's a chance.

Which leaves me alone, behind the enemy line, with few options on how to get back. I put myself here, so I'll get myself out. If I can.

My eyes fall on Merek not far away. A dark stain soaks his pants leg—worse than I'd expect. The dart could have shattered his bone. If it hit his femoral artery, he will be dead in minutes. Damn Rhain for using barbed darts. If the Fahrasi find out, they will unleash any weapon they have in their arsenal—toxic gas, bio-weapons, oxygen deprivation. It doesn't matter. They'll wipe us out, and our people in stasis will be unprotected.

I glance back, then dash from cover. Merek is my goal. This is a stupid move, but Efa's distraught face would break me if I let him die.

Another quick scan of the Fahrasi line and I skid behind a crate just across from him. I lift my head over the edge to check again. A line of darts nearly impales my head. I drop just in time, avoiding certain death. *Hyuk, that was close.*

Merek notices me then, his eyes widening. He plants his hands on the floor and pushes away from me. His lips are trembling, his face paler than ever. He shakes his head as he tries the find the words to plead for his life.

"I'm not here to kill you," I say, sliding in next to him. "But we're both in trouble. You need a medic, and I need to get back to my squad."

"What should we do?" Merek asks, breathing heavy.

"That's a good question."

"Please don't leave me here." Merek's pleading face reminds me of Efa's. Perhaps they are meant for each other.

"I can't do anything but stop the bleeding and bandage your leg," I reply, pulling out my med kit. "Once I'm gone, call for a medic. You'll be okay then."

The reality that I keep to myself is he may not have that long. Darts, even barbed ones, will take a combatant out of the fight, but unless they hit a critical part of the body, they won't kill, nor do they create the massive bleeding that is flowing from Merek's leg. I fear he is in peril, and there is little I can do about it. I cut a patch out of his pants leg and spray the blood coagulant on his wound. When it works, I spin as much of a bandage as I can get around the wound. That will have to do.

Now I must save myself.

There's a cry from the other side of the crate. The thump of a body hitting the side shakes the entire box and pushes it toward me. I skitter back, eyeing the box as if it may topple on me at any moment.

"No! Take me with you," Merek says, grabbing my arm. I tear it away from him with a glare. As he reaches for me again, I become distracted by a call coming through the comm.

"Ceri! Get your squad out of here! We're leaving!" Rhain shouts.

"Not yet!" Efa cries, her voice getting hoarse. *"She's not back yet!"*

"Where the hyuk is she?" the captain growls. *"Ceri, call in!"*

I don't dare risk a reply, but Efa may try something drastic if I fail to respond. Then if she sees Merek like this, I fear she'll forget all protocol and rush into a hail of darts to save him. One casualty is already a problem. Two is impossible.

"C Squad is going back in after her!" Efa says. *"Gather up around me. We'll break through where I saw her last!"*

"Negative, Efa! Retreat!" The captain is on the verge of serious anger. *"You will not sacrifice your entire squad for her. If she can make it back, she will."*

I won't make it back. Not now. And despite my reluctance to help Merek, I'm still thinking how I can move him to safety.

A pair of Fahrasi rush by us, headed away from the battle. I press against the crate to hide—it's unnecessary. Their focus is elsewhere. One of them is trailing blood. They have no interest in us when they're trying to stay alive.

"Can you follow them?" I ask. "I'll get you up."

"There are no medics here," Merek says. Now I understand why he wants me to help him. Fine. I will. It's better than Efa hating me forever because I left him to bleed out.

"Ceri," Efa calls again. *"Hold on, I'm coming!"*

"You don't bring the squad into the middle of a crossfire, you dimwit! Retreat, or I will order Rhain to shoot you himself!"

"Captain," Rhain responds. *"I...I can't do that. They've got us pinned!"*

"C Squad will reinforce you," Efa says. *"I'm going alone!"*

The battle continues to rage behind us. The air screams with darts moving in both directions, creating a wall of flying death. If both sides keep firing like that, soon all their ammunition will be gone, and then it'll be hand-to-hand combat. If our squads haven't pulled back by then, the Fahrasi horde will hack them apart in minutes.

This was a mess before, but now it's become a deluge of disaster. I can't protect Merek and go after Efa, even if I knew where she was. For once, the captain is right. She should have listened to him. For once.

"Please, Ceri," Merek pleads. "I know you're risking a lot for me. I promise I'll make it up to you."

"I doubt that," I reply, then sigh. "Fine, I'll get you out of here. But we've got to find somewhere else to hole up besides my side. Our adults will torture you for information, then slit your throat. I'm not saving you just to have that happen."

Merek smiles through this pain and nods. I can respect his resolve. Perhaps he has Efa as his motivation, and why not? She is mine at the moment. So then is he.

"Let's go!" I throw my shoulder under his and wrap my arm around his waist. Merek yelps and does his best to assist me in getting him on his feet.

"Where are we going?" he asks.

"Hull access. You say no one goes there. For both our sakes, you'd better be right."

We move as fast as Merek can. It is slower than I am comfortable. The crossfire has died down to random shots, each side testing the other to find out what stores of munitions they have left. My gun remains near fully loaded. I will keep that advantage for now. Our priority is escape.

Merek reaches out and twists the hatch release. We don't so much enter the hull access as fall through it. And just in time. A mass of Fahrasi repositions themselves just beyond the portal, preparing for a last charge with blades drawn.

"Shut it!" I hiss. Merek can't. I let him go to push the hatch shut with my feet, careful not to make noise.

We collapse to the grating, panting hard. We're safe for now. Likely not for long. The dart is still in Merek's leg. Someone will need to remove it. Soon.

"Don't worry," Merek says. "We're okay here."

"No, we're not. I am still behind enemy lines, and you still need a medic. Our situation hasn't changed at all."

"Yes, it has." Merek turns to me with a grin. "We've got a way out now."

DELAY

Just like the place where I first met Merek, this space is cramped, confusing, and cold. I don't want to be here any longer than required. How long that will be is unknown. But I'm to blame for this. Had I not saved Merek, my circumstances would be better. That was far from being an option. Now I've tied our fates together until we find a way out.

I push myself up, using the railing to get to my feet while Merek remains on the floor, staring up through the levels. There is little to see in the near dark, yet I become uneasy when I remember how great a distance is above our heads. Sixty-two floors to be exact. We're a very long way from safety.

"Can you stand?" I ask, offering him my hand. Merek nods and takes it, gritting his teeth to force through the pain, then steadies himself on the railing to keep his weight off his wounded leg. He attempts to give me a brave face, but his eyes show how terrified he is. I am, too.

"So you seem to have a plan. What's next?" I ask.

Merek opens his mouth to answer, then his eyes pop open, and he pauses, holding up a hand. He tilts his head, and then I realize he's listening to the comm in his ear. I had turned mine off. There was no reason to keep it on. My squads have pulled back, and they will hold the next level until reinforcements can arrive.

Efa is still an unknown, however. I should've kept my comm powered on, if for no other reason than to listen for her. If she's nearby, perhaps we can rendezvous with her, though for her safety, I'd prefer not to meet her here at all.

"Our captain has ordered the entire level searched," Merek whispers. "Everywhere. It seems your people got a good chunk of supplies before they left."

"Then we should leave, too," I say. "Up is the best direction, but...can you?"

"No." Merek shakes his head. "We're fine here."

"We are not fine here. If your captain ordered the squads to search everywhere, we are one hatch away from being discovered. That would go much better for you than it would for me."

Merek wets his lips and looks around. I don't understand his reason for stalling. He could be afraid of going off with me alone. Or he could be waiting for his comrades to spring a trap on me. I rather not consider that possibility. If Merek proves he's anything other than what he's presented himself to be, I'd have to kill him. And, for Efa's sake, I really, really don't want to do that.

"Come on," I say, tugging on his sleeve. "Let's at least make it a little harder for them to find us."

He nods and turns, heading away from the battle and toward the direction the Fahrasi horde came from. As I move, I tense, thinking about how I'm placing my life in his hands. I want to trust him, but I also want to stay alive. I glance at my pistol and check the ammunition level once again, just to feel the minor relief of knowing I have a nearly full clip.

We head around the ship's circumference, moving toward what I hope will be a way up. I know I told him I wouldn't bring him to my people, but I am becoming more at ease with the option. If I could convince the captain that Merek knows nothing, he'd go home with the next prisoner swap and we'd get a few of our own in exchange. It could work.

There. A ladder's just ahead. It won't be easy to get Merek up it, but once we're on the next level, I can relax a little. My people will listen to me. I doubt the Fahrasi will be as open-minded, now that we took a majority of the supplies they were after.

When Merek gets to the ladder, he hesitates—it's okay. He's just figuring out how he will climb with a hurt leg. Though he should power through his pain and go. We've got little time to spare.

But as the seconds tick by, I realize he is not considering anything. He doesn't want to go up at all.

"You need to get on that ladder," I say and stare him down. Merek shrinks from my gaze.

Then he shakes his head.

"No. Listen," Merek says. "Efa is looking for you. If we leave now, they'll capture her."

A moment of panic rushes through me. Could she still be here?

"No. Efa isn't stupid," I reply, trying to sound confident. "She wouldn't have risked herself. For certain she's retreated already."

I watch him as I speak, but if he caught I was lying, he doesn't show it. Right now, Efa is doing exactly what my voice in her head is telling her not to. I might add what an idiot she was being for putting herself at risk. She wouldn't be listening, though. Just as I'd be ignoring her words.

"Efa will find us," Merek says. "Call her. You still have your comm, right?"

I mutter a curse under my breath as I glare at him. So much for him believing me.

"Efa won't answer!" I hiss back. "She knows better than to give away her position. And we shouldn't, either. I doubt she's even on this level any longer."

"She is."

"You haven't known her as long as I have." I thrust a finger at the level access port. "Now get up that ladder if you want to see her again."

"No. She's here. I know it."

My eyes narrow more. I might have to get aggressive with him, though that is as foolish of an option as I can think of. He's in no position to fight me, but his wound makes it impossible to force him up the ladder. I can't carry him up, either. The portal at the top is not large enough for two to fit through at the same time.

"If she was here, she would tell me," I state. "You want to risk yourself and wait for her when she's likely not even coming?"

Merek only tightens his jaw. Bish. He'll stay here even if it kills him. Perhaps that's what being in love is about. Foolishness and impulsive behavior. Both are a deadly trait to have in a battle. If it was Efa before me, I'd drag her up the ladder by her hair and get her to safety.

"You are a fool," I growl. "And so am I, for waiting here with you."

Merek grins and pulls out his pistol. "We won't die, if that's what you fear."

"I don't fear death. I fear dying like an idiot."

"That won't happen. You're too skilled, Ceri. No Fahrasi can match you."

"One Fahrasi isn't a worry. A hundred are."

Merek looks like he is about to laugh. He had better not. I will have no choice but to silence him, and there are few ways I can do that, none of which will make Merek or Efa happy with me. She likely isn't already. Still, that's a minor issue compared to getting off this level and to safety.

The hatch we entered through grinds open. Merek and I drop to a crouch, but he can't maintain it and crashes to the grating. I grit my teeth. Whoever just entered heard that.

As I lift my gun hand to the ready, I wonder if I should have been more insistent with Merek. I want to keep him alive, for Efa's sake, and I can do that if we can get to a defensible position. This isn't it. We need to move or we're dead. At least, I am, and there's no way for me to protect him in that condition.

I glance and nod at Merek, ready to fight. I don't know what he will do, and I fear he won't shoot at his own people. He may just fire a dart through the base of my skull and end me instead.

It doesn't matter. I've made my choice and placed my fate in saving the boy of Efa's affections. For whatever that will bring me.

"Get ready," I whisper, tensing.

There's a creak on the grating just before us. A shadow slides through the status lights that line a pair of air recyclers. The movement is smooth, even graceful. A girl, for certain. Boys move with more aggression, even when they are trying to be stealthy.

I anticipate her movements and aim the barrel of my gun on the spot she's about to occupy. In three seconds, I will fire, and that will take care of our immediate problem. Then I will haul Merek up the ladder with my bare hands if I have to.

My finger rests on the trigger. One more second, and I'll fire, and this—

"Wait!" I hiss, dropping my weapon and slapping Merek's gun down at the same time. I know that walk, and I know that girl.

And we almost killed her.

"Ceri?" Efa's whisper comes floating over. I shut my eyes, thankful for my self-restraint.

"You bish-head," I reply. "What are you doing here?"

"Ceri!" Efa pops out of the darkness, her arms wide. In a single motion, she wraps them around my body and buries her face in my neck. I squirm as her hair tickles me and attempt to push her back gently.

"Efa!" Merek slides over to us. If I could see his face, I am sure there would be a huge grin on it.

"What?" Efa pops her head up. "What are you doing here?"

"Ceri saved me."

"I did no such thing," I say, but Efa isn't convinced. She beams at me, her eyes bright and glossy.

"You saved him? Ceri, I could kiss you!"

"Please don't."

Efa does anyway, planting her wet lips on my cheek. For her sake, I tolerate it, though it still gets a smile from me. I am glad she's unharmed. This isn't the safest place for her to be, but she's under my protection, and I prefer it that way.

"Great," Merek says. "Now we're all here!"

"Yes, great," I moan. "Now we can all suffer together."

ALLY

It's less of a challenge to get Merek up the ladder with the two of us. Efa can touch parts of his body that I am not comfortable touching. I've no wish to be intimate with him. My only interest is to return to my nest and crash there for the rest of my life. It may be unrealistic, yet I have little desire for anything else.

The three of us arrive on the next level, gasping for air. It's almost as if gravity is heavier, closer to the engines like this. I don't know the science well, but that seems wrong. I must be exhausted. We all are.

"We can't take him back," Efa whispers in my ear. "You know what will happen if we do."

"I know," I reply, grinding my teeth together. "I wasn't planning on it."

That's a lie. I'm just not ready to argue with her about it, but I won't fool her for long. Efa will know the moment we turn toward our fallback position. There are few paths to get him back to his faction, and that's not one of them.

"I've got a place we can go," Efa says, and my gut gets tight. I know where she means. There's no reason to go there. Not when we apply common sense.

"Bad idea," I say, and shake my head.

There's a part of the ship unclaimed by either faction, and for good reason. There's nothing there other than rumors and possibly a few rogue individuals neither side wants. It's said they're insane, driven to madness by the isolation. If that's true, then the number of reasons to go there are less than zero.

"Merek and I have already talked about it," Efa says, to my regret. Of course they have. There is no other place they could live together. It's still not an option. They should not endure hell for the sake of their love.

"I already said no," I reply. "And besides, the three of us won't get there by ourselves."

"I think I've got that problem solved already," Merek says.

"What?" I spin toward him, suspicion flashing through my mind.

"Two minutes, and you'll see. We'll have the help we need."

"What did you do?"

"Don't worry, everything's fine."

"None of this comes anywhere close to fine, Merek." I thrust my finger toward him. "If you put us in danger—"

"He didn't," Efa says, clasping her hand around mine and lowering it. I glare at her but expect it will do little good. My fate is with theirs, as I've chosen. As much as I dislike it, I am only along for the ride down this path.

Boots hit the rungs of the ladder below—they've found us! I jerk into action, gripping my gun and blade, ready to dispatch the first Fahrasi that shows their face.

Yet when I see the boy who pops his head through the level access port, killing him disappears from my thoughts.

He's...pretty. There's no better word to describe him. His dark eyes and shoulder-length hair are normal for his faction, but his skin is smoother than any girl's that I know. I'm also in awe of the length of his eyelashes. He smiles at us as he steps onto the level. Merek nods and smirks back, causing Efa and I to share a confused glance.

"I'm here for Merek," the boy says, raising his hands. No weapons in them, which is helpful, but not a reason to turn my back on him, even if I wanted to, and I don't think I ever will.

"Hey, help me here, would you?" Merek says, offering his hand to him. "I got hit."

"Woah, hold on." Sayer drops next to him, to examine the bandage around Merek's leg. It remains clean, for which I'm thankful. Though, that's the least of my concerns.

"Who are you?" I challenge.

"This is Sayer. Sayer Tak," Merek says. "He's my mate. We can trust him."

"Says you."

Sayer takes Efa and me in, a grin coming to his face. "You really weren't joking about this, were you?"

"Did you think I was?" Merek fires back with a glare. Then he waves a hand at us. "Anyway, this is Efa and her friend Ceri."

Sayer takes a longer look at us, possibly reevaluating his first assumptions. I lock my eyes on his every motion, but the blurriness in my vision only reminds me of my fatigue. At least now I can dump Merek on him, so Efa and I can get back to base. And sleep.

"Nice to meet you," Sayer says with a bit of a chuckle. "Sorry, I know this is strange for you, too. We'd all be trying to murder each other if we were down one level. Other than being pissed that you've killed some of my friends, I've got nothing personal against the Tarakh. I don't even know why we're fighting."

"That makes four of us, Sayer," Efa says with a smile, "and it is nice to meet you, too. A friend of Merek's is a friend of mine."

When their eyes turn to me, expectant of a reply, all I can do is nod. I can't find any words worth saying, and I feel the fool. I don't want to give this pretty Fahrasi any hint of friendliness, if only for fear that I might learn to enjoy his presence. That would be dangerous. Despite what he says, I cannot let my guard down.

"I'm sure Ceri feels the same way," Efa says. "She's just looking out for me, like any big sister would."

"Ceri is your sister?" Merek asks.

"No," is all I can manage. Sayer slides his eyes to Merek, seeking an explanation. Merek can't provide one. There is no equivalent to Efa's and my relationship in their faction. At least, not that I've heard. Efa is my younger sister because she is female and younger than me. I might call an older male my brother, yet he is not by blood. It is just what we do to show connection to each other.

"Anyway," Merek says to Sayer, "we're on the move. Level thirty-eight is where we're going."

"Thirty-eight?" Sayer's eyebrows press together.

"Yes. Is that a problem?"

"Hey," Sayer replies, holding his hands up, "I'm here to help you do whatever, but are you sure that's where you want to end up? Maybe we can convince the chief to take her in as a refugee or something. You'd be better off than—"

"No," I growl, lifting my gun. "She's not going to your base, and we aren't going to thirty-eight. We're going home."

"Woah, calm down!" Sayer backs up, his hand moving to his holster. "It was just a suggestion!"

"Ceri, ease off," Efa hisses at me, then turns back to Sayer. "Thank you, Sayer, but thirty-eight is the only place for us."

Sayer's eyes dart between Efa and me. He shakes his head and sighs, dropping his hand from his weapon. I watch him for a moment longer, then relax. As much as I can, anyway. My pulse's still pumping hard.

"Even if what you want is there, it's not safe for you," I say to Efa. "So if you truly think of me as a big sister, then you'll listen to me and return to base."

"And if you are truly my big sister," Efa crosses her arms, "you would want nothing more than my happiness."

I smolder as I stare at her. Her poor attempt at manipulation is obvious. We both know what a terrible decision she and Merek have come up with. There'd be no life for them there, yet there's no life for them elsewhere, either.

It doesn't matter. We'd never make it, anyway. Some patrol would either pick us off or capture us along the way. There is no chance they'll get the freedom they're hoping for, even with my protection.

Why I'm even considering any of this? Efa and I are returning to base and spending the rest of the night and the next day in our nests.

If I can convince her.

"Don't be ridiculous, Efa," I say. "What you're asking is unrealistic. Let's go."

As I reach for her hand, Efa twists away, stepping closer to Merek. I'm left there, with my hand out and my jaw slack, not believing she's about to choose him over me.

"Ceri, think about it," Merek says. "With Sayer's and your help, we'll make it. Then we can build a new life for ourselves."

My hand drops, fatigue setting in. This conversation is just as tiring. Merek and Efa are going to keep insisting on going somewhere they can never be safe, no matter what they think. Still, we can't stay here.

"The two of you should head back to your squads," I say to Merek. "We shouldn't spend any more time here."

"That's true," Sayer says. "But do you really want to return to base? There's no way they'll be able to be together if we don't get away from this constant fighting. It's less than safe for sure. Still, don't you want to see them happy?"

"I want nothing more than Efa's happiness." My gaze connects with hers, and she smiles. That her big sister is looking out for her mental wellbeing is not in question. How Efa attains it certainly is.

"Ceri, there's no reason to think that thirty-eight is any worse than anywhere else," Merek says, looking at Efa. "I promise, I'll do everything I can to protect her and to make sure she is comfortable."

Efa's cheeks, already at their maximum plumpness, redden a little. She is completely infatuated, and there is nothing I can do to change that. The pleading gaze she gives me doesn't help the situation, nor does Sayer siding with them.

I don't appreciate the pressure they're attempting to put on me. Their plan is bish, and if I don't hear something better, I'm taking Efa back to base. Dragging her, if I have to. Whatever Captain Daga's punishment is, it'll be better than leaving Efa with these two. And I won't do that. If she won't come with me, then I'll have to stay with her until she comes to her senses. If she ever does.

"Let's just suppose for a second I okay this hyuking nonsense idea," I say with a steady gaze at Sayer. "How can I trust you? Are you willing to protect Efa as much as you're willing to protect Merek?"

Sayer levels a sober glance at me. I'm sure he's remembering every friend killed by a Tarakh as he considers his answer. Good. I'm getting my point across.

"If doing this makes Merek happy, then I'm with him," Sayer replies. "I only fight because I don't want to die. I can look past our differences to make sure they're safe. Can you?"

"You ask that question as if you think either of us has a choice," I reply.

Sayer smirks. He understands what a hell detail the two of us are in. Still, we'd choose nothing else. For a moment, I feel that connection to him all soldiers feel in their shared misery, and it calms me a little. But Sayer, nor Merek, stops being the enemy with a few words or a feeling. We may share this, but that doesn't make it right.

"Fair enough," Sayer says. "We'll look out for both of them because won't do anything else. I've got no fight with you, so you and I can work together."

Even as he speaks, I'm outside myself, looking down at a person who, until half a minute ago, was planning to tie Efa up and carry her home. I'm not giving up on doing the right thing. I just don't know what that is anymore.

"And what happens if our intentions cross?" I ask as the thought enters my mind. Perhaps it's my last, desperate attempt to stop this disaster.

"Ceri, stop it," Efa says, slapping my arm gently. "There's nothing to worry about."

"Agreed," Merek says. "None of us have reason to choose sides. We're beyond that now."

"Are we?" I ask, keeping my eyes locked on him.

"Listen," Sayer says, leaning in toward me. "Honestly, I don't understand what he means, but I bet you care about Efa as much as I do Merek. He's saved my life a few times, so I owe him, and I'd still look out for him even if I didn't. I'm guessing you'd do the same for her, right?"

I nod.

"So then," Sayer says, "we have a mutual understanding and a mutual interest. I'll give you my word, whatever that's worth to you, that I will protect both of them with my life. What say you about that?"

This pretty Fahrasi makes more sense than I will openly admit. That's a small comfort in this alternative universe we've chosen to enter together. Reality be damned, we going through this.

"I'll do the same," I reply. "But know that I won't hesitate to end either of you, should you betray our agreement."

Sayer grins. "I think we're talking the same language."

"Good," I say. "Then you take point."

UNKNOWN

WE CLIMB FOR AN hour, moving up through the hull access to bypass any retreating squads. Once we're clear, we return to the main part of the levels and hit the ladders there. As Sayer does his best to pull Merek up, Efa and I take turns pushing from below while other covers the rest of us from a potential ambush. We make an easy target—a lumbering convoy that's moving too slowly and making way too much noise. I do my best to remind them of their lack of noise discipline, yet all Sayer and Efa seem to care about is Merek. They should care about him more and stop him from grunting so much, so that he doesn't get shot.

Once we hit level forty-seven, Merek groans and pushes himself away from the ladder access. He lies out flat and stares up at the ceiling. Sayer takes up a cross-legged position next to him, leaning his forearms on his knees with a heavy sigh.

"This is going to take forever," Sayer moans. "We should take a day and rest."

"Merek won't be healed by then," I say. "In fact, he may get worse."

"It's just a dart. He'll be fine."

I grind my teeth as I consider telling them the truth. I should. They won't run off to tell Fahrasi command.

"It's not just any dart," I say, my jaw tight.

The three of them turn to me, worry in their eyes. They understand.

"Should we...turn back?" Sayer asks.

"Turn back to where?" Efa shakes her head as she replies.

"No." Merek echoes her action. "We can't. Neither of our sides will be kind about us missing for so long. I'll be alright. Just give me a minute."

We continue our climb in silence for another five levels. As we move, Efa throws several glances my way, hoping to get me to explain about the barbed dart in Merek's leg. I won't. I've already said as much as I'm willing to about that. Any more will anger Sayer, and we don't need dissent in our precarious group.

Merek requests another break, but this time, we pull him into a far corner of the level. We need to be more covert about our movements. With the battle raging below us, there is a constant danger of runners ferrying wounded and ammunition up and down the levels. If we only had one of their fast-hoists, we could move faster.

Movement down the hallway catches my notice. I jump to my feet, my gun and light come out. Efa and Sayer are a second behind me as I blast the corridor in illumination.

"Ooh hoo! Light, light, light!" a male voice, hoarse with age, cries. As I turn my light on him, he throws his arms across his face and dances about like a child who needs to use the toilet.

His clothes are strange. I can't place whether they should be Fahrasi, Tarakh or something else. They're in such tatters, I'm not sure I can even call them clothes. His pants are a patchwork of materials. His shirt looks like he knitted it together from a collection of packing blankets. All of it is covered in dirt and grease smudges.

"Who are you?" Sayer shouts. "Tell us, or we'll fill you so full of darts you'll double your body weight in metal!"

"Sayer!" I hiss. He pivots his head toward me. "Keep your voice down. And there's four of us and just one of him. No need to threaten him."

"Yeah, sorry. Though." Sayer points at the man. "He's making enough noise for all of us."

"Whooo, whoo! Tell us. Tell us," the man echoes Sayer's demand. He moves closer, peeking through his sleeves to see us. I lower my weapon and turn my light toward the ceiling. I get the sense he's not a threat to us.

"So say it!" Sayer shouts again.

"Hey, no need for *all* of us to give away our position," Merek warns.

"Light, light, light," the man says. "Too much for Rabbit. Shut down, shut down."

If I had to bet, I'd guess this ancient child is a recluse. An *unangh,* as we call them—person forgotten by everyone—including themselves. I've heard the stories the older soldiers used to frighten the new recruits into keeping close to base. With the terrifying qualities they would give these people, it was an effective way to control the youth with ideas of exploration. But this man before us is nothing to fear. Even if he had a blade, he could never get close enough to any of us to use it, including Merek, with his wounded leg.

"Put your weapon down, Efa. And turn off your light," I say. "He's harmless."

Efa does as I ask. I wish Sayer would, too. He isn't ready to, and I don't feel like pressing him. I will keep an eye on him, however. He seems like the type to fire before thinking.

"Harm, harm, harmonica!" the man says, turning toward the wall. "Yes, yes. Harmless!"

"What's your name?" I ask. "Are you Tarakh? Or Fahrasi?"

"I am Rabbit!"

"So glad we've got that established," Sayer mutters. At least his gun hand is lowering. Rabbit lowers his arms, but he still squints with Sayer's light in his face.

And what a face it is. Pale, wrinkled, and dark with any manner of dust and dirt caught in his long white beard. It matches the remnants of the hair that only grows in patches on his head. This man has not seen a hygiene chamber for decades, I'll bet. Best we keep our distance, if only for that reason.

"Rabbit, my name is Efa." She takes a step toward him, smiling. "Can you tell me which level you live on?"

Rabbit peers at her, examining her face for a moment. Efa forces herself to keep smiling, but she is unsure of what to do. It's clear that his mental faculties function at a different level than ours. A much stranger one, too.

"Oh, pretty!" Rabbit says, his eyes popping open. Merek chuckles. I shake my head and roll my eyes, smiling as I do. Of all the things that he could have said, that wouldn't have been my guess. Still, I suppose Efa brings that reaction out of people.

"Thank you, Rabbit," Efa says, a blush coming to her cheeks. "But can you tell me where your home is? Where do you live on the ship?"

"Live?" Rabbit's eyes turn up to look at the ceiling. "Not here. No."

"Then what are you doing here?" I ask.

"Rabbits need to eat, too."

"Alright then," Sayer says. "We'll let you go scavenge for food, and we'll be on our way. Okay?"

"No, wait!" Efa says, turning to him. "He can help us find machine access."

Merek's mouth drops open. "Right! He probably lives there." Then he grins. "What a neighbor he would make."

"Sure, he may know," I say, my hand rubbing the back of my neck. "But is he capable of telling us?"

Efa hadn't considered that. Sayer did. He's likely decided that Rabbit is too senile to even show us the nearest ladder, which only leaves me, and I don't know what to think of this curiosity of a person. That he has survived for however long on his own means he is canny enough to scavenge for food and whatever else he needs. Maybe he could help, after all.

Still, his brain function is questionable, and getting straight answers from him will be difficult. He may not be capable of telling us where we should go and trying to get him to do so could be a frustrating effort. We should move on, while this level remains clear of potential threats.

"Rabbit, we are looking for a part of the ship that we call the machine room," Efa says. "It's a place where the ship's main environmental and power systems are. We think there's access to it somewhere on level thirty-eight. Do you know the place I mean?"

Rabbit tilts his head and flicks it a few times while he blinks. Then he walks off, only to return, muttering something to himself. Efa turns to me for help, but I have no more answers than she does.

"Well? Do you know it?" Sayer repeats.

"Machines? Know?" Rabbit nods as he picks at a scab on his arm. "Yes. I know it. I know it well."

Merek and Efa release a relieved sigh and share a look and a smile. For the first time, their hope of being together has an actual destination. We're no longer climbing with the hope we might stumble on something that would give us a position.

There's a reason we don't know where the access to these systems is. Humans don't need to go there. They're all automated and will function without human intervention for a thousand years, long enough for the *Stratford* to get to its destination. The designers never considered they'd get damaged by a battle.

"Where's the entrance?" I ask. "Is it on thirty-eight?"

"No...no, no, no, no! Not there! No! Never!" Rabbit replies.

"Then where?" Sayer asks, his eyes hardening. "Thirty-seven maybe?"

"Hoo, hoo, hoo, hoo! Thirty-seven, he says! So wrong, so wrong!" Rabbit jumps up and down in an odd sort of hop. He is more limber than I expected for a person of his age. Then again, I've only met one other person older than sixty, and that was the chief of our faction. Few awake on this ship are lucky enough to live that long.

"Forget this guy." Sayer turns away from him with a flick of his hand and looks at Merek. "We'll get you there. Don't worry."

"And where is there?" I ask as I throw my arms up. "I think he just confirmed for us we have no idea where we're going."

There's always the possibility that Rabbit is playing with us. That this whole loopy old man thing is just an act. I don't know what his motivation for that would be. He couldn't catch four of us in any trap we'd be stupid enough to fall into.

I'm fine with asking him. It costs us nothing, and we may gain very important information—if the information is accurate. I motion to Efa to ask him. She seems to get actual answers from him when she proposes a question to him.

"Rabbit," Efa says, pressing her hands together and smiling, "where is the machine access?"

"Oh." Rabbit's eyes get big. "Well, not up!"

"Then *where*, old man?" Sayer growls.

"Down. Down, down, down. Definitely down." Rabbit crouches and finds something interesting about his shoes to investigate. Not that I could call them shoes. They're more like shoe-shaped forms, secured to his feet with thick cord.

"Down?" Merek asks, his face showing signs of dread. "How far down?"

"One...two...three!"

The four of us share a look. Unlike a building, they numbered the *Stratford*'s levels from highest to lowest for convenience. Since most of the crew awake during transit—and their children, and their children's children, and so on—would live on the upper levels near command and control, it was easier for them to use the single digits.

"Levels one through three are at the fore of the ship," I say. "You just said the access was way down, not up."

"Wait," Efa says, "did you mean one hundred and twenty-three?"

"Impossible," Sayer says. "There's no such level!"

I agree. There are only eighty-one levels on the *Stratford*. Unless...did the adults lie to us?

"Wrong, wrong, wrong!" Rabbit says, waving a finger in the air. "I will show you!"

"Show us?" Efa's face flashes with excitement.

"Come! Come to one, two, three! You will see!"

Efa looks at me, her eyes begging my permission. Merek is doing the same, I'm sure. I glance at Sayer to catch his reaction, but all he does is shrug. It's up to me then.

One-hundred-twenty-three. Eighty-one levels below. It's only a coincidence the number is the same. And it's far. Too far for either faction to ever go. Perhaps too far for even the unwanted to travel. Which means it's perfect for Efa and Merek.

"We've started on this...this...hell, I don't know what to call it," I say and pluck at the collar of my shirt. "But we've got a destination now, and if it gets us away from the fight, then that's way less risky than going up another four levels."

Efa beams at me. So does Merek. Sayer seems relieved. I'm sure the sooner he gets this done and returns to his faction, the sooner he will feel at ease. If any of us could again. Merek and Efa will be free to live and love each other, but Sayer and I will face punishment the moment we return to base.

Perhaps I should envy Efa. She will get to choose her fate.

DISSAPEARANCE

WE LOWER MEREK TO the deck of the landing, then slide down the ladder after him. Our pace is as casual as our attention to our surroundings. There's nothing to be wary about. No threats to watch out for. Just the comfort of constant movement. Away from danger.

One thing I am glad about: heading down is much faster than going up. We found some scrap wire and created a harness we could use to lower Merek down the ladders. It works well enough, and despite or muscles aching, we've already gone thirty floors in an hour.

Rabbit has been no help. Other than complaining we're too slow, he's done nothing but skitter away until we signal for him to come back. I have no concerns about him getting caught. He has likely avoided detection for decades. I *am* worried that he will forget we're following him.

"Cross, cross, cross," Rabbit says when we arrive at level eighty. He shoots off straight through the middle of a field of stasis chambers. Occupied stasis chambers.

"Wow," Efa gasps, walking to the nearest unit. "I've never seen so many."

She brushes the frost off the window and peers in while Sayer and I check the room for trouble. We're not expecting any, but that's usually when it shows up. Better to be safe than dead.

As we cross the level, I turn my head up to the ceiling, far away. The openness here enhances the massive size of this space. The *Stratford* is larger toward the aft than it is at the fore. I just didn't realize how much larger. Most floors pack rooms and corridors hull to hull. Their ceilings are lower, too. Perhaps it's a requirement for all the stasis machinery hanging overhead.

"Hey," Sayer hisses to me. "Where'd Rabbit go?"

"Bish." My eyes scan the space for movement. There's none. Rabbit wanted us to cross, and that's what we're doing. He's got to be on the other side already.

I motion Sayer to hold and dash through the stasis units, jumping over the wire conduits that line the spaces between. As fast as I can run, the distance is still longer than I expect. I am winded by the time I reach the other side.

There's an entrance to a corridor at the end. I duck into it, pulling out my gun. This must be the way he went. But there's two ways to go here, and both lead to ladders. I jet down one way and look down, then race to the other side and do the same. No Rabbit. By this time, I am so out of breath that I slide down the wall and sit to take a moment.

I don't have the breath to call out to him. And I don't want to push our luck. Occupied stasis beds mean techs come down this far to check on them. They won't be armed, but they would alert command to our presence.

I force myself up, feeling the day's excess action gnawing at my muscles. I will get sleep when we reach our destination, but a sentry will need to be posted. That means none of us will get enough rest.

"Find him?" Sayer mouths to me as I return to the stasis chamber. I shake my head, and he curses and raises his fist to pound the edge of one of the stasis units, but reconsiders. One of those things could hold a relative of his.

"What's going on?" Efa asks. Merek has his arm around her as she helps him toward us. Despite how that dart must tear up his muscle, he's in no pain. At least none that he's showing.

"I can't tell which way Rabbit went," I say. "There's two ladders in the corridor, and they both lead to different parts of eighty-one."

"So you take one, and I'll take the other," Sayer says. "And we'll find that old man. He hasn't gone far."

"Are you sure?" I throw a hand toward the opposite side of the level. "Did you see how fast he crossed all this? He could be ten levels down from here by now."

"Hey," Merek says. "We should get to that side corridor. We're too easy to spot here."

Merek words are a little slurred. Between the painkiller and his blood loss, I can understand if his tongue is slow. All of ours are. We've been through a lot, and we still have far to go. But first, we need to find our guide.

I nod and motion toward the corridor, then move to take the lead. Before I can, Sayer grabs my shoulder, stopping my forward movement. I tear away, and spin on him, ready to fight. But he passes me by, taking point instead. I can only stare and wonder how Fahrasi men treat their women. Merek better not be like that.

I shake my head. That's not something I have time to consider. Sayer may have elected himself lead, but our backs still need cover. Fine by me. Let him figure out where to go if he can.

It's not long before Sayer proves he's got no better idea than I do. He runs from one ladder to the other, then back. A minute later, he realizes there is no suitable answer on which way to go.

"I still say you and I split up and scout eight-one," Sayer says. "There's got to be a hint of him somewhere."

"Maybe we should wait," Efa suggests. "It's not a good idea to separate. We can't use comms, and we don't know what's down there."

"Yes, we do. More levels." Sayer waves a hand at a ladder. "And safety."

"What if Rabbit comes back?" Efa looks between Sayer and me. "You may think he's wrong in the head, but that's not true. He understands more than it seems, but he hasn't spoken to anyone in a long time."

How long is a question. It's not as important as where the hyuk did Rabbit go? And why? The man may be strange in the head from living alone for so long, but he's still got enough brain cells to survive. And I bet some of those are the ones that enable his ability for deception.

Efa wants to wait here. That's a bad idea. It's only a matter of time before someone comes down here. It doesn't matter if it's a Fahrasi or a Tarakh. We lose if they discover us.

"Merek already said it," I say. "We're open targets here. This is just too much space for four..." I glance at Merek. "...three people to cover. It's indefensible."

"But we need Rabbit to show us where the access point is," Efa replies. "Without him, we could search for it for months and not find it. With no supplies, we don't even have days. And I'm not going back just because we could find food. No way."

"She's got a point," Merek says, then clenches his hands. "And I'm going to drag you guys down fast without some real help for my leg. I'm already dizzy."

"How much medication have you had?" Efa asks, turning to him. "Can you have another shot?"

Merek looks at Sayer, who turns to me. I huff, then cross my arms when I realize they can't answer.

"Are you joking? Don't you know how much you've given him?" I shake my head. "No. You can't give him another shot. Not unless you want to put him in danger of an overdose."

"But it's already wearing off!" Efa says. "He's going to be in agony soon."

"He already is," I shoot back. "His painkiller isn't wearing off. He's just a lot more hurt than you think. I saw his wound, Efa. The only reason he isn't screaming his head off right now is because of how many shots you dumped in him."

"Ceri, please. Let's just wait here. Let Merek rest. I'll watch him. Then maybe you and Sayer can find some supplies. Water, at least."

"She's got it right," Sayer says. "We could find a couple of canteens or bottles around somewhere. There's got to be a recycler faucet nearby, too. The techs would need it."

"Didn't you just say that splitting up is a bad idea?" I say to Efa, who lowers her head in regret. "And you cannot stay here. *We* cannot stay here. This is an active level. There's going to be techs coming down with an escort at some point. It is stupid to think we're safe here."

"And where do we go, Ceri?" Efa says. "Just keep heading aft until the engine radiation fries our heads? We have to find a base of operations."

"That's the smartest thing you've said in the last ten minutes, but again, it can't be here! We've got to go, Efa. Stop being dense about this."

Efa tilts her head as she levels her gaze at me. "Then where can it be? Do you have any idea where to go? Of course not. So don't pretend you know better."

"Hey," Sayer says as he throws up his hands between us. "This isn't helpful. You're both right. We need to find a place to hole up, we need supplies, and we need to find Rabbit. None of that is happening right now, so let's...just cool down, take a moment, and then head out."

"I'm worried about how long Merek can keep moving," Efa says, glancing at him. "And we're not doing anything that is going to hurt him, so if you want to go, you figure out how to do that."

Sayer glances at me as his lips press together. He knows I'm the only one with leadership experience here. Still, I don't enjoy having the responsibility for Merek on my shoulders. I've got enough watching over Efa as it is.

But I've already made my decision, or Efa and I wouldn't be fighting over it. If they want me to say it, then I will.

"Okay," I say. "We're going."

LABYRINTH

Level eighty-one is a severe contrast to the level above. Where that space was vast, this one is cramped, and instead of one massive room encompassing the entire floor, this is a maze of corridors, junctions, and intersections. My guess is this is where they keep the supplies and spare parts for the stasis beds.

Which means no food, but maybe water.

"Argh, I am starving," Sayer says, holding a hand over his stomach. "We'd better find something to eat soon."

"I'm not," Efa says and looks to Merek. "How about you?"

"No," Merek winces. "Just really thirsty."

"It's the painkiller," I say, even though I'm not sure it is. I'm also parched. The roof of my mouth is as dry and rough as the blanket I use back at base. I was looking forward to stealing one of those coverlets on sixty-two for myself. But just like our current supply of water, it's out of reach.

"We'll find some," Efa says, looking into Merek's unfocused eyes. He smiles at her and tries to act as if he's fine. Of course he's not. The level of agony he's feeling will only get worse.

No matter how tough Merek thinks he is, he will be screaming once the medication wears off. That dart has to come out soon.

He's lucky he's got Efa to care for him. She is a skilled attendant in that way. Efa took care of me when I got hit the first time. I was only fifteen then. A dart went right through my shoulder, cracking the bone. I cried for days. She must have wanted to run away, but she held me and soothed my pain as much as the medication did.

"Let's go this way," I say, pointing down a corridor to our right. My intuition tells me nothing about it, but we've got to get through this level, and starting off in some direction is the only way to accomplish that.

The corridor snakes right after only a few paces, turning us toward the hull. I recognize the sliding double doors of the automated rail system, dark and shut. The panel that operates the system is also unlit. As much as I wish Deryn's squad got it to work, they didn't. We couldn't use it, even if they did. That would be like getting back on comm and shouting our location to both factions.

The adults might consider us already dead, and that's for the best. If Efa or I showed our face back at base with no explanation where we were, the captain would punish us so badly, we would wish our lives had ended.

Perhaps I am already considering never going back. Though if I didn't, my squad, especially the younger ones, would lose someone who gives enough of a bish about them to make sure they stay safe. There's no telling who Captain Daga would assign to be their leader after me.

"Anyone know what a water receptacle might look down here?" Sayer asks.

"A patch of a blue wall with a spout and a basin sticking out of it," I answer as I glance at him with a raised eyebrow. "Have you never seen one before?"

"Of course I have." Sayer makes a sound of annoyance. "You Tarakh may control most of them, but we still have enough for what we need."

A spot of blue catches my eye as I hear his words. I ignore the risk and turn my light on it. Sure enough, at the end of the corridor, before it turns left, is exactly what we are looking for.

"So what do you think that is, then?" I ask, smirking at him.

Sayer frowns, then squints as he peers at the point where my light is shining. So he's got problems seeing far away. In this ship of narrow corridors and small spaces, that's rarely an issue.

"You found one!" Efa exclaims. I can tell she wants to race over there and bring her lover more liquid than he could ever drink.

"Stay there, I'll get it," I say to her. Merek can't stand without her now. As it is, he could go into shock at any moment. Water is critical to his survival.

As I jog toward the outlet, I'm reminded of the fact that I have nothing to carry water in. None of us do. I could use my hands cupped together, but it won't be much. It could be enough for Merek, however.

I holster my gun and press the button above the spout. No one has used this unit in a while, so it could take time for the water to come out. I lean on the wall and watch, waiting for the welcome sound of flowing refreshment.

But after a minute, I become anxious. After five minutes, my shoulders are slumping. The others have made it over by then and, along with me, are staring at the moistureless spout as disappointment falls over their faces. I try to swallow, but my throat is just too dry. I can only imagine how Merek feels.

"There's got to be another unit on this level, right?" Efa asks. She's got both of her arms around Merek to stop him from collapsing.

"Who knows?" Sayer says and sighs.

"Usually there's at least one on each side of the hull," I answer. Then, with more consideration, I add, "That's just the floors where we live, of course. They might not be standard on the storage and utility decks."

"Wouldn't there be one on a recovery level?" Efa asks. "They'd need water for whenever they woke someone up, right? They dropped us in a bath when they pulled us out."

"That wasn't water," Sayer says, "but you're right. They would also need it for recovery."

"Recovery level is two floors up," I state. "That's the wrong way."

"But Merek needs water now!" Efa says. "We need it, too."

"Why didn't we get some while we were there?" Sayer frowns, then shakes his head.

"We were following Rabbit, remember?" I reply.

Sayer slams his fist into the wall. "Hyuk that old man! He can fall into the nearest gravity well for all I care! What a waste of time it was to follow him!"

The booming sound rolls through the level. When Efa and I jump, he realizes his mistake. I shake my head at him, ready to give him a sharp rebuke for giving our position away. If there's someone on this level, they know we're here.

"Ceri," Efa says as she looks at me with those huge pleading eyes of hers. "We have to go back up. Please?"

"And waste more time?" I sigh and give her an apologetic look. "Merek can't make it back up the ladders, and we'd all be so tired from pulling him up, we'd have to crash there. You know that's a dangerous place to spend any more time than we have already. Besides, there could just as likely be a working outlet down a level, too."

"Down," Merek mumbles the single word. "Efa...we go down."

Merek's breathing has turned ragged and raspy. He's trying his best to stay conscious, but I just watched his eyes roll back into his head, and he didn't even notice. Sayer did, and his demeanor changes the moment he does. He hands his weapon to me and takes Merek from Efa to wrap his arm around him.

"You two cover us," Sayer says then. "Let's go, and fast, yeah?"

"Take point, Efa," I say, handing her Sayer's gun.

"But..." Efa looks down at the gun. "Can't we take a vote or something?"

"We just did," Sayer replies. "We're headed down. You know, where you and Merek wanted to go?"

"Leave her alone, Sayer," I say. "We all know the plan."

Efa looks at Merek as she bites her lower lip. I'm not sure what she's trying to figure out. She must know time is speeding by as she does. Whatever she wants, she better tell us soon.

"What if I went up by myself?" Efa says a second later.

"And break your own rule about sticking together?" I reply. "No."

"What are we going to find on eighty-two? There could be nothing down there! At least we know there could be an outlet two floors up!"

Efa pounds the air with her fist while she uses that tone of voice that means she's not thinking things through. I know it because she's only ever used it with me, and she trusts me with her moments of casual stupidity. This can't be one of them, however.

"Listen," I say, fixing her hair to distract her from panic. "We are going to find water. We're going to find food, and we will help Merek as soon as we can. I promise. The only way to do that is for us to get moving. Now will you take point, or should I?"

Efa pushes my hand away. "Okay, fine. I'll take point. No need to treat me like a baby."

I give her a smile, but the frown on her face remains.

"And I move fast," Efa says, narrowing her eyes at Sayer and me. "So you better keep up."

True to her word, Efa moves at battle speed. Sayer attempts to match her pace, but after a few minutes, he's puffing. I drop a hand on his shoulder and hold him back, motioning that we should give her space to lead. Point isn't useful if the entire squad is right on top of the scout.

We move through a serpentine layout of passages. Some bring us back to where we started, others are a dead end. There's no obvious way across the level. Efa darts in and out of rooms, searching them for something useful. There isn't anything. We're not machines. We don't need spare parts.

Merek's throat sounds like something is caught in it. The bandage around his leg is soaked red. I hold my breath and stare, glad Efa is too far away to see it. But any time we had to get him to safety is gone. If he goes into full shock, we could lose him.

As we turn a corner, hope appears. At the end of the corridor is the ladder we need to get to eighty-two. There better be water down there. We could all be in trouble if there isn't.

Efa throws up her hand and shuts it, dropping to a crouch. Sayer halts, unsure of what to do. I slide by him, motioning him to stay put, and move up to Efa. As I touch down next to her, she signals to me she's heard something. I tilt my head to listen, but nothing is apparent.

Until...

There's a tap on the rung of the ladder, and then another. Someone takes a breath, and a hand slaps on the floor of our level. We aim our weapons, our fingers on their triggers. The moment I sense the target before us has shown their head, I blast my light in their face.

"Light, light, light!" Rabbit cries. "Bright light!"

I shut the power off and sigh, bumping into Efa as I slump. She does the same to me as she sniffles.

"Where the hell did you go, you bastard?" Sayer hisses from behind us.

"Shopping," Rabbit replies as he clears the ladder and stands. "You sound thirsty. I have it. The solution!"

In his hands are a pair of bottles and another small package, what looks to be a bag of premade meals. I shut my eyes and thank whatever luck we had going for us that made him come back.

"Oh, Rabbit," Efa says. "Thank you. Bring it here right away!"

OPERATION

MEREK WAS FALLING IN and out of consciousness by the time we got him down the ladder. Sayer and I had to carry him while Rabbit led us through the level with fewer turns and dead ends than eighty-one. He promised to show us a space where we could care for Merek, and possibly ourselves. I'm hopeful, if only because we're out of options.

"Almost there, almost there," Rabbit says.

Rabbit is moving slower than before. He may have realized we couldn't keep up with him or that Merek was a heavy burden to bear. It's still slower than he'd like, but now I agree with him. We'd better not run into a patrol.

"How is he?" Efa asks, bringing up the rear. She carries a pistol in each hand. One is mine, the other Sayer's. She's an odd contradiction, aggressive in appearance, yet so very concerned for her lover, the enemy.

"No different," I reply. "Keep your focus on covering our backs."

I'd consider asking Efa to switch with me, but she'd only lock her eyes on Merek and worry herself sick over him. I told her to take the rear position for that very reason. It's good she agreed. One casualty is already more than enough.

"Here, here, here," Rabbit says, hopping in front of a doorway, his hands pulled tight to his chest.

Without warning, Sayer rips the door open and drags Merek—and me—straight into the darkness. I yelp as my tactical sense screams for visual information. Where the hyuk did he learn how to scout a room? Or did he?

"Efa! Light, now!" I hiss. With her hands full of weapons, it'll be a moment.

The door shuts behind us, locking us into complete blackness. A second later, light blasts into my eyes in a full assault. I cry out, squeezing my eyelids down as I wince. Sayer curses and jerks, losing his balance, and falls, pulling me along with him. Efa screams, her voice filling the room. Her hand hits me in the back of the head. A thump follows, and then what sounds like Efa sliding down the wall.

"Situational status!" Sayer shouts. "Can anyone see?"

"Not yet," I answer. I can see a little if I squint hard, but beyond that, I'm helpless.

Someone, likely Rabbit, shut the door and turned the overheads on. He could have warned us first, but that might have been asking too much of the old man. At least he had the sense to block the light from spilling out into the corridor.

Still, his lack of understanding about how soldiers operate has put me on edge. When I find him, I will make sure he never forgets we don't like surprises.

"There's a bed in here," Efa says.

"A bed? Where?" I ask as my eyes grow more accustomed to this extreme level of brightness. It's like Earth on a summer day. Or the overhead lamps in the stasis recovery room. I haven't experienced either in seven years. But I only miss one.

Efa grabs my head and twists it around. To my disappointment, it's not as I imagined. I won't be curling up in it for a few hours. None of us will.

"That's an exam table," I say, "not a bed."

"So this is a medical room," Sayer says, grinning as he scans the space. "That old rat brought us to the right place."

"Where is he?" Efa asks.

"Who cares? We can help Merek here." He turns to me. "Help me put him on the table."

I push up off the wall, struggling a little to get to my feet, shakier on them than I expect. Fatigue is hitting me hard. Likely all of us are feeling the same, and if Merek didn't need immediate help, I would suggest we rest before making any attempts to get the dart out.

"Bish, his leg is looking like hell," Sayer says. I give him a glare, knowing that Efa will take that hard. As it is, she's already near panic.

But he's right. A dark stain drenches Merek's bandage, and the area surrounding it is an ugly purple. I spin away to stop Efa from seeing it, but she's just behind me, struggling to keep a calm aura about her as she mashes her lips together. I wrap an arm around her shoulders to pull her away, but she plants her feet wide, refusing to move. Efa sniffles, then leans into me and clutches my waist tighter than she's ever done before. Her other hand slides up her shirt and finds a bit of loose fabric to squeeze in her fist.

We've all lost a friend to the fight, someone we liked just enough to make or stomachs turn when we heard they were gone. Efa's love for Merek is far beyond that. I don't want to imagine how she'd react if he died. Which means we have to save his life. Somehow.

"Okay," Sayer says, staring at his semi-conscious friend. "How do we do this?"

"Do what?" I reply.

"Get that dart out. That's what we have to do, right? Then use whatever we can find to stop him from bleeding to death."

Silence fills the space between us. Efa and I can do first aid, like dressing wounds, slowing blood loss, and administering basic medications. After that, the more heavily wounded go to the battle surgeon. They've got the knowledge and skill to get inside a body and save a life. Sayer also likely knows how to slow the course of death, not stop it completely. While we all understand the basic concept of removing a dart from a body, we don't have a clue what the first step is.

"So, where do we start?" Sayer's focused on me now. As if I have some miracle knowledge that'll save his friend.

"We need to get to the wound and open it up so we don't damage his leg when we pull the dart out," Efa replies. I blink at her. Ten seconds ago, she was about to break down in sobs.

"Let's check in the drawers," I suggest. "We'll need something sharp to cut with that isn't a weapon."

"Aren't his pants in the way?" Sayer asks. "We should take them off first."

Efa's eyes open up, her cheeks reddening. She's never seen a boy without pants before. Not even Merek. I'll be happy about that if we can save his life.

"So let's get them off, right?" Sayer looks at me. I can only shrug. Efa doesn't need a memory of me ripping off her lover's pants, no matter the reason.

"Are you two kidding me? You're going to be embarrassed now?" Sayer tsks us. "If we had known Tarakh girls were such wussies about boy's underwear, we'd have fought every battle with our pants off and beat the hell out of you."

"Yeah? Try fighting me when I'm shirtless," I shoot back. "You'd faint on sight."

"Can we please just do it and get it over with?" Efa says, her eyes locked on Merek.

Sayer rolls his eyes at me and motions for me to go to the opposite side of Merek. I glare at him but follow his direction. This operation's what's important right now.

"Take his boots off," Sayer says to Efa. Then he turns to me. "On three, we'll raise his back up and Efa will pull his pants off. Then we can have a better look at the wound."

Efa connects her gaze with mine. She's telling me how uncomfortable she is with this, but we've no choice. And, for the moment, it's just pants, the same kind that the two of us wear, if a little larger. That's all that's required from her. Then I'm going to force her to sit in the far corner until we're done.

The action goes as well as it can until Merek stirs. Efa gets nervous and pulls harder. It only wakes him more.

"What...what are you doing?" he mumbles.

"Just take it easy," Sayer says. "We're going to get that thing out of your leg."

"Hurts..."

Sayer throws a questioning look at me, but I shake my head. We can't give him more painkiller. Not for a while. What he really needs is blood. There isn't any here besides what's in our bodies, but it'd be a guess if any of us are compatible.

Once we lay him back down, I get a better look at Merek's wound. The bleeding has stopped. For now. Our fumbling about inside of it is sure to make it run red again.

Efa touches my arm, and I turn to her to find a surgeon's knife and some kind of tweezer in my face. I frown and pull back. She's got the wrong idea. My hands are steady, yet I'd never attempt to do this. Efa would never forgive me if I messed up, and I don't want Merek's permanent disability on my conscience, either.

"Sayer, these are for you," I say, nodding to the tools in Efa's hand.

Sayer's wide eyes dart to them. "Why me?"

"Because he's your friend, and if I had to guess, my eyesight is better than yours. You'll need someone to observe and direct you and make sure we're not doing more damage."

"Efa should do it. He belongs to her first."

"No." Efa shakes her head and backs away. "No. Please don't ask me. I can't do that. I can't."

Efa's plea doesn't sway Sayer, but it'll scar Efa for life if she does it wrong. He's the only one qualified to do this. I just have to convince him of it.

"Sayer," I say. "No one wants to mess this up. Efa more than either of us. Get it? I'll be your eyes, and you can be my hands. We'll do this together."

Panic flashes across his face as he eyes Merek's still body. Bish. I've got to calm him down. I grit my teeth and reach out to take his hand with both of mine, like I've done with the recruits when they get scared. A few gentle strokes get his attention back to me, and I give him a smile.

"We can do this," I say.

Sayer stares at me, open-mouthed, then glances down at our clasped hands. Now he's made it strange. I narrow my eyes at him and let go. Still, it works. He finds his courage and nods. Efa holds the tools out and Sayer accepts them with a reluctant motion. He takes a breath, and a moment to stare at Merek's leg before leaning over his friend.

The first cut brings a moan from Merek. Sayer jerks back, concerned he just did something wrong. I give him a reassuring shake of my head and motion for him to continue, doing my best to hide the explosion of terror that just filled my body.

"Use the tweezers and see if you can find the dart," I say, pointing to a spot on Merek's wound where it seems the deepest. "Try there."

Sayer hesitates, then tightens his jaw and jambs his tweezer deep into the hole in Merek's leg. He slides it around quickly but gently. Still, Merek cries out, and Sayer pulls the tool away.

"I can't...I can't cause him pain like this," Sayer says, shaking his head. "I can't do this."

"Give him another dose," Efa blurts out, but it's a wrong idea. She doesn't remember she's already given him too much.

"No," I reply and point to a chair in the corner. "Go sit over there. You're only going to make yourself sick watching this."

Efa hesitates, then goes when I glare at her. I should send her outside, really, but I doubt she'll go. And she'd still hear Merek's cries, which would torture her as much as we're torturing him. It's too bad there's no way to ease his torment.

Well, there is, though no one will like it.

"Sorry, guy," I say, patting Merek on the cheek. "Hang in there a second more, okay?"

Before either Efa or Sayer can protest, I swing my fist into Merek's chin. His head jerks, and Efa screams. Then, recovering from the force of my blow, his body relaxes, and his jaw goes slack. I curl my lips inward as I watch him, uncertain if I just did the right thing.

"Ceri! What the hell?" Efa shouts, glaring at me.

"Yeah!" Sayer echoes, pointing the scalpel at me. "Give me one reason I shouldn't choke the life out of you!"

I swallow and turn toward them. "Now he won't feel the pain."

Anger continues to spill from the two of them, but they do as I order. They can hate me all they want. I solved the problem, and now we can save Merek without him feeling a thing.

Sayer finds the dart not soon after, but it's a struggle to get it out. I have to get my fingers inside Merek's leg to pry the barbs free. By the time we're done, Sayer and I are breathing hard.

"Here," Efa says, slamming a packet of cauterizing compound into my hand. I look at her, and my stomach twists into agony. As long as I stared at the wound and nothing else, I could focus on the task at hand, but as I see how much she's fighting to keep from becoming a terrified mess, my legs go weak and I have to lean on the exam table to keep standing.

I rip the packet open and pour it into Merek's wound, jamming my fingers inside to make sure the medication gets all the way in. I use way more than is needed, but I don't care. The blue-gray liquid spilling over his leg seems right. It'll take care of any issues with infection, too. My hands are far from clean.

"Good job," I say, my voice weak. Sayer finds a field dressing and wraps it around Merek's leg. Our work is done—for now. Merek won't get any worse, but who knows if he'll get any better? It will be a while at least, time we'll have when we're in a safer place. It's a miracle no one heard all the noise we've made.

I stumble across the room, slamming into a wall and sliding down it as my eyes close. Sayer moves to the opposite corner and does something similar.

The last thing I see before I lose consciousness is Efa standing watch over her lover. Over Merek. She reaches out and caresses his face, looking down at him with some emotion I do not yet understand. Maybe one day I will.

Right now, all I can see is the blackness of sleep, and I welcome it.

EVASION

Despite the brightness of the room, I sleep deeply. I know I did because my eyes take a long time to open once I return to the universe of the conscious. I could feel the harshness of the overhead bulbs burning through my eyelids, and I have no interest in the torture of getting used to the light again. No one else had the idea, or the strength, to find the power switch. I am not even sure I remember what one looks like.

Once my vision returns, along with a stabbing pain in my head, I notice Efa. She's asleep, but I don't understand how. She kneels on the floor while her torso drapes over Merek's chest, her arms clinging to him as if she is trying to stop his soul from leaving his body. Efa has never expressed a belief about such things, nor have I. Death to us isn't another step in the cycle of things. It's the end of our life in hell.

I force myself up and move to her. No matter how much Efa wants to be close to him, she can't sleep like that. Her legs will be useless when we want to move again, and we will soon. Our one goal is to get her and Merek to somewhere they will be happy together. Nowhere like that exists on this ship, though if they try hard enough, they can convince themselves that one does, just like they've convinced themselves that they can be together.

Efa will not be easy to disconnect from Merek. She's light enough for me to lift, but her hands are underneath his shoulders. If I pull her up, her hands will get stuck, and that would wake her. Still, I might not have another way.

Sayer is snoring away in his corner. He won't be any help, even if I cared to wake him. Efa is my charge. I'll do what is necessary to care for her on my own.

I lean over and wrap my arms around Efa's waist, making sure I have a good grip. Then I straighten up, lifting her with me. My aching muscles complain with the effort. I cannot stop now. To drop her is to wake her up.

I catch her under her arms and move her away from the exam table, using as much gentle motion as I can. Efa remains asleep, and that is all I care about.

But then her foot catches on something, throwing me off-balance. I throw a leg back for support—too far. My ankle buckles and we fall. I twist to protect Efa from hitting the deck first. I wince as my shoulder and back come into impact with the hard metal surface, made rough for better traction.

Pain is coming, and for all my effort, Efa still wakes. She mumbles Merek's name and reaches out to search for him. When she realizes he's not there, she stirs, then jerks awake.

"Ceri?" Efa asks, pushing against me and twisting to see the person who has her wrapped in their arms.

"Sorry," I say. "I just wanted to get you to lie down. You were going to hurt yourself like that."

"Like what?"

"You were on your knees next to Merek."

Efa stares into my eyes, her brain still waking from its rest. Her gaze is both vacant and full of thought. I attempt to give her an apologetic smile, but it clashes with the wince I make as a searing heat runs up my back.

"I fell asleep?" It's not really a question. "I just wanted to be near him. His breathing must have put me at ease, and I drifted off."

"You weren't the only one."

"Did you...I...His leg is okay now, right?"

"I think so." My mind races to think of something better to say to assure her. I can't. As awake as I am from the fall, my mind is not clear enough. I don't know why I am overly worried about it.

"Thank you." Efa pulls me closer to her, pressing her chin onto my shoulder and bringing me into a hug. I jump as her hands rub against a sore spot and fight myself not to groan.

"I did nothing, Efa."

"You did everything. You saved him. Merek would not be alive if not for you."

"Sayer was the one who removed the dart."

"And you were the one who convinced him to do it. I will never forget that, Ceri."

I don't need praise. Though it's better than fighting with her. Every time we clash, I worry she's pulling away from me. Her falling in love with Merek, in some ways, seems like a sign of that. I want her to be happy, yet when I consider, I realize I'm reluctant for this to happen. I want to protect her, but I also don't want her to leave me. Her natural cheer has kept me from dark thoughts, and with Efa gone, I will be alone with them.

Efa is ready to fall asleep again. I might be as well, if I can extricate myself from her arms. That might be more difficult than I think. Like some mornings when we wake, our limbs are a tangled mess. If we were back at base, I'd just give her a good shove to get free, and she'd get the hint. That'd be rude to do now.

"Ceri?" Efa asks, her voice muffled by her mouth against my shoulder.

"What is it?"

"Can we really get to where we're going?"

As my mind drifts in half sleep, her question stirs thoughts of disaster, and I'm hesitant to reply. In reality, arriving at our destination should be simple. Climb down around forty more levels, avoid detection, and find enough food and water to survive. We can accomplish these things.

Yet plenty of mishaps have seeped in to cover all of it with doubt. The start of this plan has been a mess, and Merek, while no longer in mortal danger, will be a burden. We have no idea what we will face along the way or when we arrive. We might meet people like Rabbit, helpful and resourceful, if strange. Or they could be sinister and dangerous. We won't know until we get there.

It's good that Efa cannot see my face. It would betray everything I am attempting to hide from her. I want to tell her how much I will miss her and what I really think about this wreck of a plan. Beyond that, I still have doubt that what she is doing is right.

If I could convince her to return to base, I would accept the blame for everything. The captain will throw me into a locker for a while, but it would make her safe, and she'd still be around. Then maybe, once I was out, we could find a way for her to meet Merek from time to time.

I just don't know if I can change her mind, now we're so close.

"Ceri?" Efa asks, lifting her head. I try to turn away, but she stops my head from moving. "What are you thinking about? Tell me."

I smile at her to fend off her curiosity. It won't be that easy. Efa is persistent. Before they put us in the same squad, she badgered me daily until I promised to refuse any other partner assignment. As irritated as I was with her, I'm glad she did it. Efa is one of the best soldiers in the entire Tarakh battle force. But more than that, she's a great friend. That's what really makes all of this difficult.

"Please?" Efa begs me with her eyes.

"I'm thinking about you," I reply, "and Merek." That much is the truth, if only a small part of it.

"What about us?"

"I was just thinking I've never seen someone so dedicated to someone else like that."

"Liar. That's not it." Efa sticks her tongue out at me. "Give me the truth, or I will torture it out of you."

"Who's lying now?" I grin. "You could never get a word out of me."

Efa sighs and slides over to sit next to me. "That is true. But…"

"But?"

"You didn't answer my question."

"What was it?"

"You didn't forget it, scrap head." Efa jabs me in the side with her elbow. "Answer me."

"I will get you there, Efa. You and Merek."

"I know that's what you want to tell me, but do you really think we can make it? Please, Ceri. I want to hear you say it."

Efa knows me too well. And she should. We have been inseparable since the adults forced us to train together. We were frightened and confused, even though we had little time to be, and found comfort in each other's friendship. They pounded their words and ideas into us nearly every minute we were awake: *It is an honor to be chosen to fight. We expect great things from you. If you want to live, you will do everything we tell you.*

The truth was the adults didn't want to fight each other, and couldn't. They had to get command and control working again. They had to look after the thousands in stasis. Children had no training or knowledge of the technical, but they could teach us how to use a gun and a blade to protect our supplies and our faction. And how to kill, with no real consideration of whether it was right to murder children. Or how it would give us all nightmares.

"We will get there," I say, rubbing her hand. "It's not that far, and Rabbit will guide us. You trust him, don't you?"

"Of course!"

"Then we will make it, and you should stop worrying about it."

I feel bad for my manipulation of her hopes and for my lack of honesty. It's not right to deceive her when she has placed so much trust and faith in me. It may be a small thing, but what happens when I have to elaborate on it? I don't know if I will remember enough of what I said for my lies to remain undetected by her.

It's done. I've answered her how I thought was best. If it was another moment, I may have told her the truth. But I said what I said, and I can't take it back.

"Okay," Efa says with a yawn. "You're right. I'll stop worrying. As long as you don't move."

"Huh?"

"Don't move." Efa's command becomes clear when she returns her head to my shoulder, resting her hands on the opposite side.

Efa has the right idea. For the moment, sleep is the best action. I rest my head on hers and close my eyes, glad our conversation has ended. I don't have the strength to tell her any more lies.

DEMAND

As quickly as I return to sleep, I awakened just as fast by someone's finger poking me in the middle of my forehead. Not just once, but a few times in rapid succession. Since no words follow, I can assume it is neither Sayer nor Merek. And because I can still feel Efa's head on my shoulder, I know it isn't her.

I don't accept anyone else touching me.

My hand shoots up, grabbing the wrist of the offending hand and twisting. A yelp comes from the intruder. They bend under the force of my grip, falling to their knees before me. My eyes snap open, expecting a foolish Fahrasi boy. But it's less of a surprise than that.

Rabbit.

"P-P-P-Please! Do not hurt!" Rabbit pleads, wincing as I hold his arm in a very uncomfortable position.

"I won't, as long as you promise to never, ever touch a sleeping soldier again," I growl, gripping his wrist tighter. "We will kill you if you wake us."

"I promise, I promise!"

I let him go, and he pulls his hand close to his body, looking at it as if it was some wounded animal. His cry did not sound all that human, so his action fits. It also woke up everyone else.

Sayer springs to his feet, gun in hand. He scans the room, expecting a threat, yet finds none. Then he spies Rabbit backing into the farthest corner, his eyes focusing on the floor.

"What did you do to him?" Sayer asks, coming over. He offers Rabbit a hand up, but the old man skitters away from him, backing himself against another wall.

"Taught him a lesson," I reply.

Efa stirs, rubbing her nose on my shoulder before she lifts her head to give me a bleary smile. She turns to check on Merek, only to find Sayer glancing between Rabbit and the two of us.

Merek moans and stirs then, pulling our attention away from the cowering Rabbit.

"Hey," Sayer says as he moves to his friend. "How are you feeling?"

Merek mutters something incoherent, but raises his arm and reaches out to Sayer, who claps Merek's hand in his. A second later, Efa is up and over there, too.

"So you knew about this room," I say to Rabbit, who nods quickly in reply. "Thank you. You helped us save his life."

Rabbit shrinks under my praise. Perhaps he is not used to it. I suspect he isn't used to human interaction at all.

"So, then." I glance at Merek, gauging his ability to move and decide it doesn't matter. We can't stay in this room forever. "We're ready to move again. You promise not to run away, right? And we need to find more food and water."

"Yeah, I'm starving!" Sayer says. He turns his attention to Rabbit and me, now that Efa has monopolized Merek once again. "Where can we find more food?"

"Food you will have," Rabbit replies, scratching his arm. "First, I ask something."

"What?"

Rabbit raises his hand, sticking out his index finger and raising his thumb, then pointing it at Sayer as if to mime shooting at him. Sayer looks at me, his forehead wrinkling.

"I think he wants your pistol," I say.

"No!" Rabbit says. "Not just!"

I lean forward. "What do you mean?"

"You." Rabbit points at me, then Efa, Merek and Sayer in succession as he says, "And you, and you, and you. All you."

"You want all our guns just to show us the way?" I shake my head. "What are you going to do with four guns?"

"Yeah, and why do you suddenly want to bargain with us for something you already agreed to do?" Sayer shouts.

Rabbit's response is to duck his head while his fingers intertwine. It's not an answer I will accept. Heat runs through me just looking at him. If he thinks he can extort some kind of payment from us, he is going to learn quickly what I do to cheaters.

"Rabbit, if we give them to you, we won't be able to defend ourselves, or you," Efa tries.

"You cannot," Rabbit replies. "I am safe without you."

My jaw goes tight. This is turning into a negotiation where we do not have an advantage. Rabbit has something we need, and we only have something he might want. It's uneven, and I don't see an obvious way to win. If we can't figure this out, we'll be on our own to search for an entrance we may never find.

"There's no way we're giving up our guns!" Sayer shouts, showing his teeth. Rabbit pulls back. Just a little. He fears Sayer's wrath, but not too much. He knows he can press us and we can do little to stop him.

"I will not help," Rabbit replies and goes to stand.

"Wait just a second, you bish of an old man!" I say, reaching out to him. Rabbit pauses, eying me with suspicion. He should fear me instead. I wouldn't want to, but I will kill him to protect Efa if I must.

I crouch before him and pull out my pistol, showing him just enough of it to make him nervous. His hesitant reaction tells me I'm successful in my intimidation. I'm glad. It's the only safe weapon I have to battle him with.

"Now listen," I say. "You're going to show us the entrance to the machine room, like you promised, or I will make you regret that you ever met us. Understand?"

Rabbit watches my face for a moment. He must be searching for some hint that will tell him I'm bluffing. Except I'm not. I will make good on my threat if I must. Efa comes before any old man attempting to get in our way.

"You...will hurt me?" Rabbit asks.

"Not if you keep your promise."

"No promise. No promise. Only promise to leave the sleeping soldier alone! Alone! Alone! Let sleep, sleep, sleep."

I narrow my eyes at him. Rabbit is cannier than he wants us to believe. That makes him a potential problem. He's already proven he's sharper than he pretends to be. If I had any trust in him before now, it's gone. This old man is just another adult—no more our ally than any the Fahrasi or Tarakh captains are. I should fear them first, but they're not the ones asking for our guns. At least not at the moment.

"You agreed to take us," I growl, keeping my level of coercion up.

"Not." Rabbit shakes his head. "Did not, did not. No promise."

"I didn't say promise! I say you agreed!"

"You are trouble." Rabbit wags a finger in my face, then moves away. "No agreement for trouble!"

My body is turning red hot over his tricks. If that's the way he wants to go, then I'll make it a point to show him how much trouble we can be. Especially if he continues to press us for some kind of trade. Rabbit needs to understand what he is up against.

"Didn't you think there'd be trouble bringing us there?" I ask. "I think you already knew. Make good on your agreement, or *I'll* give you trouble!"

"Go easy on him, Ceri," Efa pleads.

I won't. Not for her sake. Efa sees something in him I don't. That's fine. I'll be the one to use force if needed. Let Efa play the part of the gentle girl, even though she is more than capable of causing Rabbit as much pain as I can. Especially if he stops helping her get what she wants.

"No. No. No!" Rabbit hops and shakes his head. "No trouble or you will go. Must give request, or else."

"Or else what, you vermin bastard?" Sayer pulls his own gun and swings it around. If it scares Rabbit, he doesn't show it. Words have no effect on him. Rabbit may talk with strange syntax, but he's as sharp as any of us. I wonder what he was before he went recluse. An engineer, perhaps. Which means logic also will not work on him. Only fear will drive him to accept our terms.

"No help, no—"

Before he can finish his sentence, I strike out, my hand seizing his throat. My fingers find his windpipe and press just enough to make him uncomfortable. I won't kill him, but he needs to think I might.

"Ceri, no!" Efa cries, leaving Merek's side and pressing toward me. I tense, unsure of what she might do in this situation. Her pistol remains in its holster, but she might pull it out if she fears I will destroy her one chance at freedom.

"You will do what we want, or I will end you here and now," I shout, using as much real rage at him as I can. His life is in my hands. If Rabbit chooses defiance now, he may just force me to take action.

To my surprise, he uses my hold on his neck for his own benefit. He pretends to choke, coughing and rolling his head around as if he cannot breathe. I've put pressure on his throat, but nothing more. He's faking. It should be obvious to everyone.

"Ceri, enough!" Efa shouts. She grabs my arm and yanks it off Rabbit's neck. The old man makes use of the moment and doubles over, his hands going to his neck. It's a lie, and he knows it. I flash Efa a glare for taking his side, but if he believes he has an ally in her, he is mistaken.

Time to press the threat again.

I power on my gun, and raise it, ready to push it against his forehead and scare him into changing his mind. It may not come to that, but it will depend on his reaction. And Efa's.

Rabbit glances between Efa and me. Merek is sitting up now, and Sayer is not far away. He grips his gun, unsure of whether to put it away or use it. His hesitation won't last for long. Rabbit had better decide quickly.

"Give," Rabbit says slowly. "Give me, or no help. I want them. Give now."

I sigh. I was foolish to think I was smart enough to deceive him. Rabbit has called my bluff, and now I must either make good on my threat or let him go.

And the rage rising in me is demanding action.

CHASE

"You're not getting anything, you little rodent," Sayer says, stepping toward Rabbit. The old man looks up, more curious than afraid. I don't think Sayer understands the negotiation is over. We either agree to Rabbit's demand, or we make our own way down.

"Leave him alone, Sayer," Efa says. "He's just trying to survive like we are."

"Yeah? Then he should know we need weapons more than he does."

"No shooter, no help," Rabbit says, raising a finger.

"And if you don't stand up and start showing us the way, I'm going to use my shooter and pop you right between the eyes!" Sayer's gun hand rises, and mine comes to the ready. Will he shoot Rabbit? I can't be sure. I know Sayer only a little better than I know the old man, and I trust neither of them.

"Hey," Merek says, taking hold of his friend's sleeve. "Let's take it easy. We can talk this out."

"Not if he keeps insisting that we give him our guns!" Sayer pulls away, throwing a finger into Rabbit's face. "I swear I will beat the life out of you, old man, if you're not up and moving in three seconds."

"Give now," Rabbit says, opening up his hands. "Then we move."

"No," I say, though I'm not sure to whom. I can feel the aggression in the air. My muscles tense, ready for the explosion.

"Sayer," Efa says, reaching out to him. I lift my hand to stop her from getting involved. It's too late.

Sayer roars and swings his foot. Rabbit throws his arms up, and they take the brunt of the hit. The old man cries out in pain. I shoot up, tackling Sayer before he can attack again. We topple, my arm and his shoulder impacting the ground first.

I wince, but plant my feet on the floor, using gravity and leverage to pin Sayer down. He struggles, then rolls to knock my legs out from under me. I fall on top of him, my stomach slamming into his hip. Air escapes my lungs, and I gasp for breath.

Sayer takes the advantage and shoves me to the floor, pinning me down. I glare at him and twist my arm to break his grip on my wrist. It doesn't work. It took all my energy to get my breath back, and now all I can do is stare up at him.

"Had enough?" Sayer asks, sneering. "Now don't try that again, or I will have to hurt you."

"You must be confused," I reply, poking the tip of my gun into his chest. Sayer's mouth drops open the moment he feels it.

"Stop it!" Efa shouts. "Don't you see what you've done?"

"What?" I glance at Efa, then around the room. "Bish!"

Rabbit is gone.

Sayer and I spring to our feet, both of us staring at the open door. There's only darkness out there, and Rabbit has already had time to allow his eyes to adjust. If we just rush after him, we're only going to smack into walls until we can see again.

Not to mention, with all the noise and light we've been making, we're now a bright, noisy target for any squad to ambush us the moment we step out of the room.

"Shut off the light!" I hiss. The room goes dark, and I drop to a crouch. "Efa, stay here and watch Merek."

"I'm fine," Merek replies. "I've got my gun. Let Efa cover you."

"No," Sayer says. "I'll go. You stay."

"I don't need either of you," I say, moving to the door. Sayer finds the back of my shirt and grabs it. I jerk to a stop, spinning around and breaking his grip.

"You know going out there on your own is dumb," Sayer says, laying his hand on my shoulder instead. "I'll cover you. No games."

I shrug his hand off me, sickened by his touch. We just fought like the enemies we are. One of us will get more than hurt if we do that again. Sayer's offering me a chance at peace. I'd be wise to accept. Besides, I might actually need his help.

"Fine, we both go." I raise a finger at him. "But if you hurt him, I will put a dart in your skull, understand? We still need him to guide us."

"Whatever you say, Captain," Sayer says and smirks.

"And none of that bish, either."

"Sheesh. So strict."

"Shut up. Let's go."

We slip out the door and head down the corridor in opposite directions. I stay low until my eyes reacquaint themselves to the dark. Luckily, it doesn't take long. They're used to the low light that's been the norm on this ship. Light is painful. And dangerous.

Even when my sight returns, it won't be easy to find Rabbit. He'll run as soon as he spots one of us. And he knows this part of the ship while we don't. I will have to try hard to find him.

Perhaps he's still willing to talk. Rabbit wants our guns and still thinks that he has an advantage in the negotiation. He would be right, of course. I am slinking around this level because we need him. My gun is staying in my hand, however.

"Rabbit," I whisper as I move down the corridor. "Come out and talk. I won't hurt you."

I should have given Sayer some operational guidelines so we could communicate. If Efa was with me, I could give her three hand signals and she'd know exactly what to do. Sayer knows none of that, for good reason. It's not his fault the Fahrasi chose him.

Though, as is typical of his faction, he's likely pounding down each passage to drive Rabbit into a corner. Or, if Sayer is smart enough, he will drive the old man toward me. Rabbit may just decide to do that on his own, since he knows I won't kill him.

But Sayer might, even after I warned him not to.

"Hyuk," I mutter and power on my light, ignoring everything I have ever learned about tactical movement. I need to find Rabbit before Sayer does, or at least scare him away. It's a foolish plan, but I have little choice. And I'm putting myself at enormous risk to make it happen. I just hope any patrol I run into is Tarakh. They might let me live.

I do my best to keep my footsteps quiet. Sound travels farther in this ship than light. The cramped corridors restrict the rays of my beam, while the echoes of my boots will bounce freely from one side of the level to the other. If I listened hard, I might hear Sayer moving. Or Rabbit.

"Rabbit!" I hiss. "We're not done talking! Show yourself!"

That would be too simple, of course. If he isn't already down two levels, then he's hiding nearby and biding his time as Sayer and I stir up the entire area.

This effort could be a huge waste of time.

I huff and rush down the corridor, checking every alcove, doorway, and ventilation grating for the old man and consider searching the hull access points. But that'd be dangerous. If someone saw a light flash, a squad would be headed down to me in seconds. Captain Daga, like his Fahrasi counterpart, would want to know who was beating them to the lower levels.

There's a blur of motion at the end of the corridor. I raise my gun, aiming for the edge of the turn. It could have been Rabbit, but it could have been anything, including the someone I don't want to run into. If anyone other than Sayer or Rabbit appears, I'll be shooting first.

I dash to the corner, dropping and sliding myself into it. My light and gun come up, blasting the next corridor with illumination. But it's empty. I press my lips tight. Something, or someone, was there. I'm certain of it.

A second later, I'm up and moving. I must. I won't find Rabbit keeping still, and I open myself to a potential attack. But the constant drive is grinding on me. I've lost my focus and my sense of direction. My chest is tightening and my only relief is to sweep the corridor. I'd better encounter something soon, if only to put an end to my disquiet.

There's a sliding door, half-open, not far away. I've got to check it out or risk opening my back to a potential threat.

My foot finds the edge of the door. My finger finds the trigger of my gun. I'm ready to go, then I realize I'm panting hard. A few breaths calm me, but now I've lost my chance at surprise. Too late to retreat now.

I shove the door open and shine my light inside, strobing it to confuse anyone there—except there's no one, and now no reason to stay. The room is a mess. Rabbit, or perhaps his co-habitants, ransacked this space long ago. The pair of cabinets and desk that are here lie on the floor, toppled by force. Their drawers are strewn about the room, along with contents not worth taking. I shake my head. I'm wasting time here. Sayer could already have his hands around Rabbit's neck.

Then I notice something out of place. A piece of metal, placed in such a way only someone with a trained eye would notice. That would include most soldiers. Whoever did it was taking a risk of the wrong person seeing it.

As I draw closer, I notice a scrawl of letters on one side. It's my name—misspelled. I can only guess at one person who might have done that. After a quick examination of the plate to make sure there are no traps on it, I turn it over and find a message—from Rabbit.

I will talk to you. Just you. Come down. No bring the boy.

A chuckle escapes my throat. Rabbit means Sayer. And he wants me to meet him one level down. I'll go, if only for Efa, though I wonder why Rabbit didn't just stay here and wait for me. Perhaps he was worried about Sayer finding him. That was smart thinking.

I power off my light, wait until my eyes are ready, and slip out into the corridor, headed toward the down ladder. If I can find Rabbit, and come back fast enough, Sayer will never know I left the level.

TRADE

By the time I touch down on level eighty-three, I feel more attuned to myself and the skills I've honed over years of fighting. My eyes are as sharp in the dark as they ever were. If someone were to attack me here, they stand little chance of success.

But I'm not here to fight. Negotiation is my plan, though that requires two parties, and right now, one is missing. I can't expect Rabbit to be on point on much, but he could have at least been waiting for me as I came down the ladder.

Now I'll have to search him out on an unfamiliar level, and that makes me unhappy. It's all storage here, rows upon rows of cargo packed away in bays that run from one side of the *Stratford* to the other. I'd guess there's more than over a hundred, and Rabbit could be in any of them.

I start down the aisle that runs parallel to the hull so I can glance down the others that run across to the other side of the ship. Perhaps Rabbit left me another clue that will tell me where he is hiding. Better he should just come out. If I have to search this whole level to find him, he will feel my wrath.

A moment before I consider how many ways I can torture the old man, a pair of knocks, too random to be anything but human mad, come from my left. I target a door not far away, where I think the sound came from. I'm right. A second later, a hand pokes out from the door and beckons me over.

I check my surroundings, then stroll to the bay that is growing limbs. I slip my gun into its holster and slide the door open.

Whatever cargo the bay held is gone now. Only remnants of packaging and empty crates fill a corner. Rabbit crouches on a box in front of the pile, watching me as a young child might gaze at an adult. I glance behind me, then slide the door shut.

"You have come," Rabbit says, almost sounding hopeful.

"Yes, because you ran away," I reply.

"Pain is not for me."

I snort. It wasn't his intention to be funny, but his comment surprised me. So much for intimidation. The smile on my face just ruined that. I've got to get back to being serious.

"So," I say, folding my arms, "you wanted to talk. Let's talk."

"*You* wanted to talk," Rabbit echoes. "That is why *you* are here."

The old man is clever. Perhaps more so than me. He's survived longer on this ship than I have, which means he knows more than a trick or two. He'll take advantage of the situation if I'm not cautious.

"We both do," I reply. "So let's get on with it. I want you to lead us to the access point, just like before. You can name your terms"—I hold up a finger—"but you can't have our guns. We need them for protection. Ask for something else, and we could have a deal."

"No. Nothing else. You give"—Rabbit points to my holster—"or no help."

"I just told you that won't work. Either you get something else or you get nothing."

"Nothing is not good. You are trouble, trouble, trouble. No reward, no risk."

We remain at a standoff, then. Threatening him didn't work before, so I expect it won't work now. Maybe I could just tie him up and torture him until he told us where to go, but that'll fail, too. Forced coercion almost never results in the truth.

Rabbit watches me, comfortable in his position and patient enough to wait me out. Seconds are speeding by, and with each one, I am losing the chance to get back without Sayer doing something careless. If I want to avoid that, I'll need to consider this problem another way.

There's a reason Rabbit wants these guns, and self-defense isn't it. He wouldn't know how to use them, and I won't be showing him. Not even if he begs. Though perhaps there's a potential way for me to bargain with him.

"What do you need guns for?" I ask. "You've survived a long time with no weapons. I think they'd just cause you trouble if you had them. Efa and Merek could protect you...if they had their guns."

"No protection. No." Rabbit shakes his head. "Not needed. Trade needed."

"Trade? With who?"

"Friends. Friends make trade."

My eyebrows collide as I consider what he means by *friends*. If there are others beside him down on the systems levels, I may need to reassess the risk to Efa and Merek. Rabbit is mostly harmless. I can't be certain of anyone else.

"You mean your trade with us?" I try.

Rabbit cackles with a dry wheeze. "You are no friend!"

I cross my arms as my eyes narrow at him. He's made it plenty clear where his trust of us stands.

"Just remember that trust works both ways, old man."

Rabbit tilts his head and shrugs in a single lazy movement. He still thinks he has the advantage, but now I know the guns mean nothing to him other than as a thing to trade. What worries me more is who he trades it to and for what. Likely something he values more, whatever that may be.

"Alright," I say as I pace around the room. "You want items to trade, I get it. The guns are worth a lot to someone."

"Yes, yes, yes." Rabbit nods to himself and smiles. "Good trade. Good trade."

I wonder what might be worth the same as a dart pistol to him. And if I don't have its equivalent on me, I'll have to get it. That's a problem, because the only place I know to find anything valuable is back at base. Going there would be difficult, if not impossible. I won't have a right to show my face there without some kind of explanation.

Which means I'd have to come up with one. I might, but it'd have to be so exceptional that I'd be able to get away with such a fabrication of the truth. Just being wounded wouldn't cut it. Captain Daga would pick out my lie in a second.

I can feel Rabbit's eyes on me as he perches on his box. He'll wait there forever if he thinks I'm about to give in to his demand. I've no intention of doing so. But it's getting me nowhere.

Rabbit scratches his arm, then looks down at it, distracted by whatever is irritating him. He reminds me of my puppy, constantly swiping at a singular itch that bothered him. It almost seems a regular action for Rabbit.

Then I remember he's been doing that since we met him. Curious. I take a few steps towards him to get a good view of the problem.

And in the same moment, I get an idea of another item we can offer for trade.

"That," I say and nod at the mass of reddish dots across his forearm. "It itches, doesn't it?"

"Yes, yes, yes. Itchy." Rabbit winces. "And hurt."

"I can get medication for you that would stop the itching."

Rabbit's eyes brighten, and he gives me a hopeful, if tentative, look. The sides of my mouth curl up. I've got his interest in something other than our guns.

"You can do?" Rabbit asks.

"In trade for showing us the way. Yes."

"No!" Rabbit shakes his head with violent force. "Not enough! You give everything!"

The curl of my lips transforms into a grin. I've broken the stalemate, and we're back into negotiation. I have or, at least, can get something he wants. The sides are even now. Let's see if I can be just as wily as him.

"The guns were never happening," I say. "But you want medication, that can be an option. Or maybe some other kind? Do your feet hurt? Or your knees? I know something that can help."

Rabbit recoils but then, after a moment, considers. After a minute, he taps a finger on his lower back and mimes a wince. That his back is causing him discomfort is obvious. Why he feels pain is beyond my knowledge to guess. I could grab some anti-inflammatory medication, which might help him, though it's just speculation. Still, it's worth a try.

"Alright," I say. "I'll get you the ointment for your arm and something for your back. Enough to last you a long time. You can even trade some of it with your friends if you don't need it. I bet if they're a veteran like you are, they might need some of this stuff, too."

"How you know?" Rabbit asks, tilting his head to peer at me with one eye. "How you know which?"

"How do I know what medication to get? Well—"

"Wait!" Rabbit holds up a hand. "You don't have now?"

"No, I don't have it with me, but I can get it."

He wrinkles his nose and glares for a tense minute. Then he waves his hand at me and nods. I don't understand his motion. I frown and shake my head at him.

"Tell me how," Rabbit demands.

"I've seen some of the adult—some of our older people with the same problem. I know what they use. We have it back at base, and I know exactly where to find it. If you agree…the medication for you showing us the way, I will go get it now and be back in a few hours. Do we have a deal?"

Rabbit hops off his box and stands. He gets close, lifting his nose at me, almost as if he is sniffing the air that surrounds me. I watch him as he makes a single orbit about me. Rabbit can't fight, but that doesn't mean he can't be dangerous in other ways, especially now that I've offered him something he really wants. Something that I am very much hoping he will accept in exchange for his guidance.

He comes to a stop in front of me, making every attempt to seem intimidating. I do everything I can not to laugh. That'd end our negotiation, and not with the conclusion either of us wants.

"Deal," Rabbit says. "I will do it. But you better not lie."

"Don't worry," I reply with a smile. "If I wanted to trick you, Rabbit, you'd already know it."

Rabbit pushes his lips out and nods again. He understands, and that's enough. Now I need to climb. But only me. Tarakh sentinels would shoot Sayer on sight, and I can't risk Efa. I can move fastest by myself, anyway.

"Go wait with Efa, and tell them what I went to do," I say. "They won't come after me. They know better."

"I can do." Rabbit smirks and nods with that near-constant bouncing he does. It's annoying, but I somehow feel safer that he will be with Efa. He will make sure nothing happens to her, if only for the sake of his deal. That will allow me to focus on my task. And I will need to. Once I leave this floor, I will head straight into uncertainty.

RETURN

My face drips with sweat as I pass up into level thirty-eight. The fatigue of climbing forty-five levels with nothing so much as a moment to catch my breath is hitting me hard. My stomach growls in complaint, caught somewhere between hunger and nausea. Even if I had brought food with me, I doubt it would help. As it is, I haven't touched my canteen, and I know that's bad. Dehydration in this arid environment is a common occurrence. If I am exerting myself enough to create perspiration, I've already lost a significant amount of water from my body.

Thirty-eight, our former destination of intent, is as good of a place to stop as any. I cannot kill my muscles trying to climb fast and then have no strength left to fight. Once I get to fourteen, there will be sentries to get by. Soldiers too. My preference would be not to harm any of my people, even a little. It will be a hard choice I will have to make if one of them gets in my way.

I press my back against the nearest wall and slide down it, grabbing my canteen and pouring half its contents down my throat. I didn't realize how thirsty I was until the water touched my lips. If I didn't start coughing from drinking too much at once, I may not have stopped. As it is, I have to throw my arm across my mouth to stop the noise. I am only a few levels away from Tarakh and Fahrasi territory. Silence is the only rule I can follow.

This was not how I wanted things to go. If Rabbit had disappeared, I planned to convince Efa to return to base with me. Instead, I've contradicted every intention I had, and now I'm climbing back to base alone, with an ache forming in my heart. This had better be worth it.

After about five minutes, I push myself up and rub my legs to get the stiffness out of them. Then I walk down past a few massive crates that dwarf me in size. Like half of the ship, thirty-eight is a storage level. The size makes me think they contain equipment for exploration and colonization—not anything I would make any use of in my lifetime. Our chief's best estimate is that we are at least four hundred years away from our destination. That is, if the *Stratford* is where it should be in its journey. There's a good chance it's not.

There's also a good chance we might crash into a star.

I glance at a few labels on the crates, a small longing in me to open one, walk inside, and touch a device that will one day be put to use on a planet far away. Habitats, vehicles, portable laboratories—I only know these words from texts about past landings. There are few pictures to describe them, so I can only imagine in my head what they must have been like.

A word on a label catches my eye: *Excavator*. Inside this crate is a machine designed to move a massive amount of soil and rock. There is little chance that I will ever get to see it in action, so I feel justified when I break the seal on the crate's hatch and climb in to examine it firsthand. I won't stay long, just enough to understand what I am missing. After that, Efa becomes my priority once again.

The adults didn't design these crates to keep humans out, only the elements, whatever they are. I would have experienced them too, had they not given me the *honor* of killing my fellow passengers.

I power on my light, unconcerned about light discipline inside an opaque container, and shine it on the monstrous vehicle before me.

The first thing I see is a wheel double my height and likely several times heavier than my weight. If I hadn't seen a picture of one, I wouldn't have known what it was. The largest wheel we use on the *Stratford* is no taller than the length of my thumb.

Next is the bucket, which is three times as long as the wheel is high and nearly as tall. The space it contains inside of it could hold every nest for my squad, with more comfort than we have ever known. A machine this size could move enough dirt to cover this entire level in twenty minutes. If they are planning to construct a city, the colonists have definitely chosen the right tool for the job.

An ache forms in my chest, and I rub a hand over my heart to soothe it. Whether through battle or old age, my fate is to die on this ship. I can accept that, but when I take in this wondrous machine, it becomes much harder to do.

Even though I understand that my fate is to die on this ship, it's not that easy to accept when I take in this wondrous machine. Just to visualize moving in my mind is exciting. I might have even become an excavator operator. It'd be fun to be at the controls of such a huge vehicle.

A sound from outside the crate catches my ear—footsteps. More than a few. It's a patrol for certain. The only question is, which faction do they belong to? I shut my light, sliding to the hatch to close it before they catch sight of it.

I curse under my breath—it won't shut. It wasn't designed to. The only reason to open this box would be to use what's inside of it, and getting the excavator out would require the near destruction of the crate.

If the patrol sees this, they will investigate. And they will find me.

A quick scan of the machine reveals no simple place to hide. Not under, not behind, and definitely not on top. I have to get out of here before they arrive.

I throw my leg through the hatch, pushing myself through once my foot touches the floor. But in my haste, I use too much force and lose my balance. My arms flail about and I hit the floor with a thump.

My hand goes to my pistol, and I scramble behind the back side of the crate. The patrol heard that for certain. Even Deryn's B Squad would have taken notice of such an obvious sound.

The footsteps pick up their pace, getting closer but staying quiet. I can tell by the coordinated patterns that this is no apprentice squad. They are so well in sync that it is difficult to tell how many there are. That's the point. It puts a potential enemy such as me off my tactics. I slip behind the next crate, down the row, and further into darkness. It is my only cover. I must make use of it as best as I can.

As I press myself to the deck, the first members of the patrol come into view. Fahrasi. A boy and a girl, but no one I have fought before. This could be a scouting team, not a full squad. That would mean less for me to deal with, though scouts, like Niah and her team, are quite skilled. They need to operate on their own for extended periods. Four scouts are as much of a challenge as an entire squad of ten.

The boy appears to be a year or two younger than Efa. The girl is older, perhaps just over my age. She has a sharpness in her eyes that is unnerving. I will need to be on top of my game if I am to match her. But that is not the plan. My mission is to retrieve medicine and make it back to Efa and Rabbit as quickly as possible. If I get caught in a battle, it will only delay me.

A week ago, such a situation would have excited me. This would be a chance to disable an important enemy team. Yet, as they come closer, I feel no desire to attack. The only thing that keeps my mind occupied is how to get away without getting caught.

And that's the question. There are others besides these two. What I don't know is where they are. A quick panic turns my head to look behind me. Of course, no one is there, and I just took my eyes off the enemy. That's enough time for them to spot me and shoot me dead.

I wish I could lie here and wait until they leave the level. But they heard the noise I made, and if they're good enough to hide their numbers, they're good enough to know that only a thorough search of the area makes them safe. They will find me if they check the level well.

What I need is a distraction. Another noise for them to investigate while I slip past them and get to the next floor before they suspect anything. I need time to consider the best approach, but I'd better come up with something soon, or I'm going to get cornered and captured.

As I watch and wait, the boy points to the open hatch and slinks toward it. The girl raises her gun, covering him. They move so well together, I almost smile at the level of their skill. These two would be a challenge for sure. I'm making the right choice.

That means I can use my gun for something other than attack. Or rather, what's inside it. I press the clip release on my gun, taking the ammo container into my hand and plucking out a few darts. They're all I have, but they'll have to do.

Another check of my surroundings confirms I remain safe. Their teammates must be investigating something else or holding back in case of ambush. The moment I make noise, I'll know.

With a singular movement, I lift to a crouch and propel the darts away from the Fahrasi pair. One impales itself into the soft composite while the rest smack against the side of a nearby crate and drop. They clatter to the ground, filling the level with a loud ping.

The boy gasps, but before he can speak, the girl holds up a hand, then presses her fingers against her throat. So they've got sublingual comm units. I won't hear what they say.

It doesn't matter. They're distracted, so I'm leaving.

The moment I move, another pair of Fahrasi appear ahead of me, just one crate's length away. My reaction is faster than the panic that hits me. I dart across the row, pressing into the shadow of the box before me and sliding around the corner before they spot me.

A flash of light tells me I'm not as silent as I might have liked. They're after me now, even if they don't know who, or what, they're chasing.

I break into a run, dashing down the next aisle and cutting down the next row I come across. If I stop now, I risk getting caught. Two against one was bad enough. Four is impossible.

But when I glance back, there's no hint of their lights. Are they not giving chase? A scout team would fear an attack by an enemy squad, who would outnumber them by more than double. And battle engagement is not their primary mission. They'll avoid it where they can.

The weight lifts from my chest as I realize I may have just lucked out. I'm taking advantage of that now. I'm at the up ladder a few seconds later, turning back only once to confirm I'm safe.

As I step off the last rung of the ladder onto level thirty-seven, my mind goes back to the massive excavator in the crate. The people who will use it to build their new world will never know anything about me and how I fought to protect them. They will never know that this ship was ever in danger. They may not even care if they did.

And yet, I cannot stop living my life for their sake.

LARCENY

DESPITE MY TWISTED STOMACH, made no better by my encounter with the Fahrasi scouts, I climb the next twenty-three levels with relative ease, stopping only to refill my canteen. By then, I was back in Tarakh territory, which meant I needed to be even more careful than I was before. Capture by the Fahrasi would mean interrogation and a long wait for a prisoner swap. Capture by my faction would also mean interrogation, but when they learned the truth, severe punishment would follow.

I push off the last rung onto the moderately lit corridors of fifteen, with its red walls and gray decking. Stacks of crates and containers narrow the space and make it a challenge to navigate in case I need to run. I'm not worried. Getting past the sentry on sixteen was no issue—I know their routine well—and anyone who sees me here might just ignore me. After the mess on sixty-two, I'm sure Captain Daga has his squads doing double duty elsewhere, so those who know me aren't around to disrupt my plan.

I'm headed to the newly installed utility ladder in the middle of the level. It'll get me close to the bay that holds the medicine storage lockers. I don't exactly remember which ones I will need to open, since I've only been in there a few times to retrieve a few tubes of topical painkiller. They've secured most everything else to keep it from the Fahrasi's greedy hands, though they've never even come close to stepping foot on this level.

An adult medical worker smiles and nods to me as she passes. I nod back and keep my head down, hoping she won't recognize me. I've never spent much time in medical, and I'm thankful for that. If she remembered me, I would have had to knock her out, and I don't know if I could have done that.

I arrive at the bay with the backup ladder but walk by it with only a casual glance inside. It's empty—good. Now I can turn back around and climb up without having to explain why.

A stack of crates in another bay catches my eye as I turn around. I pause as a symbol on one box relights a memory in my brain. There's medication in there, and potentially what I want.

My lips curve upward. If this is what I need, I can get it from here rather than risk heading up the ladder to fourteen, where there are a lot more people. Captain Daga will be there, and he's the absolute last person I want to meet.

I scan the area and turn back to the bay, moving quick enough to make time but slow enough not to attract attention. I only pause to examine the crates, checking the codes to see if I've found what I'm looking for. The numbers are close enough, so I lick my lips and move in.

"Something I can help you with, soldier?" a male voice says to my left. I startle and bump into the edge of the door as I back up and turn to face the voice. It's a sentry, around my age. I'm glad we don't know each other.

I clamp my mouth shut as I look him in the eye. A soldier should never avoid it, especially with members of their own forces. And I just entered somewhere I shouldn't be. He'll get suspicious if I act out of the norm.

"Oh. Is this not the examination bay?" I ask, glancing around to appear confused, then returning to look at the sentry again.

"Do I look like a medic to you?" he asks with a furrowed brow.

"No, of course not."

"What's wrong with you, anyway? You seem fine to me."

"Just getting an old wound checked out."

"Yeah, well, that won't happen in here." The sentry motions at the ceiling with his thumb. "Upstairs."

I press my lips together. This can't be the end of the conversation. It's still easier to grab the medication here than risk a trip up the ladder. I'll need a minute to figure out how I can get away with it.

"You know, I was sure that they told me fifteen," I say, pointing up to echo his meaning. "There was something about a new facility in a bay here."

"Maybe get your head checked before that old wound," he replies.

My eyes narrow at him. Soldiers take verbal shots at each other all the time. It is how we keep the self-important members among us down at a level where they remember to function as part of a squad. We all need it sometimes.

But sentries aren't soldiers. They went through the same training and somehow wound up assigned to the easiest and most despised post in the squads. It is a necessary job, but they're not our equals, and they don't get to insult us like they are.

"No need to take your frustration out on me. I had nothing to do with assigning you to this bish detail. It was your own lack of performance that put you here." My words come out with a venomous point. A sentry who thinks they can get away with talking down to a soldier is in for a hard lesson.

"You need to move along," he growls. "Nothing for you here."

It's hard to tell from his baggy uniform whether his extra weight is muscle or flab. If I had to guess, I'd say it was the latter. Sentries can train just as much as soldiers, but there's little point. We won't let anyone get past us, so they'll never encounter the enemy. He may be stronger than I am, but his skills are as dull as his personality.

I could take him down if I needed to. I can even visualize the three moves I need to make it happen. He'd be out, and I'd have free access to every crate in the bay.

Someone would find him, however, and then the entire base would be on alert. Troops would be crawling over every level, and if they found me, I'd need to fight my way out.

"What are you waiting for?" the sentry says. "Or are you suddenly attracted to me?"

He meant that as a joke. A terrible one at that. My fist should tell his face just how bad it was, so he never repeats it.

Though...it offers me an opportunity. If he's that naïve and full of himself to think I might like him, then I have an advantage.

"Well." I curve one side of my mouth up and push my hair back over my ear like I've seen Efa do. "You aren't ugly."

He frowns, and I get the sense that wasn't the right thing to say. I'd might know if I'd had any sort of regular teenage life. That's impossible on this ship.

"Not ugly?" He snorts and waves me away. "Thanks for the insult. Now get lost before I call an adult."

Hyuk and a half. I shouldn't have tried that.

"Hey." I hold up my hands. "I'm sorry. I don't know how to say stuff like that. I just know how to fight."

The sentry watches me for a moment as he considers whether he can believe me. That he hasn't continued to throw me out of the room is promising.

Then, when he sighs and rolls his eyes, I get the confirmation I'm right.

"Okay, fine," he says. "I get all you battle-types are a bunch of hard-asses with limited social skills. But you're still standing here. Don't you have an examination to get to?"

"Yes...but—"

I pause when he gets tense. He must think I'm playing some game with him. He'd be right, though I have no intention of admitting it. The truth appears to work on him, however, so I'll keep using that tactic and see if I can't achieve my goal.

"Listen," I say and feign checking out the door. "I have an exam, but I was hoping to get some medication for my squad mate. She's out on patrol and is hurting...badly."

"What's the problem? Why doesn't she just get checked by the medic?" the sentry asks. For the first time, concern touches his face.

"It's not that easy. If she requests to return to base, the captain will go hard on her for it. He'll assign her to all the worst details for the next month, maybe more. Word would get around to the other squads, and they'll look down on her for it. That's an awful place to be. Someone might not give her cover when she requests it."

I'm speaking from experience, partially. When I first became field leader, I was on C Squad's bish list. I made some poor decisions, just like Deryn did. No one died, but a few got hurt. I had to regain their trust, and it was far from easy. None of the squad, save for Efa, let me forget my mistake.

"So she didn't get hit? What else could hurt so much?" the sentry asks, leaning forward.

"We call it battle rash. Everyone gets it at least once." I hold up a hand when he goes to ask me to explain. "Trust me, you don't want to know. Not everything on this ship is healthy for us to be around."

The sentry's eyes widen, and I hide my smile. I'm nearly through to him.

"Yeah, I know," the sentry says with a pained smile. "One of my mates got this cough. The doctor has no idea what's wrong with him. He got some medication, but all it did was make him tired. The captain pulled him from active duty. All he does now is transcribe reports."

"Bish. That sucks," I say, attempting to appear sympathetic. "So then you get why I need to get this medication, right?"

"Yeah, I do." The sentry shakes his head. "But I can't let you have it. This is a new haul from a raid, and the adults haven't taken inventory on it yet."

"From sixty-two, right?"

"How do you know that?"

"I was there!"

He pulls back, his jaw going slack. The sentry appraises me with a new respect. If I was just some battle-broken soldier to him before, I've gained a new level of his esteem. I take the initiative and go in for the kill.

"If they haven't inventoried this yet, then it doesn't exist. All I want is just a few things. No one will miss it. My mate needs it badly. If I can help her, we can find even more than this. I heard there's ice cream down there. Do you know what ice cream is?"

The sentry shakes his head as he stares at me. I lean in and put a hand on his shoulder.

"If you let me take what I need, I promise I will bring you some. You have to try it."

"I..." He deflates. "I can't. If the adults find out, I'm dead. I can't take a risk like that for some ice stuff."

A sigh escapes from my lungs. So much for that plan.

My hand snaps around his neck. I squeeze and shove him back against the wall, pulling my gun to jam it against his forehead. The sentry's face turns red as he clutches at my hand and gags, his eyes popping from their sockets. But I can't stop. I've got to get what I need and escape this level as fast as I can.

The moment he recovers, he'll hit the alarm for sure. I'll need to be far gone before that happens.

"You have no idea how many times I've pulled this trigger," I hiss and dig my weapon deeper into his head. "It'd be nothing to squeeze it one more time. So unless you want me to put three needles into your skull, you'll hold still and keep your mouth shut while I get what I need. And don't think about pulling the alarm, or I will return and make sure you really feel pain. Got it?"

The sentry nods and tries to swallow. I ease up on his throat and back away. My pistol stays on him until I'm sure he won't try something foolish. He rubs his neck as he watches me move to the crates, break one open, and drop as many tubes of medication into my side pocket as I can. I think I've got the right ones, but even if I don't, I've got no time to search for more.

With one last warning glare and a flick of my gun at the sentry, I slip out the bay door and race, fast and silent, toward the ladder. I've got a long way to go, and my objective isn't complete until I return to Efa and Rabbit.

A lot could happen in that time. I need to stay vigilant. If I can.

EXPOSURE

Five seconds after I leave the storage bay, the intrusion alarm goes off. The corridor fills with people—adults, sentries, and soldiers. They scramble to get to their posts, joining up with their teams to defend the base.

I have a moment of panic, then realize the chaos that will occur around me is to my benefit. I'll just become another gray uniform in a mass of dark attire. It will slow my egress, but once I'm off this level, I'll be clear. All I need to do is get to the ladder.

As the corridor becomes more cramped, I struggle against the press of bodies. Most head in the opposite direction, but a few are moving the same way and help me along.

The end of the corridor is just ahead, and I can see an end to the mass of people rushing about. I double my efforts to get there, shoving a few of the slower movers out of my way. Curses and exclamations of outrage meet my motions. It doesn't matter. I'm almost there.

Someone slams into my shoulder, spinning me sideways and knocking my senses from me. I lose my balance, only to be held up by several hands that return me upright before pushing past. I take a few seconds to clear my head, then I'm moving again.

"Ceri?" a voice calls from behind, sending fear ripping through me. "Bish! It is you! When did you get back?"

I stop and turn. It's Aidan, an aide to the squad captains. I stare at him as he pushes past a few others to get to me. I search for something to tell him, some excuse why I'm here. But my head is blank. That hit took more out of me than I realized.

"Hey, sorry about that impact. You okay?" Aidan is younger but just as tall as I am. He's got more muscle, too. I'm glad to see him, but this is the worst possible moment for a catch-up.

I nod, stalling for time until I can come up with a reason I need to leave. He tells me about what happened after Efa and I went missing and asks if I know where she is. I barely hear him.

"Aidan! Let's go!" an adult voice calls. I feel a chill run through my body the second I recognize it.

Captain Daga.

"Coming, Captain!"

"Who are you talking to?"

Bish. It's over if he recognizes me.

"Hey, you better go," I say with a smile. "Better not to annoy him, right?"

"Yeah, true." He pats me on the arm. "Glad you're back."

I pivot and step, taking the first of many that will put as much distance between me and my commanding officer before he realizes it's me. Aiden told me Captain Daga thinks I'm dead or captured. I need to keep him believing that's the truth.

"Hold up, soldier!" Captain Daga calls after me. "Why aren't you with your squad?"

I pretend not to hear him and pick up my pace. Maybe I can fool him if I keep my head down. Maybe.

"You! Stop and answer me now!"

That's it. I squeeze my eyes shut and freeze. It's over. He'd order everyone in the corridor to knock me down if I continue. And the moment I face him, he'll see it's me.

With a hard swallow, I turn to face him, looking him straight in the eye. He pats Aidan on the back and pushes him off, his own gaze never diverting from my own.

"Ceri." The captain speaks as if saying my name will confirm my existence for him. "I'm assuming you just got back and were on your way to report to me? What happened to your comm?"

"Lost," I reply, forcing the word from my mouth.

"You wounded?"

"No, Captain."

The alarm goes quiet as we stare at each other, a silent standoff that will only arouse his suspicions if I keep it up. I don't know what excuse I can make to get away from him. The longer I stay here, the sooner he executes me for what I just did.

"Well, we're in the all clear," he says. "Come with me now and give me your full report. I'll have the medics check you out after, anyway."

I nod, but my feet stay firm on the deck, unmoving. They may have even turned away from him.

"Let's go." Captain Daga takes a step, then he notices I haven't moved and glares. "What the hell is wrong with you?" he shouts. "I said let's go!"

Aidan's return diverts the captain's attention as the aide comes running back, his chest heaving and his eyes wide. Aidan shoots me a nervous glance, then covers his mouth and whispers in the captain's ear. My feet are moving now, sliding back and putting distance between me and anyone who could be my potential captor.

Then a sentry lieutenant walks up, followed by a pair of his guards—and the boy I choked. He takes one look at me, then turns to the boy, who gulps and nods. His next motion takes him to Captain Daga, who listens while the lieutenant says something in his ear.

I take a step back, calculating my chances if I run. Not good. The ladder is likely covered by a few soldiers. With comm access, they'd know I was coming before I even got there.

I'm not giving up yet.

"What did you do?" Captain Daga shouts, walking toward me, his face red and his eyes piercing. I know that look. It means my life, should I let him arrest me. "What the hyuk did you do, you bish-head?"

"Secure her," the lieutenant says to his two guards. They eye me, each with a snarl, and approach, passing by Captain Daga. I move, not away, but into a fighting stance. The sentries, I might take them down, but the captain has actual combat experience, more than me by many years. If I fought him, he'd make me pay for my lack of respect for an adult.

"You stay where you are, Ceri!" Captain Daga points a finger at me.

"Remove your weapons belt, soldier!" the lieutenant says. "Drop it on the ground now, or I will order them to shoot you."

They would, and even at this range, these poor shots would hit me. I reach down for the holster strap on my leg, taking my time while I monitor the sentries' approach. Their hands remain away from their weapons, and I'm thankful for that. They may be squad rejects, but they're still Tarakh. I don't want to harm them. Much.

The sentries stop a respectful distance away, ready to apprehend me but well aware that I am lethal, even unarmed. They may hope that I'll be obedient since my captain is here. I won't. Not while Efa is waiting for me.

"*Now*, Ceri," Captain Daga growls. He's just behind the two sentries now, and unlike the two boys before me, the captain keeps his hand to his side, just above his holster. Now I've got three to neutralize if I want to escape. And I desperately need to.

As I reach for the buckle of my weapons belt, my legs bend, tensing to spring me into action. Captain Daga remains steady—he can't see what I'm about to do. But time is limited. I've got to move.

I pull my belt off, and I hold it out to the sentry on my left. He glances at it, then realizes he should take it. With a roll of his eyes, he steps forward, focusing on the belt.

Wrong choice.

I shove off the deck, shooting straight into the boy. My shoulder drives into his gut, and he flies back, smashing into Captain Daga. The two of them tumble, their arms flailing about to stop their fall.

The other sentry goes for his gun, but he fumbles with the holster cover. My arm swings out, catching him across the face with the side of my hand. I reverse and throw my fist under his jaw. His feet leave the floor as his head snaps back.

A second later, I'm heading to the ladder as he crumples to the floor. His lieutenant curses and pounds the wall.

"You're dead, Ceri!" Captain Daga shouts. "I will gut you myself! You hear me?"

I can't go straight to level access. They'll be waiting for me. I double back, and cut around a corner. Then another, approaching the ladder sentries from behind. If I'm lucky, they won't be looking this way.

The guards at the ladder confirm their readiness, shouting and directing each other into position. There's two female voices and one male, perhaps a little older than the other two. I may know one girl, and if so, she'll hesitate before attacking me. The boy is my first target. I don't know him and can't trust what he'll do once he spots me.

They're positioned well, using the corners for cover and keeping low. Their pistols are out, so I draw mine but keep my belt in my other hand. It may prove useful at close distance.

I slide up the wall, staying in the shadows. The boy, a hulking brute, is just ahead of me, clutching his gun as if it may just jump out of his hand. How right he is.

"Hey, what's going on?" I say in a friendly voice.

The boy turns, searching for the voice. His gun hand comes around. I strike, flinging the buckle end of my belt at his hand. He cries out as it cracks over his knuckles, the weapon falling from his hand. I shoot forward, closing the distance between us.

I wrap my gun arm around his neck and twist my foot to plant it behind his legs. He topples, sliding toward one girl. She springs to her feet and takes aim, getting two rounds off before I disarm her. An elbow to her head drops her, and my knee on her chest keeps her down.

"Ceri, please stop!" the last girl commands. She has me nearly point-blank, her weapon pointed at my head. I forget her name—I'd use it if I could. I taught her proper gun use in battle. If she remembers any of it, I don't have a chance.

"I don't know what they told you," I say, raising my hands and taking a moment to catch my breath, "but I'm not the enemy. All I wanted was some medicine. That's it. I'm trying to save a life. A Tarakh life."

Footsteps echo from down the hall and my pulse quickens. I've got less than ten seconds to convince her. If I can't, I'll have to hurt her, and that is not my preference.

"You know I can't," the girl says. "No more than you can. So don't make me shoot you, okay?"

I check the girl I pinned. She's still dazed, so I have a moment, but just one.

"You don't want to, I know." I step forward and give her a small smile. "I have no interest in hurting you, either. Just lower your weapon, and I'll be on my way. You can tell them I evaded you."

Shouts echo down the corridor. It's that lieutenant, and more sentries. He's not taking chances. They'll each take a turn beating me for what I did.

I keep my hands up and my smile on. It's sincere. There is a sweetness about her that reminds me of Efa. I remember then this girl took a long time to get good with her weapon. I never thought she'd use it outside of practice.

When I take another two steps closer, she shifts on her feet at her face turns pained. I'm glad she doesn't want to shoot, but she's likely more afraid of what the adults will do to her if she lets me go. I will solve that conflict for her.

"Hey," I say, keeping my voice soft, even as the beating of boots closes in. "It's okay. They won't blame you for not shooting one of your own people."

When the barrel of her gun dips, I put my hand over it and press it down. She bows her head, ashamed of her failure.

"You're doing the right thing." I take her chin in my hand and lift so I can look her in the eyes. She needs to know I mean what I say. "I promise. When this is all over, you'll see."

Before she can reply, my elbow comes across her face. Her body jerks, and her knees buckle. I catch her before she falls, bringing her down to the floor before I drop through the level access, grabbing my belt, and her ammunition, on the way.

I hit the deck with a gentle touch and sprint away from the ladder. A discord of voices blasts through the hatch above me as I fly free. They'll be coming after me, but not right away. The adults will need to organize a squad and find replacements for those I defeated. By then, I should be twenty levels down.

I still need to be careful. There are sentries on the next few levels, and they will be on the lookout. If I keep to the shadows, I will slip by them without incident. I do not relish hurting any more of my people. After all, we still need them to fight the enemy.

ABANDONMENT

I MADE IT BACK.

As I approach the exam room on level eighty-two, I notice a sliver of light slipping through a crack in the door. My jaw tightens and I curse through my teeth at the sheer lack of discipline. All of them know better, but especially Efa. She's scolded the younger soldiers in our squad for using their lights when they shouldn't. Often. Now here she is, doing what she'd reprimanded others for. How she didn't notice the door open is beyond my interest to consider. Either Efa is being lazy...

Or something is wrong.

I rush to the door, grab its edge, and throw it open. A flood of white light blasts into my eyes, forcing me to shut them in the face of potential danger.

A shout and a high-pitched screech pierce my ears. I drop and roll, ripping my blade from its sheath. It is the best defense I can make while blinded. My opponents better not have guns.

"Ceri!" Efa's squeak fills the room and reverberates into the corridor. As much as it unnerves me to realize we just alerted the entire level to our location, I lower my blade. Efa is alive and likely unharmed. That's most important.

Efa's body slams into mine as she throws her arms around me. If it weren't for her embrace, I would be flat on my back. As it is, I have to grab the doorway to stop from falling over. Still, her touch is welcome, and once I stabilize my balance, I hug her back. Efa plants a kiss on my cheek and giggles.

My eyes become accustomed to the room's brightness, and I remember to shut the door before scanning the room for signs of trouble. Merek sits in a corner, his shirt off. He curls a side of his mouth up and waves at me. I raise an eyebrow and nod, but stare at him for a moment longer before turning back to Efa. That's when I notice her shirt is unbuttoned down to her stomach. Now I understand what's going on.

"What happened to you?" Efa asks before I can make a comment about it. "Rabbit tried to tell us what you were planning, but he made no sense. Where did you go? We were worried they captured you!"

"And you were so concerned about it you felt the need to get undressed?" I motion to her open shirt with my blade.

Efa ducks her head, quickly hiding her exposed skin as her cheeks turn red. Merek also follows my hint and reaches for his shirt to put it back on. I inhale and attempt to calm myself as I wait for them. They're not the only ones uncomfortable about my sudden appearance.

That they might enjoy a sensual moment together is no surprise. I just never considered they'd find time to be intimate, not when we're trying to escape. Though I'm far from being an expert. I know little about this kind of love and am even more naïve about where or when two people decide to...whatever. They just do, I suppose. It's still a problem.

"Couldn't you have been doing something better?" I ask as I sheathe my knife. It's a rude way to ask, but I'm not happy. I just took an enormous risk to get the medication, and all they've been doing is exploring each other's bodies.

"Didn't Sayer go after you?" Merek frowns. "Why aren't you with him?"

"Yeah," Efa echoes, brushing her shirt down. "Going off on your own was kind of stupid, Ceri."

I press my lips together, attempting not to react to their verbal attack. Efa has a point. My decision was impulsive, but I did it for them. They won't accept that argument as valid, and we need to be discussing ways to find Rabbit and Sayer rather than fighting. I will attempt to push irritation aside and focus on the plan.

"Sorry, I didn't mean to cause any problems," I say, bowing my head. "Now let's—"

"Yeah, but be honest. You did," Merek says. "Sayer is missing because of you."

I inhale a slow breath as I stare at him. That he is protecting Efa from embarrassment is honorable, but he's pressing me to take the blame for their misbehavior, and that I won't accept.

"So where did Rabbit go?" I ask.

Merek shrugs, a bit too dismissive for my taste, especially after he just blamed me for his squad mate's disappearance. Sayer knows not to just walk off on his own, and Merek is well aware of that. I slide my hands to my waist—they're closer to my weapons that way—and narrow my eyes.

"Rabbit said you went to get something," Efa says, taking notice of my growing annoyance with her beloved. It's a better defense than Merek brought to bear. I'll respond in kind.

"I did." My hand goes into my pocket, and I pull out a few tubes of the medication. "This'll be what we offer him instead of our guns."

"Wow, Ceri!" Efa clasps her hands together and beams. "Where'd you find that?"

I pause, knowing Efa won't like the answer I'm about to give. The truth is still the best option. If I attempt to lie, she'll catch me in it. Efa is well aware of the weeks it takes our scout teams to discover unsecured medication. That I just got lucky and found some in a day won't come across as anything but the fabricated tale it would be. Besides, Efa knows me too well. It's near impossible for me to deceive her.

"I stole it from the supply we got from the raid," I reply.

Efa's smile disappears, and her mouth drops open as she stares. Merek does, too. Now I must prepare for the onslaught of their outrage. If they thought going off on my own was wrong, they'll consider this the worst mistake anyone has ever made.

"You went back to base?" Efa shakes her head. "Tell me no one saw you."

I shrug. "Not exactly. I had to subdue a few sentries on my way out. Daga saw me, but I made it back here in less than an hour. I don't think—"

"Sixty-seven levels in less than an hour? That's impossible!"

When she says it, I realize just how ridiculous an accomplishment it was. No one has ever done that before. No one has been stupid enough to try, though this will be the easiest part of the story for them to believe. Once they realize the risk I took and the danger I just put us all in, they won't be in such a state of wonder at my feat.

"What the hyuk were you thinking?" Merek hisses.

I rub a finger around the socket of my eye, feeling the sudden fatigue of traveling so far, so fast. I slide over to the exam table and sit. It's a bad idea. My weariness hits me harder, and I lean forward to close my eyes.

"No, no. Wait." Efa holds up a hand. "It's a joke. Right, Ceri? You just got lucky. That's all. She's just messing with us."

"No, she's not," Merek says, scrambling to gather his gear. "We need to get out of here now."

"But you need to rest more!"

"Yeah? Well, thanks to your squad mate, I can't."

I glance up to find Merek glaring at me and wonder how this conversation got turned around. He's the one indulging himself while I was risking my life. For him. He could at least thank me.

"Hey, I made this happen for you." I shake the medication tubes at him. "Now we can keep our weapons, and Rabbit, as soon as we find him, will lead you down to the machine access. Trust me. Nobody up there knows where it is."

"That doesn't matter. If we can get to it, then so can your captain."

Efa swivels her head, glancing between the two of us until she stops on me with a face that pleads for explanation.

"Is Captain Daga really coming for you?" She asks.

"You know he will. I had to take out five sentries and knock him flat to get away, so the sooner we find Rabbit, the sooner we can start moving down. Help me do that, and we can continue down. As soon as now, if you're ready."

"We can't wait for Rabbit," Merek says. "If your captain finds me with Efa, I'm dead."

"And what do you think he's going to do if he catches me?" I shoot back.

"Not my problem. If you really want Rabbit's help, you can find him, and you should, because you made this mess."

"*I did?*" My chest gets tight, like it does right before a battle. And this is quickly becoming that. "I'm not the one trying to put my hands down Efa's shirt!"

"No...come on. Don't fight." Efa swings around, searching for her gear and snatching it up once she does. "We have to stick together, right? Ceri, let's just start moving down. Merek needs you to help him walk. Rabbit will find us, won't he?"

I take a breath and do my best to back down. She's doing her best to keep us together, but panic is edging into her voice. I put it there. Merek too. I'm all for making up for my mistakes and doing what we need to get Rabbit and Sayer back, but he's got to do the same.

"We should stick together," I say, trying to keep my calm. "But finding Rabbit is our priority. Without his knowledge of the lower levels, we'll struggle to find supplies. He's a good scout, too. We need someone at point. I'll be too busy helping Merek."

"No, you won't," Merek says, "because I don't need your help."

To prove his claim, he grabs the edge of the exam table and pulls himself up, struggling just a little as he presses his legs straight. I'm feeling less than capable of performing the same feat, even with no wound.

"Let's go, Efa," Merek says, holding his arm out to her. She takes two steps toward him, then looks back at me, her eyes looking for approval.

"No, Efa. Don't," I say. "You can't protect him while you're focused on helping him. Always two escorts with a medical evac, you know that."

Efa sours at my rebuke. I didn't mean it to come out hard, but my fatigue has given me an irritable edge that is slicing straight through my patience. Now I've gone and stabbed her with it, and her face is already radiating signs of displeasure.

"Of course I know that," she says and folds her arms. "But I also think you shouldn't be the one to lecture me on tactical operations."

"What?"

"I'm sorry, Merek's right. We need to head down right away and put as much distance between us and the captain as possible. You should come. The way you look at the moment, I doubt you'll last every long by yourself."

I twitch at her words. We've had our fights before, one not that long ago over Merek. Now she's choosing his side over mine, and it's rubbing my heart raw. I know she loves him, and I sort of understand what that means, but I still have trouble accepting it in my mind. She's Tarakh. He's Fahrasi. They don't have to hate each other, but fall in love? You love your squad mates and your faction. Not the enemy.

But I'll get nowhere by holding firm. Merek is set in his plan, and he won't listen to suggestion, especially from me. All I can do is try to deescalate and get Efa to choose a little compromise.

"Alright, you can get a head start. I'll find Rabbit and catch up with you."

"We'll find our own way," Merek says. His blunt tone makes my teeth clench. I'm letting him get what he wants. He doesn't need to be mean about it.

"Don't be stupid, Merek," I reply. "You need Rabbit. And you need me."

"No, I don't. You're useless to me in your condition."

I gnash my teeth and seethe. "I just climbed half the ship for you! I'm allowed to be tired!"

"No one asked you to do that."

The next time he says something like that, I'm going to pop him across the jaw like I did before. What doesn't he understand about the sacrifice I just made for him?

"You—"

"Ceri, just stop arguing," Efa says, putting her hands on her hips. A second later, she sighs and tosses a hand up. "Or...do whatever you want, but we're headed down. And if we have to, we'll find machine access ourselves."

Her declaration stuns me into silence. What can I say, now that she's given up on me, too? Is love so strong that it can break the bonds of friendship? Or family?

As they finish packing, I just stare. Merek lays his arm around Efa's shoulder, and then, in the quiet of the moment, they shut the lights and step out.

CONTROL

As EXHAUSTED AS I was, there'd be no rest after Efa and Merek disappeared into the dark. My chest still aches from how she chose him over me. It was foolish, verging on stupid. More than anything I did. They may not want my help, but they'd need it soon enough. I figured it would be best to get Rabbit and follow them before they ran into trouble. And they would.

The old man was easy to find once I began searching. I didn't even need to look very long. He was behind the ladder that goes to eighty-one, his hands perched on the third rung, while he watched me approach. I wonder how long he had been there and how much of our conversation—or Efa and Merek's interactions—he had witnessed.

"I need a new canteen," I say as I stop before him. "Do you know where I can find one?"

Rabbit shrugs and says, "Easy. Many around."

"Good."

He tilts his head and stares at me, remaining silent. After such an aggressive demand for our guns, his behavior has cooled a lot. I would have expected that he'd badger me to no end for the prize that I captured for him.

"Do you know where Sayer is?"

Rabbit's eyes wander about the area. I frown at him and cross my arms. Save for the ladder and some emergency equipment, there is nothing to see in the alcove. He better not try to deceive me. I have no patience for any more games from him. Or anyone.

"You must have seen him," I say. "Where did he go?"

Rabbit points up the ladder, his eyes following his finger. I trap my tongue with my teeth, considering the meaning of Sayer's direction. Up makes me think he's heading back to his people, potentially to strike a bargain with them and turn Efa and me in. I don't want to believe that, but I can't trust anyone anymore. Not even Efa. Merek compromises her decision-making. She can't think straight around him.

"Fine," I say. "So aren't you wondering?"

"Wondering many, many, many things. Always."

"No, I mean, aren't you wondering if I brought the medicine back?"

"Have you?"

His lack of excitement is grinding on me. I would have thought he would welcome the medicine with enthusiasm, but his underwhelming response is giving me pause. Suspicion wells up in the back of my mind as I watch him.

Rabbit has done nothing wrong, but he isn't acting like himself. Perhaps the medicine is still a second best to him. Or perhaps he is lying to me about Sayer. He's lying about something. That I know.

I reach into my pocket and pull out a tube to show to him. Rabbit's eyes open a little wider, and he rises. So he's interested in it after all. I step closer, offering the tube to him. He sniffs at it, then reaches for it. But I pull it away.

"Do we still have a deal?" I ask.

Rabbit pouts and shrinks. Whatever. He can try to play on my emotions all he wants. It won't get him anything more than we agreed to.

"Do we? If not, I'll trade with someone else," I say, moving to walk away.

"Give first. Let me try, let me try!" Rabbit cries, stretching out his hand.

I remain still as he reaches out for the tube. So, he was just trying to show a lack of interest, perhaps as a plan to negotiate for more. I knew he was tricky, but this makes me reevaluate his true intentions, and that makes me tense.

If Sayer doesn't return, it'll be just Efa and me trying to help Merek move while keeping watch. We can't keep Rabbit under constant surveillance. It's not possible. The thoughts that cross my mind about what could happen if we miss something are disturbing. Better to kill Rabbit now than to worry about any of them occurring.

Still, Rabbit wants the medicine. That puts me in control, at least for the moment. I could use that to keep him in check. It would mean not giving him all the medication as I had told him I would, but I don't have any issue with that.

Rabbit might.

"Okay," I say. "I'll let you try. But no more until you hold up your part of the deal."

"Give then!"

Rather than just hand him the tube, I open the cap and squeeze a little out into his hand, then make a motion for him to apply it to his arm. Rabbit lifts the thick white paste up to his nose and sniffs—and quickly regrets it.

"Bad!" Rabbit wrinkles his nose and waves his hand at me.

"You don't eat it. You just put it on the spot where it itches." I make the motion again, exaggerating my movements so he understands what to do.

"Cold," Rabbit says, frowning. He gets the medication where he needs to, however. "Ugly too."

I chuckle at his childish comments. A four-year-old would have a better reaction. Rabbit must be at least another seventy years older than that. Most of the children awake on this ship will never see beyond thirty. The fighting is to blame for that. Our medical staff are skilled, especially after so much practice, and they have access to most of the life-saving technology available on the *Stratford*. Yet they can save no one if they arrive back to base already dead.

"It doesn't work!" Rabbit complains, waving his arm around. "Broken, broken!"

Oh bish.

Panic runs through my body. Was the medication expired? I bring the tube close to my eyes and search for an expiry date somewhere along its casing. There must be something, some indication of whether it's still usable. They wouldn't have just stockpiled it like that without knowing it needed to last a thousand years or more.

I drop my arm with a sigh. Even if I found a date, I have no idea what the current date is. Information like that isn't given to soldiers. It's considered a distraction. We do not need to concern ourselves with the past or the future. Survive today, fight again tomorrow. That's all they allow us to know.

Rabbit looks at me, expecting an answer. I have none, but he won't allow me that escape. The medication could still be good or it could just as easily be bad. Or maybe it just takes time for it to work. There is no way for me to tell. All I know is that if I tell him something that he doesn't want to hear, that's the end of our deal.

"It's not instant," I say. "Give it time, and you'll feel it."

"How long?"

"I don't know. I'm not a doctor."

"Then how you know it's right?" Rabbit shakes a fist at me, more to show his arm than to threaten. He wouldn't. We've already shown him what happens when he crosses us.

He has me on that question, however. I don't know for certain if it's the right medication. It was a guess. I saw it applied to a burn on one of my squad mate's backs and figured it would handle Rabbit's red itch. He won't like it if I tell him that. He'll walk away, and I as much I'd prefer to let him, I can't. Efa and Merek need him still and that means so do I.

"One adult would use it for something on the back of their neck. I remember the tube well enough," I reply. "It went away after a short while."

It's a lie. I had no other option, and I won't regret it if he believes me. That's all that matters. Rabbit hasn't been truthful, either. Ours is a partnership of mutual mistrust and joint benefit. If we both get what we want, then everything else is unimportant.

"Give then," Rabbit says. "When it works, I will help."

Hyuk. I don't have time to sit around and wait until he notices something happening. It may never work, and Captain Daga or whoever he sends to drag me back to base will arrive long before that.

"You can have it," I say. "But we go now, like we agreed. If not, then I'm not giving you more."

"Wrong, wrong, wrong! Deal is everything now!"

Rabbit is standing now, frowning at me with an angry look only a greedy old man could create on his face. Of course, he may only be playing me as much as I am him. I'll find out soon enough.

I fold my arms in front of me. "I'll only give you everything if we go now, like you agreed to."

He twitches and wrinkles his nose, then chews on his lip for a moment, considering.

"How many?" Rabbit asks.

"How many what?"

"How many those?" He points to the tube in my hand.

I feel the edge of my mouth curl up. He's looking for options, like whether he can trade them to others for something more useful, no matter if the medication is good or not. I'm impressed. Perhaps that's why he's survived so long. Rabbit can turn any situation to his advantage. He'll do the same to me if I don't watch him. Still, I also know how to survive.

I reach into my right pocket and pull out what's there. Ten tubes—more than I remember taking. That doesn't include the ones in my left pocket. They'll stay there for now, possibly for longer if I don't like how Rabbit is acting.

"This many," I say. "Enough to last you ten lifetimes and still have some for trade."

"Give."

"Not until you agree on your life." I shake the tubes at him. "These ten tubes for you to bring us to the machine access...and inside. If you try to trick me, I will kill you."

Rabbit shrugs. "Death is no fear. Happy place for me."

I puff out a laugh. We have a similar view of our existence, then. I might like Rabbit more if I didn't have to bargain with him. Though I'd still never trust him.

"Yes, a happy place for all of us on this ship who aren't in stasis," I say. I don't fear death, nor am I looking forward to it. As miserable as my life is, I'd still like to experience it for a little while longer.

Rabbit nods and purses his lips, pensive for a moment. I wonder what he did before they put him in a pod and turned him into an ice cube like the rest of us. Something that required a lot of brainpower, I bet. Maybe one day I will ask him. For now, we'll just maintain our mutually cautious partnership.

"So are we agreed, then?" I ask as I offer him the tubes. Rabbit's eyes focus on my outstretched arm. There's more of the predator in them than the harmless herbivore he named himself after. Then again, I never believed that he was harmless.

"Yes," he says and snatches them out of my hand. "Yes. Go. Down, down, down."

I grin. Merek and Efa won't have made it far. And when they see I've got Rabbit, they'll change their minds about being mad at me.

CHAOS

My brain lifts to consciousness as I lie on the exam table in the medical room. I stretch my legs, then my arms, and feel the blood rush back into them, relieving at least some of the aches in them. There are plenty more, but I'll have to push those out of my mind until the next time I rest. Whenever that may be.

As much as I wanted to get moving, I didn't have it in me. No sleep, plus racing up and down half the ship left my body wasted. If I didn't rest at least a little, I was going to fall down a ladder at some point. And if I wanted to convince Merek and Efa to stay with Rabbit and me, I needed to be sharp enough to form a reasonable argument. I was already considering what I'd say when I laid down.

At some point, my eyes closed and didn't open again until they were ready.

Rabbit had promised to stick by me. I didn't believe it, so when I woke, it surprised me he was still around. He must have gone for a while, however. I find a full canteen of water next to me when I sit up. It makes me smile, seeing it there. The old man may be a fierce survivor, but he isn't without his compassion.

I gulp half the water in the canteen down, spilling a good amount of it on my shirt. I don't mind. The feel of moisture against my skin is calming. It's like the one time Efa and I snuck off with a large crate and found a place to fill it full of water. Once we figured out a way to heat the water, we took turns bathing. I never had another chance to do that, but I remember it like it was yesterday. The bath made my skin so smooth for most of a day, I almost felt like a real girl.

"Thanks," I say to Rabbit, holding up the canteen to him and nodding.

Even though Rabbit acknowledges my gratitude, he remains stiff. I frown then and watch him. He's nervous about something, though my brain is still waking up and too slow to consider what it means.

"Not, not safe," Rabbit says, bouncing on his haunches and glancing at the door.

That's all I need to know. I grab my weapons belt and shoot to my feet to put it on. I can't tell how long I slept, but it was too long. Now trouble may have come to this level, and I have no intel about it.

"What is it?" I whisper, moving to him.

"Someone, someone, someone," Rabbit says.

"More than one, I bet," I say, my hand sliding down to my holster. "A lot more than one. Get behind the table."

At least I shut the door and turned out the light before I slept. That won't stop a true pursuit team from checking in here, but it will give us plenty of warning if they do. We'll still have to escape the room before they gas us with canisters. Some of those devices can render us unconscious in a few seconds. We aren't prepared for that kind of fight.

"Hold here," I say. "I'm going to do a little reconnaissance."

Rabbit makes a strange sound and ducks behind the exam table, his eyes scanning the walls for an escape. I doubt there is one. He would have found it already, and we would have fast used it.

I slide the door open, using as much skill as I can to keep it from making noise, and slip through. The corridor is dark, yet I can feel it. Others are here. They're keeping quiet, so I know they're soldiers. Which means they're here for me. I swallow and consider our escape.

I'll need to clear a path to the ladder. We could use the hull access to go down, but that door is in the same place, and if these soldiers have any skill, which they will—Captain Daga would only send his best after me—they'll be watching there, too. The ladder is not far away, so I'll take as much time as I need to get there and ensure I'm careful.

As I crouch and move along the wall, I pause and listen every few seconds. There's nothing more than I heard before. They may have made noise before, but they won't make that mistake again.

I freeze the moment I hit the corner that turns toward the ladder alcove. At least one soldier is there. Maybe two. They're waiting for me. No doubt there are more on the level, searching, ready to drive me toward these two. Captain Daga taught us that tactic, and while I'm not ready to believe it's him down here, I'm sure they're Tarakh.

I return to the exam room. One glance at Rabbit and he understands what's going on. He shifts on his feet, his hands touching the floor as if he's about to leap away.

"Rabbit, do you know a good hiding place on this level?" I whisper. "Can you get to it?"

Rabbit nods. It's enough. I'll trust he can make it there. He doesn't want to be captured any more than I do. The medication that I gave him will be worthless if he's caught by Fahrasi and potentially deadly to him if found by Tarakh.

We slip from the room, Rabbit first, me after. I've got my pistol in one hand, my blade in another, and enough clips for my gun to fight a war. I still feel my pulse pounding in my throat. What I have planned is tricky to execute by myself. Only their response will tell me if I am successful.

I slink toward the up ladder. It's a feint, and if they take it, we could be down two levels before they realize what happened. But I can only wound them. Dead soldiers don't share information. I want them to give each other as many false positives as I can create.

Only a single soldier there. That doesn't mean there isn't more around. I position myself to get a solid shot on him so there won't be much noise when I take him down. Once he's out, I can move on to creating a distraction around the area. It should draw others back here, and by then Rabbit and I will be gone.

As I get ready, the soldier turns. I grit my teeth. It's one of Rhain's squad. Hyuk. Captain Daga is so furious he pulled his best team from active duty to find me. This is bad. Truly. A

Squad will do everything they can to capture me. There's a good chance they'll succeed, too.

I will take as many of them down as possible before they disarm me. That's all I can do. Send enough of them to the doctor so they have to return to base, giving Efa and Merek a chance to get down to level one-twenty-three on their own.

The boy cries out as my dart gets him in his thigh. I'm gone in the next moment, headed for the down ladder. I'll take those two out and put Rhain's team into complete disarray. He'll struggle to keep control as I pick at them from as many sides as I can.

Light floods the intersection ahead. At least two of them are headed towards me. I dart back and take the first right I can, but another light is down the corridor, headed away. It won't be for long. That soldier will check their back like Captain Daga trained them to. I've got to choose another route.

I slow my breathing as I consider my options. As it is, I'm already panting. But there's reason to stay calm. I may not know this level, but neither does A Squad. At least for the moment, I have a place to hide. I duck back into the exam room, sliding the door shut so that only a crack remains.

Two soldiers rush past, their lights blasting the corridor with illumination. That's no mistake—Rhain has part of his team hidden in the dark. The two that just passed me are making as much sound and brightness to drive me toward their trap. So far, I've avoided it.

Even better, I should spring it and let Rhain find me. I can lead them on a useless chase and then disappear. Rhain will be so eager to catch me, he'll make a mistake, and then I'll have a way through their net.

I hope.

When the next pair of soldiers pass by, I slip out behind them. Two quick shots take them out of the chase. I double back, fully expecting more of the squad to come to their rescue.

A dart flies past my head. I drop and roll, racing for cover. Another one comes from the opposite way. Bish, they've got me pinpointed.

I pick a direction and charge, firing three shots out to keep my attacker's head down. I can't see them yet, but I must press my approach.

Light blasts me in the face. I drop and roll again, keeping my forward momentum. A second later, I smash into a girl's legs. She falls with a yelp, and I'm on her. We wrestle for control, but I have the advantage. My hand finds her throat, and I squeeze.

"Ceri, please!" the girl croaks. I recognize the voice and let up, not wanting to do any permanent damage. I still smash her gun hand onto the floor and disarm her. Then, with a gasp, I'm up and moving again.

But only for a second.

The rest of Rhain's squad surrounds me. They're flooding the corridor with so much light, I've nowhere to go. My gun hand comes up, waving back and forth at the glare in my face. I can't see anything well enough to hit them. If I fire, they will fill me with every dart in their clips. They'll keep their distance enough to avoid my blade. I could take a few of them in a knife fight, if I could see.

My heart pounds in my throat. I need another option.

"Back off!" Rhain shouts as he steps into the light. He grins and shakes his head, then sneers. "When will you learn? A Squad is the best. We found you in half a day. What are you compared to us?"

"Maybe you should ask your four squad mates I just took out," I reply in an even tone. Then I smirk to drive my point home.

Rhain narrows his eyes at me, but only for a moment. "It doesn't matter what you say. You're caught. And I can't wait to watch Captain Daga beat the life out of you. With all the stupid stuff you just pulled, he considers you worse than the enemy. You're about to learn what hell really is."

My eyes narrow at him. I'd expect nothing less from Daga and his pets. I just didn't think they'd find me so soon. Now I've got to prepare myself. I'm about to enter a universe of pain.

DUEL

RHAIN'S SQUAD TAKES UP positions on all sides of me. The six of them that remain standing, that is. Their lights illuminate each other as much as they blind me. Their pistols are out, but they've made one mistake—I can make out their shapes well enough to target. Whether I'm fast enough to get any of them before they get me is the question.

"Drop the weapons," Rhain says. "Or I order them to crush every bone in you legs. You may be good, Ceri, but you're not that good. My squad will take you down before you even lift your hand."

"Maybe that's true," I reply, staring at him. "But I'm not aiming at *them*, Rhain. I can get three or four shots through your thin skull before they get me, and I'll be happy to see you die before I do."

Rhain presses his lips together and swallows. I grin at him, content that I've scared him into thinking twice about ordering his team to fire.

"I wonder who Captain Daga will choose for the next field lead," I taunt.

Rhain takes a step back, attempting to hide behind their light, even though he knows it won't save him.

"Maybe we should teach her a lesson first," a squad member says. Whoever he is, he doesn't like me much. I'll be remembering that voice.

"Yes! Punish her, punish her!" someone chants. Others join in, their voices climbing to a frenzied pitch as their faces distort with a savage hunger in the hard beams of their lights. I wince and cover my ear at the sheer volume of their shouts.

Only two of them are reluctant to join in. The girl that I let go before, and her friend.

"Hey!" Rhain holds his hands up and hisses. "Noise discipline, you idiots! We don't know what's down here. And cut some lights!"

"Wow," I say and snort. "The mighty A Squad, clueless about standard protocol? I'm amazed the Fahrasi haven't neutralized your dumb asses yet."

"That's it!" Rhain pushes out from his team and draws his blade. "I'm going to slice your arms off."

"Whoa, whoa, whoa," Tegan, Rhain's second, reaches out and grabs his arm. "No weapons, or the captain will lock you up right next to her."

"Fine." Rhain hands his blade and gun to her and looks at me. "Now you."

What a fool. He just gave up his weapons while mine are still in my hands. And his squad is more interested in a fight than in monitoring me. I could easily create a distraction by wounding him and then run. I might even clear enough levels to make it safe to join up with Efa.

But as I look at Rhain, something in me desires to teach him a lesson. As long as his squad keeps out of it, I could beat him in a duel or, at least, leave him with a serious limp.

"Hey." Tegan holds her hand out to me. "I promise we won't get involved. We've got to secure the level again, anyway."

"Yeah." Rhain turns to the two girls who didn't cheer him on. "You two, go cover the ladders. Tegan, you handle the rest."

I put my weapons in her hand, but when Tegan goes to take them away, I don't let go. I want her to look me in the eye. Only when I feel she's telling the truth will I allow her to take them.

Tegan gives me an uneasy smile, then gives me a single, slow nod. It's enough. Once I open my hand, she jams my weapons in her belt and turns to direct her squad. Two more of the team disappear to retrieve their wounded. Now it is just Rhain, Tegan, and two others.

The odds are moving slowly toward my favor.

They place four lights on the floor and point them up at the ceiling. That defines the boundary where we will face off. I'll only abide by it if it's safe, and it won't be. He'll aim to hurt me as much as he can, and I will make sure I leave him with something permanent to remember me by.

Rhain drops into a forward stance. He'll attack from the moment Tegan says go. I put my weight on my back foot for more range of motion. I'll let him take the initiative and then send him into the wall. If he thinks he's going to end this with one strike, he's in for a painful reminder about just how good I am.

"Ready, set—"

Rhain jumps Tegan's call, flying forward with a front kick. I dodge left, spinning to come behind him. His elbow slams into my back. I yelp and lose my balance, dropping to the floor. Rhain's heel comes up, aiming for my head. I roll away and spring back to my feet.

He presses his attack, throwing his fist at my face. I narrowly avoid getting hit and slide right, my hand coming down to chop at his neck. Too late. His fist pounds into my stomach, and I double over, coughing from the impact. A spinning kick sends me flying across our makeshift fighting ring. I land on my side, curling up from the pain.

My hand covers my stomach, confused how he's responding so fast. I'm faster than he is, yet he's beating me. I'd expect Rhain to cheat, but if I want to win, I've got to figure out how.

"Get up!" Rhain growls. "So I can kick your ass again."

I push myself up to a kneeling position, keeping my eyes on him. He's cocky now, and I'm doubting my ability to beat him. Rhain had the same training I did, and he's not that much better than me. I need to get a hit in, or this will end with me arrested and hurting.

I spring into the air from a crouch, my kick aiming for his head. He avoids it as expected, swinging upward with a punch. I pivot and land, throwing my fist at his ear. Rhain drops and cries out, clutching his ear. I suck air through my teeth as blood seeps from my knuckles. They hit something hard.

His comm!

So that's how he's doing it. One of his squad is watching my moves and giving him hints before I attack. Hyuking cheater. But just because I know doesn't mean I can counter it. I can't call him on it, either. No one here, not even Tegan, will back me. I'll have to come up with something on my own. I can always pound on his ear again.

Rhain jumps to his feet, sending a kick toward my body. I twist and block. His arm follows, striking me in the head. I pull back and try to refocus, but Rhain follows with a flurry of punches that put me on the defensive. He backs me into a corner, and the only way I can get out is through him.

Here I go, then.

I charge forward, tackling him. We hit the ground, both of us swinging to get a hit in. Rhain manages a few strikes to my head, and I pound on his side. We roll away from each other and get back up, slower than before. We're both showing signs of fatigue. And hurt.

I try a feint, punching with my right arm and kicking with my left. Rhain avoids both, spinning around my attack to strike the side of my head. I stumble and retreat. He attacks again, striking me hard with a fist to my cheek. A flash of light crosses my vision, and I lose all sense of direction. My knees buckle. Everything spins. A second after, I'm on the deck, breathing hard.

Rhain is on me, throwing punches into my back. I grunt, struggling to get away, but he keeps on me. Hits come one after the other. My body shakes from his relentless assault. I push at his legs. It's useless. All I can do is try to crawl away, but he won't stop. I put my arms up to protect my face. It doesn't matter. Rhain is beating me in any spot he can swing at. The pain is wearing me down. I'm near collapse.

And arrest.

With my last bit of strength, I cry out, swinging my leg. My foot connects with his stomach. Rhain goes flying back, crashing into one of his squad, who tries to catch him. The two of them go down. But they're both up in a hurry.

Rhain sneers, but he's holding still as his chest heaves, gasping for air. My last strike must have got him good. I'll take it. It may be the last one I get in.

"Had enough? Or do you still think you can win?" Rhain hisses, but he's delaying. I'm thankful for it, whatever the reason. I need a moment. Maybe a few.

My hand goes to my side as I lean over, and my vision gets blurry. My body aches everywhere. I'm seconds from blanking out. Fine. I should just lie down and let the blackness take me. That'd stop the agony I'm in. Just close my eyes and it'd all be over.

No. No way. I've got to fight to stay awake—to lose consciousness is to lose everything.

"She's done, Rhain," Tegan says. "Let's pack it up and get back to base. I don't want to stay down here any longer than we need to."

"Yeah, in a minute," Rhain says with a groan. "As soon as she surrenders."

I cough. Blood drips from my mouth, and I wipe a sleeve across it to clean it up. Bish. Rhain wanted to hurt me, and he succeeded. I can only hope I hurt him enough for him to remember it.

"Give up, Ceri," Rhain says, moving to stand over me. "I won. You've got nothing left."

My eyelids lower, and for a moment, I welcome the peace that comes with it. Then Captain Daga's grinning face appears, and I force my eyes back open. Not yet. I'm not done yet.

"Oh, Rhain," I say, spitting out a wad of crimson saliva. "What a dumb hyuk you are. How did you ever become a field lead?"

"You want more? I'd be happy to put you down, you waste of a uniform." His hands balling up into fists again. "Face it, Ceri. This is the only time a boy will ever put his hands on you. Bish, for all I know you probably like it, you sick hyuk."

"Maybe." The edges of my lips curve up. Rhain is right over me, and his guard is completely down. He thinks he's beaten me.

But I never said I was giving up.

My body jerks into action, twisting as my fist fires up, hammering him right between the legs. Rhain's mouth drops open, and he shrieks like a little girl. A second later, he clutches himself and bends over, moaning.

I press both my hands into his ribs and shove, throwing him into Tegan. She catches him with a yelp. I spring to my feet, gritting my teeth from the pain but shooting forward despite it. My shoulder finds the boy who suggested my punishment, and I knock him aside.

"Don't!" Tegan shouts at my back. "Regroup first! We'll get her later."

As I stumble toward the ladder, I remember that girl is there, and I am weaponless. I can't beat a soldier with a gun in my current state anyway, but I can't stop, either. To stay on this level is to guarantee more hurt. Or worse.

What? She's not there. I thank whatever tiny miracle I'm witness to. Of course, she's likely gone to rejoin her squad after Tegan took charge. A Squad's second seems less inclined to chase me very far. Still, she may not have a choice. Returning to Captain Daga without me in custody could mean A Squad receives my punishment instead. I wouldn't envy them that.

Right now, I need to find a hole on eighty-four or eighty-five to climb into so I can check my wounds. If I'm hurt worse than I hope, I won't be able to help Efa until I recover.

And that is not a possibility I accept.

COMPLICATION

I MADE IT THROUGH level eighty-four with no issues other than the raw agony coursing through me. Rhain had not been gentle, nor had I. I did what I had to survive and have no regrets. It was a stupid duel, though. The adults would have stopped it the instant they learned what was going on. Now the Tarakh are down two field leaders, and that will leave us at a severe disadvantage against the Fahrasi.

I limp my way to the ladder down to eighty-five, considering whether Rhain is in more pain than I am. It was a dirty shot I took, but he deserved it, the way he was cheating. I'm suffering from all of his underhanded strikes. Half my torso is likely covered in contusions. It doesn't matter. I've managed pain like this before. I can do it again.

Then, halfway down the ladder to eighty-five, my legs give out.

My fingers slip from the top. I flail my arms out to catch myself, but I'm too slow. The ceiling is flying past my vision. My leg kicks out as my other foot shoots between two rungs of the ladder. It catches as I hit the floor, and my ankle strikes the hard metal. I scream as my entire leg twists into an agonizing position. I reach up to free it, but it's too far. Fire burns up from my knee, and I cry out, wary of the noise I make. But I've got no control over the pain. My head spins from the impact on the floor, and my right shoulder feels as though bone is scraping on bone.

As I writhe in anguish, I curse myself for this pathetic position I'm stuck in. Not even a recruit on their first day has ever done this. It would only take the weakest member of B Squad to arrest me now. I am alone and helpless, with no idea how to save myself.

I shut my eyes, and the entire ship spins around me—bad idea. Better to focus on my breathing. Only then can I clear my head of panic and get my thoughts in order. The pain will not win. I've trained years for a moment just like this, hoping it would never happen.

And now that is has, it's harder than I ever expected. My heart pounds in my chest from the trauma across my body. My breaths come short and fast. I will have to fight for every second. Some will prove my skill to survive. Others will only be sheer torture.

I must remove my leg from the ladder. That will be a challenge in this awkward position. If it wasn't for the deck stopping my fall, my shin bone would have snapped in two. It already feels like it has.

With both my hands on the lowest rung, I lift my body as much as I can tolerate and slip my foot off the rung. I sigh at the release, but I'm not done yet. I need more space to maneuver my leg out. The more I push up, the more I shake from the effort. I cannot handle much more. My shoulders spasm, and my fingers are about to slip off. I grit my teeth and yank my leg free.

I release the ladder and tumble, my legs going over my head. They hit the deck with a thump, and my body follows. I end up face-down, pressed against the cold deck, taking quick breaths as I manage the aches running through me.

If A Squad was planning to give chase, they'd be here by now, though Tegan wouldn't push them just to capture me. She's only interested in her squad's survival. Which means they'll head back up to recover at base. Captain Daga will learn of their failure and of Rhain's stupid attempt to show me up then and may even come for me himself after that.

Which means I am safe. For now.

I roll onto my back, wincing as my ribs press against the deck. It only makes me hate Rhain more. At least he'll get what's coming to him. Captain Daga will tear him in two, and after that, he'll be lucky to even remain in A Squad as its most junior member. Likely the captain wants to do worse to me.

When I sit up, I pause and consider how to get on my feet from this position. The throbbing in my knee makes me worry, and other than the ladder, there is no place to grab on to for support. But I have to get up, or I will stay here for longer than I am comfortable.

I reach out and grab the ladder, inhale, then pull up, using my good leg for support. Once I am standing, I exhale, tighten my jaw, and prepare myself to try weight on the other leg.

I'm shaking from exhaustion, or perhaps fear. I take another breath, release the ladder, and I recenter my balance.

Pain like an electric shock rips through my body. I gasp as my sight floods with the light of a thousand suns. The corridor turns upside down. My sense of direction vanishes. I reach back for the ladder, only to find it gone.

A second later, my head smashes into the deck with a crack.

I let out a moan of agony as my eyes threaten to roll back into my head. My senses go numb, and I shiver. All I can do is lie there until the control of my limbs returns. If it does.

Minutes later—I don't know how many—feeling returns. And so does an ache that radiates from my head down through me and ends with a throbbing in my knee. This is bad. If I can't walk, I cannot search for Efa or be useful to her at all. Worse. She could put herself in danger by coming to look for me. If Captain Daga finds us both...

He will certainly find me if I keep lying at the base of the ladder like this. I need to solve that now. Then I can worry about my lack of mobility and how I can get to Efa before someone else does.

The spot on my head where it hit the floor is turning warm. And wet. Perhaps it already was, and I just noticed it. When I reach up to touch it, I wince and jerk my fingers away, feeling the slickness on them. A glance at my fingers shows what I expect to see—blood. A lot—hyuk. That just became my priority.

I remember the tubes in my pants' pocket. If my fall didn't smash them, they might stop the blood loss out of my head. Now I have to get into a position where I can take it.

When I sit up, my stomach twists, and I wretch, doubling over. My head goes down on my knees and focus on breathing to push dizziness away. Each second that passes is another agony. I close my eyes to focus and gather the mental strength to get away from this spot.

Once I'm more stable, I grab a tube from my pocket, check it for breakage, then open it and dump its contents over my head. It stings, and the medicine is more fluid than I remember. It mixes with the drying blood on my scalp and drips a reddish line down my face. I attempt to wipe it off the first time it happens. The second time, I don't bother. It might benefit me to seem as terrifying as I'm sure I look.

The smell of turns me lightheaded. More than I was a minute ago. My vision goes from soft to sharp, then back again. But I can't wait to move any longer. I need a space to hide and recover. Any room would do.

There's a few bays straight down the corridor. No—too obvious. But I don't need to go far. Something with a locking door would be best. I just have to look.

With my hurt leg extended out, I reach back and pull myself along. I head to the first intersection and turn, letting my eyes adjust to the drop in illumination before surveying the corridor for doors.

Two on the left and two on the right. It doesn't matter which. I choose the second on the left and drag myself toward it, taking a minute to catch my breath. It's taking more effort to move than I expected. I hope I can rest soon.

As damaged as I am, it'll be a challenge to open the door. I rest my back on the wall and prop my head against it so I've got enough leverage to push the door open. It only opens partway. I have to take my weapons belt off and slip in sideways.

By the time I get in and shut the door, my arms are shaking with fatigue. A sudden sense of exhaustion hit me and I fight to stay awake. Oh hell. The medicine I just dumped on my head might have painkiller in it, and I just gave myself way more than I need. Sleep is inevitable. I'll have no choice but to burn it off while I lie here unconscious and unprotected. There's little I can do besides make myself comfortable.

It's coming fast now. I'm going to collapse right where I lay. I stretch a hand out, searching for something to rest my head on so I don't wake up with another ache. As I pat the deck, my fingers catch the edge of a soft container, and I drag it toward me, not realizing until it's too late that it is on the bottom of a stack.

The last thing I feel before I lose consciousness is the containers crashing down on me. I hardly care. I am numb to the pain of the impact.

And everything else.

REASSEMBLY

I WAKE WITH A start, shaking the boxes off my back as I break free of them. They're only full of thin fabric, and it all spills out as they tumble away. I push myself up and scan my surroundings.

The room is just more containers, lined up in rows, towering above my head. Whether they're full of fabric or something else equally useless is not my concern. What I need is a canteen or something that I can carry water in. I am painfully thirsty, and my throat is raw. I need to drink something now.

The pain across my body has lessened to a dull ache, and that's promising. Once I can get my senses back in line, I will get moving again, provided I can stand on both feet.

Damn that Rhain. On top of putting hurt all over me, he's delayed my search for Efa. If I can't find her, I will make sure he understands just how much he's to blame. What I did to him on eighty-two will be minor compared to what I will do. As soon as I can find something more than sheets to use as a weapon.

On reconsideration, I rip a piece of fabric off and cover my head with it, tying it underneath my hair in the back. It will serve as a makeshift bandage and keep my hair out of my face like it has been. I wrap a few more strips under my knee to serve as a brace.

The stacks of containers will serve a solid support as I stand up. I push one back for better leverage and lift myself. Another stack goes under my other hand, and I repeat until I am resting on my good foot.

Then comes the test. I hold my breath and place the toes of my other foot on the deck—nothing. I force my fear down and continue.

My heel goes down, slowly, as I keep both hands on a stack of boxes and shift my weight to both feet, cringing as I do. To my relief, only a dull ache radiates from my knee, nowhere near the level of agony that stunned me before. I can work with this, and if I need it, more medication is an option. Though I'd prefer not to. I need to stay sharp in case of something unexpected, and that seems likely. Let's see how long I can tolerate the pain.

I lean on the wall and push the door open as far as it will go. There's no sliding through while I'm on my feet. I have no ability to maneuver and I'm far too worried about my knee hitting something.

With a slow exhale, I push out of the bay and take my first breath in the cool air of the corridor. It's refreshing. I feel my senses—

Someone's here.

Tension presses against my lungs as I limp to the wall opposite the bay. Then I listen. And listen more. There's a sound. Someone walking. Maybe two.

I gasp. No. It's not just footsteps. It's a particular gait, and after years of hearing it, one that I am extremely familiar with.

"Efa!" My voice comes out thin and raspy. I force myself to swallow and try again. All I do is croak. I need to find another way to get her attention. If I can get to them before they leave the level, we can reconnect, and I will feel a lot better being with them.

Or will I? I don't know how they'll respond to my sudden presence. I'm just a burden wounded like this. Efa will want to care for me, but she can't look after Merek and me both. Rabbit's no help, either. He's got to lead them. Which means Efa must choose between me and her lover a second time. I expect she'll make the same decision and leave me on my own. Again.

It's alright. I'll move myself. I'll make it to them and prove that I can keep up.

"I'm coming, Efa," I whisper as I set my arm against the wall, using it for support. Then I set my jaw and shuffle down the corridor toward the ladder to eighty-six.

I struggle to get far. My heart is beating hard even after a few steps. There's no way I can catch them like this. Perhaps that's for the best. Efa may not forgive me, now that Merek has her ear. I could just be pushing myself for nothing.

No. I can't believe that. Yet I can't come up with anything else. I just overdid it with the painkiller. That's what's causing all this doubt. I just need to find Efa and look her in the eye. Then this medicine-induced delusion will clear from my head, and I'd know for sure how she feels.

But to do that, I have to hurry.

My foot lands poorly, and I stumble, barely catching myself on the edge of a doorway. A second later, I recover, pushing off the doorway to keep up my pace.

"Efa!" I try again, but it's useless. I need water down my throat or she'll never hear me. Not unless she's checking the level for sounds. Merek, and likely Rabbit, won't allow her to do that. I'd back his call if I were there. They don't have time to do anything but move.

I pause at an intersection—which way should I go? Maybe left, but that means I must cross from this corner to the one farthest away with no support. It may only be four or five paces, yet I'm terrified to try. The memory of pain too much to handle has frayed my nerves.

Still, if I want to see Efa again, I'll have to chance it.

With a sharp breath, I push off the wall and take my first step. It's more of a hop than a limp, as I take all the weight off my bad leg. I can't hurt it if I don't use it, at least until I get to the other side.

After the second step, my balance gets off and I lean far to one side, threatening a fall. I throw my arms wide and recenter my weight, briefly touching the toes of my hurt foot to the deck. It's enough to keep me on my feet, and I sigh, crisis avoided.

After that, I move as fast as I can, taking the final two hops to catch the corner's edge. I press against it and shut my eyes, if only for a second. Now that I have support again, I make all haste down the corridor, limping, hopping, and doing whatever else I can to get to the ladder. It shouldn't be far now. If I can just—bish!

I misstep and fall forward, landing hard even as my arms come up to lessen the impact. My cheekbone smacks the deck, knocking my senses from me. Vibration rattles my bones, and I let out a long, coarse wail. Pain is coming any second to pound me like the aftershock of an explosion. And when it does, I will suffer.

It hits me all at once—a flame surging through my body, from my face to my knee. I shut my eyes and clench my teeth until I cannot bear it any longer. A whimper escapes my lips as my body writhes. My hand scrapes the floor as I move it to check my face—no blood, but I will be bruised and sore there for days. Just like the rest of me.

I roll onto my back with a groan, fighting to regain my will to keep going. Efa is gone. I'm sure of it. She and Merek will be hitting the first rung of the down ladder by now. Yet, I just lie here, wishing for the minor comfort of my nest. Wishing I never agreed to any of this mess.

"Wait for me, Efa," I whisper, even as I know she won't. Can't. I'd be a burden that she doesn't need.

That sharp glance that Efa gave me before she walked out was worse than anything Rhain did. My ribs may ache from his punches, but the thought that Efa may not care to see me again stabs me to the core.

There's little point to keep on if I am no longer needed. Efa has Merek now. I can only ever be second place to him, and I hate the idea of that. I should have expected this would happen, but how could I have? What do I know about relationships like this? The adults do everything they can to discourage us from ever getting close to each other. From the moment we wake, they pound into our heads that boys and girls are exactly the same, that intimacy is bad for the squad, and those who break their law will surely suffer. For once, they may be right about something. I hate that idea the most.

A sudden urge to move builds inside of me, telling me to get my pathetic ass up off the deck and do...anything. But I've got no plan and my head hurts too much to think for very long. Maybe I should just give up and take my punishment. It'd be less to bear than watching Efa walk away from me again.

Still, I move.

I press my back to the wall and push up with my arms and one good leg. With one small motion at a time, I rise and by the time I'm upright, I'm panting hard. My arms shake from fatigue, and my one good leg feels as if it's about to collapse. Doubt creeps into my mind again and I grow reluctant to put weight on that knee. It's almost certain that it'll be painful to press on it. I don't know how much more I can tolerate.

Hyuk it all. I'm doing this.

I grit my teeth, take a quick inhale, shift my weight to my left leg...and step.

Sparks fly across my vision, and I cry out as my right leg seizes in torment. I throw myself backward into the wall. The shock of the collision buckles my knees, and I slide back to the deck.

"No!" I sob and pound my fists into the floor as despair floods over me. That's it. It's over. I'm ready to surrender.

I just can't.

I lean my head back and close my eyes. As despondent as I am in this moment, I must keep going. But which way? Following Efa is the better choice. In my current state, I will already be on my knees when I beg her for forgiveness. Anything is better than the eternal torture of Captain Daga's absolute command.

I pull a medicine tube from my pocket and stare at it, wondering just how much I need. A full dose knocked me out last time, and that was just from pouring it into the cut on my head. A direct injection might kill me.

Bish, what do I have to lose if I die?

My thumb pops the cap off the integrated needle, and I take a quick breath. I flip the tube around in my fingers and jam it into my thigh, wincing as the sharp tip punctures my skin.

The medicine takes effect almost immediately. Relief comes to me as the ache in my knee and the soreness in my cheek dissipate. The rest of my body gets heavy, but the pain is gone. I smile in the freedom of numbness and push myself up. Then, I move.

It's slow going. Dizziness comes along with the lack of feeling. I catch myself several times along the wall as I move down the corridor. If I'm having this much trouble walking, then climbing will be near impossible.

The ladder alcove is just ahead. I take a tight grip on the corner edge and check my surroundings. Clear—maybe. I doubt I'd notice anyone charging toward me. I can't hear well, either.

My ears are ringing from the multiple times I hit my head on the floor. With a little luck, it won't be permanent.

A small gray container sitting next to the ladder catches my eye—a canteen? Could it be? Yes! And I think it's mine. I'll worry about how it got here later. Right now, all I'm hoping is that there's something inside of it. I make a careful but swift motion to slide down the wall next to it and reach out to snatch it up, then freeze, my hand outstretched just above it.

As much as I want to drink, this is too deliberate. Someone put it here to send me a message. But who? Efa? Rhain?

I pick it up. It's full, and any caution I had a second ago sinks under the weight of my thirst. I don't care if someone poisoned its contents. I need water. Now. I pull the cap and lift the canteen to my lips. The liquid inside is cool, and my throat welcomes it gladly.

As I gulp it down, a sweet scent wafts out. I nearly choke as I recognize it. Water spills from my lips, splashing over me and soaking the entire alcove. I pull the canteen away and stare at it, searching for that one telltale chip on the paint that will explain everything.

It's there, just on the rounded edge. Now I know it belongs to Efa, and the message is from her. She wants—no. She's hoping I'll follow them. They can't be far. And now I've found the thing I must accomplish.

Please wait for me, Efa. I'm right behind you.

DISCOVERY

Two long days pass. I manage ten levels in that time. It's nothing, considering I covered nearly seven times that many not long before. Recruits go twenty up and down every day to build their stamina and they cover that in an hour. I couldn't even manage half of that in forty-eight hours.

I'm walking again, so that's something. And I've seen or heard no one. That's a benefit and an issue. Captain Daga, and whoever's with him, would not be a welcome sight. Only Efa matters, though Merek or Rabbit would be fine, too.

Efa left no more clues. Perhaps she had nothing to leave or had too much else to focus on. It's disheartening. I was hoping to find something, and for a second I foolishly hoped I'd be able to catch up to them. She must be all the way to the access point by now. I wonder if she is still hoping I will show.

This level—ninety-five—is odd. It's wide open, save for four large tubes that extend from the center of the level out to the hull of the ship. Each one is easily three times my height, and they're staggered, two on the far side and the other two on the hull nearest to me. Pipes come up from the floor and run to the beginning of each tube. For what reason, I can't even guess.

There is a passage between them created by several rows of lockers on each side. As I walk toward them, I notice a hatch on each tube, with a control panel next to it. The illuminated ready lights on the panels draw my attention, as do the lockers. Other than a canteen and some medicine, I have nothing. There could be something useful inside.

Food would be very welcome, but I expect none, not this deep into the ship. I am starving, but I can still manage for now. Tomorrow will be different.

I head to the nearest locker and give it a quick examination before touching it. I doubt the Fahrasi would have come this far only to set traps on storage they could have just emptied. No Tarakh would have either, at least to my knowledge. The moment someone laid eyes on these potential treasure caches, they would have scavenged every last item of value from them.

Just like I'm about to do.

I press the latch release and step away. The door pops open a crack, then I grab it and throw it wide. An orange helmet resting above a white suit greets me, a relic of another time, yet fresh and useable as the day they put it here. I suck in a breath of wonder. It's a garment for traveling outside of the ship—an EVA suit. There must be an air pack for it somewhere nearby, perhaps in the next locker, which is shaped square in an equivalent size for the pack.

So these are airlocks, though they're not like any I've ever seen before. They could be for ship-to-ship connections, possibly. I could imagine these tubes, or others inside of them, extend out and provide a passageway to another ship.

That would be a sight. Two massive ships connecting. But it would never happen. Each of the twelve ships that left Earth went in separate directions, hoping one or more would be successful in finding a new world to live on. If they did, the rest of Earth's population would quickly follow.

As my stomach rumbles, I check the other lockers in the row, then move to the other side. I find a pair of utility knives—not great for fighting, but better than bare hands—a first aid kit, and a light that still works. There were other items I could have taken, but I have no way to carry them.

At the end of the locker row, I come to a control panel, curious about its function. It's a momentary diversion from my ordeal, and I allow it so I can rest for a moment.

Its configuration, like this level, is odd. I have seen the systems we use for monitoring and controlling the stasis beds. These are different. Rather than multiple screens that interact by touch, these have banks of switches, meters, and buttons on one side and a single screen and keypad on the other. It's a rather complicated set of controls for an airlock. Perhaps these are for an inter-ship connection, after all.

Then I notice the hatch at the end of the tube, striped in black-and-yellow caution signage. No other airlock on the *Stratford* is like that. There's no need. We've clearly marked airlocks with a bright red outline around the inside door so that no one attempts to use them.

My curiosity gets the better of me, and I approach to shine my light into the hatch's port window. As I press my face against it, I make out the shape of something massive inside. I move the light around to see more detail, but none of it makes sense to my eyes. There's another hatch, small and circular, on the end of the machine. If this was a way to transfer between ships, the external airlock door should be much larger. This is just big enough for a single person, perhaps wearing an EVA suit, to fit through.

I glance at the control panel again. Bish. Now I get it. This is no airlock. This is an emergency escape pod. The tubes are for launching them out from the path of the ship. But four of them wouldn't be enough to carry all of us away. Fahrasi included. No, wait. The original plan was never to have so many of us awake at once. Only the fifty-odd unlucky people chosen to care for the ship would have needed emergency pods. Those in stasis would never know if disaster occurred. Of course, it has.

And now that I know, I can move on. There's nothing else for me here. I'm not escaping this ship, ever. I couldn't leave my parents, and there'd be nowhere for me to go, even if I did. We may be passing through a solar system, but we are still far from any planet.

At least I found something useful. Though my stomach doesn't agree.

Hold on. Escape pods are prepped and ready to launch at any moment. That means stocks of survival equipment, clothing...

And food.

I return to the four tubes and the four pods in them. Four possibilities to find something to quell my hunger and perhaps more medicine to replace what I've used. My stomach churns as I think about shoving something—anything—edible down my throat.

There could be a great deal of noise involved in getting inside one of those pods. Alarms, sirens, moving machinery. All would be an obvious call to anyone within earshot. Those sounds would travel well off this level. Not that I care much. I'm starving, and my hunger is pushing me to take the risk. There's likely no one above me for ten levels. I can be fairly sure of that after having spent the better part of two days crawling, limping, and then walking through them.

I scan the control panel, reading the print on every button until I find the one marked *pressure* and press it.

Nothing happens.

I sigh and consider. With any airlock, pressure needs to be equalized between both sides before any door or hatch can open. This is to avoid someone getting sucked through or, worse, blown out of the ship. This is an emergency pod, though. They would have designed the system for a quick startup.

Then I spot what I'm searching for. I close my eyes and shake my head at my stupidity. Of course, everything would be automatic. No one has time to learn how to operate something in an emergency. In my nourishment-deprived state, I wasn't thinking straight about that.

I slap my palm down on the one button twice as large as the others and lit orange to make it more visible. An alarm and a flashing light send me into panic. I duck down into a space between the lockers and the control panel on the opposite side.

If someone is here, they'll investigate the system in operation, and I can slip away without being seen. I may have a tiny weapon now, but I'm not back to fighting strength. Not at all. I will only stand and fight as a last resort.

A light goes on inside the tube, and a moment later, the hatch opens, swinging up to allow access to the pod. Then, to my relief, the alarm goes silent, but the light remains flashing. There must be a disable button for it on the panel. With a quick check of my surroundings, I dash to the panel and scan around it again. It's there! I waste no time turning it off and ducking inside the tube.

The hatch to the pod is open, and strips of lights on the ceiling illuminate its interior. I have to squint as I enter, but that is the least of my concerns.

It's larger than I expected. Twenty seats, ten to a side, line the walls. Safety harnesses hang off them, along with neck and head restraints. Past them is a wall of lockers. That's my target. I head straight for them and pop open every single one, shining my light inside to check their contents.

A few seconds later, I am ripping boxes of meal pouches from the bottom row and breaking them open. I grab a pouch, tear it open, and dump the contents of it into my mouth.

And immediately spit it out, gagging on the foul taste. I grab my canteen and rinse until I no longer feel like I am about to vomit.

I should have known. No one's maintained these pods. Those that do are otherwise occupied or dead. I doubt anyone alive knows how to fix them.

There might still be a box or two that hasn't expired, though I've made my search more difficult by dumping the contents of each one out on the floor. It won't stop me. I am ravenous and determined, so I will test my patience while I match pouches up with their former boxes.

It doesn't take long to find one. It's a yellow-colored protein. Not my favorite, but that won't stop me. I break open the seal on the pouch, sniff the food inside, and then devour it once I consider it acceptable. I do this three more times before I lean back on a seat and relax to finish up my last pouch.

Only then do I notice the persistent beep of a terminal. The screen is near the hatch, next to the first seat. Out of curiosity, I move to it to read the prompt.

Enter coordinates or scan for potential refuge locations, it says.

Since I have no idea about coordinates, I tap the scan button on the screen as I put the last bit of food into my mouth. The terminal goes blank and remains so for a solid minute, while I watch and wonder if this pod is older and more broken than I thought.

Then it pings, and a single line displays: *One location found. Set course? Y/N*

I stare at it. Re-read it, then read it a third time because what it says doesn't register in my brain.

Until it does.

My jaw drops. It found a planet—a *liveable* planet. In range of this pod. If I launched this pod, I could be on my way in seconds. A new life. Everything they've denied me at the press of a button. A yearning rises in my chest as I consider the possibility. What would it be like to live under a blue sky again?

It's pointless. There is no way to slow the ship down in time, nor would it be possible to ferry everyone off the *Stratford* with just four pods. The adults must know this. That is why they never attempted to scan with the pod's system. It would just be a wistful moment among thousands of wistful moments on this ship.

I sigh and tap the *N*, then gather up as many meal pouches as I can fit in my pockets and exit. The greatest gift this pod can give me is already in my hands. I will accept it as enough, because now I can live another day.

COMPASSION

The first thing I did in my renewed life was vomit. The moment I touched down on ninety-six, I wretched as nausea hit me. I stumbled to the corner and released whatever was left in my stomach.

I overdid it. Four meal packets were way too much. My body wasn't ready for all that food. I haven't eaten that much in a day since I woke. On the days with no fighting, we're allowed two meals. Other days, we'd be lucky to stuff half of one in our mouths.

Nutrition to me is just a necessity. I eat because I must. They formulate meal pouches to give us the strength to fight and little else. There are rumors that the Fahrasi grow their own food, but I've seen nothing of the sort. Not even Efa's alleged ice cream. Perhaps I should ask Merek when I see him next.

I wretch again as my head hangs. I was lucky that I tucked my hair into my collar, or it would have caught the half-digested remnants of my meal. No more food for today. Not even ice cream if I had some.

What I need is water. I grab my canteen and put it to my lips, only to find that I've drunk everything in it. I'm not worried.

There's a recycler station just down the hall. It's even marked with a blue light. I limp over to it, and with a contented smile, I put my canteen under the faucet and press the button, then watch the clear liquid drop into the black hole of my bottle. It will be good to get the wretched taste of bile out of my mouth.

A ringing, like metal on metal, pierces the stillness in the corridor. I freeze. Someone's here. And they just drew their blade. My hand goes to mine by reflex. Of course, it's not there. I grab one of the utility knives instead and get ready to defend myself. But I'm hoping I don't have to. I'm in no condition to fight.

Dammit. Why wasn't I paying attention?

There's a corridor that breaks off to the left. I can make it if I move now. I quickly scan the corner where the sound came from, and I move as my leg allows. Water splashes from my canteen as I stumble down the hall, smacking the ground with a loud plop. There's no time to put the cover back. Not that it matters. They already know I'm here.

Two pairs of boots give chase, burning down the corridor and closing fast. I slip down the next corridor on my right, then make a left. There's no outrunning them, but I may outsmart them.

I double back, heading toward my original position, making a few more turns along the way. My breaths come up short, made harder by the rawness in my throat. I'm weak from throwing up. I've got to hide. A storage bay or even a closet. Anything will do. Just until they pass.

Darts whistle past my head, emphasizing my need to find cover quick. I duck and roll into another passage, scrambling to my feet in less than a second. There's a door just ahead. I grab it and throw it open.

And get slammed from behind.

I grunt as my body goes airborne and lands hard. But I move through the pain, twisting to get back on my feet. Too slow. Hands grab my wrists and force me back down. I struggle to get free, but my attacker gets on top of me, gaining leverage.

"Stay down, Ceri," a woman's voice growls. The air goes from my lungs. It's Niah. I should have known Captain Daga would send her squad after me. Niah is one of the few who can still beat me in a fight.

My body relaxes. There's no escaping Niah, not while I'm still trying to recover from my wounds. Niah knows it too, so she releases her weight on my hands but remains over me. She taught me how to fight, so she's well aware of what I can do, even hurt as I am now.

As I lay on the deck, I shut my eyes and sigh. I suppose this is how it ends. Niah will haul me back to base and put me in front of the captain. Then he'll lock me away, and that'll be the end. I hope my sacrifice will at least allow Efa to live freely, even though her life won't be much better than mine.

Two of Niah's team arrive, prompting me to look. I know them, yet they stare at me as if I was a stranger. The boy of the pair powers on his light and blasts it into my face. I squeeze my eyes shut and turn my head away.

"You have any weapons on you?" Niah asks. It's a standard question. If there's no risk of me attacking, she'll be able to ease off.

"Just a knife," I say. The slur in my words surprises me. As does the exhaustion covering my body. This can't just be from the bad meal packs.

"Where is it?" She demands.

"In my pocket."

Niah jams her hands into my pockets and pulls everything out. Medicine, meal pouches, and last, the one utility knife that I stashed there. She might not search me for anything else, but if she does, she'll find the second one. That won't go over well.

Niah turns me over and sits me up to look at me. Whatever she sees makes her eyes go wide.

"Bish, Ceri. You look like death." Niah wrinkles her nose. "You smell like it, too. What the hyuk happened to you?"

My head droops. All I want to do is beg her to let me sleep. Or even use her lap as a pillow. But she wouldn't allow it. Not until I answered her questions. That's another problem I don't have the energy to handle.

"You wouldn't believe me if I told you," I drawl.

"Try me."

I desperately want to. If things were different, I'd blab everything to her and hope she'd help me. As I've been a big sister to Efa, Niah has been mine. She's nearly ten years older and should be an adult by now. Why she isn't is between her and the adults, though I expect it's because they're unwilling to share their authority. Perhaps that's why she became a scout.

This far from base, she can make her own rules, far beyond the adult's supervision.

But if she thinks I've turned traitor, I cannot trust her. That's difficult to know. I'd like to believe she's giving me a chance to tell my side. Or maybe demanding that I do. I'm not sure she can handle it. As it is, I barely can.

"Rhain and I had a spar," I say.

"That much I know." Niah smirks. "It took him two days before he could walk straight again. What else?"

"There's nothing else."

"That's a lie. Rhain didn't do this." Niah grabs my chin and turns it to look at the bruises on my cheekbone. Then her eyes drift up to my head. She puts her fingers under the fabric and slides it off. "Or this."

All I can do is look at her with sad eyes. Every look she gives me reminds me of the hell I've been through over the last few days. I'm finding it hard not to just collapse in front of her, but perhaps I should. Niah has never betrayed me before.

"Get me the med kit," Niah says to the boy with the light.

"Aren't we supposed to just bring her back?" he asks.

"In a minute. She's in poor condition and she needs help. Even if she were the enemy, we'd care for her."

"Is she the enemy?" the girl asks, watching me with a suspicious gaze.

"Only Ceri can answer that." Niah swivels toward her. "And we won't get any answers from her if she can't think straight. Now get the med kit!"

The girl runs off, likely to another squad member. Niah's team is usually just four, but Captain Daga may have added a few more. It should flatter me he needs so many to take me down.

Niah crouches before me, her eyes watching my face. I offer a small curl of the edge of my mouth, and she reaches out to stroke my hair. I tilt my head into her hand, accepting her touch.

"I heard about Efa," she says. "I'm sorry."

I go stiff. What has she heard? I need to find out. If the adults think she's dead, they won't look for her. It's a welcome support to her escape, and I'll do my best to make use of it.

But when I don't react, Niah tilts her head. Her compassion turns into a frown. A moment later, understanding sets in, and she exhales a slow breath while her hand goes to her collar.

"She's not dead, is she?" she asks.

I look at Niah, my eyes burning from the wetness that invades them. The medication must make me feel vulnerable, or perhaps I am just missing Efa way more than I thought. We've been together nearly every moment since they took us from stasis. I've only recently noticed her lack of interest in spending time with me. I understand why now. It only makes me miss her more.

I feel a sob welling up, and try to fight it. To tell Niah the truth means I must explain Merek to her, and she might not understand. I didn't, not until I met him and saw how much he cared for Efa. Still, Niah is sharp, and I really could use an ally.

If I can explain my reasons, then maybe she'll choose to back me.

"No, she's not," I reply. The boy makes a sound of disbelief. Niah, to her credit, smiles instead.

"Is that what you've been doing? Protecting her?" she asks. Only a big sister would figure that out.

It's then that everything I've been holding in surges from my lips. I tell her about the moment Efa confessed to me and continue though to when I met Merek, and then Sayer, and then Rabbit. I tell her about Efa and Merek's plan to find the access point, and Sayer's and my dumb insistence we go with them.

Niah listens, her eyebrows pressing together from time to time when I explain my reasons for stealing medicine or for trusting the Fahrasi. By the time I am nearly finished, the girl returns with the med kit, setting it down next to Niah as she keeps a wary eye on me.

"Good," Niah says and points out the door. "Now go set up. We're bedding down on this floor. Set a watch schedule for the night." Then she turns to the boy. "And you heard none of this, got it? This is more of a mess than your little brain can figure out. Don't get any ideas about going to the adults on your own, or I will cut your legs off. I'll report this to Captain Daga myself. Now get out. I've got this."

Once they're gone, Niah digs into the med kit and begins dressing my wounds. She's quiet as she works through each minor cut and bruise, caring for me as if I was her own child.

As she works, I feel the tension drain from my body, not having even realized it was there.

My confession to her was a welcome relief, and now that I've opened up to her, everything I've been holding in bursts from me. Tears cascade down my cheeks, falling onto my hands as they rest in my lap. My chest heaves and I sob, but for once, I'm not ashamed. I've resigned myself to Niah's care. It's the only place I can feel safe to do so. After this, I must find strength to face Captain Daga and the other adults as they crush me under their judgement.

Efa must survive without me. I will be helpless to protect her.

And I may never see her again.

Still, there is a sort of freedom in helplessness. I will cede my control to fate and allow to happen whatever may happen. Niah is here too, and she will help me through the tough moments. That thought alone gives me strength.

"Feel better?" Niah wipes my eyes dry with a clean dressing and uses the moisture to wipe the dirt from the rest of my face. "You know, you haven't cried this much since you were a recruit."

I nod and duck my head. I might have been strong a moment ago, but now I feel too exposed.

"It's okay, Ceri," Niah says, rubbing my shoulder. "We're allowed to cry. It's a part of being human. And we *are* human, no matter what the so-called adults tell you."

"It's fine...I mean, I'm fine."

"Are you? Really?"

"Maybe not right now." I squeeze my eyes shut and tighten my fists. "But I will be. I have to be."

Niah sits back, resting her arm on her knee. She presses her lips together as she looks at me, rubbing a finger on her chin. After a minute of uncomfortable silence, she takes a breath and nods.

"Good, because once the team beds down, I'm coming to get you."

I blink and shake my head. "Why? For what reason?"

"You need to be with Efa, and staying here will be your death. Captain Daga is not far behind, and he will murder you for the embarrassment you caused him. He wants revenge, Ceri. And that man is of a single mind. A trapped mind. He will never understand what you just told me."

My jaw goes slack. Niah is returning control of my fate back to me. As elated as I feel, I also get queasy. Accepting her help is dangerous. For her and for me. Daga—he is no longer a captain to me—will hunt me like I was his prey and kill anyone who gets in his way. That puts Niah, Efa and Merek at risk, too.

As much as I am reluctant to receive Niah's help, I realize I will. It's the only possibility now.

"And one more thing," Niah adds. "The machine room is not safe for you. Now the rail system is running, the chief wants us to claim as much of the lower levels as we can, and we will. I've already been down there, Ceri. That's how we found you. We came up, not down. It's only a matter of time before we return. In force."

My mouth drops open as I stare at her. "H...how can I thank you?" I blurt, not knowing what else to say.

"By seeing your mission through to the end, little sister." Niah gives me a wistful smile. "They're not right, you know. The adults. The Tarakh and the Fahrasi aren't enemies. We're all one people, and if we're lucky, one day we will be again. Now get some rest. I'll return soon."

Niah pats me on the cheek and gets up. As she walks out, I wonder just how many more believe like she does.

RISK

I FACE THE UNRELENTING darkness of level ninety-nine. This floor holds the literal example of death—it's our morgue. Other than three metal tables with overhead lights hanging over them, there's nothing but rows upon rows of frozen bodies. I don't know why we bother to keep them. These people will never wake up again. Better to set them free to drift among the stars than to lock them in cold storage for ages.

Niah brought me to the floor above before turning around. She wished me luck and shot up the ladder with me staring after her, wondering what I did to deserve her kindness. I owed her so much, even before this. Now I owe her everything. And I plan to pay all it back.

I shine my light across the level, its rays reaching far to the opposite side. The lack of corridors on this level only enhances its immense size. It's nearly twice the size of no one's ground on level eight. The Tarakh and the Fahrasi can stand on opposite sides here, firing every round we have, and hit no one. Darts aren't accurate at that distance. We haven't needed them to be.

By the time I reach the other side, I am panting. I only jogged halfway before the soreness in my knee made me stop. It won't get better until I find another place to rest, and there will be none. It's twenty-three floors to go before I reach machine access, and if all goes well, Efa.

I hope she'll forgive me when I crush her dream of safety.

The clank of a boot hitting the ladder sends me diving between the rows of freezers. That's a soldier making a lot of noise on purpose. They're trying to drive me up towards Niah's scouts. But Niah and her team will be on their way down soon enough. I'm trapped, and there's no place to hide. Daga will inspect every row and freezer to find me. But where can I go? They're already assembling on this floor and will make swift moves to secure it.

A memory from my first meeting with Merek returns, and I slide down the row toward the opposite side of the level, headed for the first hull access I can find. That could be enough, depending on how much of a rush they're in. I should think of a backup plan too, if there's time.

The hatch is at the end of the row. I crawl to it and pull the release, wrenching the hatch open and jumping inside. Closing it is more difficult. If I make noise, my hiding spot is lost.

I find an opening behind a heavy piece of machinery and slip behind it, pulling out the utility knife that Niah returned to me. She couldn't give me a gun—that would have been too obvious. As it is, she's walking a fine line by letting me go. Niah does not fear Daga. But I fear him for her.

The hull access is cool, as I remember it, even compared to the chill drifting off the freezers. I make the mistake of leaning against the second hull, jerking away the moment I feel the icy fingers of space reaching out toward me. The *Stratford's* outer hull is beyond that one. I can only imagine how dangerous it would be to touch any of the metal superstructure there. Space is an unforgiving environment, and it if wasn't for the security of the triple hull, we would be that much closer to death.

This may be a good hiding spot, but between the hum of machinery and the thickness of the hull itself, I can't hear them moving or talking. I can only keep still and wait.

Or...I can continue down through the hull. I just need to look for the ladder. Though it's not the best idea. Either faction could have sentries above watching for movement. It's a risk I'll have to take. Holding still and waiting for Daga to find me is a worse idea.

I lean over the railing and look down, searching for the ladder. I spot it quickly, though it'll be difficult to get to. It's not as easy as walking around the catwalk to the top of the ladder. I'll have to leave the safety of the railing and climb around the massive structure that's the rail system.

A chill shoots up my arms. I shiver and pull my hands from the railing—it's freezing! Any metal I touch in here will be. I'll have to gather my strength and endure it or I will fall. And if I do, there's nothing to stop me from plummeting all the way to the bottom.

I rub my hands together to warm them and reach out, straining my arms to get to the next handhold. Then I swing my leg out, but it's still a little short. The only way that I can get there is to jump, and I'm already in an awkward position. I'll need to find another route.

The clink of the hatch lock echoes through the hull. Bish, they're here. But where can I hide?

As the grind of metal on metal echoes through the hull, I make a desperate choice. My hand grabs the nearest cross-beam, and I swing down, wrapping my sleeve around the latch that opens a hatch to the next hull. The cold bites through the thin material and into my skin as I pull. This is far from a good idea, but I don't have time to consider anything better.

Frigid air smacks me in the face as I open the hatch. I gasp as air escapes my lungs. The next inhale is painful, and I must cover my nose and mouth if I want to keep breathing. I take once last breath of outside air, hold it, and duck in.

Boots hit the catwalk between the first and the second hull. Hyuk. I didn't close the hatch to the second hull yet, and there is nowhere to hide. I can't climb. The skin on my hands would tear off if I touched anything.

I am already shivering violently as I shift away from the hatch. My muscles stiffen in the chill. I must keep moving just to stay awake and alive. Perhaps I can make it around the corner far enough to keep me hidden.

"Captain! There's a hatch open to the second hull!" a voice says. I recognize it. It's a boy from A Squad. So that's who he's brought with him. It makes sense. They've got no field leader now, and many of them would want to avenge Rhain for what I did to him, just like my squad would want revenge on Rhain for attacking me. If only they knew about it. I doubt they do.

"Sir?" the voice repeats, higher pitched than before. "But we're not equipped to go in there! Neither is she! She'd never survive!"

He's right. My body is shaking uncontrollably. Thousands of needles assault every bare spot of skin on my body. The skin on my hands is purple, and I'm feeling more tired than I was before. I wrap my arms about me and rock back and forth to create some internal heat. It's a useless act. Any warmth that I create gets sucked away faster than I can replace it. This was beyond stupid of me. It won't be long before I succumb to this cold. My toes are already losing any feeling in them.

"What do we do?" another boy's voice asks. He sounds young, perhaps a recruit. "Can you just look in there, maybe?"

I drop to a crouch, bringing my body and limbs together to conserve any remnant of heat I have left. My fingers are already numb. Any longer and I might lose a few. These boys better hurry and decide.

"Hyuk no, I'm not going anywhere near that hatch," the older boy replies. "You do it."

"After you just said you wouldn't?"

"I'm senior here. Do as I say."

"But my face could freeze off!"

"Kid, we're at war. It's almost a guarantee you're going to get hurt. Just accept that and pop your head in there. We both know she's not there, but we have to check. Captain's orders."

"Aw, bish...fine. I'll do it."

My arms squeeze my body tighter and squint at the hatch. Everything is out of focus and blurry. My limbs are shaking so much. Time seems to slow, and all I want to do is just lie down on the catwalk and sleep. I can't. If I do, it's over. Maybe I should just give myself up and live one more day.

"Hyuk! The air coming out of there is killing my throat! Do I really have to do this?"

"Take a breath and hold it, then stick your head in. Then you're done. Okay?"

"Okay."

The boy's face pops through the hatch. He glances right. I hold my breath. He glances left. A wail builds inside of me I can barely contain.

But then…I notice something unusual. I blink and squint harder. This can't be reality. Can it?

When he backs out of the hatch, I know it is.

Bish. If this kid was in my squad, I would beat him for his cowardice. Instead, I will thank him for it.

His eyes were closed.

"Nothing, right?" the older boy says.

"Nope. Can we go now? I'm freezing!"

"Yeah, come on."

Me too. Before I die.

I make my way toward the hatch at a painful pace. It's all I can manage. My teeth are chattering so much they could chop my tongue in half. Of course, I'd never feel it. I don't so much climb out of the hatch as fall, my body jerking on impact. I know I hurt myself, but it'll have to wait.

The hatch.

My eyes dart to it, and only when I confirm they've closed it do I let out a whimper. My senses are dulled by the cold, yet everything hurts. As I lay on the catwalk, I rub my frozen limbs, seeking warmth even as this space feels blazing hot compared to the freezing hell I just put myself through, but it's not. I'll need to really get the cold out of my body.

But only after Daga moves off the level. Until then, I suffer.

HOPE

LEVEL ONE HUNDRED—EIGHTY-SIX LEVELS away from the place I called home. It was never really that. Only where I slept, ate, and washed. Soldiers were useless to adults if they weren't fighting. That's what they told us. We never believed them. The time we weren't killing or getting killed was ours. We did with it what we wanted, as long as we didn't get caught.

Unlike the containers of death above, this level has life. And light. This floor is one of four that contain the bio-systems for recycling air and water. There's one on level nineteen that I've been to, and just like that one, this one stinks like the boys' toilet. Even with the compartmentalized tanks of bio-muck, the design they went with doesn't stop the stench from permeating the air.

I suppose if they defrosted all the bodies on the level above, it would smell the same.

Five minutes into my arrival here, I notice I'm not alone. A pair of soldiers are probing the space, likely looking for me. Canny of Daga to hold back a pair of soldiers in case I slipped past his primary force.

By the sound of their voices and the lightness of their footsteps, these two are way inexperienced. It would be easy to snatch one and interrogate them about Daga's strategy. The chief never would have approved of him appropriating so many soldiers just to capture me. All I did was steal some medicine—well—that, and rough up a few people. Still, there must be some larger plan here.

I slip into a dark corner, one that I know these two will approach soon. All I need to do is wait until the first one passes by, then grab the other. With the way they're broadcasting their position, I doubt they'll be much of a challenge.

My guess is right on. A minute later, the two junior squad mates appear. They're young alright, just out of training. I know because one of them is from my squad—the girl, Seren. The boy is likely stolen from the other squads. I'll have to trust that he will listen to reason. I don't want to end such a young life.

As they pass by, making mistake after mistake, I prepare, but smile, recalling myself at that age. I wouldn't have remembered to use my light to clear the shadow areas, either. Only rookies left without supervision could be this mindless. They'll need to learn the hard lesson about checking everything twice, and then checking again, just like I did. Perhaps they think there's already enough illumination here, or that I couldn't possibly be here.

How wrong they are.

The moment they pass, I shoot out, wrapping my arm around Seren's body and snatching her back into the darkness.

She screams and drops her gun, grabbing at my arm to pull it off. But she's nowhere near strong enough. I clamp my hand over her mouth and close my arms about her as she struggles to get free.

The boy spins, searching for something to shoot at. His gun hand swings in every direction, his eyes growing wide at the sudden disappearance of his partner.

"I didn't teach you to scream like that, did I?" I whisper to my new captive, pressing my knife against her neck. Seren squirms, then stops. I take the risk of removing my hand from her mouth.

"Ceri!" The tension seeps from her body as Seren relaxes against me. "You won't hurt me, will you?"

"Not if your mate there cooperates."

"Seren!" the boy shouts and spins toward us. "Tell me where to shoot, and I'll kill that traitor!"

"That would be a bad idea," I say. "You've got no aim, and I can dispatch Seren here faster than you can find me. Why don't you just drop that weapon and have a seat?"

The boy hesitates. He must think that he's got me zeroed in. That's presumptuous of him. I bet his squad leader isn't all that experienced, either.

"Trust me, you'd hit Seren first, and I'd be extremely mad if you hurt her. You don't want me angry at you, do you?"

"She means it Rhys! Drop the gun!" Seren pleads. Rhys lowers his weapon but seems lost at what to do next.

"Throw your gun here and sit down by the wall," I say. Then, when Rhys doesn't move, "I won't hurt her. Sit and be patient, and when I've got what I want, I'll let her go. Understand?"

Rhys ducks his head, then slides his gun toward me. I put my knife down and reach forward to grab it. Seren relaxes more, easing into the spot on my lap.

"What do you want?" she asks.

"First, you need to know I'm not your enemy. This situation I've gotten involved in is complicated, but I'm no traitor. I'm still Tarakh, and I'm trying to protect our people."

"That's not what your captain says!" Rhys shouts. I nearly laugh. Daga is already spreading misinformation about me.

"What squad are you from, Rhys?" I ask.

"F Squad."

"That explains it. Don't shout again, or I will put you out, got it? With all the activity that your new captain has going on, there could be Fahrasi scouts down here, and they would like nothing better than to capture one of us."

Rhys glances around with nervous eyes, his hand sliding toward his blade. I feel bad for scaring the boy, but he needs to be scared. He needs to be terrified if he wants to stay alive.

"Captain Daga told us to shoot first if we see you," Seren says. "He said you were too dangerous for us to arrest."

"He's not wrong." I chuckle. "I don't want to be hurt any more than you do."

"He also said the same about Efa. Is she still alive?"

That takes the breath from my lungs. I don't know how Daga knows that, but that's a serious problem. They'll shoot Efa and

Merek down in a second if they spot them, and no one will even think to question why.

Niah was right. The machine room is dangerous for them. Daga will overrun that space and murder anyone he finds, claiming security for the Tarakh. Even Rabbit is at risk. I've got to find them right away.

I shift, adjusting Seren on my lap. When she was twelve, I would do this with ease. She's grown taller since then. Training has put some muscle on her body, too. At least she hasn't moved beyond her loyalty to me. I think. I should test her.

"What else does Captain Daga want down here?" I ask.

"Don't tell her!" Rhys hisses.

"I don't know," Seren answers with a small shrug. "He said we were securing every level for the Tarakh, but I don't get how we could hold them all."

"We can't," I reply. "We don't have anywhere near enough troops. As far as I can guess, you're down here for one reason, and that's finding me."

"Why, Ceri? What did you do?"

"Nothing. All I want to do is protect someone I care about. Like you." I lay my head on Seren's back and squeeze.

"Cut it out!" Seren whines and squirms, but she's not trying too hard. "Don't you understand you're the enemy?"

She must miss human contact as much as I do. Our training never discusses how a simple embrace could motivate a soldier to perform well beyond their own expectations. The adults didn't want us touching each other at all. Now that I've seen Efa and Merek together, I understand why.

"I'm not. Daga isn't telling you the truth," I say, "and that's because he doesn't know what the truth is."

Seren turns her head. "Can you tell me?"

"Not now. Find Niah and tell her I told you to ask. She'll explain it to you."

"Niah? The scout lead? Isn't she an adult?"

I grin. It wouldn't be the first time someone made that mistake.

"Niah will never be an adult. She understands way more than they ever will. Listen to her any chance you get. Niah will teach you how to survive."

Seren's muscles get tight. I know I'm asking her to do something unusual. But I also know she'll do it. Her curiosity will win over her fear. I chose Seren for my squad because I know she wants to do the right thing. She's just confused about what that is.

"So what will you do?" Seren asks after a long moment. "You want to help Efa, don't you?"

The answer to Seren's question is obvious. Of course I do. The real question is how. And where? There's not one safe place on this ship for them anymore. The Tarakh are leading the charge, but soon enough, the Fahrasi will go after them too. The leaders of both factions will stop at nothing to destroy the idea that two children can love each other. They can't profit from the embrace of the enemy, even if we are all the same.

An idea hits me then. The planet that the escape pod found. If Efa and Merek truly want to be together, then that's where they need to go. It's the only place they will be free to live their lives without fear of persecution or punishment.

No doubt there will be risks. An unexplored planet will contain its own dangers. Efa and Merek will need to survive with no support or assistance from anyone unless I go with them. I'm not sure I would. All I'd be is an interruption in their relationship. And the situation on the *Stratford*, even if I hate it, is one I understand. I know nothing about romantic love, nor am I sure that I'd want to.

It's their choice. They can decide when I tell them. I suspect they'll want to go, but the thought of that puts an ache in my heart. I would miss Efa something terrible, just like I do now. And I'd worry about her for the rest of my life. Just like I do every day.

Still. If that is what she truly wants, I must let her go.

"What is it?" Seren asks. I realize then that I gently rocking her.

"Sorry," I say and loosen my arms about her. "You should check in with your captain. He'll want to know where you are, and I don't want you to get in trouble with him."

Seren slides off my legs and turns to look at me, her fourteen-year-old face full of wanting. I lift my lips into a smile for her, though I know it is a pathetic attempt to ease her worries. Perhaps Seren knows it, too.

"Will you be back?" she asks. "I want to be on your squad again, Ceri."

"Honestly?" I shake my head. "I don't know. There's no way for me to guess what'll happen. And you shouldn't try, either.

You'll only make yourself sick thinking about it. Just trust in this moment, okay? Think about what it's telling you."

Seren takes a moment to consider before connecting her gaze with me again. "What does this moment tell you?"

A genuine smile touches my lips then. I reach out to brush Seren's hair with my fingers, my hand dropping to cup her cheek, sort of like Niah did to me.

"That I miss you and worry about you," I reply. Seren's lips mash together as she fights the urge to burst into tears, but she swallows and holds them back. I nod my support and say, "Be brave for your own sake, and don't think of me anymore. I am no longer a part of your world. Only consider your own survival. That's your priority now."

"No, Ceri. Please?" Seren shakes her head, reaching for my hands. I take them, but place them back on her lap. I meant what I said, even if it hurts both of us to consider it.

"I've got to go," I say. "Take care of yourself, little sister."

It's then that she throws her arms around my neck, and a small sob escapes as she presses her face into my shoulder. I rest my head on hers and give her one last squeeze. Then, before I cry, I give her a gentle push.

Seren's eyes never leave mine as she backs away. I wish I could be there for her, like Niah was for me. Fourteen was a tough age. Without someone to help me stand again when I fell on my face, I might not have survived. Seren needs a person like that too. But it can't be me.

"What about my gun?" Rhys asks as Seren wipes at her eyes and joins him again.

"You don't need it," I reply. "You can't use it worth a bish. Seren will protect you."

Rhys mutters something, then steps into line with Seren, who, with a renewed purpose, takes lead and starts acting like a real soldier. I chuckle and shake my head, proud of who she is becoming but also fearful of what she will face. No one deserves to die at that age.

Seren turns back to me one last time. "I won't tell the captain," she says, then glares at Rhys. "And he won't either, or I'll bust his head in."

"Hey, come on!" Rhys says, flinching.

Once they are gone, I sigh and get to my feet. I may have done the right thing here, but I still have much more to do.

Hang on, Efa.

TEST

Another level down, I return to the comfort of near darkness. I can still make out shelving and storage crates surrounded by machinery, tubing, and pipes that run from floor to ceiling and everywhere else. A rancid liquid drips from one of the nearby conduits. This must be a support level for the bio-systems above. It will be difficult to navigate, and I am still hurting from the succession of trials I have faced. Niah gave me a first aid kit and a few ampules of painkillers, but I'm reluctant to use them.

A sudden disturbance on the other side of the level sends me scrambling for cover. Soldiers. And not just a few. I hurdle a mass of pipes, heading toward a massive pump. It could be a spot to hide if I can slide my way into it.

Boots pound the floor behind me. Bish. I think I may have just gotten caught in the middle of a battle. Though if both sides are making this much noise, there should be darts filling the air. Blades should slip from sheaths. There should be complete mayhem.

One more spot to jump over, and I'll be clear of this fight. I'll just have to keep my head down.

But I don't make it.

Hands grab me, throwing me into a storage unit. My shoulder smacks a shelf. I bounce back and get slammed into the shelf again. Now my assailant presses themselves against me. Their arms shoot under mine and lock behind my back. I kick back with my heel and hit a shin. My attacker shouts and throws me into the shelf again with such force I nearly black out.

This is no boy or girl. It's an adult.

My head spins, and I lose my balance. My attacker puts me into a headlock and shoves my head down. Their knee jams into my spine, and my legs collapse. I go down, face forward, slowed only by the adult locking my arms in place. They pin me down even as I struggle, but they're stronger and heavier. Sheer force won't free me. If anything will.

"I've got absolutely no problem dispatching you right now," Captain Daga growls. "So unless you're looking to die, you'll calm down."

I comply, if only to save my energy. He has the advantage and could break my neck if he wanted to. He might, given his anger at me. Not that it would have mattered before. He couldn't care less what happens to the children under his command.

Boots surround us. It's A Squad, mostly, with a few of mine mixed in. Seren is there, breathing quick as her eyes widen. Rhys is next to her, grinning. So that's it. He called Daga. If I ever get out of this, I'm going to make sure that kid never grins again.

With a knee on my lower back, Daga binds my wrists together behind my back, then yanks me up to kneel. My leg burns with the forced position and I grit my teeth as I wince. He steps around to face me, grabbing my chin to force me to look up.

"I trusted you," he hisses. "I trusted you with an entire squad, and what do you do? Spit in my face. Why, Ceri? What the hyuk did I ever do to you that warrants this?"

"You would never understand," I reply, staring at him. "You and the other adults are clueless. We are not the enemy of the Fah—"

His hand comes across my face so fast, I don't catch it. My head snaps to the side as fire spreads across my cheek. Daga isn't holding back. I should be careful, or he'll make good on his threat to dispatch me.

"You have no idea what you are saying," he says loud enough for everyone to hear. "Someone put some wrong ideas into your head, and now you're all confused. That's still doesn't make what you did forgivable."

My former captain paces back and forth before me while the others stare. Most wear frowns. A few sneer. He's one to talk about putting ideas in someone's head. I can only wonder what propaganda he spread to make them believe I'm the enemy.

Daga crouches before me, staring into my eyes as if to peer inside my brain. I attempt to keep my gaze locked on his, but he's one of the few on this ship who can terrify me with only a look.

"You know, I didn't come down here for you," he says, putting a hand on his knee. "Your capture is not my primary mission, just an added incentive. I'm here to claim the lower levels for the Tarakh. With the right complement of soldiers,

I'll take them all, and perhaps keep a few to myself. As you probably can guess, there's way too many for us to hold. Our people can have what benefits them, and the rest will be my payment for all the years I've had to deal with you bish-heads."

"Does the chief know about that?" I spit back.

"The chief is dead."

My jaw drops.

"H...how?"

"Old age, of course. The man's been around since the beginning. Even with all the treatments the doctors pumped into him, his body just couldn't handle it any longer. Now his daughter, Generys, is chief." Captain Daga tilts his head. "Which reminds me. Where is Efa?"

"Efa?"

I can try to play dumb all I want, but somehow, he knows she's still alive. I don't understand why he would care. With his primary mission well defined, I'm just a distraction. Efa can't be any more than an annoyance.

"I know she's alive, Ceri. Where is she?"

"Why do you care?"

I whimper as he strikes me again. As I reel back, someone grabs my shoulders so I don't topple, but I am weary of pain. With my hands bound and not a few guns aimed at me, there's little I can do about it. Some members of A Squad wouldn't hesitate to put a dart through my skull if it came down to it, though they might sign their own death warrants if they did. Every single member of my squad would avenge me.

But that's not what I want. We're all Tarakh, and killing each other only strengthens the enemy. There is no reason to fight among ourselves.

"Don't you know?" Lines form on Captain Daga's forehead. "You spend every moment with her, and you don't have a clue why I might?"

I shake my head.

"Efa is Generys' daughter." He holds up a finger before I can speak. "I can see by the look on your face you didn't know, but you understand now, don't you? Efa is the heir to the Tarakh faction, and that's why you're going to tell me where she is, or I will put you through a universe of hurt before I end you."

If Daga meant to shock me, he failed. His words explain a lot, but his revelation changes nothing. If anything, it only strengthens my resolve to protect her. The adults can make all the claims they want. It doesn't change the fact that they treated her just like any other child.

Efa never talked about her family. Not in specifics. I wonder if she's even aware of who she is. Just like me, they pulled Efa from stasis. That means her grandfather, or even her mother, ordered her awakening. It's the why that I don't know, but it stinks of deviousness.

Still, this Generys, mother of my squad mate, might show me favor, especially if I can help her locate her daughter. Merek is a complication, of course, but if Efa became chief, that'd solve everything.

"I want to talk to chief Generys," I say.

"Oh, don't worry," Captain Daga replies. "You will. At your trial."

"No. I'm claiming the right of audience. Any Tarakh may request—"

"I don't need your explanation of the law, you stupid hyukl! I've been alive twenty years longer than you. And if you think I'm going to allow it—"

"You have to," Seren says. "It is the right of all Tarakh, even ones who have been accused."

A few voices join to support her words. Daga glares at all of them.

"You think I don't know that?" he shouts and points a finger at my supporters. "Now listen, you bish-heads. If we don't ensure the future of our faction by returning Efa to her mother, you can all kiss your ignorant asses goodbye. There must be continuity in our leadership, or someone will murder you while you sleep. That's why we can't allow traitors like this one to roam free. We must have order. You get it?"

"That doesn't stop me from claiming my rights," I say. "You can talk about lineage all you want, Daga, but we all have rules we have to follow. Even you."

Captain Daga stands, glaring at me.

"You are just asking for pain, aren't you? There's no rule that requires me to bring you back to base. In fact, it's an inconvenient task when I've got the entire bottom of the ship to cover."

"That doesn't exclude you from following the rules."

Captain Daga's foot goes into my stomach. I double over, retching as the pain spreads across my body. He pulls his gun and presses it against the back of my skull.

"Down here, I'll do whatever I want! No one is coming down to check up on me. All the other adults want is results, and they don't care how many of you brats I waste to make it happen! That means if I want to fill your skull with a load of darts, I can. Your request to speak with the chief is denied, and if you ask again, I will beat you senseless."

My hand covers my gut. I don't want to hurt anymore, but I can't allow him to just do whatever he wants. If I don't stand up to him, my squad will fall in line behind him, and I don't want that for them.

"I'm not the traitor here, Daga," I growl through my gritted teeth. "You are. You're the one breaking rules and taking whatever you want. If you think anyone here is going to fall for that bish, you're completely gone! You should step down before someone takes you down."

The children surrounding us shift. A few murmurs come from the back. My squad for certain, but maybe one or two of Rhain's former squad as well. All I know is that they all just witnessed what I did. What no child in my generation has ever done.

Daga smiles and paces before me as if I'm some kind of trophy he's won.

"Well, I suppose I should thank you, Ceri, for saving me a trip back up to base. You've given me plenty of reason that doing so would be dangerous to the faction, and we just can't have that." Daga powers up his gun. "Say goodbye to this life, you hyuking rat!"

SURPRISE

I close my eyes and await my execution. It's over for me. But that's not so bad. I won't have to suffer through this endless struggle at the hands of the adults. My one regret is that I couldn't see Efa through to freedom. She must learn to survive without me. At least she has Merek to help her, even if he is a lovesick fool.

A gun goes off. I wince, but the killing blow never comes. Then I realize it's not one shot. It's many. Someone is firing on us! The level turns into chaos as Daga and A Squad flee for cover. Darts fly over my head, coming from two directions. A crossfire. It is Fahrasi?

Seren and another of my squad grab me under my arms and drag me clear of the open space. We end up where I was intending to go, behind the massive pump I first spotted.

They cut the binds on my wrists, and Seren presses her gun into my hands. I look at it, then glare at her.

"What are you doing?"

"You're a way better shot than me!" Seren shouts.

I won't argue that point. Only Efa is more skilled when she wants to be. Still.

"I've already got one," I reply and hand it back to her. "Remember?"

Her impish smile tells me she does.

Our attackers still haven't shown themselves. That hints at only a few of them. The Fahrasi wouldn't risk such an assault, not unless they had a specific target. That has to be Daga. How they knew he was here is baffling.

Or perhaps it isn't them.

The fire pattern is familiar. One side shoots at a constant cadence, while the other is random. Then it switches to a count that I understand the moment I hear it. I've taught it to every member of my squad.

The edges of my mouth curve up. It's Efa. And Merek. It's got to be. Which means they're not here for Daga. They're trying to save me.

I turn to Seren. "Pull back. Both of you. Go back to your squad and keep your heads down."

"No! I'm staying with you!" Seren whines. "You need protection!"

"Yeah," my other squad mate says. "We're here to help you!"

"I don't need help. I need you safe. Now get there," I reply. "And that's an order."

Seren pouts. I won't allow it to sway me. She's safer away from here.

"Get out of here before I shoot you myself," I say with a smirk.

Seren presses her lips together and nods, but she's still a little hesitant. I shove her, not so gently this time, and she and her squad mate take off. I smile as I watch them. They are making me proud, remembering every detail of movement under fire that I taught them.

Now, to connect with Efa. I'll have to pinpoint her position or Merek's. Then get there—if I can. The mass of darts filling the air will make that difficult.

I peek over the edge of the pump. A Squad is well positioned and firing a constant volley toward the ladder. A few are pounding away at the top of a long duct, doing a good job of pinning down whoever's there.

Efa's there. She likes the high attack point as much as I do. But if they get around her crossfire, she's going to be in trouble, and with no way to communicate with her, I can't coordinate a defense.

A pair of A Squad rookies vault from their cover and charge toward Efa's position. They move with intention but not much skill. She could pick them off easily, but she didn't see them. I can help.

I take aim for their legs and fire three rounds. The first boy goes down. My next three darts find their target on the girl following. Their cries pierce my ears, and I grimace. They'll survive, but I'm not happy about hurting them.

I move before A Squad zeroes in on my position. And they will. Shots are already coming my way. I duck under a wide pipe and crawl past to escape.

There's a set of footholds that provide access to the top duct. Efa, if it's her—and I think it is—will hear someone coming up. She'll also be ready to drill a few shots into the top of my head if she doesn't know it's me. I'll need to come up with a way to let her know.

A dart glances off a nearby plate and scrapes past my arm, tearing a gouge in my shoulder. I twist from the impact, gritting my teeth to stop myself from crying out. The motion sends me into the side of the duct with a bang.

Efa will know someone is down here now, and that bash into the ductwork will attract attention from elsewhere. No reason to remain quiet any longer.

I press my lips together and whistle. Three short chirps, one long, two more short, and another long. It's Efa's name in an old code we found in the archive and taught each other. Others might know it, if they had half a mind to learn it. For now, it works.

"Ceri!" Efa hisses from the duct.

"I'm hit!" I reply. "Not bad, but let's get out of here before they send another attack forward!"

"Coming down!"

I lean against the nearest flat surface and fire a few rounds toward A Squad's position. By now, they're preparing to climb through the machinery and flank us. They might already be doing that.

A Squad responds to my fire by hurling a volley of shots across our entire position. I push against the wall to gain cover. The barrage is stronger than expected. They're coming for sure.

Efa slides down the duct access, grabbing my waist and pulling me back. I stumble, but she holds me up. A quick spin of my body and we stand face-to-face. Efa stares into my eyes, joy overcoming her. She regains her battle senses a second later.

"Where are you hit?" she asks, twisting me to check.

"I'm fine. Don't worry," I reply, putting my hands on her shoulders. "We need to move."

"Okay. Let's go. Merek is holding the ladder. I'm point."

I nod, and she takes off, routing back through a pair of massive air tanks. I check our backs and follow, close enough to move fast but far enough so we're not one big target.

The ladder is nearby. Efa will get us there before we have issues. A Squad will pursue, of course. If Rabbit is helping, he might have an idea on how to evade them. I wonder where he is.

Efa holds up a hand and crouches. I drop and spin, checking behind again. We're clear. Still, I maintain vigilance in as many directions as I can keep my attention on. We're almost free, but still at risk.

There's a yelp. Efa tilts back and collapses. Bish, she's hit!

I'm to her in seconds, grabbing her under her arms and lifting her up—cover first, wound next. If they surround us, that's it.

"Can you stand?" I ask, but Efa only moans. That's when I see the dart sticking from her ribs. And it's got barbs. My throat gets tight as I panic over what to do, but the only logical answer is to drag her to the ladder. As fast as possible.

"This is going to hurt," I say, dropping her gun back into her holster. "Hold on."

I wrap my arms around her and move, shuffling backward. Efa gasps and clutches to my arms. Her face devolves into a harsh grimace.

A Squad attacks from our right, forcing us into cover. I make for the rows of shelving just off my left. They're tall and thick—enough protection for me to mount a defense, but not to care for Efa at the same time. I fear she'll faint from the pain and I'll have to carry her.

I grab Efa's gun and put a heavy volley of darts in A Squad's direction. That should give them pause, maybe even long enough for me to remove the dart. I'll have to try.

The first aid pack opens as I rip it from my pocket. Painkiller is first. I take an ampule, pop the cap, and jab it into her shoulder. Efa whimpers in response and begs for more. Not yet. I need her awake. Another will put her out, and she will become difficult to handle.

"I'll give you another as soon as I can," I whisper. "Just try to hang on."

A quick check between the boxes on the shelves shows A Squad is holding. Good. I have half a minute at least, just enough time to get the dart out and patch the hole. Then I'll need to fight our way through to the ladder. The longer we wait, the tougher it will get. I can't fight all of Daga's troops at once, and I don't want to.

With one glace at Efa, I wrap the dart with my sleeve, take a breath, and pull, twisting as I go. Efa's back arches, her mouth flying open to let out successive, harsh breaths. I press her face to my body, muffling her cry. Efa grabs my leg and my arm, digging her nails into me and forcing me to bite my lip. But it's out.

I waste no time dropping the coagulant into her wound and covering it as best as I can. A raw ache in my shoulder is a reminder of the dart that grazed me. It may not be bleeding anymore, but it still needs to be patched up.

A few shots fly through the shelves, probing for us, perhaps trying to force us out into the open again. Daga won't commit his entire team until he's got situational awareness. That's to our advantage, but it won't last long.

Another dart shoots through the boxes, nearly missing my face. They've spotted us. I slide both guns through the boxes and squeeze off a few shots. It's met with a cry and the sound of bodies scrambling for cover. Bish! They were closer than I thought.

I put myself in front of Efa and prepare to let loose with another round. They'll be back, perhaps a bit more cautious than they were before. There will be more of them, too. I must be ready for anything.

Without warning, a hail of darts fly through the shelving, sparks exploding around us. I cover Efa to protect her. Each projectile whistles over our heads, the torrent of shots not stopping for over a minute. They're making their move, getting into position to surround us. We've got to escape. Now.

As the last of the shots ricochet off the metal shelves, I cover Efa's mouth and drag her back another row. She struggles, then relaxes, allowing me to move her. Everything gets silent then, our position hidden once again. I breathe through my nose until I've built up enough air in my lungs, then hold it, listening through the eerie quiet.

Seconds later, I hear their footsteps pressing softly on the deck. They're cautious, but not quiet enough. I follow the sound as they search the rows ahead of us, drawing closer with each step.

There's five of them, staggered well to avoid getting hit all at once. It's standard tactics for any side, and they're pulling it off well. These are no longer the rookies of A Squad. These are the soldiers I know. They'll beat me, given the chance.

My back hits a wall. I freeze. No retreat from here and no winning in a shootout. If I don't think of something, we're done. They're moving quickly to flank us.

Efa groans and reaches out for me. I've got no free hand to comfort her, not without giving up half my defense.

One of A Squad's soldiers throws up a hand. They heard her, and now they'll find us. Then Daga will end me for certain.

Their acting leader motions for their team to get into position. They scramble, silent and efficient in their movements. It's still enough to wobble the shelving units. I'm surprised they're not secured to the deck. Perhaps someone moved them. Still, it's dangerous. They could topple with enough force.

They could topple...

With a single movement, I rotate onto my back and press my feet against the lower shelf. I inhale and, on the exhale, shove with all my strength.

Our attackers cry out as the shelves crash onto them, knocking over the next two rows with their bodies in between. That's it. I scoop Efa up and dash from the aisle, keeping my eyes open for the remnants of A Squad's assault.

Merek is right where Efa said he would be. Sayer too. He waves us on as Merek stares at Efa's limp body in my hands. I hope the bastard who shot her broke every bone in their body underneath those shelves.

Still, I pride myself on taking them out without killing them. I wonder if they would do the same to me if I was the one after them. A few might. The others can spend the rest of their lives as base workers for all I care. If they were stupid enough to fall for my maneuver, then the Tarakh do not need them as soldiers.

Not that I think of myself as much of a Tarakh soldier anymore.

OPTION

"It's bad, isn't it?" Merek asks as we slip into a room on one-hundred-seven. It's a berth, complete with two bunks, two desks, and a pair of lockers so close together they threaten to topple over each other. The plastic wrapping remains on everything. I can only think this was to be a spillover level, used to accommodate additional people managing the ship, should they need it. Had anyone known it was here, we might have all enjoyed a comfortable place to sleep every night. Instead, I had to construct a nest from old clothes and torn fabric. It is a wonder I could sleep at all.

Merek lays Efa down on the lower bunk and kneels beside her. He whispers some words into her ear that she nods her head to, then he brushes the hair from her face. The medicine is keeping her calm, but it's only a matter of time before her agony returns.

"I can't tell," I say in reply to Merek's question. "She needs a doctor, for certain."

"Don't we all," Sayer mutters, watching me care for my shoulder wound.

He goes still, hearing something. Impossible—there's no way they found us this quickly. Not after the chaos we put them in. But if it's not A Squad, then who?

Sayer slides to the door, opening it a crack and peering out. After a moment, he whistles low and slides the door open. In steps Rabbit. He is wide-eyed and breathing heavily, and I tense at his unease. He shakes his head.

"No, no, no. Cannot stay here. Coming. They are coming." Rabbit glances at Efa, then beckons for us to follow him. "Bring her. We must, we must…"

Rabbit is right. To stay here for too long is to invite capture. Daga will tear every level apart to find us. I suspect he's become unhinged. All the adults are manic in their own way, but Daga is a special kind of disturbed, and I fear it's only gotten worse. Not only will he kill us without a second thought, but he will waste every soldier under his command to accomplish it.

"Okay," Merek says, moving to scoop Efa up again. "We're ready to go. Take us all the way to the machine access, Rabbit, and don't stop."

"No. We can't go there anymore," I say, knowing full well the reaction it will get.

"What? Why?" Merek turns on me, his eyes full of fire. When I don't answer, it only enrages him more. "Did you just come up with that? Why? Are you trying to get us back for leaving you? You went off without telling us! We had every right to be mad at you for that."

"Hey, man. Noise." Sayer raises a hand to stay Merek's approach, but his squad mate pushes past and continues toward me, leaving Efa on the bunk.

"Hyuk noise." Merek points a finger at me. "Explain yourself before I think you're trying to push Efa and me apart."

"Why would I do that?" I shake my head and stare back at him, stunned at his reaction. I'd expect him to be upset, but to accuse me of trying to sabotage their relationship after all I have sacrificed for them? "You're overreacting."

"Am I?"

"Merek, please..." Efa moans. He turns a worried glance at her, then comes back at me, his rage intensified by his concern for her.

"Not until Cerl tells me why she's trying to ruin everything. And we just saved your life! Is that how the Tarakh repay kindness? No wonder we've lost so much to your faction. You just take what you want and destroy everything else."

"Come on, man," Sayer says. "Back down already."

My eyes narrow at him, and I realize my hand is on my gun. It's a reflex, not an intent, yet that's how much his words have disturbed me. The boy before me isn't the casual infiltrator that I first met and nearly killed, were it not for Efa's interference. No. Before me is the embodiment of the faction I call enemy.

"Remember, your beloved is also Tarakh," I spit back. "What you say about me, you say about her."

Merek's mouth drops open, and he steps back. Perhaps he did not expect me to say that. I am glad that's all I've done.

We're already in a treacherous situation. There is no reason to make it worse by fighting with each other.

"Go, go, go," Rabbit hisses, peeking out the door.

His words snap me back to our immediate crisis, clearer in my mind than it was before. I remember that I have a solution—a way to keep them safe that I've already chosen, yet am still reluctant to share because it means giving Efa up to a serious unknown.

Unless I go with them. Sayer could too, should he want. He'd stop me from feeling like an unwelcome extra. There's little point in leaving with them if I disrupt the two lovers, no matter how much I'd hate losing her.

Forget it. This is not about me. I'm not doing this for my benefit. Efa and Merek deserve to know that there's another option. Then they can decide what they wish, as long as it's not returning to base. We can't go back. Not when we've just become wanted criminals.

"We don't need to go to the machine access," I say. "I found another way."

Efa lifts her head and turns it toward me. A sparkle of hope pierces the weariness in her eyes. Merek and Sayer also let anticipation slip through the confusion on their faces. Even Rabbit distracts himself from his vigilant watch to pay attention. Now that I've said it, I can't withhold my secret any longer.

"There is no place safe for you on this ship," I say to Efa and Merek. "Nor for Sayer and me. But there's a way to be free of danger *off* the *Stratford*."

"What?" Merek shakes his head. "What do you mean?"

"I found a capsule. An emergency pod. I suppose it's there in case of a serious disaster. It's got enough space for twenty and supplies for the same that could last four of us half a year. Some of it is bad, so we'd need to scavenge from the other pods, but—"

"Wait." Sayer holds up a hand. "Are you saying there's more than one pod?"

Rabbit makes a sound of delightful surprise at the idea. It's strange to consider it, but it seems like he wants to go with us. I'm not sure I understand why. He's not in danger of being executed.

"There are four, at least on ninety-five where I found them. There may be more, but we only need one."

"No," Merek says. "No, it won't work. They'd find us there before long."

"But Ceri said we could be free *off* the ship," Sayer says as he considers my words. When he realizes what I meant, he looks at me, his eyes widening. "You want to launch the pod!"

"And go where?" Merek asks.

"The pod detected a suitable planet...nearby. I'm not saying it would be easy, but no one would come after us. Not even if they wanted to. We'd have a real chance, better than anything we'd ever have here." I look at Sayer. "You wouldn't have to go, but the rest of us are criminals now. This is our only real option."

Sayer shakes his head and says, "I'm not staying here."

Merek gasps. He's thought of something, and I wonder if I should be wary.

"We should wake our families up and take them with us!" Merek's voice is close to shouting. "We can get them. Right now. I know where they are!"

Sayer glares at his squad mate once again breaking noise discipline—so does Rabbit. They're right to. One hint of our location and every squad will come down on us.

Regret presses me down, and I drop to a crouch, resting my arms on my knees. Merek is asking for something we cannot realize. He's so desperate to have it, he doesn't even understand the problem with trying.

"You can't," I say. "We don't know how to wake them. If we do it wrong, they'll die. Your family is better off in stasis until the ship reaches its destination. They'll be better equipped for survival than we'll ever be. And they may not want to go with us, even if we begged. I'd take my chances here, too, if I wasn't being hunted."

Merek hangs his head, knowing my words are truth. I wish they weren't. Yet what kind of connection would we have with our families now? I am not sure my parents would even recognize who I've become, and none of them would understand the hell the adults have forced us into.

"But Efa," Merek says, pointing at her with his hand. "We can't take her somewhere with no doctors or medical facilities. That could kill her as much as staying on the *Stratford*."

"True." I nod, considering. "I know someone we can trust. They will get her help before we leave."

"Then I will go with you. You'll need help to—"

"Not a good idea."

"Then take Sayer. He can help to carry her."

"No. I may know you, but no other Tarakh does. I don't want to complicate the situation. Go to the pod and wait for us there. That is the safest place for you now. Rabbit, you should go with them too."

"I will, I will. Going is good," Rabbit says as he hops in a crouch. "Let's go."

Merek narrows his eyes at me. I get that I've damaged his trust. There is little I can do about that now. If he truly wants to be with Efa, he'll have to risk me stealing her away from him. I would, given the opportunity. He may make her happy, but his love for her has only ruined her chances here. I won't call it a life. It was never that.

Still, what we knew before was easy in comparison. We fought the Fahrasi. They fought back. It was familiar. If we go, it will turn our lives upside down for the second time. Only fools would try this.

"Ceri's right," Sayer says. "Let her take care of Efa. While we're waiting for them, we'll pack the pod with as much as possible and have it ready for the moment they show up. Better to have more than we need than not enough."

Merek sighs, drawing a hand across his chin. His brow wrinkles and his body droops until he turns to Efa. Their eyes meet, and they gaze at each other for a long moment. Efa presses her lips into a smile for him, and his body lifts. It's only then that Merek gives me a nod. This may not be what he wants, but he knows this is their best chance.

Now to find Niah.

SEPERATION

EFA CLINGS TO MY back as I scale the ladder to level one-hun-dred-five. It's a risk to be moving toward our pursuers, but the pods are in this direction, too. After waiting an hour, Merek, Rabbit, and Sayer will all come this way, though they'll be moving up through the hull. I don't have that luxury, not if I want to meet Niah.

The one advantage I have is knowing Niah and her scout team will be out ahead of Daga's primary force by a few levels. I think I can spot them, but if they don't want me to know they're coming, I might not. That would mean trouble, of course. Niah may have told her scouts that I escaped, and they'll believe it—until they spot me climbing right toward them.

That's why I'm hoping this level, with its increased illumination, will benefit my plan. The extra light comes from monitor screens lining the walls just down the corridor, and there are many more here. We noticed them on our way down. There are a few shadows for them to hide in. But that's a problem for Efa and me, too.

I am doing my best to stay quiet, but Efa's weight on me adds an extra challenge. Plus, with all the medication in her, she's not aware of how much noise she makes. I gave her another dose to keep her calm, but all it's done is make her brain muddled. She needs constant reminding to keep her mouth closed.

Especially now that I just heard something.

"Efa," I hiss. "This time you really need to shut up. I need to listen."

The sound happens again. No doubt it's a footstep. A rustle of a pack, too. That's not good. Niah and her team wouldn't be so careless. Unless...

"Bish!"

I drop as a dart ricochets off the wall just beside us. It's not Niah. It's A Squad. But why are they here?

Then I understand. Daga wants revenge so badly, he'll do anything, including break his own rules on tactical movement to get me.

The whine of guns surrounds us. Darts scream over our heads. They're trying to flank. It's too obvious a move. I can stop them, but not with Efa on my back. I've got to hide her so I can fight back.

There! I grip Efa's arms and dart in between a bank of machines, sliding Efa off my back and ripping my gun from its holster. A quick check on her and I dash out, sending a volley of metal down one direction of the corridor. Let them think I'm only firing one way. That'll bring the other side to me. I'll be ready for them.

Seconds after, a young soldier appears and freezes, surprised by my sudden appearance. A sharp strike with the butt of my weapon takes him out. I won't kill children if I have the option.

More rounds impact the wall—too close. I dive away from the machines and take cover across an intersection. There's little here to protect me, though. I'll have to keep moving.

As I peek out, two young boys charge down the hallway. Daga is throwing raw recruits at me. They raise their pistols and fill the air with half their ammunition, hitting nothing. I almost feel bad for hurting them.

The moment they pass the corner, I spring out, knocking one back with my outstretched arm. The boy yelps and piles into his partner. Before I can neutralize them, two more fire at me from the cross passage. I spin and fly down the opposite way.

Right into the trap.

Two veteran A Squad fighters pop out from behind a machine bank. The first takes a swing at me with his blade. I dodge and catch his wrist, moving past him. His arm wrenches back, and he screams in pain, his body twisting as he tries to stop me from dislocating his shoulder.

The other raises her pistol and fires. I release the boy and pivot to dodge. A dart slices across my forearms. I wince as I lunge forward, driving my elbow at her face. She deflects the hit, but my fist comes around to pound her cheek. The girl grunts as the impact sends her into the wall.

The boy charges me, his blade aimed for my chest. I drop and punch him hard in his gut. He doubles over with a loud cough and drops to his knees. A strike across his jaw knocks him out.

The two other boys are back, firing so fast they endanger their own squad mate. She reacts by tackling me. We hit the floor and wrestle for dominance.

The girl is quick. She climbs over me and pulls her blade out, swinging at my hands. I jerk them away but realize my mistake. My body is unprotected. The girl plunges her blade toward my chest with both hands.

I roll my hips just enough to destabilize her. Her attack goes wide but still catches me on my shoulder. I cry out and drive my hand into her middle, knocking the air from her lungs. She clutches at her chest, gasping.

She's off me in the next second. I grab my gun and run, but the darts keep coming. They're driving me away from where I left Efa. That's a problem. I need to find a defensible position and make a stand.

I spot an open storage locker and slip in, taking up position on the near wall, my weapon at the ready. If any of them come in here, they're done.

The wound on my shoulder burns something fierce. I suck air through my teeth and touch two fingers to the wound. They're wet. The cut feels ragged, but it's shallow. The girl's blade must be old or chipped, and it only sends fire down my arm. I'm going to get her back for that.

"Where'd she go?" one of the young boys whispers. They're close. I take a deep breath and hold it, anticipating their entrance to my hiding spot.

"Don't know," another replies. "Weren't there two of them?"

Someone's radio crackles then, loud enough to give their position away but not for me to understand what's being said. I press against the wall and aim for the entrance. The moment one of them comes in, I'll fire.

"Hey, you two," an older male voice hisses. "Go that way, find the other one. She might be wounded. You can handle that. We'll take care of Ceri. She owes me for what she did to our squad."

I know that voice. The boy who enticed Rhain to fight me. He thinks I owe him, but it's the opposite. I bet he's the supervisor of these kids, too. This bish-head is putting rookies out front in hopes they'll slow me down enough for the experienced ones to take me out. I should be careful. Their plan almost worked.

If I can create a distraction for the toddlers, I can get back to Efa and get off this level. There seems to be more of them than regular A Squad vets.

I grin. We put such a dent in Daga's team that he had to pull in recruits to fill up the space. He needs the extra bodies because he's making a serious racket down here. The Fahrasi are sure to notice. Daga can't be caught short-handed while he's pounding on each level to find me.

Time to go on the offensive. It's the only way to get back to Efa. I push myself up and once again take a breath and hold it, listening for anything. A Squad is skilled, but they didn't learn from Niah the way I did.

There's a click. That guy turned his radio off. He's thinking it will help him be stealthy. Too late, I heard it. Now it's to my advantage that he can't warn anyone when I attack.

The moment his shadow appears, I tense—not yet—I'm waiting for his gun. Only when it sticks through the doorway will I move.

Now.

I strike, grabbing the barrel of his gun and shoving it upward. He yelps and jerks back as I rip it from his hands. The girl appears and blasts me with her light. I squeeze my eyes shut and plow forward, squeezing off a few darts. She shrieks, and I know my aim was good.

But the second I open my eyes, a fist slams into the side of my head. I'm knocked back into the locker, sideways. The boy charges in, his blade coming down. I raise my pistol to block it. The two weapons clash with a loud ping, and the gun flies from my hand.

He swings again while I'm still off balance. I pivot to evade, barely avoiding the edge of his knife.

My blade comes out, slashing up at his arms. He blocks it, but my foot slams into his knee and he drops. I thrust the pommel of my knife into his mouth. His teeth crunch and break under the force of my attack. The A Squad veteran moans as he bucks and topples over.

I scramble for my gun, quickly snatching it up and aiming for him. There's no need. The boy remains collapsed on the floor, writhing as he covers his mouth.

I'm out of the locker in the next second, ready for my next target. Only the girl is there, propped up against the wall and breathing heavy, her hand on her side. She looks up and glares at me.

"Go ahead, traitor. Shoot," she says and spits. "But Captain Daga will find you, and he will avenge me."

I scan the corridor for combatants. Clear. My attention returns to the wounded girl. She's terrified, though she's fighting hard to hide it. Even if I had no pity for her, I could no more kill her than I could Rhain. She's Tarakh.

I also don't have time to make conversation. Efa needs me.

"Sorry," I say. "You don't get to die today."

I swing my foot and put her out. Someone will find her soon enough.

All seems clear as I approach the spot where I left Efa. I don't expect it is. To test my suspicion, I aim my pistol at a monitor and pull the trigger.

Sparks fly across the corridor. Someone yells out and fires their weapon. A second one joins in. They've set up a defensive line by the ladder. Good thinking, but I couldn't care less. We're not headed that way.

I grin and dash across the intersection, continuing to run until I reach the wall of machines. Efa's on the other side. I'll grab her, and we'll be gone before they realize what happened. With a quick check behind me, I rush between the machine banks, ready to scoop Efa up and keep moving.

But she's not there.

"No! Hyuk!" I scream, careless of giving away my position. They got to her first. I pound my fist into a computer, letting out my rage for my stupidity in neglecting my friend and squad mate. Efa was relying on me to care for her, and I failed her.

A boy no older than twelve flies in, shouting at the top of his lungs in a pathetic attempt to scare me. My pistol comes up, and I thrust the barrel into his forehead. He gasps and drops his weapon, throwing his hands into the air.

"Where is she?" I shout. He can only whimper as his face turns into a bawling mess.

Darts fly past my head. Another attacker from behind. I grab the boy's shirt and whirl around, tossing him at the new threat. The two go down like a pair of toy blocks.

A Squad zeroes in on me, firing lights and rounds in my direction. I bolt from the bank of machinery, headed across the level to the other ladder. A pair gives chase, followed by a taller, larger individual. An adult.

Daga.

"There's no escape, Ceri!" he calls. "I've got Efa, and I'm coming for you. And once I find you, I will make sure you understand how wrong you were to defy me."

My body aches at the thought of leaving Efa with that monster. All the more reason to find Niah and beg her to take custody of her. She'll take care of Efa and make sure she gets to a doctor quickly.

I stop and look back, and for the first time in my life, I say a prayer. For Efa.

Then I'm gone.

REFUSAL

Level one-hundred-three. I stop near a doorway to…No, what it is doesn't matter. I'm exhausted and wounded, and I need to rest, if only for a minute—anything to get strength back into my legs. At least I've stopped bleeding. In my rush to escape A Squad's vengeful assault, I forgot about my wounds.

Other than away from Daga, I don't know which direction I should go. I can't bring Efa to Niah for help, and with Daga's change in tactics, Niah's team won't be where I need them to be. If I run into them now, it would just be sheer luck.

I've severely messed up, and that I've no plan to save Efa from that bastard twists my insides hard. I pull my knees up to my chest to soothe my worry, and I feel better almost instantly. The desire to rest my head upon them is strong, and a moment later, I give in. All I need is a minute.

Just a minute.

As I close my eyes, Efa's smiling face comes into view. A year ago, we had a day that I can only consider a miracle. No fighting, no training, no danger. Even the adults were too busy to deal with us. Efa and I stole some provisions from the pantry and found a spot far away from everyone. We did nothing but gorge ourselves and giggle for twenty-four hours. I long to have a day like that again.

A deliberate patter of feet sends me into alert. The sound came from just down the corridor. I press into the doorway, sliding my pistol from its holster. I'm going to be mad if A Squad caught up to me this quick. It would be a wonder if they moved all those newbies and wounded up even two levels.

No. Wait. Did I fall asleep?

I curse my stupidity for giving into my fatigue like that. Now I'm about to be surrounded by who-knows-what adversary. The way they move makes me think they're experienced, possibly familiar. I won't get away with any lazy combat maneuvers here.

Unless...

On a gut feeling, I put my gun away and pull out my light, blasting its beam down the hallway in both directions. If it's Fahrasi, they'll just capture me, perhaps even treat my wounds and give me some food. That's more than I've had in two days.

But if it's a Tarakh squad, I don't want to fight. They're likely not even be a part of Daga's group. I should be able to convince them I'm returning to base.

Steps approach from all directions now. They're making no secret of their presence, just as I did. They're still disciplined enough to stay out of my light, however. Hope wells up within me.

This could be Niah's team, after all.

I place the light on the ground so its beam hits the ceiling and illuminates the surrounding area. We'll all know who we're dealing with now. I stand to show I'm not a threat.

"Hands behind your head," someone hisses. "Down on your knees."

Before I even get my arms up, someone kicks the backs of my knees and presses down on my shoulders. I drop and grunt, the shock of the sudden fall sending ripples of pain through my body.

"Easy, bish-head," I say. "I'm wounded."

"Like I care, traitor," a male voice shoots back. "The only thing you deserve is to die a painful death."

He kicks me again, and I drop onto my hands, coughing. I grit my teeth at this boy's overblown sense of self-righteousness. If he tries it again, I might have to remind him of who I am.

"Enough," Niah says, stepping into the light. Her face goes hard when she looks at me. A shake of her head communicates her displeasure well. I attempt to lighten her mood with a smile and hold my arms out for her to help me up.

"You don't touch her!" The butt of a pistol slams into my back, and I snarl as I catch myself from collapsing.

"I said enough!" Niah growls out a flurry of curses at her squad member, slapping the gun from his hand. She points to someone behind me. "You and you. Go watch the ladders and the rail system. And you let me know if you hear so much as the air move. Got me?"

"But—" the boy says before Niah's raised hand shuts him up.

"We don't need any hyuking incidents. I've got Mari here to watch her. She's a better shot than either of you, so go make yourselves useful and make sure no one gets on this level."

"Aye." His voice makes clear his reluctance, but a moment later, he and his partner take off. Niah sighs and folds her arms, moving closer until she towers over me. Mari comes to her side—as close as Niah will allow. Neither seem glad to see me.

"What the bish are you doing?" Niah asks me through clenched teeth. "You're going to die this time, you know that? Captain Daga is planning to make your execution as painful as he can, and I'm sure he's already made the preparations. I should just save him the trouble and push you out an airlock myself. At least then I wouldn't have to watch you do the hyuking stupidest thing I've ever seen. Why are you here, Ceri?"

I gave away my position, and Niah knows I wouldn't have done that without reason. This is when I beg her to get Efa away from that evil man. Of course, Niah will go into a rage and curse me to the end of my lineage for being so reckless, yet I've got a feeling after all that she may just say yes.

"I'm sorry, Niah," I say and bow my head. "Efa needs your help. A Squad shot her with a barbed dart. I got it out, but I can't tell if she's got internal bleeding. They attacked us and took her."

"And you want me to what? Go ask Captain Daga, 'Pretty please, may I have Efa?'" Niah presses her hands to her hips and leans over me. She's about to lecture me until I hate myself for coming to her at all. "Did you even consider how that will happen?"

"Yes, I thought about how that could be a risk for you," I reply, remembering to stay humble, even if it's only for show.

Niah curses under her breath and shakes her head again as she stares at me with more anger in her eyes than I've ever seen as a recruit. I did some stupid stuff back then, but this might top all those mistakes combined.

Now all she'll need to do is make more of a show for her squad member and then send her away so she can talk to me alone. Just like last time. Efa's going to be alright.

"I can't help her," she says, her tone flat. "But you still can. Go back to base and fall at the mercy of the chief. Tell her..." Niah tosses out a hand. "It doesn't matter what you say, but at least your trial will be fair, and Efa will get help from a doctor."

I suck in a breath and hold it. If Niah is pretending to turn me down, she is doing an impressive job of making it seem real.

"You're going to trust her to go back on her own?" Mari turns to face Niah, waving her hands at her squad leader as she complains. "She escaped the last time! What makes you think she'll listen to you?"

"You'd do the same for any of your squad mates," Niah replies. "And you're dead."

"Huh?"

In a single movement, Niah snatches Mari's weapon away and grabs the girl by the back of her neck to swing her toward me. Mari yelps, but she's helpless to stop it. Niah holds her in place, making sure Mari looks at me.

"You just turned your back on the deadliest Tarakh soldier who ever lived," Niah hisses. "It's only out of respect for me she didn't break your neck in the three seconds you got distracted. Now until I tell you, keep your gun on her and do nothing else. That's the only way you get to live. Get it?"

Mari nods with a nervous shake of her head as she eyes me. The whites of her eyes are more apparent than they were before. Niah drops the gun back in her hands and turns her glare on me.

"You shouldn't have tried this, idiot. Now you're in a position you can't defend. Did you really think I would just make everything all better with a wave of my hand?" Niah clenches her fist and shakes it at me. "There's something seriously wrong with you, Ceri. My orders are to hunt you down and bring you to Captain Daga and only him. Understand? You were wrong to expect something else."

I only stare at her, biting my lip to stop the emotion from reaching my face. Her words have turned my insides fragile. I can't tell if they're real or how much of it is just an act. Even if it's all a show, it's still hurtful to hear her yell at me with such fury. It was only two days ago that she was wiping tears from my face. Now they're threatening to return, just because Niah has turned cold to my plea.

"I had nowhere else to turn," I say, my voice breaking. "You've been the only one who cared for us. There is no one else I can trust."

Niah's lips quiver, but only for a second. She recovers way faster than I ever could, yet that small moment of truth is enough for me to regain my courage.

"The only thing you can trust me to do is turn you in," Niah says. "Now you can return to base on your own, or I can drag you up ninety levels by your hair. It's your choice."

It's impossible for me to know how I should react to her ultimatum. I suppose I should just go along with the game, if it's a game at all. Perhaps my showing up like this has taken away her space to maneuver. Perhaps this is all she can offer me. I hate the uncertainty of it all.

"I'm not the criminal you think I am," I say.

"That's a lie," Niah shoots back. "Nobody made you attack the captain. And nobody made you steal that medicine. There are witnesses. And casualties. So you're going to accept your punishment and pray our new chief will have some crumb of compassion for you. Now get moving, or I will make you move."

I hang my head, defeated. She's as stuck as I am and giving the best advice she can, given the circumstances. There's no chance of her getting Efa, not unless she has the backing of the chief. And the only way for that to happen is for me to beg for it. I'll have to if I want to protect Efa. There's no telling what that deranged man could be doing to her right now.

Niah pulls out her pistol and powers it on. "Do I need to make myself any clearer?"

A shiver runs down my back as I shrink from her rage. It's not the first time that she's aimed her weapon at me, but it is the first time I believe she'll use it. I shouldn't have tried this, but I was out of options, and desperate to save Efa. Now I've backed Niah into a corner, and all she can do is protect herself.

"I will return on my own," I say, even as my throat gets tight.

I look into Niah's eyes, attempting to find some hint that she's still pretending, but she's closed off her emotions and pushed me away. She's trying to survive, just like all of us, and I've become poison to her. To disobey Daga's orders a second time is risking death.

"Mari will escort you to the ladder. I have to report this to the captain." Niah turns to Mari. "Give her your doses of painkiller and your canteen."

"What?" Mari blinks. "Why?"

"Because you won't need them, and she will. And you're dead again." Niah pokes Mari in the forehead. "Get that through your skull if you want to live another year."

Mari sulks all the way to the ladder, even as she makes every attempt to be vigilant. I give her no reason to be wary or afraid. Not until we reach the ladder. Then I stop and turn to face her. Mari steps back as she raises her pistol. Even now, when she has the advantage, she's still terrified of me. I suppose I've been putting that fear into soldiers, Tarakh and Fahrasi alike, for years now.

"Niah's right, you know," I say. "Follow every word she tells you. It'll keep you alive. It has for me."

Mari can only stare, unsure how, or even if, to respond. She doesn't need to. I was her five years ago and can guess every thought that's running through her mind. I wonder what fourteen-year-old me would think of this situation. Likely nothing. At that age, I didn't expect to live this long.

OBSTACLE

As I leave the ladder coming from level ninety-eight, I take a deep drink from Mari's crescent-shaped flask, draining almost all of it. I can afford such a luxury and a minute to rest. When I reach Merek, Sayer and Rabbit, I won't have time to do anything but talk.

I'll do as I promised Niah, but not yet. First, I must tell Merek what happened. I'm looking forward to that as much as I'm wishing for my arrest and sentencing. He'll blame me for losing Efa, and he'll be right to. What happens after that will be a mess.

Merek will need to be convinced not to make any hasty decisions. Having a doctor look after Efa, even if she's locked away, is still preferable to her being on some remote planet with nothing but basic first aid. As tired as I feel, I know I've got a major challenge ahead of me. Thank the ancestors that Niah let me keep my weapons. Mari didn't catch that little detail.

A beam of light hits me from down the corridor. I drop the canteen, my hand flying to my gun. There's a scramble of boots charging toward me. I crouch and raise the pistol at the light, ready to take it, or the person behind it, out.

"Ceri, wait!" a female voice says. It's Tegan. "We only want to talk!"

"Who's we?" I hiss back.

Rhain steps into the light, an intense stare on his face. He bares his teeth at me in a sinister grin. I turn my gun on him, knowing full well that Tegan and whoever else is behind the light will shoot if I do.

"We don't want to talk," Rhain says. "We want to bust your head in and drag your body to the captain. Just like you deserve, you traitor."

"Well, then—"

Rhain holds up a hand. "But I'm willing to make you an offer. Give me a rematch, and I'll let you continue on to base. That's right. We know where you're going. So does everyone else, and the more you delay, the closer they'll get. Captain Daga is looking forward to driving his knife straight through your heart."

I frown as I stare at him. Niah made her report on a wide broadcast. Smart. She's protecting me by letting everyone know my destination. Now Daga can't justify murdering me with some made up excuse. There are hundreds of witnesses who expect me to reach base alive now.

And here Rhain is, attempting to use it to his advantage.

"And if I refuse?" I say as the tip of my finger presses against the trigger. Tegan lowers herself into a stance, her hand halfway between raising it to plead with me and lowering it to grab her weapon. There's someone else next to her too, but the light makes them hard to see.

"You won't," Rhain replies.

I consider as I watch him. He won't be in any better condition than I am. That means he'll cheat again, and my body can't afford that. The alternative would be to take out the three of them before they can react to my first shot. Even at my best, that would be close to impossible.

"Perhaps not." I shrug. "I put you down hard last time. What makes you think this time is going to be any different?"

"Oh, it'll be different alright, because I'll be making sure I get payback for your dirty trick."

Leave it to Rhain to hold a grudge against me about a fight he forced me into.

"Yeah, about that." I grin. "How are the boys feeling?"

"Never better. Are we doing this, or am I going to turn your body into a pincushion?"

I tilt my head at him. The temptation to beat him senseless is strong, but I've got to get to Merek. That's the priority. My enjoyment of pummeling Rhain for the second time will have to wait.

"No," I reply.

"No?" Rhain shakes his head, his brow furrowing. He opens his mouth and shuts it, then raises his finger.

A volley of darts flies from down the corridor, catching one of Rhain's squad mates. The girl drops with a scream as the rest of us flatten on the deck. Tegan spins her light around, blasting its rays down the hall. I note five tall figures dashing for cover as I return fire.

"Bish! Fahrasi!" Tegan says. "We're exposed!"

"Beka!" Rhain dives for his squad mate, pulling her back from the firefight. She's hit in the shoulder—not lethal, but she'll be out of the fight. I slide her gun from its holster and toss it to Tegan.

"To the corner," I say, dropping to a crouch and moving.

Tegan and Rhain hurl a mass of darts down the corridor. A second later, they're dashing after me. I make sure our flank is secure, then ready myself for the attack. It's got to be a full squad after us, which means there are four more lurking, perhaps ready to circle around. We can't allow that.

"Cover the other side!" I say to Tegan, who nods, but Rhain holds her back.

"I'm still your field leader!" he shouts. "You go when I say!"

"Then say it!" Tegan shouts back.

"Not until Ceri agrees to a rematch!"

"Are you hyuking kidding me?" I put my gun around the corner and fire. "We're in the middle of a battle!"

"And you'll be responsible for getting us killed if you refuse again!"

I glare at him, wondering if he's joking. The look on his face says he's not. The Fahrasi may not kill us, but I won't take the chance to find out. We might evade them and slip past their line of attack, or we could slip back down the ladder, but for me, that's the wrong way. Ninety-five is where I need to be. Down guarantees my capture by Daga, and I'll choose the Fahrasi over him any day.

"We don't have time for this," Tegan says and dashes to the other corner, leaving me with her wounded squad mate. I look down at Beka, who stares back, a grimace on her face.

Her eyes dart past me, returning my attention to the attack. The Fahrasi may have gained ground. I slip my head around the corner to check.

And nearly smash into a charging Fahrasi.

The boy's eyes go wide. He tries to raise his gun, but I slap it from his hand. Beka grabs his legs and trips him. I drag him behind the corner and shove him against the wall. My hand covers his, and my gun goes against his head.

"They're coming!" Tegan hisses from her side of the corridor.

"How many?" I mouth to her. She raises four fingers. I was right—a full squad. We don't stand a chance without some leverage.

Rhain fires a few shots to keep their heads down. It gives me a minute to think. I'll only need five seconds.

"Hold your fire!" I shout. "We've got one of yours!"

"What are you doing?" Rhain's face is a tight fist of rage. "I'm in charge!"

"Not of me."

Everything goes quiet. The Fahrasi field leader is assessing the situation. If they're any sort of human, they'll want to save their squad mate from whatever evil fate they believe the Tarakh will force the boy into. Perhaps we should show them we're not the monsters they think we are.

"Okay," a male Fahrasi voice calls from down the passage. "Name your terms."

"You want your soldier—" Rhain shouts. I cut him off with my fist in his gut. He doubles over, clutching at his stomach. That will keep him quiet for a minute or two.

"All we want is to return to base," I say. "You let us off this level and agree not to follow us, and you can have him back unharmed."

The corridor goes silent again, except for the boy, who is panting hard as he stares at me. He looks to be about fourteen. A rookie, then. I suppose he's learned his lesson not to be so reckless. If his leader is a reasonable person, he might live to remember it.

"Acceptable," the field leader says. "But if you try something, we will attack with no hesitation and no mercy."

Tegan glances at me. I nod and rise, reaching down to pull the boy up. Better we're on the move before the Fahrasi decide to go back on their word. And they might, because that's what I would do.

I move to the other side of the boy to keep him between us. Tegan helps Beka up and looks to me for an order.

"Keep ahead of us. Rhain will cover our backs," I say to her. "Let's go."

We turn the corner and slip down the passage, moving fast and steady. The Fahrasi take up positions in the side hallways, their lights on to give us their location and to show just how outnumbered we are. Their threat is well taken, and I press my gun against our hostage's head to make sure mine is just as clear.

The ladder to ninety-six comes up fast. Tegan wastes no time in pushing Beka up the ladder. Then she drops to cover next to Rhain, who only smolders as he eyes the Fahrasi around us. His dislike of me taking charge is obvious, but he'd enjoy getting caught by the Fahrasi a lot less.

Without a word, Rhain flies up the ladder. I throw Tegan a glance, and she can only shrug, having no excuses for her field leader, though I thought he'd be an ex-field leader by now. Perhaps Daga forgot because he was so obsessed with finding me.

Tegan gives me the okay to go. I motion to the boy to move and fly up behind him, allowing Tegan to follow up just as fast. Once there, I turn to the Fahrasi boy, ready to release him back to his squad.

Until the barrel of a gun presses against my head.

"No, you don't," Rhain says. "We still have a duel to fight."

Tegan makes a noise of disbelief as she stands up. The Fahrasi's lights are already aiming up from below as they get into position and wait for us to return their squad mate. They won't have patience for a duel, and they'd quickly take advantage of our foolish distraction.

"Let it go already," I growl. "I never said I would, and you've got wounded to care for. You know that's the priority here."

Rhain's face goes red as he snarls. He knows I'm right, yet his ego would rather risk it all to fight me instead. I guess that's why Daga made him A Squad leader instead of me. I'd never be that stupid to put my squad at risk for my own selfish desire.

And right now, he's putting me at risk, too.

"Hyuk the priority. You and me. *Now*." Rhain hands his gun to Tegan, and he drops into a stance. I just stare at him, sighing over his severe level of stupidity. Rhain won't stop until one of us goes down.

So I shoot a dart into his thigh.

Rhain drops with a cry, grasping his leg. The Fahrasi shout from below, threatening to come up if we don't return their squad mate now. I wave a hand at the boy, releasing him, and he wastes no time sliding down the ladder. They ask a few questions to make sure he's okay, and I think the boy answers in the positive.

Then I turn to Tegan, who presses her lips together, unsure of what happens next. She doesn't want to fight me, and certainly I have no intention of doing that, either.

"You coming?" I ask, to which Tegan takes a breath and nods with a glance down at Rhain.

"What about him?" she asks.

"He can cover our retreat, like he should have been doing. Then he can call for someone to come get him," I reply and dig a shot of pain medicine from my pocket and toss it to him. Rhain snatches it up and slams it into his leg. Once it kicks in, he glares at me with an expression I'd expect from a five-year-old who just had their toy taken away from them.

The Fahrasi will leave him alone. He's got no worth to them, and I suspect their direction is down, toward Daga and his team. We are not the threat they seek.

Tegan kneels down and gets her shoulders under Beka's arm to help her up. The girl winces as she stands, unsteady on her feet. Beka needs help now.

So we shoot across the level, together, yet each with our own motivations: Tegan to save her squad mate, and me to deliver the worst news Merek will ever hear.

FAREWELL

As we ascend to ninety-five, I catch the flash of a light and the clunk of something heavy. The door to the pod. Someone just went inside. Or more than someone. Sayer and Merek. Rabbit too. They must have been moving fast to get here this quickly. The edges of my mouth curl up before I catch myself so Tegan doesn't see. But I was too slow. She just heard and saw everything I did.

"What is this level?" Tegan asks as she kneels to lay her unconscious squad mate down on the deck. Beka couldn't handle the pain and collapsed twice, forcing us to carry her. So we patched her up as best as we could and gave her an extra dose of pain meds to make it easier to move her up the ladders.

"Emergency pods," I say, once again taking in the four massive tubes that cross the length of the level, opposed only by the rows of lockers that run perpendicular to them. Inside those lockers is the means to help Tegan's squad mate.

Yet I'm hesitant to move. I haven't found the words to explain to Merek how I failed Efa. And him. And the moment I do, he will turn his every emotion against me. I won't blame him for it. Everything I promised him may never happen now.

To my relief, I realize we've got to clear the floor of threats before we cross the open space and make ourselves easy targets. There's no sense having a difficult discussion with Merek if I'm about to walk into danger.

Which means I will need to explain the situation to Tegan before she meets him...and shoots him, fearing another attack from the Fahrasi. I don't know how she'll take what I have to tell her, but there will be a disaster if I don't.

"How do you know that?" Tegan asks, a hint of suspicion in her voice. To answer, I will have to tell her how Efa and I came to be down this far—a question that I expect she wants to ask but hasn't yet.

"Listen, Tegan, I am going to tell you something, and it is going to be hard to believe. But I swear to you, every word will be true, and you must trust me that what I've been doing is the best for everyone involved."

Tegan shifts and curls her lower lip in. Perhaps somewhere in her mind, she knows I am no enemy. It'd be good if that was true, as I don't know how she will react to what I'm about to tell her. It's promising that she hasn't made a move for her weapon. Still, what I will say will challenge her beliefs.

"I'll listen," Tegan says. "But I warn you, Ceri. If you confess to me you're a traitor, I will do whatever I need to protect our faction, and that means we could fight. I don't want that."

"I'm not a traitor," I say, shaking my head. "We only hope to—"

Tegan throws her hand across my mouth, but I've already stopped talking. I heard what she did—the hum of an electrical motor getting louder. The sound comes from the far side of the level and sends small vibrations through the deck.

"The rail system is active," Tegan whispers.

That means Daga and at least part of his team are on their way up. It will be bad luck if they stop here.

"Rhain called for help," Tegan says, stating what we all knew would happen but also adding a concern. Daga would have asked Rhain what happened, and Rhain would have had told him the truth.

I squeeze my hands tight. They're after us. I'm certain of it.

"We need to move Beka," I say.

"Why?" Tegan asks. "They're only after you."

"Do you really trust Captain Daga to believe you when he catches the two of you with me?"

Tegan presses her lips together. That's enough of an answer. I motion to her to help me lift Beka and get moving again. Tegan nods and gets behind Beka's shoulders, resting the girl's head on her forearms.

I scan the level for a hiding spot. There are plenty of shadowy spaces here, but we can't rely on them. Daga is thorough. If he stops here, he will check every dark space on this level. No good.

But then a better idea hits me.

"Let's go to the pod! Merek and Sayer are there! We can…"

Bish. What have I done?

Tegan pauses, her eyes narrowing. I sigh and lower Beka's feet back to the deck. Tegan continues to stare.

"What are you planning, Ceri?" Tegan hisses. "Tell me. And who the hell are Merek and Sayer?"

"You shouldn't know. It's dangerous for you to know," I reply to dissuade her. It's useless. Tegan has made the connection.

"You're escaping on one of those pods, aren't you?"

I swallow hard. Tegan might want to come if I gave her the answer. We'd have space, of course, and enough supplies. But she might also hate I'm running away and do everything to stop me. And then, Merek and Sayer. And Rabbit. What do I tell her about them?

Before I can make a reply, light streams out from the rail system doors, flooding the dim level in a bath of illumination. I'm frozen in trepidation, wondering if it means Daga is here.

My wait for an answer is short. A few seconds after the light, the doors open.

Five members of A Squad burst forth, setting up a defensive line as the rest of Daga's team slips out. The captain follows, a glare running across his face as he searches the level.

The breath in my lungs escapes as my chest gets tight. My body screams to move. Now.

"Come on!" I say, picking up Beka's feet again. "We still have cover!"

Tegan holds in place, and I stop short, throwing my foot out to keep from tripping. I shoot her a glance in confusion.

"Beka and I will take our chances with the captain," Tegan says. "I have no idea what you're up to, and I'm not interested in finding out. Captain Daga, to me, is a known risk. You..."

I glance towards the approaching soldiers. We're still hidden from view, but not for long. If I can get to the corner between the lockers and the tubes, I may slip by as they search.

"Fine, but I'm warning you, Tegan," I say, letting go of Beka's feet to move my hand to my gun. "If you even so much as hint that I'm here..."

"I won't." Tegan watches me for a moment with a wistful look in her eye. Then she nods toward the pod. "Go."

She's made her choice, and I can't wait. I bolt—slinking toward the tubes where deep shadow still exists—and drop, skidding on my knees into the corner and dragging myself under the curve of the tube.

"Over here!" Tegan shouts. "A Squad! Beka needs a medic!"

Daga barks a command, and several pairs of feet rush down the alleyway toward her. Someone shines a light on her as she kneels, resting Beka's head in her lap.

"Sir! Beka's been shot!" an unfamiliar boy soldier shouts.

"Send the rail car up," Daga says. "Get a medical team to come down."

"Sir? Shouldn't we just send them up?"

"When I am satisfied that they're clear and not a second sooner. The rest of you secure the level."

Bastard. He's making Beka wait until someone else can come deal with her. Meanwhile, she suffers. Tegan will care for her as best as she can, but getting shot hurts like hell, and the longer it takes to get the dart out, the higher the chance of a complication. Beka may never fully recover.

I peer out to scan for any sign of Efa, hopeful to see her. It's doubtful she's here. Daga should have sent her back to base already. Not to make sure she's properly cared for, of course. He'd want to remove any chance of me getting her back, and as wounded, she'd only be a burden on his team's movement.

Daga's already questioning Tegan about me. That was guaranteed to happen, but if any of my C Squad is here, it could also create an opportunity. They'll be eager to know what's happened to me, and while they're trying to find out, they won't be focused at all. I can move with less risk of being found.

Tegan better do as she promised. My threat to her wasn't a bluff. I will keep my pistol out and my finger on the trigger in case she gives me away. The first two shots will be for her. The rest will be for Daga. Who knows what happens then, but if A Squad shoots me dead in revenge, it will still be worth it. We children need to be free of him. For good. Even if I have to die to make it happen.

To her credit, Tegan skirts around the truth. She can't deny that I shot Rhain, but she mentions how I helped carry Beka a few levels before leaving. Daga isn't impressed and shakes his head in disgust. Still, a few others shift at Tegan's words. They believe her and wonder if I am really the enemy the adults have made me out to be.

"Captain!" one of my former squad mates calls. "The rail car is back!"

"Good. Escort the medical team over here immediately," the captain calls back.

That was fast. Maybe the system moves at a quick clip, but it would still take time for a medical team to assemble and bring themselves and their equipment back down here. For children, adults never move with urgency.

A high-pitched tone blasts from speakers in the ceiling, followed by a pair of lights flashing just outside the pod's hatch. I catch my breath, thoughts racing through my mind as to the meaning of the alarm. Whatever is happening, it doesn't sound good.

"What the hyuk is that?" Captain Daga spins toward the tube, staring at it along with everyone around him. They remain confused for longer than he does. In the next moment, he waves a hand at it and says, "Someone shut that off!"

Before anyone can move, the whine of guns screams from the rail car. There's a mass of cries and shouts as soldiers burst through the car doors, firing in every direction.

Fahrasi.

The level turns into pure anarchy. Weapons fire multiple times every second. The hail of darts screeching through the air cuts down anyone caught standing. Daga and his team race for cover wherever they can find it and unleash their own deadly storm of metal at their attackers. Tegan drags Beka toward the ladder and attempts to slide the girl down it.

And in this chaos, I see my chance to escape.

I jump to my feet but pause. Those lights are still flashing, and the hand that squeezing my gut gets tighter. I don't know what a launch signal sounds like, yet I fear that is what I am hearing. Are Merek and Sayer launching because of the attack? Don't they realize what happens if they leave without us?

I can stop it. Maybe. Cancel the procedure or something like that. The only way to do that is on the control panel, which means I'll need to put myself in the middle of the battle. Right where Daga can see me.

My breath quickens as my muscles tense, ready to move. A heartbeat later, I go. My pulse is pounding as I spring from the dark, dashing toward the end of the locker row, risking exposure. If anyone spots me—

A dart impales the locker next to my head. I find my assailant—an A Squad rookie. He snarls at me and goes to fire again. I shoot first. My dart grazes his arm, and he drops his gun, clutching his biceps as he falls to the ground.

The alarm turns into a series of shorter bleeps, getting faster. The lights on the tube blink in sync. It's a countdown! I race to the panel, flicking every switch and pounding every button I can get my hands on. The tone stops, and the lights go out. I gasp. Did I cancel the launch? Did I make it in time?

My answer comes when the interior of the tube goes dark, and a heavy clunk vibrates the floor. There's a rumble from the tube, and I feel the force of something move at an extreme velocity away from me.

A few combatants around take notice, stunned as I am by the sudden halting of light and sound. But they can only wonder for a few seconds. In the next, their enemy fires upon them, and all curiosity about the tube disappears as they're pulled back into the battle.

I drop, clutching the panel in a vain search for a message or a status light. Anything that would tell me what just happened. *Please.* I'll pray again if that's what it takes. Just don't let this be the last of Merek and Sayer. I couldn't explain that to Efa. She'd never accept it.

The screen on the panel lights up. Green letters show up there, one by agonizing one. I hold my breath, numb to the surrounding battle, as I wait for the message to display.

When I read it, my body goes stiff. I understand the words, yet I just don't want to believe it.

Purge...successful. Pod launched.

They're gone.

"No!" I wail, and pound on the control panel. How could they be so stupid? There's no way to track them from here, not with the whole of command and control a blackened mess of melted electronics and slag. Why didn't they wait? Doesn't Merek love Efa? Was all of it just a lie?

The battle rages around me, but I'm numb to the violence. I slump to the floor, becoming overwhelmed with the thought of explaining this to Efa. Nothing I can say will be a comfort. With the pod untraceable, Merek, Sayer, and Rabbit, if he's with them, are as good as dead. She'll never get over him, and with me either imprisoned or executed, I won't be around to console her.

Forgive me, Efa.

"Hey!" a Fahrasi shouts, spotting me. I react and fire. She hits the deck to avoid my darts. Another joins her and fires a shot that burns across my cheek. I wince and hurl a volley at him before pulling back. No reason to stay here any longer. Not when everything I came here for is gone.

My chest heaves as I make a straight line to the rail system doors. Tears streak my face, stinging my eyes and cheeks. I make the last steps into the car by feel alone. I dive into a corner for cover and reach up to slam any button that will take me away from here. Up or down. It doesn't matter.

The doors shut on what I will only remember as hell, and everything becomes quiet. I curl myself up and lean into the wall, the depth of what just happened sinking in. Everything I've fought for, everything I've struggled to achieve for Efa, everything the two of us have sacrificed.

Gone.

SOLITUDE

A chime from the rail system pulls me from my darkened stupor. I raise my head as the car slows and prepares to stop. My thoughts are not so much curiosity as they are subconscious standard protocol. Situational awareness. The skills of war have been so driven into me, they are a part of my mind and my muscles. I wish they weren't so automatic. I need to think about anything other than what just happened.

The rail car announces its stop at level forty-seven, far enough away from the battle that I can get out and not concern myself with securing anything. I'm not sure that I could if I had to. My body aches, and my muscles are stiff. The past ten days, if I'm even counting the days correctly, have been one never-ending nightmare. All I want to do is to sleep for a million years and wake up having forgotten everything.

As the doors to the rail car slide open, I push myself up and out with little haste. I pass through a corridor running perpendicular to the doors and come out into a sea of white pods. Stasis beds. A cackle bursts from my lungs. How ironic. This would be the ideal place to rest for an eon or two. Of course, I should still be asleep. So should every child.

I pause as a familiarity about this space touches me. High on the wall is a symbol—lines inside of a square, symbolizing hands. Or wings. It represents our ancestors. The adults put it there so that they would watch over us while we were in stasis. If any spirit was truly here, they wouldn't have let the adults steal me from my pod. Maybe that's why I never pray to them.

Still, I'm curious...

I move to the nearest pod and wipe off the thin layer of frost that covers the bed's port. Inside is a middle-aged woman with graying blond hair and pale skin. Her face is peaceful, at rest, like someone should be who has no idea what level of hell we have brought the *Stratford* into. I move to another. It's a young boy, perhaps five or six. If he was four years older, the adults would wake him, tear him from his naïve bliss, and send him into battle with barely enough training to keep him alive for a short time.

Those adults would be my adults. This is a stasis level for the Tarakh. It was my level, too.

An urge to connect with someone or something drives me deeper into the rows. My mother. She's here, somewhere. Perhaps my father is, too. I'll find him if I can remember what he looks like.

It would be pure joy to see my mother's face again. Even as I race through the aisles—my hand turning numb as I wipe away the delicate, opaque layer of ice that covers the faces of the dormant—I sense a warmth cover me, though it remains distant. Its touch is soothing, and I become so at ease I only desire to connect with it more. I must find its source, and I will search every pod to locate it if I have to.

But fatigue floods over me as I push myself to complete a check of the first two rows. My legs give out and I drop, my head smacking into the hard side of a pod. My sight gets twisted and everything spins, forcing bile up into my throat. I clamp my hands around my skull, hoping to right myself. I can't. Nausea hits me hard, and suddenly I've got to do anything I can to stop from vomiting all over the deck.

After a minute of struggle, I press against the base of a stasis bed and drop my hands to the floor. My sight clears, but all I can focus on is breathing. My mother will have to wait, at least for now.

It occurs to me I've made more rookie mistakes in the last few minutes than I have made in my entire time as a soldier. It's amazing no attacks have come. Though no one here is a threat. Or awake. I am, for all practical requirements, alone.

Yes. I am very alone.

A laugh escapes me, even as tears flow down my face. I'm stuck somewhere between amusement and sorrow. It is a strange place to be, yet it's exactly the pathetic situation I am in. I share a common status with the people who surround me. Stuck between two states, they are neither alive nor dead, and having entrusted their lives to the *Stratford*'s caretakers, they cannot change their fate.

If they knew what these bish heads have done to their vessel and to their dream, there would be no freedom for adults like Daga.

"Get up," I say aloud. No one will hear it but me, yet no one needs to hear it more. It's the spark that reignites the desire to see my mother's face. I feel as if I will gain something from it. Perhaps just the comfort of knowing she still exists, or there could be more. Maybe I'll gain the courage to do something, whatever it may be.

And that's the question. Efa's dream is gone, and so is my ability to protect her. Everything she hoped for, and all that I hoped for her, is impossible now. There's no reason, no worthwhile sacrifice to make, that changes anything or saves anyone. I'm without a mission or a clue about what I should do.

My fingers find the edge of the stasis pod's control panel and wrap around it. With a sigh, I reach down to find whatever energy I have left and pull myself up. My head still spins, and a dull throb on my forehead reminds me I should rest and recover, rather than attempt this foolish quest.

And it is as stupid of a task as it is enormous. There are hundreds of pods, and people, here. Searching will take hours. Still, I will do it. It's the only motivation I have left.

I cut through the rows toward the other side of the level. My parents could be there or not. I'm not sure what I will do when I find them, other than stare at their faces as I search my mind for an answer to what comes next.

Efa will know the truth, eventually. She'll blame me and call me every bad word I've ever taught her before she breaks down from the weight of the truth. At that moment, I hope to be there to comfort her. But I might not be. She'd have no one to ease her misery and I quickly push away any thoughts about what happens then.

A pod two lanes away calls to me, and I stagger towards it as if drawn by some magnetic power. My pace picks up as I get closer. I must know who is there.

I take a last step and flop on top of the stasis chamber, clutching at its sides to stop from slipping off, having spent the last of my energy. As I struggle, my hand slides across the window, revealing the face that is there. I gasp and peer inside, but if I had hoped it would be the angelic face of my mother, I am sorely disappointed. The entombed person is at least female, though somewhere in her twenties.

And again, just like everyone else here, I return to a state of limbo. My parents remain elusive, as does my decision about what to do about Efa.

Perhaps Efa's fine without me, receiving the proper care for her wound from the med techs back at base. She'd be safe there while she healed. Then, once she's healthy enough to debrief, the adults might go easy on her. They'll need veteran soldiers to rebuild the squads, especially after the disaster that Daga has brought on the Tarakh troops. They'll need new field leaders, too. Tegan might fill one of those roles. Efa could too, if she so wished it.

But I doubt she would.

As I stare at the woman in the pod, I realize I am acting like a true child at this moment. My wishes are pathetic, and my fears are unfounded. It's wrong. I am a squad leader, and I don't collapse into a fit at the first sign of trouble. Efa may be safe for now, but she won't be forever. And the rest of my squad, like Seren...they're in trouble *now*. Hyuk, all the children are at risk while Daga remains in control. If he's not stopped, they're all dead.

We'll all die—adults and children alike—if Daga continues to use this ship as if it was his own gameboard. The constant war between factions will either destroy everything or use it all up. Those waking up a month before their arrival on a new world will find nothing left. Where will they be, then?

These people allowed themselves to be put in stasis on the promise of a better future. My parents deserve to wake up and find the promise had been kept. Everyone who lies in stasis on this ship deserves that. It doesn't matter if they're Tarakh or Fahrasi. Those people didn't choose sides. There were never sides until the custodial crew got greedy.

I leave the woman's pod and make my way down the aisle, step by agonizing step. I want to view the residents of these pods and learn just who it is the adults have deceived.

There are girls, boys, old women and men. Heavy people and skinny people, pretty people and ugly people. Perhaps they know each other, or maybe they don't. Who knows if any of them would get along once they woke from their frozen sleep? Even if they didn't, I doubt they'd call each other enemy. They never went through battle training. No one ever conditioned them to believe another human, not all that different from themselves, would shoot them on sight.

I stop at a pod and draw my hand across the window, just like I've done more times than I can count. A woman with long, silky black hair comes into view. The deep wave in her dark mane brings a smile to my face. It's like...mine.

And her jawline, her skin...her lips...

"Mother!" I gasp.

It's her. There's no doubt in my mind, not when my heart is pounding in my chest like this. She's possibly twice my age, maybe younger. I wonder about how old she must have been when she gave birth to me. Perhaps not much older than I am now. Ancestors. To think someone that young could raise a daughter like me.

A sob runs through me, realizing I've missed her more than I ever could have expected. She's the person who gave me life and the one who soothed my sorrows. Even now, I wish she were awake, if only so she could embrace me, hold me tight, and banish this miserable chill that permeates every part of my body.

No. I'd never wish for her to wake up to this mess. Let her journey feel like a moment in time, where she closed her eyes, only to open them a second later to find that she had arrived.

I want to do that for her. I *will* do that for her. No one is going to ruin her chance at a new life. I'll stop anyone who tries. Efa deserves whatever I can give her, too. She and I won't get to see that new world, but I can show her what it might be like. Right here on the *Stratford*.

For that to happen, the Tarakh and the Fahrasi must end their fighting and learn to work together again. No more of this hyuking battle. Right now this is just a dream, but I'll work on it, like a mission. My mission. One that I would willingly give my life to complete.

This will require my appearance before the new chief. I'll accept whatever punishment she chooses, but only if she listens to what I have to say. There's no guarantee she will, but I have to try. This is the only battle worth fighting now.

I take a last look at my mother—at least until I'm successful. Then I will come back every chance I get to tell her everything I've been through. I have no idea if my words will get through, but she would want to know what happened to me. She'll want to know how much I love her for being the person who gave me the strength to survive this hell.

A light hits the corner of my eye, and I turn. The rail car is still here. It's good for me, but it doesn't bode well for the squads down on level ninety-five. I will take it as a chance opportunity and as a gift. It will be a long time before I recover enough energy to climb all the way back to base.

And I will need all the strength I can gather for the struggle that awaits me.

SACRIFICE

I STARE AT THE empty corridor before me, hesitating to move through the rail car doors once they've opened. I am home, yet it feels like anything but that. To the people here, I am an outcast. A criminal. I've not only defied the commands of the adults, but I've done physical harm to one of them. If I hadn't hurt my comrades too, I wouldn't care. My fellow soldiers didn't deserve that. The only thing they're guilty of is ignorance.

My real guilt is having failed Efa, and if there was a punishment for that, I would gladly take it. That must be why I'm here: to accept my sentence. Efa put her trust in me, and I didn't come through when it mattered most. Now I must do what is necessary to protect her.

And everyone else who desires to be free.

I take a breath and put my foot through the doorway. It comes down onto the composite decking firmly, with the confidence that I have made the right decision. Then I step again. And again. The doors close behind me, signaling the finality of my choice. There is no running away from this. Efa would only suffer more if I changed my mind.

Chief Generys is on the floor above. I have no illusions about walking into her office and having an easy chat. There are sentries that guard her door and more than a few adults surrounding her. All I need to do is surrender to one of them and make my request. Once made, only the chief herself can deny it. I have a feeling that she won't. Too much has happened as of late, and the chief needs to hear a report from the front line, untainted by greed.

The ladder to level fifteen is down the passage and just around the corner. All I need to do is get there, and the rest will take care of itself.

I set my mind toward movement. This is a walk I have done many times before, yet never so weighted with significance, save for the very first. I remember that moment clearly. The medical team had just released me from recovery and told me to see the head office for assignment to a training squad. Every second of that walk is sharp in my mind, so sharp it's as if I was experiencing it now.

Which is why I don't see the baton that swings out and pounds into my gut.

The attack is fast and harsh. I've no chance to react. My arms fly out as multiple strikes slam into me, first my stomach, then the backs of my legs. I drop, my knees slamming into the floor. Boots and fists join the assault until I crash to the floor.

Hands yank me up and slam my back into the wall. A punch strikes my jaw. I'm slammed into the wall again as I struggle against blacking out, forcing myself to sit upright as my eyes roll back into my head.

"She's subdued," someone says as my head spins. "Get her up."

They haul me up by my armpits, doing everything they can to be as rough as possible. Straps wind around my legs, binding my legs together. Then they rip my arms back and tie my wrists. Pain runs down my shoulder and through my body, and I cry out, squeezing my eyes shut in a failed attempt to control my agony.

This isn't the way I had wanted to surrender, though I should have known better. I am a threat. It was only right of them to neutralize that threat. It was just my stupidity to think otherwise.

"Secured, sir," someone says.

"Did you knock her out?"

"I don't think so."

My body turns icy. That voice. The one I have heard and feared so many times. He's here. In front of me. Right now. I'm not Chief Generys' prisoner. I'm Captain Daga's captive. It doesn't matter how he beat me here, and I can't think clearly enough to figure it out. He's here, and nothing could be worse for my plan.

"Ceri," he says. "Wake up."

Sparks fly across my vision as his hand slaps my cheek. My head jerks to the side, and I lose my sense of balance.

"Yeah, you're awake, alright," Daga says. "No use in pretending. Look at me."

Another slap opens my eyes. I grit my teeth and glare. He returns it with a smile. It's what he wanted—to see me suffer.

He'll want a lot more than that before he turns me over to the chief, if he ever does. If I want to survive this, I'd better speak up.

"That's better." Daga grabs my chin and forces my head up. "I'm glad you decided not to pass out. I want you awake for this."

"For what?" I spit back. Daga only grins.

His fists pound my body, indiscriminate in their strikes. I bend and twist, making every attempt to protect myself. But his guards keep me upright so he can pummel me again and again. My arms go numb first, then my legs. They buckle under Daga's brutal pummeling.

I must have fainted at some point, because the next thing I remember is the shock of freezing cold crashing over my head. I shake and wail, doubling over to find warmth. Water, colder than I've ever felt. The bastards must have left it to sit by the airlock for a long while.

Still, the chill of it numbs the agony that runs through me, and I realize I'm still alive. Daga couldn't finish the job. Either that, or he's going to finish the job later. Stupid. He should have killed me and ended his problems. I can't think of any good reason he didn't. Perhaps he wants to torture me first. I hope not. I don't know if I could survive any more of this.

"She's awake, sir," someone says. I glance up from the chair they dropped me in. It's that A Squad boy, the one who has had it in for me ever since my duel with Rhain. I got him good during their ambush, but it seems he still wants more.

Footsteps approach from outside. Daga is coming. I assess my location. This looks like a storage room on level seventeen. They're trying to hide me from others who may not be loyal to their deranged captain. If I want to survive, I'd better fix that. And now.

"I demand—" My chest screams from the effort to talk, and I cough, blood dripping from my mouth as I force air back into lungs that feel as if a thousand darts have impaled them.

"You don't get to do anything but die, hyuk face," the boy says. "Unless you want to beg me for your life."

"Back away, idiot," Daga says. "She'll bite your arm off if you get too close. Or was one beating from her not enough for you?"

"Sir!" The boy jumps back and straightens into a salute. Daga only acknowledges it with a wave of his hand, then grabs his arm and shoves him out of the room. Then he gets a chair and slides it in front of me, dropping himself into it.

"I know what you're thinking, Ceri," he says. "You want to know why I haven't crushed your windpipe or driven a blade through your heart, right? That's easy to answer. I need intel on Fahrasi movements below level one hundred, and I know you have the information I want. That's the only reason you're still alive. So tell me what I need to know, and I might let you live long enough to have a trial."

I stare at him, my eyelids half-open. My brain is even less functional than that. I will use whatever I have left to focus on what I came here to do. It's the only thing that will save me from more pain.

"Tell me." Daga motions at me with his hands. "Let's go! Numbers, locations, armament. You're not that gone that you can't answer me, you little bitch. I know how tough you are. A few punches only softened you up."

"I..." The rest of the words get caught in my throat. I lean over to stop myself from choking.

Daga folds his arms and leans forward, stuck somewhere between confusion and annoyance. It won't take much to push him toward the wrong side. If he decides I don't have the intel he needs, he will take his frustration out on whatever life remains in me.

"Out with it," he says. "I don't have patience for your drawling."

"I..." A gulp of air inflates my lungs, and I use it to regain a croak of a voice. "I want an audience!"

Daga smiles and chuckles. I suppose it amuses him to see me fight to survive like this.

"Oh, Ceri. You want to know what's funny?" He shakes his finger at me. "It is hyuking hilarious to me you still believe you're a Tarakh. You're not. You have no rights and no say about anything. So go ahead. Claim whatever you want. I will give you nothing, and you'll get even less. Now, tell me what I want to know, or I will start cutting fingers off."

"Yours or mine?" I taunt.

That gets me his fist across my face. I react in slow motion, my head rolling to one side as the bile in my stomach finds its way up into my mouth. I'm left with a sharp tang in the back of my throat that saps the rest of my brainpower. All I can think of is that I don't want to die with that taste in my mouth.

Daga becomes irritated at my lack of a reply. He stands, kicking the chair back. It crashes into a cabinet with a sharp crack that resonates down the corridor.

"Who launched the emergency pod?" Daga growls. "Does that have something to do with the reason the Fahrasi are massing fighters down there? Did you tell them about the rail system? Answer me!"

The sound of voices just outside grabs my attention. I can't make out the words, but there's a female voice repeating something over and over. A demand, maybe. A male voice answers back, his tone growing in intensity.

"Fine, have it your way," Daga says, breaking me away from the voices. He pulls his blade from its sheath, then grabs my arm and jerks me across the chair. My stomach slams into the armrest. I cough, spitting out bile as I hang helplessly over the side.

Daga cuts the tie on my wrists and twists my arm up and back to lock me down. I feel the cold metal of his weapon dig into my small finger. My pulse quickens. I cannot bear any more torture. If I black out, I fear I may never wake up again. Daga won't stop causing me pain until he has cut me apart. I can accept dying in battle, but not this. I don't want to die like this.

"You brought this on yourself, you know," he says. "Now you'll have to accept your punishment."

A half sob fills my damaged lungs with air. I must use it. I reach deep inside and focus on speaking. Anything will do. It just has to be loud.

"I want an audience!" I cry.

His blade cuts into my pinky, and I scream. Daga grins wide and slices deeper. The icy edge of his weapon shocks my hand rigid. My entire arm is ablaze. I shake and howl, attempting to gather strength to end my torment.

"Stop!" the female voice I heard before shouts. Niah. My eyes fly open. Niah is here! "Stop now, or I will end you!"

Daga stops and turns, keeping hold of my wrist. He attempts to appear unconcerned, but I felt a tremor run through his body the moment he laid eyes on her. If Daga was ever afraid of me, he must be terrified of Niah.

"Be careful what you say. You're threating an adult," Daga says.

"Get the chief," Niah says to someone in the corridor. "And if any of those other bish-heads so much as breathe, you've got permission to use them for target practice."

"Do you think I will let you interfere?" Daga challenges. "This traitor has valuable information, and for the sake of the Tarakh, I intend to get it."

"The only traitor is you," Niah shoots back. "I heard Ceri make a claim for an audience. So did my entire squad. That means her request goes to the chief. You want to take the chance she'll believe you over us? Drop your weapon and let her go."

Mari pushes in behind her, her weapon out. The girl's eyes are wide as she takes me in. I can only imagine what I look like—a half-dead body covered in blood and bruises. If I saw my reflection, I might scare myself.

"Niah," Mari gasps. "Look at her!"

Niah glances past Daga, and her face goes hard. It's my fault. I put myself into this situation. Yet I'm sure Niah blames herself. She has only ever wanted to look after me, even when she was acting tough about it.

"I hope they strip your command for this," Niah says. "Now drop her arm, or I drop you."

Daga shifts and tenses, sensing the seriousness of her words. Niah will not hesitate to do it. She has no illusions about the adults. She's only followed their orders for the good of the rest of us.

Until now.

Daga makes a show of letting my arm go but keeps his blade. My bleeding hand is my only concern. I grab it and bring it close to my mouth, pressing on the cut with my lips to stop any more of my life from spilling out onto the floor.

"What the hell are you doing out there?" Daga calls outside the room. "This is a mutiny! Shoot them all dead!"

All he gets is silence. Either the scouts have A Squad well covered, or Daga's kids have done the smart thing and surrendered.

"We secure out there?" Niah asks Mari.

"No need," Mari replies. "They all dropped their weapons and ran."

I close my eyes and slump in the seat. Only part of my night-mare is over. I still must face the chief and hope she will accept the strange truth I have to tell her.

PARTNER

I'VE BEEN ASLEEP FOR a long time, though I don't remember how I ended up here. In a bed. A proper bed. The soft and supportive cushion beneath me is a luxury I've only experienced once before. When I was younger, they put me in medical quarantine to let me sweat through an infection. It was the best sleep I have ever had.

"She's coming around," a male voice says.

Alarms scream across my nerves. I shoot up, my eyes scanning the area to assess the threat before me. Bright light assaults my eyes and I squint. Then something hard grabs my wrists, and I struggle, unwilling to surrender to anyone other than the chief.

"Easy," a male adult in a med jacket says. "You're going to hurt yourself again."

I glare at him, even as pain rips through my body. He's Tarakh, which means I'm still at base. I swallow and do my best to relax. There's no danger here. At least for the moment.

"Where's Niah?" I demand.

The med tech shrugs. I'm not sure if that means he doesn't know or has no idea who she is. If he was a soldier, Niah would be as familiar to him as his weapon. There is no one more senior in the ranks of the Tarakh fighters, unless I consider the adults. And I won't.

"Is she awake yet?" Efa's excited voice comes through from the other side of a curtain. "Can I see her?"

My heart stops. As much as I want to see her, I have no plan on how to tell her what happened. I don't have the strength left to help her through it, either.

The med tech motions me to lie back down, then reaches for the curtain. Efa's face lights up as the curtain comes back. She squeaks in delight and pops off her pillow, darting back and forth to look past the man. He raises his hand in apology, then signals he'll leave us alone for a while.

As soon as Efa gets a solid look at me, the joy goes out of her. I know I must look frightening. Every bit of me aches, especially my finger, which stings something fierce. I'll accept the pain as confirmation it's still attached.

Efa's appearance is less worrisome, save for the one thing I notice: the restraints across her wrists, secured to rails on the bed.

"How's the wound?" I ask, though I'm unsure if she heard me.

"Ceri..." Efa takes in a quick breath and leans over the rail as she gawks. "What did they do to you?"

I drop my gaze. Her worried stare is difficult for me to handle, and to see her locked to the bed like that only reminds me how badly I've failed her.

"They made you a criminal," I say.

"You too," she replies, the curve of her lips turning down.

It's true, though my restraints seem thicker. Not that it matters. Neither of us can do much more than talk.

"I'm sorry, Efa," I say and close my eyes, knowing my mistake put her here. "I'm sorry it turned out like this."

If she knew what that really meant, it would wreck her. Efa is so in love with that boy, all she can think of is him. I suppose if I felt that way about someone, I'd die if I found out that they had left me. But I'd never choose to fall into the trap of desire. It's proven to be more dangerous than our enemy.

Efa attempts to reach out to me, but her restraint stops her before she can even extend her arm past the bed rail. She drops her hand onto it and sighs as she stares at it.

"Me too," Efa says after a moment. "I wish...I wish I just had one more chance to be with him."

I nod, biting down hard on my lower lip. To see Merek again would bring her so much joy, but it can never happen. Efa can't go there, and he won't return. Even if Merek survives, it would be impossible to locate him. The *Stratford* will transit through the solar system soon, and any hope of contacting him, even if the equipment was working, will be gone.

Efa gets a hopeful look in her eyes, one I pull back from. I'm already feeling my chest getting tight as I wait for her to speak. Whatever is on her mind will be difficult for me to handle.

"Did you see him?" she asks, her tone almost pleading with me to say yes. "I mean, after they took me. Did you make it to the pods? Is he okay? Did he say anything to you?"

I get sick with panic from hearing Efa's words. I double over, retching hard. A hacking cough takes my body over until blood flies out and covers the white sheets. I collapse into the bed, gasping.

"Ceri!" Efa cries. "Someone! Help! We need help here!"

The med tech returns, though not in a hurry. He frowns once he sees my bed, then pulls a small machine from a cabinet and places it on top of my stomach. Efa watches, her face pale.

"No internal bleeding," the med tech says once the machine beeps. "Maybe just a residual blood clot from the lungs. I'll give you something to help clear it up."

"So...she'll be alright?" Efa asks.

"Eventually. She needs to rest and let the medication work," he replies, then looks at me. "Don't worry, I suspect you'll have plenty of time to do that."

"So then, no execution?" I ask, the sarcasm in my voice obvious.

He only shrugs again as he connects a bag to the line in my arm. Once he's set up the machine to administer the medication, he leaves without another word.

Efa watches me, thoughtful. Perhaps she's unsure about the med tech's reply. Or worried about our fate. At some point, she'll return to her question—the one I dread to answer. I'll have to tell her something, or she'll never stop asking. I don't have it in me to fight her off, and I'm not sharp enough to come up with a story she'll believe. It's wrong to keep her hoping, yet that's exactly what I'm considering.

"Ceri, please talk to me," Efa pleads.

I realize then that I must have gone spacy for a moment and rotate my head toward her bed. Efa's face is pained and on the verge of tears. I go to turn away, but Efa stops me.

"Please don't," she says. "I want to see your face, so I know you're okay."

"I'm fine, just like the doctor said," I answer.

"He's not a doctor, and I'm not talking about your cough. Something else is bothering you, Ceri. Talk to me? Please?"

Think. Come up with something quick. As if I could. Still, some truth could put her off for the moment.

"I'm just thinking about having to be locked up with you for the rest of my childhood," I say with a small smile.

Efa returns it and giggles. "Why would that upset you? You'd never have to pick up a weapon again." She waggles her eyebrows. "And you could still cuddle with me as much as you want."

"Don't you mean the other way around?" I say.

Efa rolls her eyes and blushes. It's my attempt to tease her and evade her prying. It may even turn the conversation to something happier. But it's not to be. Just as quickly as Efa turned to humor, her face darkens once again.

"Seriously. Tell me what's wrong," she says, the pleading in her tone replaced with something more insistent. "Or if you won't do that, then tell me what Merek said. I know you're holding out on me."

Bish and a half. How'd she turn that around on me so quickly?

"He didn't say anything," I reply, feeling my lower lip tremble. "I didn't see him."

"Liar. Don't tease me."

It's the truth, but if I expected her to believe me, then the new medication the med tech gave me has already gone to my head. As it is, I want to slip under the sheets and hide from more of Efa's questioning. Maybe this bed could swallow me up and that'd be the end. Now that she smells blood, she'll be more relentless in getting me to talk than Daga ever could. I didn't fear answering him.

Efa will chip away the remains of my resistance until I have nothing left to keep my friend away from the horrible reality that faces her. It'd be better if I could just tell her Merek was dead. At least then there would be a body she could see. All she has now is her memory, one the truth will surely destroy.

"I'm not," I say.

"Then tell me what happened after we got separated."

That, at least, I can do.

I describe my battle with A Squad and escape from Daga and my misery about losing her. Then I tell her how I ran into Tegan, Beka, and Rhain and how that idiot wanted a rematch but was interrupted by the Fahrasi raid. Efa listens, nodding here and there and pushing me for details when my report trails off. I wish I could relax as I speak, but my story only leads to one ending, and I don't want to finish it.

"I know Beka. Poor aim, that one," Efa says, curling her lips in. "I'm glad she'll survive. What happened to Tegan and her after you left Rhain?"

"She chose to save Beka over going with me, so when we hit ninety-five—"

Oh hyuk.

"You were on ninety-five? I knew it! So you saw Merek! What did he say?" Efa slaps her legs for emphasis. "Come on, Ceri! I'm dying here!"

A different ache fills me, one that starts in my heart and races outward through my body as my muscles tense. I have to shut this conversation down now.

"I didn't see him. That's the truth, Efa. I swear it," I say, then tighten my jaw to stop the spread of emotion on my face.

"Then why do you say it like you know more?" Efa shifts, her hand clutching the rail as her voice drops to a whisper. "Did...something happen to him?"

I try to roll onto my side, facing away from her, but the restraints stop me from turning fully, and my struggle to escape her fails.

"I'm tired," I say. "Just let me sleep."

"Let you sleep?" Efa's voice rises. "How can you ask me that? You know something about Merek that you're hiding! Out with it!"

"Please, Efa, don't ask any more about him. Please." My voice shakes as my eyes get wet. It's over. Efa won't stop now. I'd rather die twice than tell her, but I can't resist any longer. All I can hope is that Chief Generys listens to me and chooses imprisonment over execution. That way, I can comfort her until the pain goes away. If it ever does.

"Oh…no. No, Ceri. No. You have to say it now. Tell me. I want to hear it. I don't care how bad it is. I need to know." Efa sniffles. "You can't keep that from me."

Efa's right. Either I tell her, or she'll figure it out soon enough. All I can do is brace myself and await that dreadful moment.

"Is he dead?" Efa asks, asking with firm resolve. How she can be strong at a moment like this is beyond my understanding.

"No."

Efa sighs with heavy relief. "Okay," she whispers. "He's still alive, then. It's not that bad."

As I close my eyes, all the wetness that surrounds them runs down my cheeks, some of it dripping onto my lips. The salty tears sting the cuts there, reminding me of the mess that I've become. I don't know how I got here, but even as I break down, I know in the back of my mind I will find my strength again.

For Efa.

"It's worse," I say, cringing from the emotional blade I just drove into Efa's body.

"What? How could it be worse?" But even as she asks, she realizes the answer. "No. No, he couldn't have left without me. Why? Why would he do that?"

"Efa," I gasp, "I'm sorry. I'm so sorry."

"No!" Efa shouts. "No, it can't be true. Did you see the pod launch?"

I turn back to her, and she sees how soaked my face must be. Without speaking another word, I give her the answer that will haunt me for the rest of my days.

The wail that comes from her lungs sends every tech and doctor into our berth. They spot her collapsed over the edge of the bed and rush to save her. Efa shoves them away, even as four adults attempt to hold her down.

The doctor glances at me, as if I could do any better to provide an answer.

"Please," I say, my voice muddled by sobs. I raise my arm as much as I can and show the restraint to the doctor. "Please, take this off. Let me go to her."

His eyes swivel between the two of us as he puts his hands on his hips. Then his jaw tightens, and he shakes his head. "Not a chance. You're to see the chief tomorrow so you can stand trial." He turns to the others then. "There's no emergency here. Just a bunch of crybabies. Let's go."

The one female med tech in the room frowns at him.

"Please!" I try again to force my voice through. "She needs me!"

The doctor walks out, followed by two of the techs, but before a third one can leave, the woman grabs him by his arm and motions to Efa with her head. She reaches under Efa's bed with her foot and, with the help of the other tech, pushes Efa's bed next to mine.

The tech grabs a blade and cuts Efa's far restraint. Efa rockets toward me and buries her face in my shoulder, wrapping her one free arm around me. I try to return the embrace, but my restraints stop me from doing anything more but putting my head on hers. I look at the female tech, begging her with my eyes.

"We'll be right outside, so be good," the tech says, warning me with a look. She glances at her fellow tech, then sighs and cuts one of my restraints before the two of them walk out. My arm goes around Efa the moment it's free.

"Why?" Efa's body heaves. "Why did he leave me?"

I can only hold her and hope she cries herself to sleep at some point. No words will make her feel better about what Merek did, because he did it to her. On purpose. No other kind of betrayal could hurt more than this. She trusted her heart to him, and he threw it away.

The adults have constantly impressed upon us that relationships between children are not only wrong, they're deadly. They forbid us from having them because we're not emotionally mature enough. I don't believe that. Every adult on this ship would break down like Efa did if their lover left them.

"I can't live without him, Ceri," Efa whispers, her body sagging. "I can't."

"You can," I whisper back, trying to sound confident. "I'll help you."

I wish I knew more about love to be certain of my own words. I don't. All I can do is hope, even as I wonder which one of us is right.

Ancestors, please. Take my side for once.

TRIAL

"Wake up, traitor," a man says and shoves my shoulder. I stir, stretching my neck to cure the ache in it from the odd position I lay down in. There was no sleep for me last night. With so much assaulting my mind, I didn't even try. The soreness in my muscles didn't help, either.

With a little assistance, I slide out of the bed, and before I can even grab my pants, two adults haul me out of medical and down the corridor. I couldn't say goodbye to Efa, either. She was sleeping, by her own accord or through whatever drugs they gave her. There wasn't much to say, anyway. I used all the words I could think of last night.

The two adult guards bring me to a conference room—one I've never seen before—and lock me down into a chair. I shiver as the cold seat sends a chill up my bare back. My blood-stained hospital gown covers the front of my body, but little else. I can handle it. If the adults are trying to humiliate me, they'll need to try harder.

A middle-aged woman with silver hair enters, flanked by two more adults—a woman and a man. The man shuts the door behind them, and the two of them sit.

"What is this?" the silver-haired woman says, irritation in her voice. She points at me and glares at the one guard who brought me here.

"Ceri d'Sengshuy, Chief," the man answers. "You requested her trial for this time."

"I know that, idiot. Why'd you bring her up here half-naked in a bloody gown? Go get her a blanket, at least."

"But..."

"I don't give a hyuk what we have accused her of. We don't treat any Tarakh like this. Go!"

So this is Chief Generys. I might find a reason to like her if she wasn't about to punish me. She seems like the type of person who would sentence me to die and then have lunch without another thought about it.

I shiver again. If she chooses execution, I could be dead before the day is done. Then Efa will truly be alone. I fear for her sanity if nobody is there to care for her. This love thing has done her mind in something terrible.

Chief Generys sizes me up as a guard retrieves a blanket and drops it over me like a death shroud. Perhaps she is asking herself if a half-dead girl like me could do any of the things I'm being accused of.

"Alright," she says as she sits. "Let's get this started...No, don't waste my time repeating what's in the report. I've already heard that a thousand times from Captain Daga. Where is he, anyway? He should be present for this hearing."

No, please. Not him.

"Confined to quarters by the colonel, Chief," Generys' female aide says. "Apparently, there were a few complaints from the squads about his command. He's under investigation."

My sigh catches the chief's attention. She stares at me, and I shrink under her powerful gaze. This woman is faction head because she took it. The job may have been hers by law, but she's claimed the position as her own and no one else's.

"Something to add, soldier?" the chief asks.

I avoid catching her eyes. To do so would wreck my confidence, and I can't have that. I will need as much determination as possible to defend myself. After last night, I'm completely wrecked. If there's any chance of winning my survival, I'll need to be on equal terms with her. But this woman could crush me with a single word. The best strategy is to hold my position until I can think of a better one.

"No, ma'am," I mumble.

"I don't fight for a living," the chief replies. "You call me chief. Got it?"

I nod, continuing to stare down at the table.

"Now, as per our procedures, I'm to ask you if you understand what you are being charged with. A nod will do if you're that set on not talking."

"I understand," I say.

"Fine then. Do you admit guilt to these charges? If you say yes, I'll take that into consideration. But if you don't..." She waves a hand. "Well, you still have that right."

This is trickier than it sounds. If I say I attacked my own troops, stole medication, and assaulted an adult, the chief could just decide my sentence right then with no other chance to speak. Though what would I say, even if I had the chance? What stops her from condemning me to death and Efa to loneliness?

"Chief," I say, my voice dry.

"What? Speak up, soldier! And look at me when you address me. Did your captain neglect to teach you manners?"

"Ceri's captain is Daga, Chief," the female aide reminds her.

"Right." Chief Generys runs a hand through her hair. "I remember now. That's why this situation is so interesting. In that case, let's pass through this nonsense and get to the point. The captain wants your head, soldier, but it seems like you're more popular with the troops than he is. Why don't you just start at the beginning and tell me your side of things?"

My skin goes cold. I'm caught between the possibility of a real hearing and giving up too much. Efa would hate me forever if I disclosed her love for a Fahrasi soldier. It could put her life in jeopardy, too.

"Come on!" The chief slaps the table hard. "I'm giving you a chance to tell your side here!"

I look at her and set my jaw. The chief curses and rises from her chair to lean on the table and get close to me.

"Ceri," she says, her voice softer than before. "I know you don't want to die. That's what's going to happen if all I have is Captain Daga's reports to make a judgment with. He was keen to do it himself, and that's why you're sitting here now. I don't take anyone's word for granted. Only facts are valid.

Everything else is hearsay. So, for your own sake, why don't you give me something I can turn into a fact?"

"I can't, Chief. I can't betray my friend."

Chief Generys stands up and paces in a tight loop. "Loyalty to your squad mates is a good virtue, but it won't help you here. Besides, you just told me something. Give me the rest. What secret does your friend have that is worth your life to keep?"

This is becoming a repeat of last night. Only the chief is much stronger willed than Efa, and I have no debate about hurting the chief. She's not the one in love.

I let out a slow breath, considering the options. Maybe if I can get the chief to agree not to charge Efa with any crimes, then I'd be free to test the chief with a bit of information. If she reacts well, then I can continue.

"I will tell you...everything," I say. "But first, I want you to assure me Efa will be free of any charges. She is innocent in all this."

"Any *more* charges, you mean." The chief shakes her head. "She may be my daughter, but I can't promise you that, not when I don't know what you have to say. How about this? Give me something, and then I'll let you know what I can agree to, if anything."

Take a risk, Ceri.

"I stole the medication and hurt my comrades, which I regret. Even Rhain, who deserved it."

A guard chuckles. Chief Generys turns to glare at him before motioning me to continue.

"And I fought with Captain Daga, but I did it all to protect Efa."

"Oh? All for her?" The chief folds her arms. "What a squad mate you are. We don't teach the recruits to sacrifice themselves for others though, my dear. The Tarakh don't have the numbers for any of us to be falling on our blades like that. So, again, what's so important that you'd die for her? What did she do that you're willing to take to your death?"

"Promise me first," I say.

The chief scoffs. "I think you're forgetting who you are and where you are, soldier." But after a minute of chewing on her cheek, she says, "Alright. I'll give you your promise. No charges from what you tell me."

I look up then, into her eyes. I want to see how much this is going to hurt me to say. Efa will never speak to me again after this. Her secret just became my attempt to save my life.

"Efa is in love with a Fahrasi," I say.

Chief Generys' eyes go wide. Her two aides go stiff with shock. They stare at me as if I just told them I was changing sides. In a way, they wouldn't be wrong.

"Now you have my attention," Chief Generys says. "Tell me the rest. And don't leave any detail out. I want to understand how you moved around, found food, went to the toilet. All of it. There could be a fault or lapse in our security, and we need to know that right now. *Right* now!"

Telling her the rest isn't hard. I've already given up Efa's secret, and Merek and Sayer are no longer here to worry about.

Rabbit might have gone with them, or he may have gone back down to the machine access. I have no way of knowing.

But as I get to the part about the emergency pod, I realize there is a very important detail that needs to be mentioned. It could change our situation—no, not just ours. It could change everything for every single person on this ship. Just like I promised my mother I'd do.

When I tell them, the female aide gasps. Chief Generys' reaction is more subdued, yet I can tell the possibility of a new home has quickened the pace of her heart.

"Wait," the male aide says. "The scanner on the pod found a habitable planet? And the two Fahrasi boys went there?"

"Yes, but,"—I drop my head—"I don't understand why they would just leave us like that. Merek truly loves Efa. I've seen it for myself."

Chief Generys presses her lips together. Perhaps she has some sympathy for her daughter. Or maybe the chief is only thinking about her own future. It doesn't matter. Efa's life is back in her own hands, and I can save mine if I give the chief enough reason not to take it. I think I have that reason.

"Chief," I say. "Contact the Fahrasi and tell them!"

"No!" the female aide cries. "What's wrong with you? We don't contact them about anything."

"Wouldn't we if it meant securing a truce and fixing the ship?"

The chief looks at me as she strokes a finger down her throat. Her hand is shaking, though she tries to hide it. What this means to her is more than I can, or care to, understand. If it gets me free, then that's all I need it to do. There will be time to think about everything else later.

"I need time to consider your suggestion and to verify your statements," she says. "I won't execute you for your actions, but you are still under arrest, pending the investigation. That means there could still be imprisonment for you, Ceri."

I swallow and duck my head as relief floods through me. Tears threaten to crash the emotional wall I've kept up, but it's a struggle to hold them back. When I entered this room, I didn't expect to see tomorrow.

The Chief pulls a seat out and sits in front of me, leaning her elbows on her knees and clasping her hands together. I pull back, keeping my distance. She doesn't get to see my face and believe I am grateful for her mercy. I'm not.

"When I was your age, I was in love, too," she says, a faraway look appearing in her eyes. "Madly in love. All I could think about was him. He was such a wit...and his eyes...I thought we would be together forever. But when I found out he was seeing someone else, I wanted my life to end. I didn't know how I could go on."

I blink as I stare, slack-jawed. "Why are you telling me this?"

"Because if what you say is true, Efa is thinking the same things." Chief Generys nods to the door. "Go. Be with her. Give her as much comfort as you can. You're the only one she can trust right now."

RESSURECTION

As the guards return me to medical, a sense of achievement comes over me. It's strange, since there's not much to be excited about. I'll likely spend years locked away, and Efa will be pining over Merek for a long time. Even as she sits next to me in prison. I suppose I should be selfishly glad for her company, no matter her mental state. It would be terrifying to be alone there.

Chief Generys will find I told the truth. Niah, her team and C Squad will back me up. B Squad might as well. The big revelation for her will be when they use the emergency pod scanner and find that planet. Then, anything goes.

A cry comes from the medical bay as we enter. I dodge and hit the wall as a squad medic nearly runs me over. Chaos rips through the room. Med techs scramble about, throwing equipment into packs and rushing out.

"What's going on?" one of my escorts asks.

"Massive battle down on ninety-five," replies a soldier in the bed before us. Half his face is covered in bloody bandages. "There's dead everywhere. Both sides agreed to a cease-fire just to clean up the mess."

My jaw drops. The Fahrasi must have found out about the emergency pods.

"Which squads?" I ask.

"All of them."

My body goes cold as faces and names run through my head. There's too many to consider. Niah, Mari. Aidan and Seren from my squad. Even Deryn, leader of B Squad. They all could be seriously wounded. Or dead. And there is nothing I can do for them.

A med tech stops before me, scanning my face. When recognition comes to him, he jabs a finger at me.

"You need to find your friend!" he says and takes off.

My friend? No. Efa...

I rip away from the grasp of my guards and rush into our room. Empty. Efa is gone...Where? And how did she get away? They reattached her restraints. Of course they did.

The torn fibers that lie across her sheets tell the truth. She cut herself free. How?

I spot a surgical knife on the floor. That's the answer. Still... Where'd she go?

I spin on my guards, catching their gazes as my mouth attempts to form the words I need. I don't know why Efa escaped without me, but wherever she is, I fear she needs me more than ever.

"No," one of them says, understanding my unspoken question. "You're still under investigation, and until the chief says differently, you go nowhere."

"But so is she!" I shout.

Niah appears in the doorway, breathing hard. Her uniform is torn and bloodied, and her hair sticks to the grit and perspiration on her face. When she spots me, she frowns, then eyes my and Efa's beds.

"I wanted to be here for your hearing..." Niah says in between harsh breaths. "I'm sure you've heard by now."

"How bad is it?" I ask.

Niah coughs and leans on the doorframe and closes her eyes. I can only imagine what it took for her to get here.

"No," she replies in a half whisper, then hangs her head. "You don't want to know. There's too many. Way too many." Niah shakes her head, then glances at the guards. "Where's Efa?"

"Missing!" I cry. "We need to find her! Niah...It's all a mess. I told her everything."

"Like I said, not happening," repeats the guard, but then his demeanor softens. "She's also our responsibility, so don't worry. We'll find her. She couldn't have gone far."

As a yell and a crash come from outside, the other guard spins and pushes past Niah. The first guard's eyes follow his partner out, then turn back to me, hesitant to do the same.

"I'll stay," Niah says. "Ceri won't run away from me."

The guard watches me for a moment, sending me a warning about doing something foolish, then disappears out the door. With such a disaster down on ninety-five, a suspected traitor is no longer a priority. Nor is a missing prisoner. They might search for Efa, but not now.

"Niah, we've got to find her," I say. "She's really in a terrible state. I'm worried."

"Worry isn't in your vocabulary," Niah replies, but even as she attempts to lighten the mood, her eyebrows draw together. "Besides, you heard them. She couldn't have gone far. Lie down and rest. Maybe I will, too."

"There's no way I'm resting. Efa needs us!"

"You don't have a lot of choice. They've—"

A young sentinel pops her head in, searching for something. "Where are the adults?" she asks. "The guards. Someone said they were in here."

"Gone," Niah replies. "What do you want them for?"

The sentinel looks Niah over as if she's trying to decide if Niah is one of them or not. Maybe she answers then because she decides it doesn't matter.

"A med tech down on twenty-one just said he saw Efa wandering around the stasis beds. She didn't seem right, he said. He's afraid she's going to hurt herself," the sentinel girl says, then shrugs and presses her lips together. A second later, someone calls for her, and she disappears.

I lock eyes with Niah as my entire body screams to move. She's going. There's no doubt of that. And Niah must know I'm planning the same. Now how do I plead with her and get her to agree not to stop me?

"Niah, please—"

"No," Niah says, pointing at me. "You're not going...like that. I don't want to see your pimply ass hanging out when you use the ladders. Clothes first."

Before I can even search for something more than a medical gown, she rips open a closet and tosses a med tech uniform at me. I pull the gown off, throw the shirt on, and stumble after Niah as I rush to put the pants on.

We dart through the turmoil that surrounds us, a disturbing route through this hell. Screams and cries fill the rooms as med techs and bloodied soldiers flood in with body after body. A doctor kneels on the floor, cutting into a boy's abdomen. The smell of death is everywhere. I wouldn't want to be here even if I chose to stay.

As we slip out, Seren appears, and I freeze. In her arms is a lifeless body. Rhys. Seren looks up at me, her face stained and soaked with tears. Words form on her lips, but I don't get to hear them.

"No, wait," I say as Niah grabs my arm. "She needs— "

"That girl's alive," Niah hisses into my ear as she drags me along. "That's all you need to know right now. Keep moving."

We catch the rail system down just as it's returning to ninety-five. The car is full of hollow-eyed soldiers. They stare right through us as their bodies slump against the walls. And these are the lucky ones who didn't get hit. I feel my chest tighten as I gaze back. Level twenty-one can't come soon enough.

A med tech comes into view the moment we jump through the car doors. His face is flushed and his eyes wide. He fidgets with his hands as he watches us approach, stuck in a moment of disbelief or fear. Or something else.

"Efa," Niah says. "Where is she?"

"You? You're here for her?" The med tech shakes his head as if something doesn't add up for him.

Niah grabs the tech by the collar and shakes him, her eyes in a full rage. I've never seen her like this, not even with Daga. She's ready to kill him if he doesn't answer.

"*Where?*" she shouts.

"Pod 988!" the med tech cries. "But you can't stop it! She's already closed the hatch!"

The breath goes out of me. Efa put herself in a pod, knowing full well what would happen. The body can't handle going under a second time. There would only be one reason she'd do that. One I won't accept. Efa would never do that. Not her.

"Shut it off!" I shout.

"I can't!" The med tech turns to me, helpless. "She could die if we stop the process!"

"You bish-head! She'll die if we leave her in there!"

I dash into the aisles as Niah calls after me, but her voice is a distant sound to my ears. All my focus is on finding that pod. Finding Efa.

Row after row, I scan the numbers. My heart is threatening to burst from my chest. My legs are on the verge of collapse. But I have to keep going. I won't allow Efa to die. Not while I'm still breathing.

I spot a blinking light and charge toward it. As I get close, my bare feet slip on the freezing floor, and I slide into the pod, smashing against its control box. I catch myself from falling, throwing myself forward to peer through the stasis pod's window.

And there, lying inside, her eyes closed, is Efa.

"Efa!" I scream and pound on the pod's window. "Efa, wake up!"

As much as my fists impact the unit, I realize it's futile. It doesn't stop me. I punch the machine and cry out Efa's name until my voice gets hoarse.

"Ceri, stop!" Niah calls as she limps her way toward me. "There's nothing you can do!"

No. There must be a way to turn the machine off. I scan the control box, frantically searching for some clue. Nothing. I reach for the power leads and yank as hard as I can. Impossible. There's no way my hands can break wires that thick.

My heart crushes inside my chest, pain worse than I've ever felt before. It's like someone has reached into me and torn it loose from its vessels. I can feel my strength sagging as my mind fights to deny the reality before me. Yet as I struggle in vain to save the only person I could ever fully trust, I sense the inevitable about to arrive.

"Efa!" I scream again, both fists coming down on the pod's hatch. "You can't do this!"

"Ceri, you're just hurting yourself!" Niah is close. "It's over!"

"No! No! There's still time to save her!"

I look for something heavy to break the window and spot a large metal wrench. Four steps later, it's in my hands. Four more and I'm battering the window with it again and again. But the heavy tool only bounces off the composite material. Wrong angle. I shift position and raise the wrench above my head.

I can save Efa like this. I *will* save Efa.

With the full force of my strength, the wrench comes down on the window. Shards blast out, shooting in all directions as the head of the weighty tool buries itself into the thick material. The window cracks and splinters. Gas erupts, and a second later, I yank the wrench from the hole and thrust my hands into it.

The full force of Niah's weight slams into me. We fly off our feet and land hard as the wrench falls from my hand. It bounces off the edge of another pod and hits the ground with a loud, ringing clank, like that of a bell tolling.

I try to recover, but Niah is faster, climbing over me to pin me down. I struggle, but Niah has no intention of letting me hurt myself and uses all her strength to keep me on the floor.

"Let me go!" My voice comes out as a hoarse croak. "We can still save her! She's still alive!"

I roll, slamming Niah into the side of a pod. She cries out, her lock on me loosening. I grab the edge of the machine and haul myself up, leaning over Efa's smashed window. The frozen gas rushes into my lungs and I choke, doubling over, but I force myself back up.

My hands grip the edges of the jagged material and rip pieces off as fast as I can. They go numb, and my fingers get bloody. My body be damned, I'm working against time. It's a small price to pay if my sacrifice saves Efa's life.

Without warning, Niah's arms thrust under mine, and she jerks me away from Efa's pod. We stumble back, smashing into a pod and toppling to the ground.

"Let go!" I cry.

Niah's hold on me only gets tighter. She entwines her legs in mine and locks them down. I struggle to escape, but my energy is spent. Without it, I cannot break free.

"Ancestors, what have you done?" The med tech's hands speed across the control box, checking the stasis pod's systems as he tries to shut it down. "She could be dead because of you!"

The tech races off and returns a few seconds later, throwing on a heavy smock with thick gloves and a mask. He slams his palms into the pod's hatch release and lifts the top of the pod up. Coolant spills over the edges of the unit, turning into gas before it ever hits the floor.

"Her body may not have cooled down all the way yet. If so, there's still a chance," the med tech says. "I'll take her to a recovery bay, but there are no guarantees."

I get to my feet and stumble after the med tech as he carries Efa's body to an exam table and lays her down.

When I see her face, I gasp. Her skin has turned dark orange—no color that a living human should be. She is almost like a replica of herself, built from composite and painted with the only hues that we might have on this drably toned ship.

I want to touch her, to feel if she is real. To know if she's alive. Yet my hands don't seem to work. I bend over and put my ear close to her mouth to listen.

"Don't!" the tech cries. "You could do irreversible damage to the cell structure of her skin."

"Then wake her up already!" I shout back.

"It doesn't happen just like that. A body coming out of full stasis could take up to a day to recover normal body temperature. I have no idea how long this will take! Sit down and stay out of the way!"

All I can do is wait, and I hate it. I hate thinking that I could have stopped this. I hate thinking that Efa saw no other option. And I hate thinking that this could be my fault. I didn't hear her cry for help or refused to hear it because I thought I could fix her. What a fool I am.

Minutes pass, then hours. My mind wanders through the happy memories of Efa and me together. No one has ever made me feel at ease like she has. But then all the terrible moments of the last two weeks flood my brain, and I feel the ache of loss for what we used to have.

Someone coughs. I think it was Niah, but when I glance at her, she's slouched in a corner, asleep.

Could it be?

"Positive vital signs!" the med tech yells. He rushes to a counter and pulls out a hypodermic gun and jams it into Efa's arm. He checks a monitor, then goes back to refill the device.

I rocket to my feet and race to the table, my heart pounding in my chest.

"Not yet!" he shouts. "She still needs to be stabilized!"

"Ceri, don't!" Niah rushes to stop me, but when she sees the edges of my lips curving up, she pauses and frowns. I can't help it. The euphoria in my body only continues to rise, even as I try to catch my breath.

"She's alive," I reply, my smile growing. "Efa's alive."

UNION

LEVEL EIGHT. THIS IS where everything began. Where Efa first confessed to me about Merek. Where I almost—and should have—killed him. And now, this is where the chiefs of both factions, Tarakh and Fahrasi, choose to meet. No one's ground. Neutral territory. We're all equal here. Anywhere else, it is only the sleeping and the dead that can find commonality with each other.

The adults forced me to come. They needed someone to verify or discredit any Fahrasi claims. Despite being a convict, I am one of a few still alive who have gone deep into the ship. Former Captain Daga is another, but they sent him down to watch over the emergency pods along with his Fahrasi counterpart. I hope they skewer each other.

They've illuminated the overhead lights to tolerable levels so each side can have a clear view of the enemy. I find it ironic that the one level they choose to brighten is also the location where the largest amount of death and violence between the two factions has occurred. We've put the spotlight on everything evil we've ever done to our fellow passengers.

As the chiefs sit at a makeshift table, I find the deepest, darkest corner to hide in. A blanket covers me, as all I'm allowed to wear is a prisoner's coverall. They took my soldier's uniform, along with everything else I could have called mine. Not that I care. I don't need any of it. All I ever wanted was to be with my friend.

Efa remains in medical, alive yet suffering. She misses Merek with every cell in her body. I have tried to comfort her with little success. I've begged the adults to give me more time with her, but all they've allowed is one hour a day. It's not enough, yet I don't have any other options. At least not yet. I should be thankful my hands still work.

"Ceri d'Sengshuy, come out of the dark. We want to speak to you," Chief Generys calls.

"Get up, convict," my guard says and tugs on the restraints around my wrists. I don't feel like fighting, so this time I obey. The guard still makes a show of dragging me in front of the chief and kicking the backs of my legs so I kneel before her. Chief Generys shakes her head and glares at the guard. She won't win any favor from me with an attempt at humanity. She's the one who sent me to prison.

"I wanted to share with you what we've accomplished at this historic meeting...what the information you brought me has accomplished." Generys puts her foot on a collapsed ventilator and leans forward to look at me. "Hope, Ceri. We have hope now. We'll dispatch a pod to the planet, with both Tarakh and Fahrasi explorers. They will bring back as much data as they can, and then we will send another, and another, until the pods can no longer make it back. In the meantime, our factions will work together to repair command and control, so that if this planet proves fruitful for human colonization, we have an option to bring everyone there."

I catch my breath as questions pop into my head. The *Stratford* can be fixed? How are the pods able to come back? I'm not sure I care what the answer is. I can't return Efa to normal with it, and Merek and Sayer are better off living on the planet. There's not enough reason for them to return, even if they knew how.

"If you can fix the ship, why wouldn't we just continue on to our original destination?" I ask.

"That destination is still hundreds of years away, which means none of us would be alive to see it," Chief Generys replies.

My forehead gets tight. "So? That was your job anyway, wasn't it? To live your life here? Isn't everyone in stasis counting on you to do your job?"

"That was never the mission directive. The parameters—"

"You made my parents a promise! And when they wake up, they'll expect to live on the planet you told them about! This is just using this as an excuse to end the mission!"

Chief Generys' eyes narrow. If she was expecting me to be happy about her news, she was mistaken. All I see is another adult bending the rules to suit their own needs.

"Everyone knew the risks of this mission," her male aide says. "There was never a guarantee anyone would make it."

The chief throws a hand up, then takes a breath to calm herself as she attempts to regain her regal state.

"As a reward for your efforts and sacrifices, I have reduced your sentence in half," she says. "Despite what you may think, we are grateful to you. As part of the reason for this historic moment, you are welcome to remain here for the celebration."

"I have nothing to celebrate," I shoot back. "Send me back to my cell."

The chief lets out a long sigh and stares at me with troubled eyes. I couldn't care less. Her dissatisfaction with me is her problem. I won't pretend to be some great savior of our people. The adults made me an outcast the moment they pulled me from my peaceful sleep. I lay down in that stasis pod, expecting to wake up next to my parents in a new world. And now I will never speak to them again.

"As you wish," Chief Generys says, pivoting on her heel and walking away.

As hard of a rejection as I gave to her, I am in no real hurry to get back to the stifling closet they keep me in. They dragged me and my nest into that cramped space and locked the door. If that wasn't punishment enough, its tattered hulk smells like Efa. Every night I lie down in it, her scent reminds me of just how much I've lost.

"Let's go," my guard says, yanking my restraints up. "I don't care what the chief says. You don't deserve to be here."

Before he can move me two steps, Niah approaches, motioning for the guard to stop.

"Give me a moment," she says. "I need to talk with her."

My guard eyes Niah warily, but he relaxes his arms and nods at me. He doesn't want to get on her bad side. Even though she remains a child, like all the other soldiers, she has enough influence in the faction to make the adults fear her.

"You might find this strange, but I've just met two Fahrasi who say they know you," Niah says, a playful smirk appearing on her face.

"I don't know any Fahrasi." I say. It's only half-true. I don't count Merek and Sayer, because for any practical reason, they don't exist.

Niah watches me for a moment, considering something. My skin tingles at her look. Whatever she is about to say could either break me or elate me. I don't know which it will be, and it's terrifying to wonder.

"They say they know Efa, too," Niah adds.

My heart drops from my chest. No. It's impossible. I saw the pod launch. It was gone. *They* were gone. I can't risk my mental health to trust her words. If this turns out to be a lie, it will wreck me. But now that Niah has said it, my mind will cling to whatever tiny scrap of hope I can use to bring cheer back to Efa's soul.

"Get them," I growl. "Bring them here. Now."

Niah pulls back at my insistence. She turns her head to stare at me with one eye as her eyebrows crash together.

"Who are they, Ceri?" Niah asks.

"I don't know," I reply, shaking my head. "I really don't know, but I...no. No. I'm sorry, I'm not telling you what to do, but please, get them."

Niah snorts, then smirks and nods. She's off a second later, moving with the speed and ease only a scout could have.

My mind flips between hope and denial as I wait for her return. Every combination of possibilities dumps into my head. I wrestle with my thoughts to put them into a logical arrangement, yet the one that overpowers them all is the vision of Efa's face, soaked with tears of joy. After all she's been through, this would be the greatest of all mercies.

But I'm cautious about letting my mind wander into a dangerous space. I've got to keep hope at bay and proceed as if this was a battle, keeping my defenses up and my weapon ready to fire.

That plan collapses the moment Merek and Sayer come into view.

I shoot to my feet so quickly my guard barks and rips my restraints back. He must think I'm attempting to escape. He's wrong. The only place I want to be is here.

"Back off, Fahrasi," my guard growls.

"Give it up," Niah says. "We're all friends here."

"She's a prisoner!"

"And you'll be without your hands if you keep treating her like that."

My guard tenses. He's afraid and should be. Niah is more than capable of making good on her threat. And I'd be willing to help.

"In fact, why don't you take a break and leave her in my charge?"

"Forget it," the guard shoots back. "I know what happened the last time we let you do that."

"Yeah," I say, turning to glare at him. "I saved someone's life. That's what happened. Now get out of here. Find me here or at medical later. I have no interest in being anywhere else."

Merek, Sayer, and Niah step closer, their stance as threatening as they mean it to be. The guard glances between them, calculating his chances of surviving a fight.

"Bish it all," he says and turns to me. "You better be where I can find you, or I'll put three darts in your head before I ask questions."

He tosses my restraints to Niah and stomps off, likely finding a place to hide out until we're done. He won't want his captain finding out about this. It will reflect as poorly on him as it would the rest of us.

I spin on Merek, my pulse pounding in my chest. "How? How are you here? I saw the pod launch!"

Merek blinks. "Pod? Oh, yeah. You won't believe it. We had to get off the level when that captain of yours showed up." He chuckles. "We got caught by our own troops, but they let us go once we told them about it."

"Who was in that hyuking thing, then?"

Their eyes go wide at my anger. Niah glances between the two of us, unsure of what she should do.

"Rabbit wanted to stay in there to hide," Sayer says as he frowns at me.

I gasp. Rabbit. I suppose he got what he wanted. But his selfish action crushed Efa's dream. And now he's alone on an unknown world, with a broken mind. If Rabbit survives for long, it will be a miracle.

My knees get weak thinking about it, and before my legs give out, I throw myself at Merek, hugging him as best as I can with restraints on. He jumps at the sudden closeness, but then wraps his arms around me, patting my back as if I was a baby. Tears fall as I rest my head on his shoulder, the constant torment of Efa's despair lifting from my body.

"Hey, what's wrong?" Merek says, pulling back to look at me.

"No! I mean, nothing." I sniffle, shut my eyes and take a breath. "Efa. Go see Efa. Now."

Merek watches me with a puzzled expression. "Well, of course I want to see her. Where is she?"

"Medical," Niah answers for me as she gathers up my restraints. "Let's go, lover boy."

Niah and I move so fast, Merek and Sayer have trouble keeping up. They're in unfamiliar territory, as curious about their surroundings as they are wary. Tarakh of every age and position pause to look at them as they fly by. But we're not stopping. We cannot get there soon enough. Efa has already suffered more than any lifetime deserves. To let her hurt any longer is cruel.

As we enter medical, Niah drops my restraints, and I move to Efa's bedside. She's asleep, likely sedated by the techs so she can do what they prescribe. What she's about to learn will do her far better than any medication ever could.

Merek freezes at the doorway when he sees her. The breath goes out of him as the blood drains from his face. Efa's body still shows signs of damage, none more obvious than the discolored skin on her face.

"What...happened to her?"

"It doesn't matter," I reply, holding out my hand to him. "Come here. I will wake her."

He hesitates, and my stomach gets tight. Merek better not run away now, not after all Efa has been through. She needs this. I won't let him leave until she opens her eyes.

"Efa," I whisper as I press my head against hers and stroke her hair. "Efa, wake up. I have a gift for you."

Efa's body stirs. Her hand moves up to touch my face and push it away.

"Come back later," she mumbles. "I want to sleep."

"Not for this, you don't," I say. "Open your eyes."

She moans and turns away, but I pull her back.

"Efa...I've brought Merek."

"Not funny, Ceri. Go away."

I motion to Merek, yet he remains in place. There's anguish in his eyes. He wants nothing more than to touch her. I can see it. Perhaps he just needs more of a push. I am more than willing to oblige.

"It's now or never, Fahrasi," I growl. "Be with her, or lose her forever."

That does it. Merek shoots forward and comes next to me. I raise Efa's bed so that she's sitting up and then retreat to Niah, who takes me by the shoulders and allows me to lean against her.

And then, I experience a moment of beauty that I will never forget.

As Efa stirs, Merek looks upon her as if he has never seen anything more precious. Perhaps that's true. He reaches out to touch her face and I hold my breath, terrified that even the slightest sound will destroy this fragile reunion.

She responds, tilting her head toward him. He strokes her cheek, running his thumb down the side of her neck. He leans in, pausing only to take her in again before his lips touch hers. Efa lets out a soft moan, the edges of her mouth curving up.

But then her body recoils, hands shoving against her unknown assailant. In the next second, her eyes are open and searching for the culprit. Merek stands steady, gazing down on her as Efa's widened eyes meet his.

"What?" Efa gasps as her jaw goes slack. Further words escape her, and all she can do is shake her head in disbelief.

"Hey," Merek says. "Sorry to scare you."

Efa's chest rises and falls faster and faster as she stares into his eyes. It doesn't last. Her hands wrap around his head, and she pulls his mouth to hers, their lips connecting once again. Efa kisses him with a desire so deep, it's like she has been without water for days, and the only source to quench her thirst his him.

"It's you," Efa whispers once she has finally drank fully of Merek's passion. That's when the first sobs come. I move to go to her, but Niah holds me back. She's right to. Efa has all the comfort she needs in Merek.

Sayer clears his throat, drawing my attention. He nods out of the room, hinting that we should leave the two of them alone for a while.

I nod, pressing my lips together, reluctant to leave Efa when she is in such an emotional state. But she no longer needs me in that way. I've done what I've promised. Now the two of them can be together for as long as they desire. Despite my joy in reuniting them, it pains me to realize I am no longer needed. But that is my problem to handle.

"No, wait!" Merek says as I turn with Niah to walk out. "Don't leave. Not yet."

I pivot toward him as my eyebrow arches. He smiles at Efa, then faces me with a proper stance, his head held straight. I don't like it. Whatever he's about to do is wrong and unnecessary. Merek is going to embarrass himself, and I am not about to let him.

"You saved her," Merek says. "Hyuk. You saved *us*! I owe you everything, Ceri." He kneels before me and bows. Then he tries to take my hand to kiss it, but I snatch it away before he can enact any such nonsense. He bows his head then. "Whatever you want, just say so."

My nose wrinkles at his statement. He is acting like a complete dolt. Love must have struck him in the head so hard he believes he can just conjure anything I desire.

Still, there is something that Merek can get me, and to have it might just make my time in prison all that much easier.

"There's only one thing I want," I say.

"Name it, and it's yours." Merek lifts his head, awaiting my demand. As Niah and Efa look on with curious faces, I step closer so that I tower over him. Now he'll understand just how serious this request is.

"Bring me as much ice cream as you can carry. Then we're even."

EPILOGUE

I KNEW THIS DAY would come. It was too easy to guess the adults would choose to preserve their own lives over the thousands in stasis. They'll wake some of them, of course. Anyone critical to the survival of a new colony will go, whether they want to or not.

That includes well-trained child soldiers.

The door to my tiny prison is unlocked and opened wide. Chief Generys stands there, flanked by two adult guards. Her face is stolid, hiding any hint of what is coming. I've been expecting that she'd punish me for my disobedience that day, but that was nearly two hundred days ago. Whatever. I've achieved what I needed to. Efa and Merek are together in a way none of us ever thought possible. They're even petitioning the chiefs for the right to marry, though I don't think they'll gain that approval soon. At least no one has stopped them from being together.

"Ceri d'Sengshuy, you are hereby released," the chief says. "As a model prisoner, I have decided that you have served your time. You are free to leave this cell."

"What?" I shake my head. There must be more to this than a simple reprieve. "Why?"

"Our situation on the *Stratford* has changed. We have done enough surveys of the planet's surface to determine that this is where we will begin our new colony."

I bet she was planning this ever since I first told her about my discovery. I still have plenty of question, but I hold off on asking until I understand how I fit into this scheme.

"Come with me," the chief says, motioning with her hand.

I hesitate, but only until a guard fires a threatening glare at me. They're no longer wary of my fighting skill. After six months of being locked away, I am out of shape, out of practice, and in doubt of my strength. I will go with them.

"We are making preparations for the final transfers," the chief explains as we head toward the rail system doors. "Many are already there, including some you know."

I catch my breath. Have Efa and Merek gone? Niah? I'm reluctant to believe they'd just follow orders. Yet this is a chance at real life. A world with sunlight and fresh air. A place where everyone will have the opportunity to do something new.

Save for the children.

I understand then that Chief Generys wants me to go. The reason isn't clear, and she isn't explaining. I suspect, however, she needs my skill to protect the new colony. To serve the adults as a soldier, once again. What else would I be good for?

"How many other children are going?" I ask as we step inside the rail car. A guard taps in the code for level one-twenty.

So there are more pods.

"All of them, of course," Chief Generys replies with a smile. "We're giving all of you a new life, free of war. The factions have been dissolved, and there's no need for us to fight each other any longer. From now on, we'll all work together to create the grand new community we have always intended."

There's a lot being left out of her glorious statement. Perhaps that's why she's using big words—so she can cover over everything she's hiding.

"What about those in stasis?" I ask as we pass level fifty. "Are you waking everyone up?"

"We have taken everyone we have deemed necessary."

"What about my parents?"

"Efa and Niah are below, Ceri, waiting for you. So are those two Fahrasi boys. We're all leaving now. You'll all be reunited in your new home. Aren't you looking forward to that?"

Her non-answer tells me everything I need to know, as does her attempt to change the topic of discussion. They're leaving people here, on a ship with no way to arrive at its destination and with no one to look after them. I'll bet the adults never even tried to fix command and control. And now they're abandoning thousands who put their trust in them. If I had something more than words to fight with, I'd do something about that.

The rail car stops, and the doors open to a level that looks almost identical to ninety-five, save for the additional four tubes here—double the number of pods that I'd discovered. No wonder they could move so many off the ship so quickly.

As we step out of the car, I notice the crowd of people putting on suits and stepping into the pods. There's fewer than I'd expect could fit. Does that mean...

"Is this it?" I ask, pausing. "Are we the last?"

"Yes, this is the last group," the chief responds with a tight smile. "Then we'll all be free of this disaster."

It has been a disaster, one that the adults brought upon themselves. How many have died because of their stubbornness? How many more will die because of their selfishness?

My shoulders slump as names, faces, appear in my thoughts. What did they sacrifice their lives for, if not to save the passengers of the *Stratford*? What were we doing here all this time?

I suppose it doesn't matter. It's over. I cannot fight them, and they will never agree to stay and do the job they had promised to. I just wish I could have said goodbye to my parents.

"Ceri!" Efa calls and waves as she spots me. She links her other hand with Merek's. Sayer and Niah stand nearby. They both turn when Efa does.

"See?" Chief Generys says. "Just as I promised. Get your suit on and join them. We're departing soon."

That, I don't need to be told to do. They, and many more, came to visit me in my cell. It feels different now that I'm free. At least for the moment. Chief Generys will demand our obedience again once we're on planet. This is just a trick to get our compliance.

Efa breaks from Merek to charge at me. I freeze, unsure of what she's about to do. With a leap, she flies into my arms, wrapping her legs around my waist as she assaults me with kisses on my face. I stagger backwards, my arms wrapping around her to stop the both of us from toppling.

"Easy," I say, half laughing while attempting to fight her off. "Your beloved might get jealous."

"Let him," Efa says, and plants a sloppy one on my nose. "I haven't done this in months, and besides, I never had the chance to say thank you."

"Yes, you have. Every day you could. Which, by the way, was every day."

"No, seriously." Efa slips down onto her feet, her arms still about me. "You don't know how happy you have made me. You saved me, Ceri. Twice! There aren't enough thank-yous in this universe to show you my gratitude. You are the best friend anyone has ever known."

I put on my best smile for her as she puts her head on my shoulder and squeezes me tight. For a moment, it's like we used to be, but better. Her closeness warms me, just as much as I've done for her on sleepless nights. And there were many, usually before a major battle. Our connection cured our unease, and I will forever be thankful for the time we spent together.

"And now we're going to be living on a new world," Efa says and bounces up and down. "How exciting is that?"

"It is, I suppose." I press my lips together, thinking of my parents. Of Efa's parents, too. And Merek's. Everyone's. Most will never have the chance that we will. That they will never know it doesn't matter.

"Let's go!" Chief Generys calls. "Departure in five minutes. Suit up!"

Efa untangles herself from me and makes a motion to a row of lockers nearby. Nearly everyone else is ready to disembark. I find a locker with the right size suit in it and pull it out, moving over to a bench to get the lower half of the suit on.

As I fumble with the legs, a memory floats into my head, one from when I was young. For my sixth birthday, my parents had convinced the actress of my favorite video show to stop by. It was called *Stargazer* and was about this heroine who saved those who couldn't protect themselves. Even though she wasn't in costume, she did her best to act out her role. Her genuine kindness and enthusiasm made a serious impression on me. After that, I wanted to be just like her.

Yet, at this moment, I'm very much not. I'm running away from people who are helpless to care for themselves. There will be no one here for them once we depart, and unless the ship crashes into something, they'll just continue on an endless journey. Forever. The *Stratford* will become their eternal resting place and they will never have a choice to change that.

"Get your gloves on," Efa says, pressing them into my hands. "I've got your helmet."

Niah helps me stand in the rigid suit and checks the re-breather on my back. With a quick scan of the rest of my suit, she catches my eye before she heads toward the pod. She has something to tell me. And it could be important.

Merek says goodbye to Efa and reluctantly joins Sayer in a pod full of Fahrasi that is mostly children and soldiers. Why the adults still need to be separate at this point is beyond me. Efa watches them go, then slips into the pod that will carry the two of us, along with Chief Generys and her team.

Once the chief boards, I stand alone, the last person on the *Stratford.* Except I'm not. There are many, many others, my parents included, who will remain, frozen in stasis, ignorant of the hell we are about to commit them to.

"Well?" Chief Generys says to me, leaning out of the pod's hatch and motioning me to get in.

I nod to her, yet my feet hold fast. The more I consider it, the less I want to go.

"Ceri, get over here now!"

Efa pops her head out of the hatch and frowns at me. Then, when our eyes connect, she gasps. And that's when I know I've made my choice. Ever since I woke up, I've been preparing for this moment without even realizing it. I just hope that I don't end up like Rabbit—half-sane from a lifetime of talking to myself.

"Soldier, if you don't get over here this instant, I swear I will leave you on this ship!" Chief Generys shakes her fist at me. She's serious. So am I.

"Go ahead," I reply.

The chief blinks as she stares, her jaw going slack.

There's commotion as others peer out of their pods. The children are watching me and wondering what the hyuk I must be thinking. I feel my lips curl upward as their eyes fall on me, the confidence in my decision becoming stronger by the second.

Efa slips past the chief and steps out. She walks to me, our eyes locked the entire time. Once she's before me, she smiles and takes my hand.

"Are you sure, Efa?" I ask. "What about Merek?"

"Don't worry," she replies.

Seconds later, Merek steps out, followed by Sayer. They grin at us as they approach.

"You fools can't be serious!" the chief shouts as she watches them. "What do you think you're doing?"

"What's right," Merek replies, coming to stand next to Efa. Sayer moves to my other side.

Then the floodgates open, and children from both sides rush out. Niah, Seren, and Rhys, Mari, Beka, Deryn, Tegan, and Daga's former aide, Aidan. Fahrasi and Tarakh alike. Once they all come out, there's nearly thirty.

As I glance around at all of them, I feel a warmth run through me as they look back, grins on their faces. I am thankful I won't be alone, but still concerned about how we will survive.

"You brats! I am ordering you to get back in the pods this instant!" Chief Generys yells, her voice going shrill.

"Make us," Niah says, folding her arms.

The chief pulls back, her eyes going wide. She has no interest in fighting us, nor does she care enough about us to try. Perhaps that's what the others realized, and that's why they stayed, too. I know it will be a struggle, but perhaps one day, we will regain control of this ship and take it to its true destination.

"Listen to reason! This is not a safe place for you! Without the adults, what can you do?" Chief Generys makes one last attempt to coerce us to return, but we, the children of the *Stratford*, remain where we belong. She gives me one last glare, an attempt to single me out for this coup. I'm sure she regrets freeing me now.

The hatches shut on the pods, and one by one, they depart. Quiet descends upon the level, and all those who remain turn to me, expectant smiles upon their faces. I cannot return it. As glad as I am to have company, I wish they had listened to the chief.

"I don't think you realize what you just gave up," I say, especially to the younger soldiers. "You'd have a real life there. Hope for a future. You should have gone. This ship is a lost cause."

"Then why'd you stay?" Tegan challenges. "You know as well as we do that living under the adults isn't a life. They'd just use us the only way they know how to—as expendable weapons."

"But things could change."

"But they wouldn't," Deryn says. "I don't regret my choice."

"Me neither," Seren says.

"You don't even know what you're saying," I shoot back. "You can't imagine what this is going to be like now that we're alone."

"Neither can you," Niah says, dropping a hand on my shoulder. "Don't think you're so old now that you understand everything. You don't know what awaits you either, but you chose this, and so did we."

I press my lips together. Perhaps they've put more thought into it than I expected. Perhaps this is what they've always dreamed of. Ever since the adults stole their childhood, none of us had any choice of how to live our lives.

Until now.

"Ceri," Efa says, squeezing my hand in both of hers. "This is all Merek and I ever wanted. To be together, without fear of punishment from the adults. We know it's going to be difficult. I have no illusions about that. I'm ready...We're ready to face whatever comes."

The determination in Efa's eyes gives me strength. I will do my best to make sure she can hold on to her dreams. The others are telling me the same thing. Maybe together we can create some miracle and save the *Stratford*, and the thousands on it, from its uncontrollable course.

"Thank you, Efa." I smile and squeeze her hands back. "I'm ready, too."

Books by Marc B. DeGeorge

Origin Story Series

The Starship Sneak

The Reckless Rescue

The Traitors' Trial

The Conspiracy Clash

The Deadly Discord

Air Born Series

A Call to the Sky

A Challenge for the Sky

A Crisis in the Sky

Stratford Series

A Universe Upon Us
A Universe Against Us

About the Author

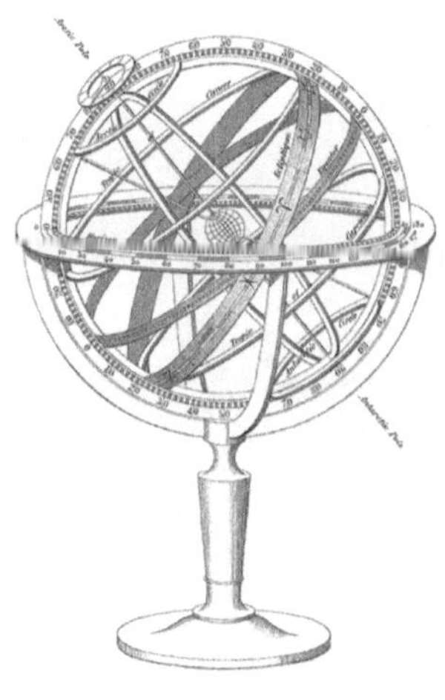

Marc B. DeGeorge has made every attempt in his adult life to maintain a balance between how much science and how much art he dabbles in. Sometimes, he's even successful. When he was young, he wanted to be an astronaut, and then an aeronautical engineer—he even went to Space Camp! But then he learned how to play guitar and his space dreams took a back seat. He spent a decade playing professionally in bands and studying music in college (university only took five years). These days, things have come round full circle, and Marc envisions the future by writing books that imagine what challenges humanity may face, and what we might accomplish together.

When Marc isn't writing, he performs traditional Japanese music on shamisen and writes, shoots, and edits performing arts photos and documentaries under the MuseMarc Studio name.

a amazon.com/Marc-B-Degeorge/e/B09LDCNVHV/

f facebook.com/MarcBDeGeorge

instagram.com/marcbdegeorgeauthor/

g goodreads.com/author/show/22081012.Marc_B_DeGeorge